The Memory Project

ANDREW C. YOUNGSON

Billington
Publishing

First published in 2021 by Billington Publishing.
www.billingtonpublishing.com

Second edition published 2022

ISBN: 9798844053962

Cover art: Keith Hale

For the past.
Always changing.

Prologue

Olivia and I would hide ourselves away for hours on end, building fortresses of chairs and bed sheets. Far from the world outside, inventing games and secret words, cackling together with chocolate-smeared lips.

Other times we would trek into the woodland that spilled out from the play park boundaries. Brave souls venturing into the wilderness, we'd set about finding sticks strong enough to fend off monsters. Neither dog walkers nor luminescent joggers could spoil the fantasy of our quests through the magical forest.

And sometimes we would just lie on Olivia's bedroom floor with the lights off. Flat on our backs, crowns of our heads touching, staring at the glow-in-the-dark stickers on the ceiling.

Sweeping constellations of green.

Recently, my mind has been resting on those moments with Olivia. Those beautiful years before she died.

Good memories, some of my finest.

I think.

"Olivia," I whisper into the night. "I remember, remember, remember, remember. This is you. I remember."

My back is pressed against the mattress. The acid yellow streetlight throws the Artex on the ceiling into monstrous relief, like a beast's gaping mouth. I close my eyes and try to repaint it as a black canvas strewn with green stars. As the oblivion of sleep descends, the stars wink out one by one. Before I slip completely, a thought wrinkles my mind:

Please, Olivia. Don't make me have the dream again.

Part One:

OTHER

Chapter 1

A sweat bead trickles down my back. The droplet's determination is laudable, but it can't make it past the blockade of my underwear's elasticated waistband.

I try to catch my breath as I scan the cocktail bar. Tea lights dance in the darkness as my eyes struggle to adjust. *Powder blue shirt, powder blue shirt, powder blue shirt. Nope.* I begin an awkward path around the tables, like a water boatman making his way through a twilit lilypond. I make it to the end of the room, then turn to take in the view. The place is half full. People huddle in twos and threes.

To my right a bartender adds a green sprig to a tumbler while her colleague waits with an empty tray on the other side of the bar. Jazz acrobatics fill the room's empty spaces. If only you could still smoke indoors; it would complete the picture beautifully.

"Douglas?" A voice calls from a booth behind me.

Powder blue shirt.

"Oh hi. Dhaval?"

He's trapped behind the table but does his best to reach across the wooden expanse. After a short hesitation, preparing for contact, I take his hand. Warm and dry, compared to the clamminess of my own.

"Shit, so sorry I'm late," I stumble, "Missed each train by a millisecond".

"Don't worry about it, mate, seriously," he smiles. "Go on, sit, please."

"God I'm such a sweaty mess, sorry." I peel off my jacket, nearly taking out the glass in front of him with my sleeve. He catches it before it topples.

"Sorry." I slide on to the curved banquette and shuffle inwards. "That looks good"

"Yeah. Long Island Iced Tea. Pretty strong actually."

"Nice. Haven't had one of those in years. Got trashed off too many last time. I think."

He makes a little laugh and nods. He's so composed. His gaze bores into me. I pick up the menu and scan without reading.

"I have...no idea what to get. Um, is it...?" I crane my neck towards the bar.

"Table service, yep. They'll be round soon. They're really good here."

"Oh, is this a favourite place of yours?"

"I wouldn't say favourite, but it's good. It's a little more traditional than the rest of the hipster bars around here. I like that."

"Shoreditch," I nod, widening my eyes for effect. This corner of east London is a notorious hotspot for entitled, middle-class creative-types. *Oh to be one of them.*

"Shoreditch," he bounces his head in agreement. "So anyway. Nice to finally meet you face-to-face. I mean you look like your picture so that's always a big tick off the list."

"Ha yeah. You too. Definitely the guy in the picture. Have you ever met up with someone who doesn't–"

"What can I get you?" The waiter with the empty tray hovers above my shoulder, a thick brown moustache tapering in waxed curlicues on either end of his shit-eating grin. *Shoreditch.*

"Oh. Uhhhh, one sec." The list of options swims in front of me. "You know what, could I just get a beer?"

"You got it. Which one? We have a range of locally–"

"The top one's fine. Thanks."

I turn back to Dhaval.

"So," he says with those attentive eyes. "Tell me about yourself, Dougie. I want to know everything."

I catch the waiter's arm. "And a whiskey chaser, please?"

***

"...and then there's my little sister, Zara. So that makes four of us."

"Wow. A lot," I say, doing my best 'I'm normal and listening' face.

"I guess it is. Didn't feel like it growing up. But then we always had my Nani around to help. And you said it was just you and your folks?"

"Yep, just the three of us."

"Sounds quiet."

"That's a good word. Yeah. It puts quite a lot of focus on you as a kid. Being at the point of the family triangle. All eyes on you."

"I bet you were a right handful as a teenager," he says.

"Maybe a little. I wasn't their problem by that stage though. Boarding school."

"Ohhhh. Even worse. You were Harry Potter, then."

"Ha. Man, I wish. Not so much. Fewer broomsticks and castles; more air con units and rice paddy fields."

His lips pinch to form a question.

"I went to boarding school in Thailand," I say quickly. "Went there when I was a kid."

"Really? That's so cool. I'm jealous. I just went to a comprehensive in Luton. What took you out there?"

"Just a, uh, scholarship thing. Sounds more special than it was. But anyway yeah, it means I was more raised by the faculty and matron than my parents. Probably why we're not that close," my voice trails off. *Why did I get on this track?* He just looks at me, waiting intently for me to continue. "Boohoo, poor expat kid," I add, filling the silence.

"It can't have been easy," he says, reaching over to brush my hand with his index finger. I slowly retract my hand, making as if to finish my drink.

"Another?" I ask.

***

"I can't believe that line worked. It was terrible," I say with a giggle. *A fucking giggle. Seriously.*

"Well it worked on you, didn't it?"

"Yes. Yes it did. Well played sir." I raise my glass to him. I finally feel myself settling into the bench. Three pints and a chaser radiate in my stomach.

"They're awful things, those apps though. I mean, how much can you really know about someone from their vital statistics and hobbies. So I'd rather be funny."

"Better that than sleazy," I reply.

"Nothing wrong with a bit of sleaze, in my opinion," he says deadpan. "Kidding. So what made you say yes?"

"Jeez, put me on the spot. I dunno. We seemed to be similar ages and stages. You seemed funny? A nice guy? As much as you can tell from these things, as you say. What? You want more? Okay….Uh, you seemed quite interesting? Y'know 'a lawyer but not-that-kind-of-lawyer."

"Environmental lawyer," he corrects. "Go on."

"Aaaaand...God I dunno." I can feel my ears reddening. "Cute?"

"Cute?" He breaks his mock silence.

"Yes cute. Shut up."

"Forget cute. I was hoping for 'hilarious', 'intelligent', 'intriguing'. I mean I have both surfing *and* poetry down as my hobbies, for crying out loud."

"I agreed to this date *in spite* of those," I laugh.

We laugh.

***

"…so there I was, at a huge gathering of my extended family – most I'd never even laid eyes on in my life – in the arse-end of nowhere in Kerala, having to explain to my great aunt why I hadn't found the right girl yet."

He's animated as he speaks. Wide eyes, legs shifting around in his seat, slender brown fingers dancing in time to his story.

"Oh God. So what did you say?"

"Just came up with some shit about London being quite a difficult place to meet people. Thankfully my brother and sister came to the rescue. Changed the conversation to their weddings and kids. Works every time."

"What a nightmare. So your folks are cool with–?"

"Oh yeah totally. I mean, if I was the only kid they had, my being gay might have been more of an issue. Actually no, I don't think even then they would care too much. They're great people. Really great."

"They sound it," I reply, hearing the smile in my voice. Now I'm the one who's quiet.

***

"A therapist?" he says, astonished. "I would never have pegged you for one of them."

"Yeah well, like I say it was a while ago. Anyway, it's all change now I'm doing the journalist thing," I say, trying to divert the conversation away.

"Freelance, you said?" he says.

I nod and take a sip of warm beer.

"Anything I would have read recently?"

"I've got an interview set up tomorrow morning actually. A playwright, really interesting woman."

He raises his eyebrows in what I can tell is polite interest. His smile widens. "Back up, though. What kind of a therapist were you? Like a shrink? A physio? Massage?"

"Something like all of that. Anyway, it wasn't for me. I think I'll be a better journalist than I was a therapist," I squirm in my seat. *Why the hell did I start this topic? Damn you, booze.*

"Hmm, strange." He sits back in his seat.

"What?"

"No, nothing. I just wouldn't have seen you as a therapist. Whichever kind you were, mystery man. I mean...never mind."

"No, what? Say it."

"It's just...I mean don't get me wrong, but you don't seem the most, I don't know, confident isn't the right word. Sure of yourself? And I just imagine that a therapist would be...more comfortable in their skin."

"Well," I shrug, and swill the dregs of my drink.

"I've offended you?"

"No, no. It's fine."

"Shit, I have. Look don't listen to me, I'm five drinks in," he shakes his head. "Anyway, I don't mean it in a bad way. You're just a little less...forward, in person. Maybe different than what I expected."

And there it is.

"I mean some of those texts you sent," he continues.

"Ah. Those."

"It was hot."

"Mmmm," I nod, still unable to look up from the glass.

"No?"

"I mean yeah it totally was," I add quickly. "It's easier to be like that when someone's at the other end of a text. To be someone...else." I can feel my neck reddening as embarrassment and frustration bloom, at odds with my drunken light-headedness.

"Look I'm sorry if I've disappointed you," I snip, sounding more pissed off than intended.

"Don't be silly. You're great. Look..." he says, again reaching over for my hand.

Before he makes contact I slide out of the booth and stand.

"I'm...I'm just going to get us some more drinks," I say.

He looks up at me startled. From this vantage point, I realise it's the first opportunity I've had to take him in properly. The sheen of light glancing off his dark hair, the softness of his eyelashes, the warmth of his chestnut complexion. What a shame it's this expression on his face.

***

"A Long Island Iced Tea and a beer please?" I ask the bartender.

He smiles. "Sure which kin–".

"Just a beer please. Any will do," I cut him off and return to berating myself.

Why do I always do this? It was going so well. I always spoil it. Maybe it's too soon to be dating? I'm not ready.

I daren't look back at Dhaval, so keep my eyes on the bar top.

To my right a woman sags on a stool, staring into the depths of a glass of red wine. Her hair hangs like a limp curtain, her shoulders are slouched. The way she's peering into the wine, it's like she wants to dive in. I know the feeling.

I open my mouth to ask if she's okay.

"Here's your beer," the bartender beams.

"Thanks," I say, then reach over to a stack of napkins next to Red Wine Woman's hand.

But she beats me to it, causing the tips of my fingers to brush momentarily against hers. At the merest touch, a deluge of imagery and emotion rushes through me. I experience the woman's memories as if they were my own.

I'm slumped on the avocado tiles of a bathroom floor. One leg bent, the other splayed out in front. An open bottle on its side. A handful of white pills grasped in my hand.

My trembling fingers clasp the powdery tablets. My clammy back presses up against the cold grooves of a radiator. My shallow breathing, clenched toes, and hollow stomach. Mildewy air fills my nostrils. I raise my head and catch a glimpse of myself. Greasy tendrils of hair snake down my face, past my bloodshot eyes, under my trembling chin, just above my pale breasts.

I close my eyes, raise a hand to my lips and cram pills into my mouth. The salty tang of the painkillers makes me choke as I crunch down on them, awakening me to the reality of what I'm doing. My eyes fly open as I gag and spit the contents down my front.

I suck in a ragged breath then release a guttural roar.

I thrust backwards from the bar, nearly tipping over a stool. Panic surges as I glance up at Red Wine Woman. *Did she notice?* She just looks back at me as if nothing has happened, then returns to her drink. I try to regain composure, but struggle to form a coherent thought, to cut a hole through the haze of the memory I just Read. My throat tightens, tears threaten to spill.

"It'll just be a minute for your cocktail," the bartender says. His expression shifts to concern. "You okay?"

An open bottle on its side. A handful of white pills grasped in my hand.

"Y-yes thanks," I say, mind reeling. "I'll…uh…be back in a second."
Oh God. Please don't make a scene. Not now. Please.

Chapter 2

My clammy back presses up against the cold grooves of a radiator...

I find the door to the gents, mercifully without too much difficulty. I try to absorb all the sensations of the here-and-now to bring me back to myself. I grip the door handle, brass, smooth.

Bathroom's empty, even more luck.

Then another surge of the memory.

Greasy tendrils of hair snake down my face, past my bloodshot eyes...

"Fuck fuck fuck!" I say under my breath, rubbing temples as I lurch towards a stall then lock myself in.

I close my eyes, raise a hand to my lips and cram pills into my mouth.

"Shit! Get out of my head, lady. Shake this off, come on Dougie. You used to do this all the time." I ache to roll up into a ball, but fight the impulse.

The salty tang of the painkillers makes me choke... I suck in a ragged breath then release a guttural roar.

The Echoes are so strong. That poor woman. If only I had the strength to pull myself together, to go back to her, help her.

Clumsy fingers feel their way into my jacket pocket. I pull out my phone, type in the letter 'A', and hit the handset symbol on the first name that pops up.

Three rings. Come on come on come on. Answer!

"Hi Dougie," a voice says with an upward inflection.

"Uh hey Adrian." My voice sounds thick. "S-sorry to call out of the blue."

"Don't be silly, man. That's how this works. You all right?"

"I, uh, not really, sorry." I feel on the verge of crying, but I push through it by taking shallow sips of air. "Slipped up. Don't know how...happened but I, uh, accidentally Read a...a really dark memory off...off someone. Really dark. Can't seem to, to get rid of it."

"Okay, okay," Adrian croons. I press my ear to the sound, grateful for his Caribbean lilt. "Just breathe for me, okay? Just breathe. Sounds like it's been a tough one. Caught you off guard didn't it?"

I nod, tears finally forging down my cheeks.

"This isn't you. This is just the Echo. You know how to deal with Echoes. Are you sitting?"

"Yes," I croak, lowering the toilet lid and settling on top.

"Good. Now straighten your back. Close your eyes. Shut everything out but my voice."

I do as he says.

"Now. Gather it all up, all the shards of the Echo, every scrap of it. They're not yours, so don't let them become you. You can do this."

I turn my thoughts to the memory. But instead of being within it, of it, I'm watching the scene from the sidelines, looking on to the Echo – the memories of others as seen in the mind's eye of Weavers. I line up the sequences of the Echo like a stretch of celluloid: the avocado tiles, the smell of mildew, the brown bottle, the pills. The face.

I push away the vines of emotion that grope for me from within the horrific scene, desperate to drag me back in.

"Okay?"

"Okay," I whisper.

"Now take hold of it and push it all together. Smaller and smaller. Until it's a small orb in your hand. You've caught it all, yes? Nothing remains outside of the orb?"

"I've got it." I can practically feel its pulse in my hands.

"All right. Now, go to your Safe, and drop this in it. I'll wait for you."

Out of the darkness, I visualise a yellow door. Immediately I feel its warmth, its strength. I created this door more than half my lifetime ago; this door and what lies behind it.

My Safe.

The panic within me, once so present, dissipates as I approach the door. The handle squeaks as it turns and opens away from me. A light beckons. I walk in, clutching the orb of Red Wine Woman's Echo.

My childhood bedroom wraps around me like a hug. The trappings of my youth lie about; the bed to my right is unmade, the duvet still bearing the rumpled impression of a child as if only vacated minutes ago. The glassy eyes and fixed smiles of soft toys stare upwards.

To my left, light spills in through a bay window. The world beyond, though poorly defined, holds the steadfast promise of summer days without end, of friends calling to me from the garden below, holding with anticipation to the handlebars of their bicycles. Beyond the garden, on the other side of the street, is a park, hemmed with trees. At its centre is a mighty pine, its broad trunk and towering height making it stand out from the others.

My attention comes back to the bedroom. In the centre lies a wooden trunk. I kneel down to its level and feel its warm lid. I find the groove at the centre of its lip and lift.

Within the trunk are countless items, each as dusty and unremarkable as the rest. A single high-top canvas shoe without laces. A VHS tape with an illegible scrawl on its label. A plastic figurine frozen in a heroic pose. A cinema stub with curled edges.

I look back to my hand. Where once a glowing orb had pulsated, I now feel the cool indifference of glass and plastic. I relax my fist to reveal an empty brown pill bottle. I stare at it for a beat then place it inside the trunk and close the lid. Business-like, I rise back to my feet and walk out the door, careful to hear the click as it shuts behind me.

A voice in the distance comes to my attention through the surrounding blackness. It becomes clearer as I walk towards it.

"…ack to yourself. Feel your hands, your toes, the air around you," Adrian says. "This is you. Now open your eyes."

The world slowly comes into focus. The bathroom stall, its artificial jasmine scent, the sound of my own breathing.

"You okay there, friend?"

"Yes," I smile. "Thanks Adrian. Thank you."

"You're very welcome. That's what I'm here for."

"This is ridiculous though – I should be able to do this without help."

"Give yourself a break. It's going to take time."

We talk like this in gentle tones for a while longer, then sign off, Adrian requesting I see him in person tomorrow afternoon for a proper check-in, me agreeing, too tired to resist.

In time, I emerge from the stall and make my way to the row of sinks, splash some water on my face and wipe it away with a hand towel. The guy staring back at me in the mirror looks tired. A lot more tired than his 34 years should allow. I hold his gaze for a long time.

It's funny. If you stare at your reflection long enough, your features begin to drift apart from each other and fade. Hold on long enough and you lose all sense of yourself. You're just a blur.

I remember this one interview I did with an old rock star who'd come to perform for the British troops at Helmand Province. So strange. A makeshift stage in the middle of a desert military base, with this aged rocker strutting about it in front of an audience of Royal Marines too young to know who he once was. At his peak he could hold an audience right there in his hand. Now, he could barely keep a crowd of soldiers (with nowhere else to go) interested for one song.

He was barely recognisable. All that remained of his once glorious mane were frazzled wisps. Years of cosmetic surgery, chemical peels and lord-knows-what-else had all but erased the boy the world had known. I was fascinated.

Afterwards, as we spoke in the makeshift greenroom behind the stage, he joked about his appearance. Called it his 'witness protection programme'. A good line. I used it as a framing device for the article I wrote up. In retrospect, it was that interview that made me realise I could make the change into profile writing. To leave all the horrors of war behind.

I don't know why I'm thinking of that interview now.

A different life. *Someone else.*

"Douglas? Dougie?"

Dhaval's voice comes into focus. I don't even turn from the mirror.

"Are you okay? Did you puke?"

My eyes are the first of my features to come back into view in my reflection. They look so empty.

"Nah," I say quietly.

"What is it? Anything I can do?"

He's so calm. What I wouldn't give to be like that.

"Look man," I say, turning my head towards him, "I think it's probably best if we call it a night."

"Okay. If you're sure. Maybe we can do this another time?"

"Jesus," I say. "Why would you want to? This was a car wreck. Clearly it's been a long time since I did this. Seriously, fly free dude. You've been lovely, but I don't think this is what you had in mind for tonight."

"Maybe not this here right now," he chuckles. "And yet…"

"And yet wha–?"

His lips are on mine before I even realise it. I flinch, but something about the way his hand cups my face gives grounding; ballasts me against the rolling room and the disquiet inside. My hands go to him, one to the small of his back, the other to his neck. I inhale. The embers of his scent warm me as I drift into him.

A shimmer glides closer to me out of the blackness. As it comes nearer I can make out figures drifting in and out of view. I can hear the muffled swoop of a female singer's voice, and the tinny descant of trumpet.

The waif-like flicker of a candle comes into view directly in front of me. It spills around the booth, and casts long shadows across the grooves of a table top. Out of the distance I see someone approach. He's picking his way through a lake of faces and their indistinct babble. He looks nervous as he searches. I recognise him instantly from the dating site. He comes right up to me. I open my mouth, but then he turns his back. Don't go.

"Douglas?" I call softly.

"Ummm, that's *your* name, buddy," Dhaval says, bringing me back to myself. I can feel my irises contract in the bathroom light. We slowly unclasp.

"Sorry," I mumble.

"You really need to stop apologising," he smiles. "If there's something wrong I'll let you know. For now? I'm intrigued. Mr Sermanni…"

He grazes the corner of my lips with his thumb. Another spark of an *Echo* from his mind flows into me, an Echo of looking at me from across the table…

He runs his fingers through his sandy blond hair and laughs.

"…you're a mystery."

***

I sink on my bed with all of my weight. Take in a deep breath, hold until it begins to burn, then push it out long and slow. A little smile tugs at the corner of my mouth.

Dhaval and I parted ways soon after our kiss. I felt like a kid, giddy and alive from the clandestine moment. We split the bill, despite his protestations that a lowly journalist's wage couldn't cover it. As we wrapped ourselves against the cold, he made a suggestion that I could come back to his. I declined.

Of course the thought had occurred to me. It's been so long since… But my desire to leave the day on a good note far outweighed the tightening sensation in my pants.

Seeing myself in his mind helped somehow. Before he got there, I felt so lost. Kind of how I've been feeling all these months since the breakdown. Adrift. This past year has been such a shit show since I had to leave the Mnemosyne Project. My boundaries have come crashing down. No wonder Red Wine Woman's memories hit me so hard.

But when Dhaval and I kissed and I saw myself in his memory, it seemed to push everything else away, to quieten the Echoes rumbling around in my head. Helped me draw a ring around myself. Ironic that the only sense of myself I've been able to find in months is in someone else's memories.

So no, I didn't go home with him. Satisfied that the evening had finished on a far better note than it could have, I headed back to east London.

I hear the rattle of a key in the front door. Erica's home. Instinctively I reach out with my foot for the bedroom door and nudge it closed. The joy of cohabiting with a nurse is barely having to see them. For all intents and purposes, she and I live alone.

I wrestle free of shirt and jeans, kicking them off the side of the bed, and lie back again with one hand behind my head. Something pokes at my back. I try to manoeuvre around it, but eventually have to give in. A white padded package. One that arrived this morning but I haven't had time to open – too busy rushing for ill-fated dates with beautifully normal men. The package crinkles in my hand. It's come a long way, bearing numerous stamps and official-looking postal imprints. My current Hackney address is written by hand on a fresh-looking label. Beyond its edges is my previous address in Hampstead. Must have been forwarded by the new tenants. God I miss the old place.

The underside of the package is blank apart from some writing on the bottom corner:

'Thailand.'

I don't recognise the writing. I reach across the bedside table for keys, then poke the sharpest one into the packet and saw along its edge. Inside is a cardboard box, not much bigger than something to contain a wedding ring. I tip it out and peer back in the package. Nothing. Inside the box is some crumpled up tissue paper, and beneath it, the coiled metallic links of a necklace. I pinch at the necklace and pull it out. Dangling at the bottom of the silver chain is a pendant about the size of a twenty-pence coin.

It's an upside-down triangle with its point facing the floor like an arrowhead. An intricate design of interlocking loops is cut into it, allowing me to see my palm as I lay it on my hand. It doesn't weigh much at all, though it feels reassuringly solid as I pass it between my fingers.

Almost imperceptibly, I feel the pendant begin to thrum. *What the hell?* I put it down on the bed to see if the sensation is coming from my hands. But no. I pick it back up. Again, a quiet tremble.

I feel drawn to it, clasping my hand completely over it. The thrum builds slightly, though never to an alarming level. After who knows how long, it recedes and fades to nothing.

Weird.

I lift the pendant up by the chain and dangle it in front of me. It's left no mark on my hand. I try holding it again, holding it close, but no effect.

Man, I must be exhausted.

Tiredness washes over me in great waves. I place the pendant on the bedside table and shut off the lamp. The pillow feels soft. My mind drifts as I fall towards sleep. The dreamless sleep of a *Weaver*.

***

We're running. She's laughing. She's pulling me onwards by the hand. I pull back slightly. She turns her head, but I can't make out her face. She pulls again. I don't want to. Stop.

The scene shifts. A melt of colour. Now we're sat on the floor. I look down. Many pairs of legs crossed together. We form a circle. I hear voices, but no words. My own are a muffle of indistinct sounds. The floor is warm.

Suddenly a set of hands over my own. I feel the cold pang of metal inside my grasp. 'Angel'. I hear my old nickname. Someone's explaining something to me. I feel a tear run down my cheek. I close my eyes.

Another shift of scene.

We're running again, but she's ahead of me now. I'm shouting at her. She screams. 'Help me. It hurts. Help.'

No! Ice cold fear runs through me. I kneel beside her crumpled form on the ground. I try to look up, but still I can't see her face. Her breathing, so shallow.

She clasps her hands over my own. A white light flashes in my mind. I can't see anything. But a voice, clear and sharp, pierces the haze.

"Remember me," she says. "Remember me."

NO! I yell. NO. DON'T LEAVE ME, PLEASE.

***

"Dougie? Dougie? Are you okay in there?"

A sharp rapping on the bedroom door wrenches me awake.

"What?" I mumble. I'm disorientated, heart thumping, a sheen of sweat coating my forehead.

The door opens ajar and Erica peers round it, her hair looking tousled.

"Are you okay? You were shouting?"

"Um...I....uh...yeah I'm okay." I can barely gather my thoughts to answer her.

"I was so worried. You sure you're okay? You still look half asleep. Didn't realise you were such a noisy dreamer."

"Uh yeah. Sor...sorry to startle you. Just...dreaming."

"Okay. Well I'll leave you be. Glad you're all right."

The sliver of light from the hallway disappears. I remain upright in bed. A muddle of Erica's words and the dream whirl around my mind.

The dream. My dream.

What the actual fuck? Did I just have a dream?

Chapter 3

I make it onto the tube two seconds before it pulls away. I spot the holy grail of London life – a vacant seat – and fill it before anyone else can.

My notepad and dictaphone are still in my hand, fresh from their use at an interview on the Southbank. This one was with the playwright. Her first original piece in years, it'll be premiered at the Young Vic. Really edgy stuff. She was as fascinating as I hoped. I've got a good feeling about this piece, think it could work. Some editors will be keen on it, surely.

I just need a break. One lucky break.

I rub my eyes and take a few long blinks. I'm still exhausted after last night's adventures. The date. The dream. But I've had no time to process either.

My face distends in the carriage's curved window, forehead swells like a gourd as I lift my chin up, then pinches suddenly in the middle like the centre of an hourglass. I become transfixed by this morphing reflection, shifting slowly up and down in the seat to make the effect extend as far down as my shoulders.

I've attracted the gaze of an elderly traveller. She peers at me over the top of her newspaper. I slink down in my seat, making my face snap back to normal proportions in front of me. A sandy wave of hair in need of trimming sits high above eyebrows a shade darker, curved towards each other in an expression of worry.

I still feel the old lady's eyes on me. You think you're being subtle, don't you lady? If only you knew. A freak is sharing a carriage with you. A *mnemosyne*. Does that official label mean anything to you? No? How about our nickname for each other: *Weaver*. Still no? Didn't think so.

As if hearing every word of my internal ranting the old lady shuffles off at the next stop. See you later then. Go stare at someone else.

We slide back into motion, I return to my reflection. The tint of the glass casts shadows on any sunken features, making voided pools of eyes, temples and cheeks. This accentuates the normally muted evidence of Italian-American lineage; my mother's Celtic genes having largely won the genetic landgrab over my appearance. I may have a Roman profile and thick hair on head, arms and chest, but the angles of my frame and lack of dancing prowess are British through and through.

A hiss of air escapes my lips, the sound mingling with the squealing of metal wheels on metal tracks. To my left a heavy-set man with shaved head is losing the battle with sleep, nodding solemnly as if at some ancient truth. I flick through my phone, too tired to do anything requiring brain power but still too fidgety from the morning's ordeal. And last night's dream. An actual, honest to God dream. What is going on?

I spot a recent email chain with my mother. She and Dad are heading up to London for the day soon. *Meet us for lunch? Your choice, even Thai if you want it.* She hates Thai, Dad too. Neither could stomach the spicy food on the few trips they took to meet me in Bangkok when I was at Weaver school. *Sounds great. I know a cute Thai place near me in Hackney.*

We always do this dance. Whether by text, phone or email, we've always been very good at keeping up a veneer of normality. Which I guess in some ways is true. Apart from the fact we haven't lived together since I was a child, we're a fairly regular family unit. 'Regular' in that we barely talk, and when we do it's usually perfunctory exchanges, empty questions and answers dotted with obligation and guilt.

Ugh, enough of this.

I flip over to text messages. Remnants of conversations lie stacked on top of each other – some exchanges with friends completed with x's and emojis, others from ex-colleagues and ex-flatmates left hanging in perpetual limbo:

> 'Sorry I didn't get a chance to say bye, Dougie. If there's anything I can do, just call.'

> 'Sorry to text. What's the code for the door again?'

> 'No worries at all, seriously. Gimme a shout when you're next free.'

I come to rest on a chain belonging to a group chat titled: 'It's nem-o-see-nee, bitch!'.

The profile image for the group is of Dante Gabriel Rossetti's oil painting of Mnemosyne; the Greek Titaness of memory, lover of Zeus, mother of the muses. Very grand. Nothing like those of us who have been branded with her name. Mnemosynes. Weavers. In the profile image her expression is stoic. Aquiline nose, pursed full lips, a halo of chestnut hair. Her long neck plunges into an exposed collarbone, a leaf-green tunic drapes across her asymmetrically, exposing the right shoulder. Completing this divine impassivity are a pair of sunglasses, a crude addition superimposed by one of my oldest friends, Kaito Taniguchi.

When I click into the group chat, Kaito's face grins back at me next to a post featuring a looping animation of Elmer Fudd chasing after a panicked looking Thanksgiving Turkey. The thread has been dormant for over a month, and it appears Kaito's was the message to end the conversation. Classic Kaito.

I skim down. The group chat comprises only four people. Kaito, Venny, Nina and me. I imagine that a stranger looking upon the stream of texts and images would immediately recognise the hallmarks of a decades-long friendship; the inane chat, the sarcastic banter, the veiled affirmations of long-distance love.

'Proof of life, pls', I type with a single thumb, bumping Kaito's cartoon turkey to second position. And then I lose signal as we head into another tunnel.

Eyes dry, I put the phone away and let myself be lulled by the swaying of the train.

***

"...amygdala, hippocampus and..?"

"Corpus striata," I say under my breath, nudging Kaito. He looks at me, all wide eyed.

"What was that?" Mr B calls out.

Mr Bordelais looked around the class with those grey eyes of his. His straight, white teeth shone through the bristles of his goatee. A young and somewhat 'hip' Canadian, Mr B was one of our only teachers at the Mnemosyne Project Bangkok. But despite the amount of contact we had with him, his pop quizzes were always met with silence. I can still remember the rattle of the aircon in those moments.

I nudge Kaito again, poking his pudgy flank with my elbow.

"Um, coppus oblongata?" he eventually says without looking up from his notebook.

"Hmm not quite, Mr Taniguchi, but close enough," Mr B says.

Kaito flushes. A few of the other kids giggle so I shoot them a look.

"Corpus striata," Mr B says, drawing out the last letter of the word as he writes it on the whiteboard. Man, even his handwriting's attractive. "These three regions of the brain – the amygdala, hippocampus and corpus striata – are key regions of the memory system. And in people like you and me, they are what?"

"Hyper-developed," all ten or so of us chime in with unenthused voices.

"Very good," Mr B says.

He tossed the black marker on his desk then clapped his hands together. A few of us shifted up in our seats at the sound.

"You all look so goddam bored," he says. "This stuff is cool, people. Super cool. I mean, sure, it's all science jargon on the board, but it's incredible in real life. A tiny genetic quirk, that's all it takes, and these regions go supercharged. Only 0.00001 per cent of the world's population can do what you do," he dots each number with a forefinger.

"And of that tiny amount an even smaller amount have abilities of Grade 2 or above and are therefore 'on the radar' to the Mnemosyne Project. I mean, come on people: You are so rare! Doesn't that blow your mind?"

Mr B looked around the room once more, the positivity practically crackling off him. I glanced around but didn't see the same energy reflected back. Some of my classmates were pretending to listen at least, but to my right, as ever, Nina was making jagged doodles across the cover of her notebook. And on the other side of the desk Venny was looking out the window at the fierce afternoon sun. Out in the courtyard a couple of Project agents – shirts and ties despite the humidity – walked by, deep in conversation.

"Ms Angsakul," Mr B says, *opening a palm towards Nina, "you are a very talented memory Reader. What a gift."*

Nina didn't respond. Just rested her freckled cheek against her fist and offered Mr B a 'so what' expression.

"Mr Taniguchi. You can actually Write your memories on to others. A Grade 4 Weaver. That's incredible, isn't it?"

Kaito flushed even redder, his eyes glued to the desk.

"And Mr Sermanni."

My heart plummeted at the mention of my name.

"Well, we'll figure you out some day, I'm sure," he beams through his tidy goatee. *The class titters at his joke. Asshole.*

The only one not laughing was Venny, who just muttered something and shook his head.

"Yes, Mr Kotto?" Mr B says, smile fading.

Venny turned and met eyes with the teacher dead on.

"I said, it doesn't matter a damn what we can do if the Mnemosyne Project won't let us share it," Venny says in his Pittsburgh drawl.
Now everybody is staring at their desks.
"I don't think that's a fair summation, Venedict," Mr B says, his voice suddenly quiet.
"No?" Venny says, matching the teacher's coolness.
"I'm afraid not. The Project does a lot of good. Treating trauma victims. Helping people navigate their experiences in ways contemporary science can't begin to explore. Granted, it's all confidential and for good reason. So no, Mr Kotto, I don't think that's fair. The Project has done a damn good job of keeping us safe for a long time, wouldn't you say? Trained us. Protected us. You feel differently?"
"Does it matter what I feel?" Venny says with a smirk.
"Don't choose this very moment to become a surly adolescent, Venny," Mr B says. There's some grit in his voice. "You're too young to be so bitter."

I didn't like where this was headed.

Venny responded with a 'pshhhhhhhhh'. Which was maybe the most adolescent response possible.

"Sorry to disappoint you so much, Mr B," he says, tipping his chair back on two legs. "I'll just be a good little Weaver and stay quiet and hidden from view."

"Venny," Nina whispers, half hiss, half plead.

"Fucking Project goon," Venny mutters. Some of the other kids breathe in loudly.

Mr B used the silence to ridiculously good effect.

"I hate to say it, Mr Kotto," he says in a way that doesn't sound one bit like he hates to say it, "but Erasers such as you and I should know the dangers our abilities represent. More so than anyone else in this room."

Venny stayed silent, but his look could've cut Mr B from nose to tail.

The teacher carried on, the veins on his neck standing out more with each word.

"Or maybe you're supremely confident that the world would be fine if it found out about us," he says, pointing outside the window. "Unshakably sure that we wouldn't be torn limb from limb by regular people. Certain they would simply accept that their memories, their very privacy and inner beings are an open book to us. No, you're probably right, Venedict. They wouldn't mind at all. They wouldn't just lock us up in institutions. Or herd us into labs. Or set us on fire. It's happened before, but don't worry. Of course you know bett–"

"That's enough!" I shout.

I was more shocked than anyone else at my outburst. It was like someone else jumped out of my throat. I retreated deep into my chair when Mr B's red stare switched to me.

"I mean...I just think that's enough. Sir," I say.

He looked up, as if he'd just remembered we were all there. One of the students looked at the guy next to her with wide eyes. Nina was pressing her pen so hard into the notebook it dug a hole. Kaito was unpicking stitches in his uniform. Venny was back to staring out the window.

"You're right, that's probably enough for today, class. Off you go," Mr B says then turns to the board and starts wiping away the writing.

Chairs squeak against the linoleum and one by one everyone heads out into the humid afternoon.

"Oh, Mr Sermanni. A word?"

My blood freezes. Nina, K and Venny look at me, but I motion for them to keep going.

"Close the door, please," Mr B says. His face is back to its usual expression. Handsome, kind even.

"Take a seat."

***

I can't remember what Mr Bordelais said to me that day. There were so many times one of us was held back for some sort of private chat. A reprimand, a check-in, a word of wisdom – there was always something, some impromptu therapy. Especially for four boarding school kids like us. The misfit toys. But like so much of my childhood, heck, my whole life, the specifics are hazy.

God, I'm sick of feeling sorry for myself. I tilt backwards, bumping the back of my head on the train window. The striplight on the carriage ceiling wobbles around in my vision.

Mr B's words haunt the edges of my mind.

They wouldn't mind at all. They wouldn't just lock us up in institutions. Or herd us into labs. Or set us on fire. It's happened before, but don't worry.

An allusion to a history lesson we were given throughout our schooling. Of the way Weavers like us used to be locked away, covertly experimented on, and worse. Every day I'm thankful yet guilt-ridden to have avoided the fate of my mnemosyne forebears. But for a handful of years, their fate would have been mine. So I guess I have to be thankful to The Mnemosyne Project. Grateful for the way it's helped keep the secret of our existence.

"Trained us. Protected us."

***

We're running. She's laughing...pulling me onwards by the hand....
Now we're sat on the floor. We form a circle...
I feel the cold pang of metal inside my grasp...
...A tear runs down my cheek...
We're running again...She screams. 'Help me. It hurts. Help.'
I kneel beside her crumpled form on the ground. I try to look up, but still I can't see her face...
...She clasps her hands over my own. A white light flashes in my mind...
"Remember me. Remember me."
"NO!"

What the…? I'm still on the train, fell asleep, heart hammering, where are…still a few stops until home. Nobody looking at me. Phew!

Stupid sod, falling asleep on the tube.

The dream again. Just like last night.

I sit still for some time, willing the panic to leak away, to stop replaying the scene over in my mind.

The girl without a face. We run together, she's just out of reach. Then a shift. Now I'm sitting in a circle with others, holding the pendant I think, hands clasped over mine, shift again, she's in pain, she holds my hands. *"Remember me"*.

Is this what dreaming is like? A twisting carnival of sights and sounds every time people fall asleep? How do they deal with this every night?

A Weaver's blessing and curse; we tend not to dream. As in, at all. Something about the way our brains are wired, plus the training we get for dealing with memories does the job that regular people's dreams do. So we sleep in blackness. God I miss it.

Maybe I'm not dreaming. Maybe this is my brain bursting, the masonry of my mind finally crumbling, giving way to the river of other people's Echoes it's held for so long.

It's all such a mess. The more I look at the pieces of the dream, the more they drift apart.

It all started with the pendant. Without realising, I've fished it out from my desk and am now dangling it above me, watching as the morning light glints off the upside-down triangle inset with intricate loops, pivoting slowly on its chain.

We slide into Bethnal Green, my final destination, and I make my way back up to street level. As I clear the barrier, a persistent rumble begins in my pocket; my phone buzzing like a trapped roach.

I find a spot across from the station, outside a mosque, and drink in the cold air.

From the preview screen of my phone, I can see a thread of messages from my far-flung friends.

The conversation goes like this:

> **Kaito:** Waddap bitches?! Konnichiwa and a belated happy new year from Bangkok. Everything is very good here. Keepin it real. U no me. [Wink emoji]
>
> **Nina:** Hi everyone. Happy New Year too! I'd say sorry for the silence but we're all as bad as each other so I won't take the hit. So I'll ask THE question instead: Resolutions anyone?
>
> **Kaito:** Srsly? Since when do u ask cute questions?
>
> **Nina:** Yes seriously. Shut up. (And 'konnichiwa from BKK'? Mixing your Asia there, butthole)
>
> **Kaito:** Duuuuh. Gimme a break. Sawatdii, then. Happier?
>
> **Nina:** Much. So, resolutions?

Venny: Good morning from a rainy Pittsburgh, dearest friends. All alive and accounted for here. Proof of life as requested.

The message is accompanied by a short video of a toddler in a high chair with orange mush smeared across his chubby cheeks. A deep voice coaxes from behind the camera. 'Jamal. Hey, Jamal, look at Daddy. Look at Daddy'. The kid looks up but just keeps grinding breakfast between his gums. The screen wobbles then flips to an extreme close up of Venny's beaming grin. 'Sup guys'. That smile. So at odds with the grimacing teenager I once knew. It's wonderful to see that grin, but I can't suppress the twinge of jealousy that follows. Because Venny's smile says so much. Says 'I got out', 'I'm free', 'Fuck you Mnemosyne Project'.

Kaito: Oh heeeeeeeey. Cutest little monster ever. Sure he's urs, V? Gagagaga :D
Venny: Pretty sure, man. He doesn't seem to have much interest in you guys, so I would say that's pretty strong evidence. Hehe.
Kaito: :O
Nina: Wow he looks so big, Venny. Look at that hair!
Venny: I know right? Takes after his daddy. When I had hair…
Nina: Ha!
Venny: To answer your question: no resolutions yet. Maybe something work-related? Promotion? Too boring?
Nina: No that's perfectly legit. Nothing wrong with more cash, Mr Family Man. Mine is to move somewhere new. Seriously I've been in Stockholm for yeeeeears. Need to get my shit in order.
Kaito: Come here! The Thai underground art scene is just waiting for ur arrival, dude. U would smash it up with ur dark twisted shit.
Nina: Kop khun kah, but no kop khun ka. Not sure the militar…sorry, government could handle me. ;)
Kaito: Nah, they're ready, believe me. That's my resolution then. To get yo ass out here. The mothership is calling. You can't ignore the call, Ms Angsakul.
Nina: I don't hear anything…

This is followed by a photo of Nina wearing an inquisitive expression, a hand cupped against her ear. Emblazoned across her exposed wrist is a tattoo of a snake – its skeletal tail wraps round her wrist out of view. Nina's eyes are rimmed with liner. Splotchy freckles spread across the smooth bridge of her nose. I've always loved Nina's face. The juxtaposition of Scandinavian cheekbones and Thai almond eyes and button nose were always such beguiling betrayals of her dark temperament as a teenager. When she was a teenager. God. When we were teenagers. Almost half our lifetime ago.

Kaito: Very funny. Like ur hair, by the way. Very sleek. I'll always miss the buzz cut tho.

Nina: Creep. But thanks. Where's your proof of life, then?
Venny: No dick pics pls, K.
Nina: **Vomit emoji**
Kaito: No dick pics? Okay. But I'm pretty sure this counts as the mother of all dick pics. Check out the view from mah penthouse, bitches.

A video arrives in the thread; Bangkok's night-time skyline. A hazy yellow blanket atop a chess board of skyscrapers. You would barely know any buildings were there, but for their neon outlines, lit windows and the glinting slogans on cranes perched on unfinished spires. Bangkok, Krung Thep, City of Angels. It's not the most distinctive of Asia's modern skylines, but I'd spot it anywhere.

When Kaito reaches the farthest extent of his wraparound view, he flips the camera to himself. He holds it high so we can take him in from head to toe.

'So what do you think, guys? Pretty nice huh,' he says, clearly in reference to himself as much as the vista. Gone is the tubby Japanese boy of our youth. In his place stands the chiseled cut of a man who has made a conscious effort to look every bit the playboy; a slick of black hair flanked by closely shaven sides and a creaseless shirt that clings to the evidence of hours at the gym. Yet the strain of moulding his body into a shape it doesn't want to be, plus the early lines of approaching middle age, are evident.

'The only thing that's missing are some of my oldest buddies to come enjoy it with me. So whaddaya say? New Year's resolution – big reunion in the BeeKayKay?'

Hearing the bounce in Kaito's voice brings a smile to my face. His accent, like all of ours, is a mashup of a mid-Atlantic American baseline mixed with occasional inflections of our individual heritages. Me, for example – in London people just think I'm American: in the States they think I'm English. It takes a fellow expat to identify an accent like mine, Nina's and Kaito's. Even Venny's voice bears the melody of a foreign upbringing, no matter how much he's re-embedded himself in Pennsylvania. You can't wipe that slate clean.

Venny: My MAN! What a sweet pad. Just need to find a way to book Jamal into a crèche for two weeks and I am there… Or maybe a business trip. You could hire me! Even a crook businessman like you must need an accountant right?
Nina: The answer is yes, K. The mother of all dick pics. We're all very impressed...
Kaito: Aww u guys. I've missed this. The old gang ripping the shit out of each other. Gagagaga. Speaking of, where u at, Angel? You called this meeting, but I don't see u at the table.

"Angel". A childhood nickname used by anyone other than childhood friends would seem awkward. I remember the horror when Nina discovered my middle name. Angelo. A name chosen by my father – another attempt to bring out the Italian within me to displace some of the Celtic, like dropping a family-sized lasagne in a bath of Scotch whisky. The mock chanting of 'Angelo, Angelo' among my fellow inmates at the boarding school quickly morphed into 'Angel'. 'Angel face'. 'Angel of the morning'. 'Angelcakes'. Could be worse, my adolescent self had acquiesced.

I enter the fray.

> **Me:** Hey guys. Sorry to have texted and run. I've actually been asleep. During the day. On the train…I know, shame shame shame. Anyways, new years resolutions eh? Hmmmmmm. Staying in bed count?

Without even checking my appearance I take a quick picture. I hold my fingers in a peace symbol over one eye. *Click*. Terrible. The bloodshot eyes are a particularly good look. Hey, maybe the three-day shadow will distract them. Fuck it. Send.

I back out of the chat, but immediately notice a red notification dot over a separate text thread. I press into it. A jolt hits me the millisecond I see the message.

> **Adrian:** Hey there. You still okay for 2pm, Hyde Park?

The clock reads 1.35pm.
Fuck.

Chapter 4

"So how're you feeling?" Adrian asks as we crunch our way around a chilly Hyde Park.

"Yeah, not bad. Just, you know...not bad. You?"

"I'm fine, thanks. You know me."

"Actually I don't really, even after all this time."

I flash Adrian a smile, or as much as he can see above the heavy-knit scarf.

"Touché. Well, what do you want to know? I'm an open book, man," he says with a coffee-tinged grin.

"Really? All right then, you asked for it." I arch then invert my gloved fingers as if preparing to type the Great American Novel. "Favourite colour? Where did you go to school? What's the meaning of life? Do you say 'aitch' or 'haitch'? Do you know the way to San Jose? Aaaand...what's a nice man like you doing in a park like this? Go."

He releases a steaming roar of laughter into the air. "Very good, my friend, very good. Joking's a good sign."

"I must be on the mend then, huh?"

We continue our meandering journey around the park. It's one of those crisp winter days people love to wank on about; heavenly in the sunlight, desolate in the shade. The Serpentine lies almost motionless. A few months from now gung-ho swimmers will plonk into the lake like captive manatees being released into the wild. But for now, only a few ducks skim its surface.

Recently Adrian's been kind enough to bring our sessions outside of his office. He understands it's not easy for me to sit on the reclining chair when it's not been that long since I sat where he does.

A recovered-memory therapist. That's what I was for years. A *Stitcher*, as it's more commonly called – a healer of people with ghosts in their pasts. Turns out I wasn't very good at it. Not that Adrian's my Stitcher. No. He's my mentor, my go-to guy to talk all things *Weaver* with and has been ever since I moved to London. Every Weaver has one. Well, *has* to have one. Even Adrian. If you were the paranoid type, you would consider mentors to be the eyes and ears of the Mnemosyne Project, the front line of control and surveillance. Me? I try to think of them as sponsors. Weavers Anonymous. So no, he's not my Stitcher. I tell myself this, burying the feeling that recent check-ins have seemed more like therapy.

"Done anything fun recently?"

"Fun?"

"Yes, fun. That thing people have from time to time. Bowling, cinema, dinner parties. That sort of thing"

"Hmmm. Fun fun fun fun fun," I mutter. "Nope doesn't ring a bell. Oh wait, no, I did meet up with someone a couple of nights ago. An acquaintance if you will. Well not really an acquaintance. But we're acquainted now I suppose.”

"Dougie?”

"Hm?”

"Did you go on a date?”

"Well…” I burrow into my scarf

"You dog,” he barks, then wraps his arms around me.

"Hey man, what the hell? Professional boundaries, jeez,” I jest, but nudge him off all the same.

"Oh hey, you're right sorry.” He holds his hands aloft. "A date! How'd it go?”

"Pretty good. Pretty good.” I can't contain my smile. "I mean not so good at the start, then bad in the middle, but good in the end.”

"Did you guys–”

"What? No. What do you take me for?”

"Well, I mean I don't wanna presume. But it's been a while, hasn't it. What, five months? Six?”

"Jesus, I share *far* too much with you, man.”

"Well come on, that's how this thing works.”

"That's exactly what you said to me last night when my head was full of that woman's damage,” I say, cocking my eyebrow.

Adrian stops then looks at me.

"Well it's true isn't it, Dougie?” He lays a hand on my shoulder and squeezes. "This is good news, let me enjoy it.”

"Sure. Sorry. You're right. This is good.”

"Normal problems for a normal life,” he says. "That's what it's all about.”

A normal life. I try to suppress my bullshit gauge – something I always do when Adrian says things like that.

"What's he like?” Adrian says.

"Who, the guy? He's nice. Dhaval. He's refreshingly...normal. You'd be pleased.”

"You know what I'm going to say,” he tilts his head, suddenly serious.

I don't give him the satisfaction of a reply. Just stare ahead, letting him sing his tired old song.

"You know the deal, Dougie. If it's going to turn into an ongoing thing, I need to report it. I don't want to use the word 'vet' but I will need to have a little...chat...with him. Just due diligence, a formality.”

A formality, sure. If profiling someone is a formality. Digging into their history, their every movement, to seek anything that might suggest they pose a risk to the Great Secret is a formality. If putting someone on a register of people to be Erased at the slightest leak is a fucking formality. But I don't say any of that.

"Yup. Totally. I'm not going to tell him what I am, Adrian. It's too soon.”

"I think I'll be the judge of that,” he says with a note of warning in his voice, but a smile creeping back onto his face. "I'd like to *see* him. May I?”

Something small twinges in my stomach.

"Uh...sure. Sure,” I say.

I pinch the tip of my glove, slide it off then hold out my hand open-palmed for Adrian. He clears his throat, cradles the underside of my hand in his, then with the other lightly drags the tip of his middle finger down my palm. His eyelids flutter, then close.

"Show me."

I feel him searching. An electrical tickle deep inside my head. I concentrate, focus on the evening with Dhaval – the bar, the drinks, his eyes. I gather up everything innocuous I can recall and offer it to Adrian, package it up nice and neat and push it towards the tiny buzz in my mind.

"Oh," he says, eyes still closed, eyebrows arching. "Great bar, think I know the place. Mmm, whiskey chaser. My favourite. Tastes expensive too. Oh. You felt so nervous. Now where is he...oh. Hello there. Lovely smile. Good kisser? Let's see..."

"C'mon man," I say, pulling my hand and the memory back. He grips my wrist.

"Ts ts ts," he tuts. Then rushes forward.

The bathroom. My reflection. The Echo of the rockstar interview at the desert *military base. Dhaval's face approaching mine. His lips. The softness of his tongue. His face again, this time outside of my taxi. My bed. The parcel. My exhaustion. Her. Running. Screaming. 'Help me. It hurts. Remember me '" –*

"Fuck off," I shout, yanking out of his grasp. "What the hell are you doing?"

"Dougie, whoa now, shhhhh, take a breath," he sings. "Just *chillax*."

We stand there, breath evaporating into the space between us.

"I just needed to see," he says, "you know I need to see. To make sure you're okay. What did we say about you fighting me on these things?"

I look down at my shoes and take in a deep breath. "Sure, sorry."

Silence.

"He's still in there, isn't he? The journalist. Kieron. I thought we got rid of him," he says with an air of disappointment.

"Yeah," I breathe out. I can't bring myself to look at Adrian. "He's still there. But he's mostly gone. Seriously, it's not bad. Not like it was. His trauma, all that's gone from me, I swear. These are just little Echoes. I'm fine honestly. If anything, he's helping me."

"Helping you?"

"Yeah," I mutter, and kick a pebble along the pathway. "His skills, you know. All that experience. I think maybe I...maybe I could–"

Adrian's voice booms, making me jump. "Could what? Jesus, Dougie, maybe you could what? Be a hotfooted reporter, a prize-winning writer extraordinaire? God, how many times have we been over this? Don't you see, this is just him, his Echo still bangin' around inside your noggin." He screws a finger against his temple.

"Maybe it's not though. Maybe this is something I could be good at.

Maybe this is me. He's just showing me the way to find a new direction for my life, away from–"

"Oh come on, you can't be that deluded, Dougie. See sense. This is–"

"I know I know I know," I say through gritted teeth. "You've said it a million times, but you're not listening to me. Look, I know it was bad. I mean c'mon, I was the one that had him in my head. But he's gone now, I swear it. Just let me...this could be good for me. I'm good at it, I think I could be really good at it."

He looks at me stone cold. Then realisation dawns.

"Wait. Is this why you were late in getting here today? You weren't– Dougie tell me that wasn't you…"

I feel the blood drain from my cheeks. "I just wanted to try–"

"Oh for God's sake, Douglas," He walks a few paces then doubles back. "You were playing at being him, weren't you?"

"No, this was me. All me. Look I'm trying to explain to you that this is something I could be good at, just me. To hell with being a Stitcher, that was never for me. The Project's benched me, for fuck's sake. But this… Okay look, I just set up an interview with this playwright woman. That's all. Told her it was an interview for a newspaper."

He groans, and pinches the bridge of his nose.

I continue: "Which okay, might have been a lie. But I had a plan. I was going to write it up and get someone to publish it. I had a plan, don't you see?"

He shakes his head and shoots me a pained expression. "Dougie," he whispers.

"I know," I say. "But you've got to believe me, this is me. *I* want to do this. It's not him. He's gone. It's just a few of his skills are still there and I'm making use of them."

More silence.

"I'll be reporting this. You know that?" he says quietly.

A flash of rebuttal almost bursts out of me, but disappears just as suddenly as it ignites – the icy look in his eyes extinguishing any fight in me. I close my mouth and look up to the sky. A single green parakeet darts high above our heads, flitting through the canopies of oak and silver birch, and then out into the free air.

"I know," I say, defeat spreading through my frame, followed by a tiny spark of panic. "What do you think they'll do? More therapy? Another trip to the Erasers?"

"Don't worry about that now. Let me handle it."

"But maybe you don't need to report it? I'm doing well. This could just be between us."

"Shhhh," he shakes his head solemnly, his expression softening. "I have to. You know I do. It's for your own good, for all our own good. The Project protects. Always remember that. Sure, one day it's a Weaver accidentally picking up journalist skills, but the next it's some rogue government regime forcing Weavers back into the espionage game. So it's not just picking up journalist skills, Dougie. It's a direct threat to the Mnemosyne Protocol – the *one thing* that stops people out there from abusing us again. We stick to the rules; they stick to the rules. That's the deal."

"You don't need to lecture–," I mutter.

"Apparently I do," he says. "Look. Maybe...maybe they'll be fine with just upping your sessions with me."

"Okay," I feel my chin crease and tremble. "Thanks Adrian. You know I appreciate your help. I just–"

"Hey, come on now." He closes the gap between us and squeezes my arm.

"I just wanted something–"

"I know you did. I know."

"Thought this could be good for me. A new direction." I wipe my nose on my sleeve then sigh. "Aw man. What a mess."

"Not a mess, my friend. Just a work in progress."

This makes me chuckle a little.

"I think that's enough for today, don't you?" he says.

"God yeah."

"Okay then. Shall we get out of this park? I'm freezing my nuts off."

"Sure. Actually I'm going to head home this way, if that's all right," I say, pointing in the opposite direction.

"Of course. You'll be fine?"

"I'll be fine."

We hug, then part.

"Oh Dougie," he calls. "Who was the young woman?

"What?"

"The one that was running. Screaming for help?"

"Oh. Uh, just a movie," I blurt, heart lurching. "Watched it just before I fell asleep. One of those murder mysteries. Shouldn't do that right before I sleep, eh? Give me nightmares."

He makes a little nod to acknowledge my joke, but confusion doesn't leave his face.

"Nightmares. Good one. Well, I'll be seeing you then. Be good to yourself, yeah, Dougie? I'll be in touch."

I walk on, pretending I'm out of earshot.

Chapter 5

It must be ten minutes before I realise where I've walked. Unthinking feet were desperate to carry me away from Adrian; if they'd been thinking, they wouldn't have taken me here.

Victorian terraces line each side of the South Kensington street – alabaster regiments standing to attention, protecting their prestigious inhabitants. And yet, nestled between the embassy workers and Russian oligarchs are occasional oddities, like the people in this building.

Out of pure habit I've stopped halfway down the street, at the portico-framed footsteps of a townhouse I know all too well. No plaque or sign indicates who or what occupies the building. If it had, it would read 'Mnemosyne Project UK'. But it doesn't.

When I first came here, immediately after graduating, I stood agog at this entrance. I remember the swelling pride as I walked through these doors.

"Ahh, first day. I remember mine well," the woman says as she leads me up the stairs past a series of empty rooms.

"Are these…?" I begin.

"Oh, we have plenty of space," she waves at the air. "We're very lucky you know. Gifted a long term lease way back in the seventies. A luxury really, having this all to ourselves with so few of us kicking around in it. Not like the bigger branches, I imagine. Bangkok, did you say?"

"Yeah that's right."

"Fancy."

"If barbed wire and lino are fancy," I venture.

She laughs too quickly. "Gosh you are funny. Anyway this is the kitchen…"

Back then the excitement at having finally left school put a sheen on everything. But now I see it so differently. I see the mould creeping up the columns, can practically smell the damp therapy rooms, feel their peeling plasterwork and crumbling cornices, hear the gurgle and wheeze of the plumbing. What once seemed ostentatious and supremely 'London' now seems decrepit and forgotten.

For all its highly classified status, its intergovernmental heft, this Project branch is operated on a shoestring. There are only a few hundred thousand Weavers in the world, so no need to throw too much cash at maintaining the secret. Only the three big branches get the real money anyway. Atlanta. Cape Town. Bangkok. Small ones like London are all but outposts left on the fringes.

And yet, for all that, I'm stuck to the spot, hypnotised by the silent power of this place. Its bedrock mission. The words of Dr George McNamara ripple in my mind. The Founder. The guy who helped lead Weavers out from the clutches of the covert government operations and into the protected shade of The Project. I guess anything would be better than what he found in those awful labs. It's no wonder his journal, shocking and stark, is still a primary text for any Weaver.

> *"What has been done to them is unspeakable. Mnemosynes young and old, gaunt and glassy-eyed, transformed into weapons by means of torture and cruel conditioning. Reduced to zombified arms of war, haunted by the Echoes of the minds they were forced to hook into."*

Have we really come so far since our 'release'? Since quiet laws have been ratified in our name – our existence prised from cruel hands only to be hidden away in top secret vaults alongside God knows what other threats that have been deemed too mind bending, too existentially crushing for the general public to contemplate. Isn't The Project just another covert agency?

In every way that matters, my whole life has been orchestrated by this little institution. From my induction, to the training I received in the Far East, to my recent expulsion. Now here I am, on the other side of the door.

In spite of myself and the anger I feel towards The Project, a contradictory part of me still longs for its embrace. But I can never go back. My own recklessness saw to that.

> *"Are you going to fix me? Put me back together again?*
> *"You bet I am. Just you wait and see."*

Words from the fringes of my fractured memory. Taunting me, holding up a mirror to my hubris. I stumble out of their trajectory, cursing myself with each step for coming back here. Back to the scene of the crime.

***

"Dog. Hey, dog!"
The █████████████████████████████████████ *sharpens my senses. Suddenly I feel every* █████████████ *on my body all at once. Cheekbone, shoulder, ribs, lower back, eyebrow, thigh. They all* ████ *with a keen throb.*
Lost all sense of time. We could've been at this for minutes or days. ██████ *still ripples in my heart, but with each impact of* ████████████████, *a new sensation is taking its place. A dull and* █████ *feeling. Don't know what it is, but I know I should be* █████ *of it. Feels like approaching sleep. But not the kind you feel at the end of a day when your head settles on the pillow. God, pillows. How long has it been since I laid my head on one? No, this isn't like that. It's like sleep that offers no* █████. *Only emptiness.*

"Hey!" A fresh ████ *on my cheek.*

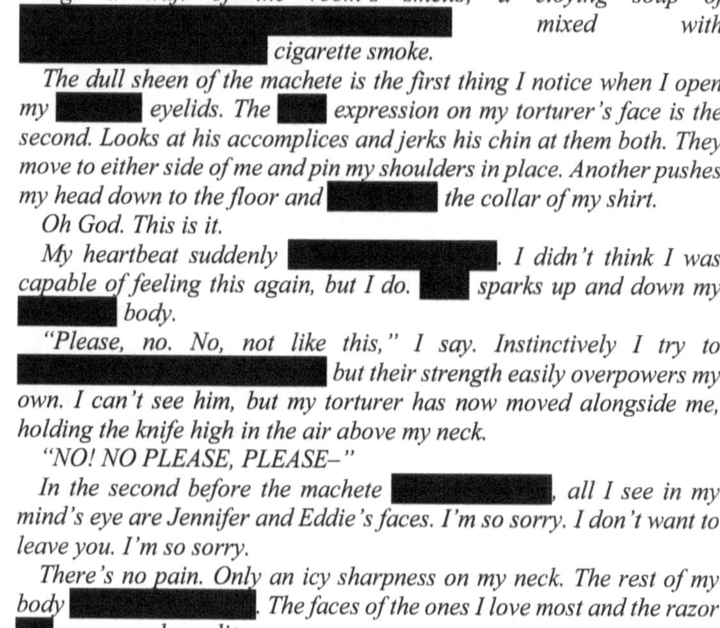

Lift my face up, as far as I can from kneeling. The cable ties around my wrists ████████████████████████████. *Shifting like this brings a waft of the room's smells; a cloying soup of* ████████████████████ *mixed with* ████████ *cigarette smoke.*

The dull sheen of the machete is the first thing I notice when I open my ████ *eyelids. The* ████ *expression on my torturer's face is the second. Looks at his accomplices and jerks his chin at them both. They move to either side of me and pin my shoulders in place. Another pushes my head down to the floor and* ████████ *the collar of my shirt.*

Oh God. This is it.

My heartbeat suddenly ████████████. *I didn't think I was capable of feeling this again, but I do.* ████ *sparks up and down my* ████████ *body.*

"Please, no. No, not like this," I say. Instinctively I try to ████████████████████ *but their strength easily overpowers my own. I can't see him, but my torturer has now moved alongside me, holding the knife high in the air above my neck.*

"NO! NO PLEASE, PLEASE–"

In the second before the machete ████████████, *all I see in my mind's eye are Jennifer and Eddie's faces. I'm so sorry. I don't want to leave you. I'm so sorry.*

There's no pain. Only an icy sharpness on my neck. The rest of my body ████████████. *The faces of the ones I love most and the razor* ████ *are my only reality.*

Silence.

And then laughter. I didn't expect laughter. Slowly the shapes and sounds and smells of the room come back into focus. I'm on the floor, ████████████████████, *and above me the raucous laughter of men reverberates.*

I open my eyes and I see him kneeling down to my level. My torturer bears the widest smile I have ever seen. Between his fingers he dangles a cloth, water dripping from the end of it to the floor by my face. At this sight I become aware of the true sensation on my neck: the cold wetness of water, and the sharp sting of the cloth having been whipped against it.

I moan with ████████. *Mirth rings around the room in response.*

I thought it was all over. My ████ *finally brought to an end. But they were only toying with me. Their cruelty cuts deeper than a knife.*

***

His name was Kieron Marber, and he was a foreign correspondent for a national newspaper. Redacted memories like this, plus a few case notes, are what I remember about my time treating him.

Three years ago Kieron was getting ready to leave his beat as a war reporter for a more stable position as a profile writer – politicians, artists, celebrity-types, that kind of thing. It was a bold move, but he was ready to make the change for the good of his wife, Jennifer, and their toddler, Eddie. His last assignment before the career change was covering civil uprisings in the Middle East. It was supposed to be a simple job. Get in, gather some civilian vox pops, thread it together with some colour, and get out. He'd written that story countless times before. But within a day he and his fixer were taken hostage by a militant faction and for the following twenty-six months he was beaten, starved, and moved from one hidden location to another.

Within six months his fixer, a brave young man (*what was his name? I'm sure I used to know*) with an unwavering vision of what his country's freedom could look like, had been killed. At this point, Kieron began losing hope that he would be rescued.

He had some idea about the efforts probably being made to do so, though obviously they hadn't been successful. He knew diplomats would try their bit, that his newspaper would splash it – 'Our reporter, kidnapped behind enemy lines'. Poor Jennifer and little Eddie, they would have had cameras thrust in their faces.

Kieron felt the campaign for his release would have begun to wane by now and the news would be moving on.

By 12 months, his mind had all but closed off thoughts of home. Too painful to reflect on life before now. Windowless rooms with stained walls, tattered mattresses, buckets for shitting in. This was reality now.

The periodic beatings and mock executions he became numb to somehow. If once the fear had ripped through him, making him wail with noises he never knew were within him, now he felt little when they came for him.

'Dog'. That was the only English word he heard for more than two years. He was able to make out a few snippets in their own tongue. None of them nice words.

He began to drift. Day by day losing his sense of self, becoming more body than soul. Faces of those he'd known, those he'd loved, melding into featureless canvasses. Occasionally, his captors would delight in flashing him his reflection in mirrors. An emaciated stranger looked back at him.

Two months before his rescue by local oppositional forces, the dynamic changed. The beatings began once more, but this time they weren't for extracting information or even recreation. They had long since learned 'Dog' had nothing of value to offer them. No, this fresh bout of torture was to prepare him for the camera.

"My name is Kieron Marber, I am a reporter, a British citizen. In ten days, I will be beheaded, unless a ransom of $100,000,000 is paid."

In a strange way he welcomed the resurgence of terror into his life. It had been a long time since he had felt any fear of death.

A handful of nights before his planned execution, armed men in scarves stormed the house he was kept in. Later, he would discover the location was only a few miles west of the village he had been abducted from. For now though, he finally let himself go. Into the hands of his saviours he flowed. Hands, faces, voices, the growl of a vehicle carrying him into the night. A single thought rose above the fog in his mind.

'Is this the end?'

"Are you going to fix me? Put me back together again?" he asks, eyes raw.

"You bet I am," I say. *"Just you wait and see."*

Kieron Marber wasn't supposed to be my client.

For trauma cases such as Kieron's, Erasing is usually the prescribed treatment. *Erasers* – Weavers with a special talent for removing memories – are a rarity. They're feared and valued in equal measure by the few that know of their existence. Imagine being able to reach into someone's mind and simply cut out memories, like a surgical scalpel excising a tumour? Valuable, maybe even lifesaving. But in the wrong hands? That's why The Project keeps such tight control on Erasers.

The Mnemosyne Protocol dictates that any licensed Weaving, especially Erasure, is prescribed to only very special cases where conventional therapy won't work. Prisoners of war are one of the most common clients. This is one of the ways we earn our keep, justifying the meagre funds governments around the world give to The Project.

All treatment is conducted on the downlow of course. No patient ever remembers being treated by Weavers, at least not the superhuman elements of the therapy. That's Erased along with any trauma they're being treated for. It's very clever, really. If a tad chilling when you think about it too long.

"I think I'm a lost cause, Doc," Kieron says while picking at a deep button on the Chesterfield.

"I disagree," I say. Poor guy looks so hollow. Defeated. *"Your situation is challenging, sure. But there's always a treatment."* Damned if I know what it is yet.

"Challenging," he repeats. *"Please just tell me like it is."*

"Okay then," I say, taking a deep breath. Fuck it, he's not going to remember any of this anyway. *"The problem is, Kieron, your trauma of the past few years, your wholesale acceptance of your new reality as prisoner 'Dog', has formed an impenetrable wall in your mind."*

He looks at me blankly, comprehension far from his grasp, way out there along with his will to even care.

"You've locked away so much of your former life before the abduction that you need to be brought back to yourself before the trauma of the past two years can be Erased. As awful as your new reality is, to remove it could leave you as little more than a shell."

Many questions quiver on his lips.

"But that's why I'm here."

Kieron needed a Stitcher.

If Erasers are the surgical knife, then we Stitchers are the needle and thread. We are trained to do what no-one else can.

"How do you do it?"

Even after all these years it still feels weird talking so openly with a regular human being about this. Like I'm breaking some sacred rule.

"Well, we work with the frayed edges of memories. Traumatic memories which are buried deep in the subconscious, festering and malignant. Just like yours. We bring these memories into the conscious part of the mind where they can be more safely processed. You see, Kieron, traumatic memories only have power in the inaccessible corners of our minds. Bring them to the light and they shrivel and die."

"Oh," is all he says. "Is it safe?"

"Completely," I say.

I was so naïve. Yes, the danger for patients is minimal, but for the Stitcher? That's a different matter. The darker the trauma, the higher the risk for us. And the kicker is, I knew this, had been told about it. The trauma of countless other patients was already swimming in my mind, loosening the foundations of my Safe – my mental vault – to its limit. But I didn't care. Was too caught up in my own cleverness, inflated by a superhero complex. I could fix anyone. Even someone as damaged as Kieron Marber.

And so I started his treatment. We began small, as much for me as for him.

"Lie back and close your eyes. Yes, just like that. Okay, now I'm going to lightly touch your temples just like this. Is that okay?"

"Sure," he says. Even this far along he doesn't believe what I've been telling him. Thinks I'm some crackpot shrink. The saddest part is that he just goes along with it anyway.

"All right then. Now, I'm going to try to bypass your memories of the past two years by making 'a call'. What I mean by that is I'm going to ask you to cast your mind back to a life episode from long ago. So how about a first day at school?"

"I really can't remem…I'm sorry," he says, straining through his lids.

"That's fine, don't worry. How about a childhood party? Balloons, cake, something like that?"

"Maybe. Yes actually. I think I remember something. Party games in the back garden maybe?"

"Great, hold on to that. Visualise every element of it. The sights, the sounds, any smells. Don't push, just let it flow."

We started to gain ground with this method. Kieron's Echoes – his memories as seen in my mind's eye – showed a lot. Beyond the terror of his prison years, I could feel the warmth of his past. Like the first glimmers of spring after winter, I could practically reach out and grasp the shoots of Kieron's former life. He was there waiting for me to free him, just on the other side.

But for the current Kieron, these Stitching sessions were swiftly becoming a fresh form of torment. Each flicker of his early life was accompanied by roaring flames of his recent abuse.

"I can't! Please don't make me see it. I can feel it, please don't!"
"It's okay, Kieron, it's okay. I'm here, you're safe. Just breathe. In and out. In. And out. Shhh."

I couldn't continue this way. It wasn't helping. Kieron was coming apart at the seams, and I wasn't faring much better. His trauma was burning me too. No, I needed to find a new method to break through his walls in a way that didn't traumatise him further, for both our sakes. So I got experimental. I tapped up a contact who worked deeper in The Project. She sent me some research papers, classified to low graded Weavers like me. They showed me some new potential methods for reaching into deeper memory systems. By a combination of these experimental techniques and some I knew from training, I hypothesised that mixing hypnosis and Weaving could be the key. And in a way it was.

I felt like I was on some new frontier. Tipped for greatness.

"Are you going to fix me? Put me back together again?" he asks, eyes raw. My heart breaks for him.
"You bet I am," I say. *"Just you wait and see. Now just listen to the sound of my voice, and let everything else go."*

I was pleased how quickly Kieron fell into a trance. This meant he wouldn't have to endure the pain of therapy any longer. I prepared myself for a deep dive. Dimmed the lights, emptied my mind, settled my breathing, then reached for Kieron's hand and closed my eyes…

What happened next has been heavily redacted from my mind courtesy of Erasers. Ironic, I know. But between the snippets of Echoes I retain, and the reams of notes written about this case, I know the broad strokes.

I drowned. Dived into the depths of Kieron's memories, through the tumult of his years of torture and out the other side. I found him, the real Kieron, before the claws of captivity had dug into him, and pulled him towards me. But I wasn't prepared for the flood. His memories rushed to the surface, gasped for air and continued straight into me. His pain, his relief, his defeat, his hope – now mine.

I was eventually brought out of my coma a few weeks afterwards. My mind had gone into spasm at the onslaught of Kieron's Echoes. But through careful Stitching and the heavy hands of Erasers, I was brought back to myself. Well, a close proximity.

I was put on leave. Permanently. By conducting unsanctioned techniques

I had violated the Mnemosyne Project code. My saving grace, the thing that saved me from prison, was Kieron. While misguided, my efforts had healed him, taken down the wall. Erasers were then able to do their thing and cut out the tumour of his years in captivity, plus the superhuman elements of his treatment by me, and let him get on with his life. His memories of the life before were untouched. Only Echoes, duplicates of his memories, had flooded into me.

I never saw Kieron again, though in some ways I see him every day. The benign pieces of his psyche, the Echoes left on the cutting room floor by Erasers, they live on in my mind. Most of it's harmless, useful even. Kieron's talent for journalism has stayed in me. I've tried to put it to use, hoping it could be my gateway to a new career, a new life far away from the Mnemosyne Project.

I can barely feel Kieron's trauma within me. Erasers removed the horror, the pain, the fear, but the emptiness and untidy scars left by Erasers have an eeriness all of their own.

Chapter 6

The air bites my lungs.

In. Out. In. Out.

It's been a while since I tried anything even close to exercise and my body's telling me all about it. I push harder.

In. Out. In. Out.

The sharpness of it all feels good, brings me clarity, blows away the looping dream that's wrenched me awake for the past four nights. *Remember me. Remember me.* Push it away, leave it behind.

I slalom round morning commuters, dog walkers, bundles of newspapers, gaggles of school kids. A homeless man sits up in a sleeping bag. What worlds would I find within his psyche if I touched his hand?

But I don't stop. Just pass by everyone, leaving them for dust.

Mornings have no routine since I was fired. A trickle of sick pay from The Project has sustained me, but only just. Hence why I had to move from my beautiful apartment in north London, to this flatshare out east. Money. Who needs it. Just keep running.

In. Out. In. Out.

Fifteen minutes in I feel a surge of endorphins. The rush is timed perfectly, just as I break free of the chewing gum-splattered pavements and down to the smooth banks of the canal. Houseboats of unique shapes and colours hem the waterside, with faded names on their bows. *Go Fish. Samphire. Tenacious B. High Life. Uptown Girl.*

I push on through the morning mist. My lungs begin to burn, my side cramps, but it just spurs me on.

In out in out in out in out in out…

Enough! I thunder to a halt, legs wobbling, fingers planted on thighs. Breathe in. Hold. And out. I lift my head up. My eyeline's level with the prow of a boat. In chipped calligraphy, a single name: Olivia.

I graze the name with a finger. I smile at the hazy memories invoked by the name. Olivia. It's been more than half my lifetime…

We were friends. I feel that fact somewhere deep inside. Fortresses built out of chairs and bed sheets. Imaginary quests through a magical forest. She was a little older than me. I think. For all our adventures together, I can barely remember her. Like most of my life, my childhood's a jumble.

Now that I think of it, Olivia's come to represent everything before I was taken away to the Mnemosyne Project's South East Asia branch for schooling. Cut away from home and thrown into a new life as a Weaver, joining my fellow freaks: Nina, Kaito, and Venny. Maybe I've always held friendships up to the memory of Olivia. Nostalgia creates very high pedestals, but then it's difficult to compete with the dead. An accident, a car maybe? Immediate death on impact. Or was it falling from a tree? Either way, she was gone in an instant. All I have left are the fragments of our time together. It was all so long ago. When was the last time I even thought about you, Olivia? Why am I suddenly holding on to your memory again, when I can barely remember you?

Is it you, Olivia? Are you who I'm dreaming of? The young woman without a face. No, not without a face. A blur, yes. But more a feeling of a person than the sight of their face…the sense of a person…

I plod on to ease the stitch in my side. It's just above freezing, but my body's a furnace. Keep moving.

Thoughts drift back to the dream. They're never far from it. As the mystery of it all has consumed me with each night's repeat, I've fallen into a research spiral. Starting with the pendant; does the emblem of the intersecting circles mean anything? Can I find any other examples of it anywhere? No luck. Just an ordinary pendant.

I feel it shifting along its chain. I've taken to wearing it in the past few days. Something compelling about having it near. I reach inside and bring the warm metal to my lips.

What does it actually mean for a Weaver to start dreaming? This has been almost impossible to research. My mind snaps back to the old textbook I was reading just before heading out. What little reference I found was less than comforting:

'Dreaming is a rare phenomenon for Mnemosynes. Particularly for those of Grades 3 and higher. The experience of dreaming should be investigated and closely monitored. Dreams could be a product of the imagination, but could also signify early onset psychosis.'

Wonderful.

And what of the dream itself? Where are we running? It feels like it could be outside somewhere, but the environment is so vague. All a blur. And the circle we sit in? That feels like somewhere else, somewhere inside. Dark and warm. And I feel younger. If it even is me. No, it is me. "Angel". I hear them saying my nickname from years ago. From school.

And then I feel it again. The lightest thrum of electricity emanating from the pendant. My lips, so sensitive, pick it up immediately. I stop dead and close my eyes, determined to not let the sensation evade me. Focus. Empty your mind, just like I was trained. Flow with it...

I'm there in the circle again.

But also here by the canal. Lucid. Don't lose it, hold yourself between it all. Focus.

I feel the grain of the wooden flooring. A fan rotates above us. Us. Many pairs of legs, crossed on the floor like mine. I hear the mumbling of voices. What are they saying? I can't make it out. Try. Focus. No, it's all soft and indistinct.

"Here, like this." A voice much closer cuts through the haze. She's right next to me. "Here, close your hands over it." The pendant, I feel it between my palms. "Now listen to it, talk to it, pour yourself into it. There's so much in there. A world within a world."

The scene drifts out of reach. I come to, on the banks of the canal.

"Olivia?" I whisper. "Is it you?"

My heart's not thundering this time. I feel more control than I have in ages. I know more now. The floor, the fan, that's my boarding house in Thailand, I'm sure of it. But why would Olivia be there? She had died long before I left England. So if not her, then who was talking to me?

More questions. But the answers are in here, in the pendant. I don't know how I know, I just do. I think...I think I just Read the pendant. Read the Echoes buried within it. Is that even possible?

A Grade 3 Generic. That's all I've ever been. A straight-down-the-line, generalist, middle-of-the-road-Weaver. An ability to do almost anything, but without a major affinity for any of it. I mean, I got by okay at school, I was a decent student, so I picked up the basics of memory Reading and Writing well. Even learned a little Erasing.

The Project has always had trouble with people like me. What to do with a Generic of my middling level? And then there was that self-aggrandising desire to help others. I practically had 'become a therapist' written on my forehead. That's how I got trained up as a Stitcher. Didn't fight a single step of it. Generalist by name and nature.

But Reading the Echoes in objects? I've never heard of that before, let alone done it.

I open my phone up and head straight for *'It's nem-o-see-nee, bitch'*. I'm about to start typing. But no. I don't want to discuss this with everyone, I need to contain this. I back up a level and scan down the list of text conversations until I find her, then type:

'Hey Neens. Weird question. Have you ever dreamed? Like, fallen asleep and had an actual dream?'

My thumb hovers over the send button. *Come on, this is Nina. You can trust her.* I hit send, then back out of the chat.

Am I crazy? Am I finally losing it? If I am, why have I not felt this focused and in control in months?

Fuck it. I'm taking control of my life.

Without a second thought I search my phone book and hit the call icon. No hesitations. The phone rings two, three, four times. I hold out.

"Hey Dougie," he says with a note of surprise.

"Hi Dhaval. Sorry to call in the morning. I just, uh–"

"The morning? It's 2018, nobody calls full stop," he says with a chuckle. "I'm kidding. It's nice to hear from you. I wasn't sure if... What's up?"

"I, uh, well..." *Come on. Do it.* "I just wanted to see if you were free for date number two?"

Chapter 7

The water glass begins to sing; at first low and indistinct but growing more sonorous as I hit the right circular rhythm. Like the hum of a prayer bowl the note blends in and out of my consciousness. A pair of eyes glare at me from across the room, so I halt the glass's tune.

I let out a sigh. When I first took my seat at the empty table I was nervous, but fifteen minutes on I'm descending into boredom.

"Are you sure I can't get you a proper drink while you wait?" She wears an electric blue Thai formal dress, hair pulled tightly into a bun on top of her head, but her accent is pure Leytonstone.

"No thanks, honestly. I'm happy to wait." *Not entirely happy.*

Alone once more, I dip my finger into the glass and raise it back to the rim, careful not to let the droplet fall. For a moment my fingertip and the glass become one, joined by the translucent bead.

I wonder…

Eyelids drop as my fingertip travels along the rim. *Focus, just like before, let your mind flow.* The crystalline song begins again. *Focus. Come on.* The mystery girl's words. *'Listen to it, talk to it'.*

For the longest time, nothing. But then, I hear the murmur; the life within the glass. The stories it can tell. Nothing concrete, little bursts of sound, light, taste, smell, emotion. Only the hint of an Echo, not like with a human being. *'Hello'*, I call into the very fabric of the glass, *'I'm here. Talk to me'.*

The flash of an image.

> *I'm reaching for the glass. It's full of wine. The red imprint of my bottom lip is smeared across its edge.*

The scene is gone as quickly as it appeared. I try to follow but it's useless. *Find another. There must be more in here.* Again I hear it. A cacophony of voices dialled down to a whisper. *Come on, speak to me…*

"Dougie?"

My eyes spring open and a face leaps into view; a bob of white hair, searching eyes and thin lips.

"Mum, hi," I say, rising to my feet and planting a kiss on her cheek.

"Sorry we're late. Your father insisted he knew where he was going without the need to refer to your directions."

He stands a few steps behind her, arms hanging off his broad shoulders. His hair's swept back in imitation of its former lustre, an effect mocked by the standard issue spectacles which perch on his Roman nose.

"Hey Dad." I raise my mental barriers then reach out a hand to shake his. It's warm, clammy. "Like the beard. Is it new?"

"Ish," he says.

"Are you okay Douglas," Mum asks as she drapes her jacket on the back of a seat, "You looked a million miles away there."

"Oh no, I'm good," I wave.

The waitress returns for our drinks order. We agree on a bottle of white wine; the option probably neither of us wants. Mum busies herself over the menu, a laminated booklet containing an overwhelming array of dishes and combinations. Dad peers over his glasses to do the same, while making little 'hmms' and 'pum pum pums'. I was never sure if they wanted me to take the reins over a Thai meal when I was a teenager and I'm even less sure now. I order vegetable skewers and satay sauce, a papaya salad which the waitress promises isn't 'too spicy', followed by red and green curries, plus a tofu Pad Thai noodle platter. Each dish is a diluted Westernised twist of the kind of things I used to order for them when they visited me in Bangkok, except then I ordered in Thai, using my smattering of the language to maximum effect. *'Look how well I'm doing, your boy's flourishing, love me please'*. That kind of thing. I don't attempt a single Thai word here.

"So how are things?" we ask in unison, followed by a threefold chorus of "no you first".

"Well, you know pottering along," says my mother, her Scottish lilt enduring despite all these years away from the homeland. "I'm still doing some volunteering at the library which ticks the time over nicely. And your father…" She offers a hand in his direction to pass the conversational ball, but he just looks back at her. "He's still winding down his hours at the office."

"I thought you retired," I say, forcing the ball firmly into his court.

"Yep, I did but they needed some extra support, so I've come back on as a consultant. Nothing big, just a few hours here and there."

Mum makes eyes at me and shakes her head.

"Well retirement isn't for everyone, eh Pops," I say.

"Hey I like retirement, but a few extra bucks don't hurt." Even after all these decades, his Californian accent remains intact, nasal and drawn out. I already feel my own being caught in its orbit.

"Sure thing. So are you still fighting the good fight with your eco warriors?"

"Oh they're doing great things," Mum chimes in. "The most recent beach clean-up was a great success, wasn't it darling?"

He nods and pushes his mouth together in a white man smirk, beard hairs splaying outwards.

My dad, the eco warrior, still holding on to his hippy dream. I used to admire him for that, or at least the ideal of it. A love of Mother Earth is what brought him and my Mum together all those years ago. She was on a post-high school tour of the States, escaping her Catholic upbringing on the West Coast of Scotland, and ended up finding love on the hedonistic West Coast of America. Somewhere around Haight-Ashbury, among the plumes of pot smoke and 'Save the Earth' placard-making, they found each other. I often wonder what happened to that anti-Capitalist duo and why they ended up trading it in for a half-life on the southern coast of England.

Though I understood Dad's reasons for leaving the States. A romantic perception of the world outside the US. To him, America felt like an island largely on its own, unlike Europe's interconnectedness and multiplicity of peoples, faiths, tongues. And yet one step on English soil and his foot became embedded.

Silence descends on the table. This is where Mum's going to ask me what news I've got.

"But enough about us. What's your news," she says. "How are you?"

This is where I'm going to do my little evasive manoeuvre.

"Good. Yeah. Nothing much to report really. Just, you know, getting used to the new place, exercising a bit. TV and books. You guys watching anything good?"

This is where Dad is going to take my bait – anything to keep the conversation light – but when my mother is going to kick it to the sidewalk.

"Well yes actu–" he begins.

"But how are you feeling? Any...clearer?" she intersects.

She doesn't really want to know. She's never wanted to know. But she asks anyway. That's what mothers do.

"Uh yeah," I bob my head, joining my Dad's gaze on the cream tablecloth. "Like I say, I'm good, just trying to live well and let time do its thing."

"Well that's good, that's very good. Your father and I, we were worried when we heard you had stepped away from your job."

"When I was fired," I prickle. "I mean let's call it what it is, Mum."

"No well…" She looks hurt. That's the worst.

"Look it's fine," I say evenly. "I was never any use at it anyway, so this is a positive thing in a way. A chance to find something new, far away from, from…" *Weaving.* I still can't bring myself to say it in front of my parents, even though I'm allowed to. They're on my safe list, The Project has vetted them serially over the years. The secret is safe. But even though, the words – Mnemosyne, Weaver, Stitcher, Generic, Reading, Writing, Erasing – have always tasted like swear words when I'm with them.

"Of course, away from...it all," she finishes for me.

***

Ironically, I don't think I remember the first time I Wove. My childhood was always kind of hazy, though I've accepted it as a simple fact of my life. Memories have ever been either mine or someone else's. I've never known a time when they've solely been my own.

What I do remember is my parents' reaction, and the understanding that my memories were something to be hidden. The awakening of my *otherness*.

The first – and therefore maybe worst – incident was when I was about three years old. We hadn't long moved to the UK from the States where I was born. The southern coast of England had seemed so green and rolling, or so my father always says. Anyway there we were, newly ensconced in

Kitsford, a pocket village of Sussex whose once tiny population may have bloomed in recent years, but has remained the Caucasian middle class enclave of my youth.

Mum hadn't long rejoined the workforce after taking time away to raise a family. Well, to have me. Finding childcare wasn't difficult in a village where everyone makes it their business to help, or at least get close enough to peek inside the doors of newcomers. Soon I was in the daytime care of Mrs Landing, an elderly local woman who filled her long-since empty nest with broods of other people's kids. The recent death of her husband Tom left even more room in her schedule to fill.

I remember her kindness, but also her old-school approach to discipline. One afternoon I wet myself, caught off guard after drinking too much juice. Instead of the fuss and cuddles I expected, I was shamed in front of my toddler peers for being so childish.

"Big boys don't wet themselves, Douglas," Mrs Landing says.
My pants are so soggy, getting cold. Everybody's laughing at me. I want to run away.
"Well if you're going to cry, then I'm just going to clean you up and send you to bed for a nap. Just like a little baby. Do you want that? Hmm?"

I didn't piss myself ever again.

Yet for all her strictness, Mrs Landing was very maternal. I still think of her sweetness, of our quiet times together, of her hand's warmth as she stroked my blond curls while reading to me, of the crooning sounds she made whenever I was hurt.

"There there, little one. Shhh shh shhhh. I'm here, don't you worry."

I was bereft when my mother told me I wouldn't be going back to Mrs Landing's again. I cried for weeks. 'That awful woman'. That was how she was referred henceforth. Had I done something wrong? Did Mum not approve of my love for Mrs Landing?

It wasn't either of those. It was more to do with the recollections I had begun to share with Mum. Memories of the long summers I spent in a cottage on the banks of Lake Windermere. Of the time my dear little William lost his first tooth. Of the night my friend Jean lost her leg while firewatching during a London air raid. Of the happiness of my wedding day, and the nerves of my wedding night.

I remember Mum's face blurring from mild interest, to curiosity, to horror as I shared my stories.

"It was so sad, Mummy. When Tom said his last words to me. I just held his hand and he stopped breathing," I say.
Mum looks at me, her mouth is open. Is she going to cry too?
"Don't be sad for me. It was good that I could be there for Tom. At the

end of our life together. In sickness and in health, Mummy, isn't it."

Of course I now understand why my mother acted the way she did. Here was her three-year-old son speaking in a vocabulary far beyond his years. Here was her three-year-old son who suddenly she could barely recognise.

I must have terrified her, yet I don't remember feeling any fear. Didn't question why the more contact I had with Mrs Landing, the more I could recall memories that weren't my own, that I could reflect on episodes of someone else's joy and sadness. It felt natural and right to me. This must be the way humans live. By sharing. By blending.

The shame only came when I saw my mother's face that day, when I realised that this wasn't how humans live. In the years that followed, I strove to forge an iron curtain between myself and others. Physical proximity, skin-to-skin contact, is how Weavers connect. So I learned to shrug off hugs, to pull my hands away from any attempts to reach for them. This compulsion to separate Self and Other waged internally too. Any memories I accidentally Wove, I became desperate to push away. But without training, I usually failed. They collided inside me as they grew in number. Attempts to hide my Weaving began to fail, and cracks began to show.

I was sent to a therapist, Dr Jansen, who seemed to understand my issues.

"Well hello there, Douglas. Come take a seat here next to me. That's right. Now, your mummy tells me you've been having a little trouble. Don't you worry. I can help you keep all those busy thoughts nice and tidy."

She was a Mnemosyne Project scout. My journey into the great secret had begun. She helped me build a construct in my mind where I could lock down the memories of others that I Read. I created my Safe.

I've always wondered what would have happened if I hadn't seen my mother's face that day. Would I have been able to stay in that serene state of balance forever? Away from The Project's reach.

***

"...and then your father, well he just knocked on their window and when they wound it down he threw the rubbish into the car and said...and said..." Mum can barely get the punchline out for heaving with laughter. "He said...why don't you stick your trash up your *ass* and dispose of it at home, ya *bleepin'* litterbug?"

She purses her lips shut and opens her eyes wide.

"Dad, you did not." I don't know what I find more funny; how much of a lightweight drinker my mother is, or my Dad bringing vigilante justice to the mean streets of Sussex.

"I did, I really did," he says, cracking a smile. "I don't know what came over me, I just saw red and had to do something about it."

"Well I'm proud of you, man. Jeez I'm sure as hell going to watch which recycling bins I place my trash in. Don't wanna confuse the brown with the blue and get taken down by the Bad Ass of Kitsford."

We chuckle together, then Mum makes a contented sigh, places her fork on her plate and sits back in her chair. "Oh but you should come and see the house some time, it's been so long. Won't you?"

"Sure Mum, I promise," I say. She knows I'm lying but doesn't let it spoil the mood. "How is the old place anyway? And jolly old Kitsford? Has it reached the 21st century yet?"

"Oh shoosh," she says. "It's lovely. Listen to you, you're such a hardened Londoner now. You were so *chillaxed* when you arrived from San Francisco."

"Oh God, Mum. *Chillaxed?*"

"Yes chillaxed. That's what we love about the south, isn't it Nico," she looks to my father who shrugs. "It's so *chillaxed*. You used to love it as a wee boy, just running around the village happy as you like."

"Whatever you say, Mum."

"I do. I do say." Her eyes are bloodshot, cheeks rosy – the papaya salad was indeed a little 'too spicy'. "You would spend hours out in the garden, or in the park across the road doing lord knows what for hours on end."

"Making fortresses on the private estate that backs onto the park as I recall," Dad says, one eyebrow lifted. Mum giggles.

"It's true, I did. Hey, is that huge pine tree still there?" I say.

She squints.

"Man, I loved that tree," I say. "Olivia and I used to dare each other to climb that thing but I was always too scared. She did it though, she was always so brave..."

"Who, darling?"

"Hmm?"

"Who did you climb the tree with?"

"Olivia, my friend. You remember?"

"I..."

"Come on, we lived in each other's back pockets. Remember that time she bumped her head on the tree and I came running to you and Dad. I was crying. I can't remember more than... it was all so crazy–"

And just like that the air leaves the table. My mother's colour drains. Her eyes, bright only a millisecond ago, are now small. Like she's gone somewhere else, somewhere far.

"Lisa," Dad croons quietly, placing his hand over hers on the table. His expression has fallen too, somehow ashen.

Mum lifts the water glass and takes a long slow sip.

"Mum? Are you okay? Was it something I–"

"Why don't you tell us about the job hunt, Doug," my Dad jumps in, his expression brightening. The effect is more forced than natural. "What's the plan?"

"I, uh...Mum seriously are you–" I reach out with my hand but she retreats. "Mum?"

"I'm fine, I'm fine," she says, her expression trying to correct itself but eyes still damp. "Just the chilli in the salad, you know I'm not used to it. It just hit me all of a sudden. But anyway, yes, tell us about the job."

"You said something about journalism or something," Dad says.

What just happened? What did I say to make Mum so...so...Wait. Did he just say..?

"I never said anything to you guys about journalism," I say slowly.

A glance between them both.

"Oh my mistake, Dougie," he says.

"Yes, ha! The things your father comes up with. Anyway–" she says, flustered.

"When did you... how did you know about that?" I press.

"What?"

"About me wanting to become a reporter?"

"No no, like I said just a mistake. So anyway–".

"No, hold on, I want to know how you heard about that." I can feel my face burning. "How the *fu*... how the *hell* did you guys hear about that? There's no possible way you could know about that."

"Now Douglas, calm down, you're starting to make a scene," Mum says, a note of warning in her voice.

"No I will not *chillax* Mum. Just answer my fucking question. I want to know how you knew about that. I'm one-hundred percent sure I never mentioned it to you. So how the hell did you know?"

Another look between them; a note of assignation on her face, but unmoving stoicism on his. And then I understand.

"Adrian. Adrian told you."

"Douglas," Mum says. "Dougie. He only wants what's best for you–"

"I can't believe this," I shout, pushing myself away from the table. The chair legs screech. Heads turn towards us from all directions. "He's calling you up about me? That's it, I'm going to–"

Dad's hand clamps over my own as I try to leave the table.

"Doug, calm the hell down and just listen to us."

Our fellow diners reluctantly turn back to their food. Dad continues in his best damage-limitation tone.

"Your helper, therapist–"

"Mentor," I hiss through my teeth.

"Mentor. Adrian. He's only been in touch with us once. Maybe, what, a few weeks ago? He said you were making good progress from whatever it was you were going through. He didn't tell us many specifics, I promise. Just that you've been going through a tough time, had been let go from work and that you could do with some extra support. Okay?"

His words are an ambling baseline to the buzz of my own thoughts. How could Adrian do this to me, betray our trust like this? I don't give a shit if he thinks he's doing it for noble reasons. He knows my relationship with my parents isn't the best, so why would he crowbar himself into an already strained dynamic? Unless...unless maybe Dad isn't being completely honest, telling me the whole picture.

My eyes rest on his hand. I can't think of the last time we were in such close quarters. It would almost be nice if it weren't for the context. His hand. Touching my own. Comforting me. No. Stopping me. Holding me in place. Controlling me. No harm in me taking advantage of the situation then?

My mind goes to the point of contact between our skin. I reach out with my mind, beginning to formulate a call into him. *What was Adrian phoning you about Dad? What did he tell you?* I begin to feel the flow of Dad's mind, the stream of his memories whispering just ahead –

"Dougie don't–" he bellows, whipping his hand away.

"I didn't, I wasn't…" I splutter. I feel like a child caught in the act. Embarrassed, ashamed, angry, defensive.

He just sits there staring at me hard, pondering his next move.

"I think," Mum pipes up, "we should maybe just park this conversation for a wee while. Let's get the bill shall we? Our treat, okay Dougie. Dougie?"

"Sure," I reply.

Three minutes of silence later and my parents have settled the bill. They get their coats on and head out of the restaurant. Through the window, I see them exchanging words. Mum touches Dad's arm. He looks away from her, off into the distance.

I'm about to join them when I stop and look back at the table. An idea dawns. I head back to the table, take an unused napkin and wrap it around a glass. Mum's glass.

A quick look around to check no-one's watching. Then place it in my bag.

Chapter 8

The lamplight dissects the bedroom. The ochre striations of his iris, the sinews of his shoulder, the rumpled bed sheet, the knot of a wooden floorboard, a discarded pair of briefs.

Our bodies move together in waves. His thrusts issue the call, my thighs give their response. Hands travel the plain of his back, nails marking tracks as they dig downwards. The bristles on his cheek crackle against my ear, breath caresses my collarbone.

His mind, so focused, so present, there's no danger of falling into his past. We're locked in the moment. No thoughts, only action.

We want this.

***

"What's this?" The silvery trace of a scar on the back of his hand.

"Broke it when I was a kid," he says sleepily. "Fell over my handlebars straight on to the tarmac. Needed surgery and then had a cast on it for months."

"Ouch". I hold it to my lips and kiss away the pain of it. I see the memory of it, taste the blood.

> *"Mama" I cry. My hand, so sore. Feels crunchy when I move it. My tooth is on the road. A big gap in my mouth. Tastes like metal.*

"What about you?" He asks, pulling me back to the present, away from his past.

"Just this." I raise my knee into the light, feeling along the three inch scar. "Taxi clipped my leg on the roadside. Didn't break anything thankfully, but left a bad gash."

"Oooh," he winces, then rises up on one elbow, folds his head down to my knee. Kisses it softly. He runs his hand down my leg, squeezing lightly as he goes.

"You seem calmer now," he says after a while.

"I am. You helped a lot."

I smile. We kiss.

He breaks the silence again. "Before, when you got here you seemed so, I dunno, on fire. Angry, horny, upset. All of that."

He's right, I was. The events of the day had built to a crescendo. My father's indifference then even colder disappointment, my mother's mysterious sadness, my sense of betrayal by Adrian and my parents, my shame at having tried to Read my father. All squirming within me. I tried to let it go, to flush the adrenaline from my system, but it didn't help. The more

I dwelled on it, the more it multiplied. Then Dhaval's face came to mind. I needed him.

I didn't call, just went straight to his apartment. I knew where it was – I'd dropped him there a few nights earlier following our second date, when once again I had made my excuses not to be alone with him, to be intimate, vulnerable. No excuses this time. I knocked on his door, he answered. Surprised, confused. I leaped.

I guess this is our third date, then. Things are progressing quickly. Doesn't feel like it though.

I meet his gaze. "I know, I'm sorry. It's been a rough day. A rough couple of days. But this? This is the best I've felt in a while. Thank you, Dhaval."

"You're welcome," he whispers, brushing my fringe to the side. For as primal as we just were not ten minutes ago, now we're completely relaxed, contemplative. *This guy.*

"So tell me about it. Your rough day." His expression, so open. I don't want to offload any more, to poison what we're creating, but his eyes and his good heart reach out to me. So I do. I tell him about my rough day. But only the basics, none of the specifics. No Weaving, no Adrian, no breakdown. Just me and my parents, our difficult relationship, a spoiled lunch, a cold departure. And he seems to get it. Doesn't push for any more than I'm offering, just happy to listen.

The conversation drifts to his family, their brief episodes of friction, yet the ties that bind them together. I ache at the absence of such a bond with my own family, but hearing him talk and catching glimpses in his memories soothes me. I know that the familial love he feels isn't mine to share in, but it feels good to be swept along nonetheless, to feel those smiling faces beaming on him from around so many meal tables, to feel their pride from across the graduation hall, to share their holiday joys.

So many happy memories. Such a charmed life. I just lay my head on his chest, tracking the crop circles of hair as he shares his life stories.

A small thought occurs. A gift. In return for showing me his happy Echoes, I'll give him a present from my past. Something little but perfect.

Writing. Weaving one's memories directly into the mind of another. It's difficult, but I can do it when I try. Not nearly as well as Kaito, but adequately. The thing with Writing, unlike Reading, is that the Writer ends up losing the memory. They give it away. The facts of the memory remain, its 'skeleton' stays, but the emotional resonance and the vibrancy of the recollection fade.

Writing a memory is an intimate thing to do. A gift not to be given lightly.

Dhaval is worth the gift.

The time I swam in the warm waters of the Gulf of Thailand. Yes, that's a good memory. I'll give it to him. To say thank you. Thank you for sharing. For being with me.

Here…

The crystal waters of the sea, the soft sand between my toes. In the distance, the white hull of a fishing boat makes the sunlight wink on and off. Nina, Kaito and Venny wave at me from the shoreline. They're inviting me to grab some food with them. 'Ten minutes' I indicate with my splayed hands. I turn back out towards the horizon and bask in the moment.

As soon as I Write the memory on Dhaval, I feel its richness fading in my mind. Like a kiss blown on the wind, I bid my happy little memory farewell, releasing it to its new home.

***

"Remember me."

I startle awake. Didn't mean to sleep. I was afraid of this exact thing happening – of the dream coming to me while in Dhaval's presence.

I whip my head in his direction, but he's still asleep, arm splayed out across the pillow. I wait for my heartbeat to level out, then slip out of bed and tiptoe over to my backpack. I sit on the floor and rest my naked back against the bedframe. A sliver of the city glints through a gap in the blinds.

I twirl the pendant from front to back then press the flesh of my thumb into its patterned surface. I feel its same story, looping within its metallic prison. It wants to talk to me, to tell me its story again and again. But I don't want to hear it anymore. The pendant and the dream show me the same scenes. Disparate pieces of a jigsaw puzzle.

All they do is taunt me. So I try to lock the Echoes away. I pull them all together in my mind, try to compact them into an orb, just as I would a normal Echo from a human being. I want to put them into my Safe.

I stand there, in my mind's eye, above the wooden trunk which contains all the Echoes I've collected and locked away over the years. But it doesn't work. The Echoes from the pendant and dream refuse. It's like trying to hold on to a beehive, to contain all the crawling insects. So I stop trying. They're not going to be silenced easily. They're insistent in telling me what they have to say, and won't stop until...what? Until they're answered?

I reach inside my backpack and feel down to the bottom where the glass is nestled. I bring it out and slowly unwrap its napkin covering. The light bounces off the tumbler.

The pendant can't answer my questions, but maybe this can. I think back to the moment when lunch with Mum and Dad soured and fell apart. I was talking about my childhood, of playing by the big pine tree opposite the house, of Olivia hitting her head. That's when the energy changed around the table, when my mother suddenly looked so stricken. She tried to hide her pain, to swallow it down with sips from this glass.

I focus on the tumbler, let my mind go loose, breathe in and out, then close my eyes. I issue a call to it in my head. *I'm here.* Just like with the pendant. *Talk to me. I'm listening.* After long seconds I begin to hear them, the Echoes in the glass, the fragments of memories of its users, like a haze of radio static. I can't grasp onto them. Not like with people – when I Read people, there's a liquidity to it all, a flow to the way their memories sing. They want to be heard, just like the pendant.

But these Echoes, trapped in the glass, don't want to be heard. The multiplicity of voices buzzes at me angrily, evading my calls.

I change tack. Instead of trying to capture an Echo, I focus on her. On my mother. Her face as it fell from rosy-cheeked contentment to ashen sadness. I freeze that image in my mind, and hold it up to the static, trying to find a match.

There. Fractured, incomplete, but it's there. My mother's Echo. I rush towards it.

A burst of shock. A swell of sorrow. Never forgotten. Never gone.

–

Oh Dougie, what happened? Are you hurt? No! Oh no! What did you do?

–

His hand on my arm. "Lisa". The water cools me. A moment, I just need...

The Echo fizzles away. I try to get it back but it's no use. I'm exhausted. This…what, Reading objects? Whatever it is I'm doing has drained me. And for what? It's given me nothing but more questions.

***

"Hey. Hey, you there. On the floor. Whatcha doin'?"

His husky whisper rescues me from the looping dream. I look up, one eye open, to see him smiling down on me, head resting sideways along his forearm. The morning's first rays break through the blinds.

"Sorry. Lookin' in bag and must've fall'n sleep," I mumble.

"Well get back up here, I've got something to ask you," he grins.

I roll on to the bed and slide into his arms.

***

It's only after we're done that I remember he had a question.

"Oh that," he calls, coming back from the kitchen with mugs of coffee. "What are your plans this morning?"

I don't even try to fabricate an answer. "Nothing."

"Good. It's the strangest thing. I dreamed of a beach and now I only want one thing. Wanna go swimming?"

***

We glide through the water in opposite lanes. The pool's empty. This might be one of London's only heated open air lidos, but that's not enough to coax anyone else out of their warm beds this early.

Steam rises from my arm as I raise it out of the water, then disappears as I plunge it back in. My stroke strengthens with each lap, my heart leaps with each passing splash from Dhaval. As he reaches the water's edge he skims under, twists and then pushes out with strong legs. I duck under the lane divider to intersect. He sees me coming and reaches out to pull me under. I take a gulp of air a second before submerging.

We roll and wrestle, bubbles tickling our skin. It's quiet down here. Just him and me. We burst back through the surface, spitting with laughter. Sea otters gambolling in the wild, wild surf.

After a few more laps, I pull myself out of the pool and shiver over to a mound of towels, then curl up in a ball on a sun lounger. A sun lounger, in February. I could go inside, but the view is too enjoyable. I sit there for some time just watching him slice through the water. It parts for him obligingly.

A dull buzz goes off in my bag. I reach a soggy hand in and take out my phone. With some trouble I unlock it and read the message thread:

The first is my own from days earlier:

Me: Hey Neens. Weird question. Have you ever dreamed? Like, fallen asleep and had a dream?'

The response is from seconds ago:

Nina: Angel. I think we need to talk.

Chapter 9

'A prayer for the wild at heart kept in cages'.

The quote's scrawled multiple times over the notebook. Different styles, some slanted like calligraphy, others more blocky.
"What does it mean?" I whisper to Nina. I shouldn't be in her bedroom with the door closed. Not that anything's gonna happen, but still, I can feel the judging gazes of the paintings and portraits she's made and stuck up on the wall.
"It's from a play. Doesn't matter," she says without looking up, adding the finishing touches to her latest version. It's like typewriter text, all inky and splotchy, making it look like the paper is more absorbent than it really is.
"It's really cool," I say. "I can't believe you're really gonna do this, Neens."
She flicks her eyes up then grins.

One winter when Nina and I were fourteen or so, we were orphaned for the whole Christmas break. For one reason or another neither of our parents could take us home for the holidays. It didn't really bother me. Mine hadn't brought me home for Christmas since I moved to Thailand for schooling. Nina, however, didn't take the news so well. Her folks, a Thai mother and Swedish father, still lived in Stockholm where Nina had partly grown up, and were taking some time to themselves. They blamed it on the expense of flying Nina home, which might have been true, but Nina took it hard. In many ways, this was the start of her retreat into herself, and the sullen persona she began to adopt – the make-up, the piercings, the black clothing.

"You're sure this is what you want? You're not just permanently marking your body to piss off your parents?" I say.

In retrospect I blame myself a little for Nina's act of rebellion. I was excited at the prospect of breaking rules, but the idea of doing so myself was too daunting.

She rolls her eyes but doesn't say anything. She loves being mysterious. Knows it gives me a thrill.

To my mind, we hadn't been that close before this winter break. Sure, we were two troubled souls, reeling from the life changes we were going through. But we didn't spend too much quality time together sharing our innermost thoughts.

She snaps the book shut, making me jump. "Okay. Let's do this. Remember the story?"

I nod and salute, which makes her laugh a little.

"You're such a dork."

I open the door quietly. Nobody here. Phew. Then we head downstairs, me first then Nina thirty seconds later.

The boarding house we lived in was on the outskirts of Bangkok in a beautiful estate. It was a stunning construct of white walls, teak panelling and steep orange gabled roofs. Split over three floors, if you counted the mezzanine, the house was what Nina, Kaito, Venny and I called home for the duration of our schooling. We were the only boarders in our class at the MPB, the Mnemosyne Project Bangkok, which doubled as an administrative outpost for The Project and a school for us. There were other students, some whose names I can recall – Shalini, Jonathan, Mai, Daisuke – others just faces in my memory. But the four boarders, we considered ourselves a sub-unit, the most broken of the misfit toys.

Nina nudges me and jerks her head in the direction of the dining area.

"Su? Khun Su?" I call, voice bouncing around the ground floor. It feels so empty here since everyone else left for Christmas break.

"Aah?" a voice calls back. Nina and I shuffle in. Khun Su is at the end of the long dining table, holding papers and bill-looking documents.

Su was our matron. She ran the boarding house for the entire time we lived there. Hired by the school, yet operating at arm's length from it, she did her job with a fierce dedication. She had a wizened complexion way beyond her years, yet sharp dark eyes, and sleek hair that hung below her shoulders. The combination gave her a spectral quality. She could be terrifying when she wanted, but in quiet times like this, with so few of us around, her edges softened.

"So Nina and I were wondering…" I start, flashing Su a cheeky smile I know she can't resist. Except maybe she can, because she's looking back at me without any expression. "…it's really boring around here with nothing to do. It would be really great if we could go out for the afternoon? Into the city? Get some food, go to the movies?" She just stares back, which makes me feel sweaty. "Y'see there's this awesome new film, about uh this asteroid thing that's going to hit the earth but there's these people that–"

Nina's toe presses against my heel.

"–anyway it would just be so much more fun than sticking around here all day. And clearly you're busy with work. So…" I kind of finish.

Su breathes in, puts her pen down, looks at me, then to Nina, then back to me again.

"Okay okay," she says. Then smiles a little. I try not to look too relieved.

"Cinema, food, then home. Go. But be good, yes?"

"Yes, thank you, thank you. We'll be good. Promise," I say then run back upstairs. I hear Su speak to Nina in Thai. I catch a few of the words, something about looking after me.

"Chai chai," Nina says. Yes yes.

The journey to the city was quieter than usual so our taxi skipped on to the freeway and zipped through Bangkok's labyrinthine *thanon* and *soi* street system. The house was a twenty-minute walk to the school, but anywhere between forty-five minutes and three hour's drive to central Bangkok depending on how bad the traffic was. 'Rod tid mak mak' – 'very bad traffic jam' – as the taxi drivers used to say to us.

We were at Siam Square in less than an hour. I followed Nina who strode through the shopping arcade's pop-up stores and eateries. Within another fifteen minutes Nina was leaning back into the cracked leather chair of a tattoo parlour.

The music is freaking me out, so loud. How can the artist concentrate? Room smells like a doctor's surgery but also like a temple, alcohol and incense. The walls are full of designs and words in tribal black. Thai characters, kanji, some just pictures and angry looking doodles. I'm trying to keep my cool, but from the way Nina's looking at me from the chair, I can tell I'm failing.

"What?" I screw up my face at her.

Then the needle starts buzzing, and the artist slowly lowers the tip to Nina's inner thigh.

I'll never forget her face while the tattooist did his work. I was so worried for her, but she just sat there without expression, as if somehow outside of the situation.

'A prayer for the wild at heart kept in cages'.

The quote was a subtitle from Tennessee William's play, Stairs to the Roof, though its origin held little interest for Nina. The words alone were what grabbed her. They spoke of her new life as a Weaver, of her parents' abandonment, of the cage-like existence we were living. No matter how beautiful the boarding house was, we knew that we were caught in The Project's grip, and probably always would be. So dramatic. So teenage.

Later that night, safely back home, Nina did something that I would never have expected. Something that deepened our friendship by many shades.

The quiet of the evening had fully descended on the house. Khun Su had already gone to bed. Nina and I were sitting in her bedroom with the door closed. The day's experiences had left me less afraid of Khun Su's ire at breaking house rules. Not that she ever did tell me off for it – an astute woman, she knew that no fraternising was likely to happen between Nina and me, or between me and any girl for that matter.

"How does it feel?" I look down at Nina's thigh where surgical tape is showing underneath the edge of her shorts.

"Fine," Nina shrugs, folding a candy wrapper like origami.

"Neens. Why did you get it?" I ask, finally brave enough.

She places the wrapper down and looks directly at me, first all serious, but then softer.

"What is it?"

"I just...there's something about you." I'm not used to seeing her so relaxed. It's freaking me out.

"What do you mean?"

"I don't know," she shakes her head. "You wanna know why I got it? Here."

She lays out her hands flat on the bed, palms facing upwards.

Maybe it was loneliness, maybe it was because I had become her co-conspirator. I don't know, I didn't question it for fear the moment would pass. Instead I just lay my hand on top of hers and closed my eyes.

Leaf by leaf, she opened up to me, revealing answers to all my questions.

She showed me how the pain of the needle offered her reprieve from the sadness within; showed me her joy at experiencing something new, yet indifference at marking her body indelibly in this way; showed me the faces of her parents gathered around a Christmas tree years before, grinning as she opened her presents; showed me the pain on their faces as they left her behind in the boarding house, trying their best to block out pleading calls.

The Echoes begin to fade. I can feel Nina pulling away from me. I do the same, drifting back to myself.

Our hands feel sweaty together. I lift mine off and rest it on my knee. We stare at each other. Her face doesn't seem passive to me any longer. It seems full of feelings and thoughts.

"Thank you," I whisper.

"You're welcome, Angel."

This act of sharing, of baring her inner world, would set the template for the intimate friendship that Nina, Kaito, Venny and I would develop. The school would train us in the responsible use of our abilities; it would shape us into the citizens we would need to be to survive, hidden in regular society. And we would let it. But The Project, would never fully understand us, or truly appreciate what it was like to be us. To be individuals yes, but porous individuals, protean and fluid. The Project wanted us frozen into rigid shapes, to teach us to construct thick boundaries between Self and Other.

As far as we were concerned, the only people who understood us, was us. In sharing herself with me, Nina taught me that we were more than we were being told.

That 'we' could be more than 'me'.

***

"So we said our goodbyes outside the restaurant and headed separate ways," I say. "We met up this morning for coffee – it was so awkward. Neither of us could mention the argument, well not until a few minutes before they had to catch their train south."

"So then what happened?" Nina asks. Her face on the screen has been focused for some time while she's listened to me recounting the whole story of lunch with my parents. She looks tired, drawn even, but is clearly making the effort to pay attention.

"I said I was sorry, I guess, for causing a stir in the restaurant. They both said it was okay, but that they were worried about me. They want me to go home for a while, to spend some time with them. Away from the city, to help me get my head together blah blah."

"And?"

"I said I would think about it."

"Will you?"

"Hell no. I'm not going there. If we can't even make it through one lunch, why would I stay with them for some indeterminate length of time? I mean, they clearly don't want to tell me anything more about how they knew about my...my situation. So as far as I'm concerned, they're as untrustworthy as Adrian. Ugh. Shit, sorry Nina. We haven't spoken in months and here I am just offloading on you. I'm sorry."

"What are you talking about? *I'm* sorry. I can't believe you've been going through all this alone. You should've called, Angel."

I should have, but somehow this whole catalogue of crap feels like something anyone else could have avoided. A more talented Weaver, a more stable personality.

"I know, I know. I just...I think I'm beginning to make some progress, though"

"But...you did try to Read your dad. Against his will. That's not okay, Angel. It's just not, and you know that."

I grab a fistful of hair.

"I was just so angry. The opportunity presented itself and I just thought...I don't know what I thought. You're right, it's not okay."

This dynamic feels a little strange, Nina berating me about the ethics of Weaving. When we were young, she was the one more likely to act recklessly. But since growing up, it's like she's so much more together, more comfortable in her skin. I was the one riding on her coat-tails, but now? I don't think for a second she would grab on to mine, not on this crazy ride.

"How do you do it, Neens? Reading person after person, but not losing yourself?"

From the second Nina arrived at school, her Weaver ability was immediately clear to the faculty. Far above her talent for Write memories was her talent for Reading. It was just so natural to her.

"I don't know, for me it's just always been about them, not me. I don't come into the equation," she says.

It sounds blissful, the way she describes it. Reading people, only seeing what they're willing to show her. Her years as a Project consultant, seconded to Interpol – helping to crack the most difficult criminal cases – have secured her good favour with The Project. I've always envied that. Where I graft to the bone, grinding my Weaving to breaking point, Nina is only drawn upon by The Project when absolutely needed.

"It's kind of a clean transaction when I Read. Does that make any sense?" she says.

"Yeah it really does," I say. "You take the memory in then push it out. I just take it all in until it festers. Jeez, listen to me. Anyway, tell me, how's the art going?"

Art was always Nina's first passion at school. In class, and every spare opportunity in between, she would be creating dark and twisted characters and landscapes. Her flair was picked up by our art teacher who taught Nina to channel her anger into paint and ink.

When she graduated school, Nina walked straight into her Reader job at The Project's Stockholm branch, and was quickly guided towards her consultancy work with Interpol. She was efficient and discreet; ideal traits for operating within the parameters of the Mnemosyne Protocol. We aid special branches of governments and intergovernmental agencies around the world, and in return they help us keep the secret of our existence.

At first I didn't understand how Nina, rebellious and tempestuous as a teenager, accepted her role with The Project without resistance. But then I realised that she had managed to cut a deal. *You want me? You gotta meet me halfway. I do work for you when you need me; you let me keep doing my art.* I guess compromise can tame even the wildest of hearts.

"Is that one of your latest?" I say, looking beyond Nina where a huge canvas is propped against the wall, emblazoned with swirls of purples and blacks with occasional flecks of yellow, and in the foreground the silhouette of a figure. Even from the pixelated video screen I can feel the energy of the painting.

"Yeah it's pretty recent actually," she says dismissively. "Anyway, listen Angel. About your text message…"

"Oh, that. Look maybe we should talk about it another time," I say. "No offence but you look exhausted, Neens. I appreciate you being my agony aunt, but I think I should do you a favour and let you–"

"What did you mean by a dream?" she says.

"Well I…oh God I can't believe I'm going to tell you this. Do you…do you think they're listening?"

"Who? The Project?"

I nod.

"I think they have bigger fish to fry than tapping your phone, Angel," she chuckles. "Paranoia much?"

"You're right. Guess I'm just a bit…okay anyway, here goes. So." I take a deep breath. "A couple of weeks ago a package arrived in the post. No sender address on it apart from one word: 'Thailand'. Very strange, right? Inside was this pendant." I pull it out from around my neck.

"It's beautiful," Nina says, leaning in to her screen. "What are those markings?"

"They're interlocking circles. I've looked online, spent hours, but can't find anything that matches. Anyway, the weirdest thing happened when I first held the pendant, Neens. It started pulsing. Like a low level vibration, barely there, but definitely there, if you get what I mean. After a while it stopped. But then I got super drowsy and then the next thing I knew, I was asleep. And...dreaming."

I wait to see surprise, shock, incredulity, anything. But Nina just holds her look of concentration. So I tell her about the dream. About the girl who's running and laughing. Then how I'm in a room sitting cross-legged. Then I'm back with the girl who's now screaming, dying.

"...'remember me' over and over. Then I wake up. And this dream, Nina. I've been having this dream every night since. Every goddam night. I'm just...okay you've gotta say something, Neens," I say, rubbing my stubbly cheek. "Am I going mad?"

But she doesn't say anything. Instead she reaches down, below the screen. Her face blank.

"Nina?" I ask.

She stops. Her eyes come back to me. She lifts up her hand and in it she's holding something white, dog-eared. Opened.

A package. Just like mine.

My stomach lurches. Overlapping emotions and thoughts rise; surprise at what I'm seeing, relief that I'm not alone, confusion over what this means. And then sadness when I finally understand the shadows under Nina's eyes.

"You too?" I say.

"Yup," she says, resting her cheekbone on her fist. "Me too. I haven't had any rest since this arrived in the post last week. Since I touched this."

"A pendant?"

"Nothing quite so elegant."

She picks up something else from her desk; something vibrantly green and orange, spherical with a knitted texture. She tosses the object lightly in the air and when she catches it I hear the unmistakable crunch of dry rice grains.

"A hacky sack?"

"A fucking hacky sack," she confirms with a growl.

It was just as I described it, she explains. The package arrived out of the blue. Within seconds of extracting the sack she could feel it vibrating. Next thing she knew she was drowsy and heading to the sofa.

"You dreamed?"

"I dreamed. It's so weird to say it out loud. I had to let you tell me your story first, Angel. I'm sorry, I just wasn't brave enough to admit it. This is all so nuts. I mean, what the hell?"

"I don't know, Neens, I don't know. I'm so sorry that you're going through this. What have you been dreaming?"

A beat of hesitation, then she tells me. It comprises two seemingly distinct scenes.

"So in the first," she says, "I'm sitting in a classroom taking an exam. I say *I*, but I mean *the onlooker*. Anyway, I'm in a classroom sitting next to a girl. I can't really see her face. It's like seeing someone in the periphery of your vision, y'know? So this girl is playing with a pencil, balancing the tip on her finger and catching it just as it begins to tip over. I feel worried that she's going to get in trouble with the teacher who's at the front of the class. That maybe I'll get in trouble too. But when I turn back to the girl, she's holding the pencil in both hands. Focusing quietly. Then, so weird, she suddenly bursts out laughing. The teacher spins round in the girl's direction just as the scene shifts."

"Is that everything?" I interrupt. "The mystery girl – you're not running in your dream? She's not calling to you?"

"No. No she's not," she says.

"Does she say her name at all?" *Olivia.* My heart rate quickens.

"No she doesn't. Why?" Nina asks.

I boulder on. "What's the second scene? You said there were two?"

"Sounds like the same as yours, but I guess from a different perspective? I'm in a circle of people, sitting on the floor cross-legged. It's all dark and quiet. I look around the circle and recognise Venny, Kaito and you. You all look as worried as I feel. I lean over to you and say 'are you ready?' You nod back at me. Your face, Angel. My God. It's the most serious…solemn of us all. But behind the seriousness is this crazy intensity. It's like there's a fire inside you."

My mouth is dry. "What happens then?" I ask.

"Nothing. This is where I always wake up. The exact same point every time."

Chapter 10

My exposed ear feels raw against the wind. It's late afternoon and the sun is dimming. Streetlights spring to life, their amber glare reflecting in glassy pavement puddles.

"I'm pretty sure I know the difference between dreams and memories," Nina says down the phone into my warmer ear. "And these visions or whatever the hell we're having? They are not dreams. But hey what do I know, I'm only a professional Reader."

I can just imagine her gesticulating as she paces around her studio. I smile at the image and almost bang into a fellow pedestrian.

"I didn't suggest you weren't, Neens. But yeah I totally agree," I say. "These are just too vivid. As weird as they are, they're just too real."

During the past few days, we've been utterly captivated by our investigation. The initial excitement of finding each other has become channelled into a forensic examination of our mutual situation.

The only breaks I've taken have been for Dhaval. A coffee here, a quick make-out session there. Speaking of, I was supposed to be using this afternoon to prepare dinner for him. Poor guy showed up on my doorstep ten minutes ago with cocktail ingredients in his hands and a big grin on his face. I've rushed out to grab 'last minute supplies' while he fixes the drinks.

I couldn't resist another call to Nina en route. Once again, we're caught in the wave of each other's energy. Feels like the old days.

"Okay so we're agreed. That's one off the list then. Tick!" she laughs.

"Ha. Yeah, mystery solved."

We consider the next questions to be solved, namely 'why the hell do we not remember these memories', 'who is this mystery girl', 'how did the memories in these objects transfer to our psyches'? And for that matter, 'who sent these packages to us'? We've agreed that the 'Thailand' imprint on the packages is the best and only clue we have to go on.

I pull my scarf tight against the icy breeze while revisiting my hypothesis, that I'm pretty sure the dreams take place in Bangkok. She asks how I can be so sure. I hesitate at first, but then something inside me says *come on, this is Nina.* So I tell her I seem to be Reading the Echoes in the pendant while I'm awake, that the memories within it are exactly the same as the dream only more rich and detailed.

"O-kay," she scoops after a long pause. "You're right, that sounds nuts."

I come to a standstill in the doorway of Tesco and rub my eyes.

"I know, I know," I say, ducking into the store. "Are you going to call The Project on me or something?"

"Jesus, no. Sorry, I'm just a little stunned. I mean, Reading memories in objects? I didn't think that was possible. And, y'know," she says with an uncharacteristically sheepish note, "if you were able to do it we would've known by now. Don't you think?"

"Yes you're right," I snap a little too harshly. I've always been touchy about being the only Grade 3 Weaver among my friends; their Grade 4 status seeming to mock my mediocrity. "Look, I've never been able to do this, and to be honest I'm not great at it now. And yet it's happening, I swear. You have to believe me."

"I do, Angel. God knows it's probably the least crazy thing going on in our lives right now. Have you researched it at all?" she says.

"I can't find anything about it. Nothing in any of the books. I'm too afraid to search online."

"Yeah maybe don't do that," she says with a little huff. "What's it like?"

"Reading the objects?" I say. "It's weird. Kind of like normal Reading but more fractured. Like the Echoes are all broken up and dancing around. Difficult to get hold of, and even when I do it's like they're only one piece of a bigger picture. Leaves me exhausted too. I think I might be getting better at it. Maybe. Neens, are you sure you've not…never mind," I clam up.

"Have I started Reading objects?," she says with a chuckle. "No, no I haven't. I wouldn't even know how."

And so there and then – me standing in the vegetable aisle and Nina in her studio – I try to teach her how to Read her hacky sack. Or rather, what little I know of the process. It's like the blind leading the blind.

"…try to block out all other sensations. Hold the hacky sack but try to ignore the feel of it. If that makes sense," I say.

"That makes no sense whatsoever, guru."

"I mean, try to listen to what's inside it."

"I know what's inside it," she says. "Beans."

"Very funny. Just try this, Nina. For me? Please?"

"All right, okay!" she groans. She takes a deep breath, in and out. "You were saying. Listen to the hacky sack."

"Yes. Close your eyes and just listen to it. Remember the feeling when you first held it. A low vibration. Try to focus on that. Let it talk to you."

For long seconds all I can hear is Nina's breathing. I close my eyes too, as if transmitting a prayer through the airwaves straight to her mind. I sync my breathing to hers. And then…

"I'm not gonna lie, all I can feel is beans, Angel. I really don't think I'm an object Reader."

I can't deny the disappointment that follows. "It's fine. It was a long shot," I say.

"I'm sorry buddy. For what it's worth I really do believe you," she says.

"Thanks," I say. "God this is so frust–"

A series of beeps chime in my ear. I hold the phone away to see who's calling. Adrian. *I really cannot deal with him right now.*

I hear Nina's tiny voice from the handset.

"…you?"

"Sorry I didn't catch that."

"I said, where are you? It sounds busy."

"Oh, I'm out shopping for groceries. I'm cooking tonight."

"You're cooking? Now *that* is the craziest thing I've heard you say all day."

"Hey shut up. I can cook. Sorta. Kinda. Question: does making a chicken salad count as cooking?"

"Definitely not. That's just assembling."

"Ugh. But I'm following a recipe and everything. Surely that counts for something?" I'm now wandering up and down the aisles filling a basket with whatever leaps out from my mental shopping list. The smells of floor cleaner and a thousand different foodstuffs curdles in my nose.

"So who are you 'assembling' for? Your fancy man?"

"Maybe," I mumble.

Talking about my love life with Nina has always been a strange thing. A couple of times as teenagers we fooled around (Khun Su wasn't right about everything). Strictly second base stuff. That was a lifetime ago and yet I still feel a nugget of guilt about somehow misleading Nina or something. That I couldn't be straight for her. Although I realise this is incredibly narcissistic and doesn't give Nina any credit. After all, she was the one who instigated our hook-ups.

"Wow. Cookin' a salad. This must be serious," she needles.

"Well, kinda yeah. I think it is. In fact he's waiting for me at my place right now," I say with the appropriate amount of bashfulness.

"You know a romantic dinner is all about the dessert, right?"

"It is?"

"How can you not know that?"

"I'm not sure I wanna take romantic dessert advice from someone who loves that horrible Thai jelly cake. Y'know the green one in all those layers? What's it called again?"

"Khanom chan," she says, "and I think you'll find it's delicious".

"Whatever," I say, lobbing a chocolate bar into the basket.

"All this meal prep sounds pretty serious, Angel. Does that mean you've…?"

"Had sex? Uh yeah Nina, I'm in my thirties."

"I was gonna say, 'are you thinking of telling him you're a Weaver'. But good to know where you're at, hotshot."

"Oh. Well I've thought about telling him, but I just don't think…"

"Angel."

"…I mean, how the hell do you even tell someone something like this? Any time I've tried before it just screws everything up–"

"Angel, it's fine. I was kidding. Telling someone is a big deal, I should know. Especially with all the strings that come attached."

"Tell me about it. Adrian is all over me about it. He's desperate to start vetting Dhaval. To be quite frank he can back the hell out of my personal life for a second. Anyway, enough about my love life. How about yours?"

"Well deflected, Mr Sermanni. Let's just say I'm taking some 'me time' and leave it at that."

"Shit, you and Theis broke up?"

"Yup. A few months back."

"Aw Neens, I'm sorry. I feel awful, I should have asked sooner. Man. Theis was a great guy."

"He cheated on me. A lot."

Shit.

"Man, that Theis was a scumbag. I always knew it. What an asshole."

She makes a little 'heh' of laughter.

"Seriously though, I'm sorry Nina. That sucks. No-one deserves that, especially you. You know what? Fuck him."

"Yeah, fuck him."

"So what happened?"

I do my best to sound like I'm listening closely – lots of 'uh-huhs' and 'oh nos' at what I think are the appropriate breaks in Nina's story – all the while negotiating the self-checkout. I need a bag so cast around for an attendant. A woman with dead eyes and a two-sizes-too-small branded polo shirt spots me finally.

"Could I have one of those," I mouth, pointing at her haul of carrier bags. My finger connects with her bare wrist.

His eyes. Bloodshot and wild. His teeth. Gritted and grinding.
"What did you fucking say? You fucking stupid cunt. What the fuck would you know?"
His breath. Toxic and sharp. His fist. Scabbed and clenched.
"Just calm down, all right? I'm just saying you should lay off it a bit."
"And who the fuck are you? My fucking sponsor? I only drink so you look half fucking decent to me, you stupid fat fucking pig."
He steps forward. My ribs. Still ache from the last time.

I come away with a bag in my hand and my heart in my throat. A flicker of confusion crosses her eyes, but they reset to a vacant stare almost immediately.

Nina's voice comes sharply back to focus as I hover over the checkout.

"...made some bullshit excuses about how much of a mistake it was, how he would never do it again. He even, get *this*, he even tried to blame me for accidentally Reading him and revealing it all. I mean, Jesus Christ, what a dick!"

"Yeah, what an asshole," I say, still absorbed in the Echo I just Read.

"So anyway, that was it for me. I was out of there. Best decision of my life. And now the Erasers have swooped in and 'poof' I'm out of his life now too I guess."

I finish filling the bag one-handedly and am about to walk away when I spot the assistant with her bags.

"Sorry hold on one sec, Neens." I cup my hand over the receiver and approach the assistant. She turns slowly to face me.

"You need to leave him. He's no good for you," I say simply.

Her mouth opens a little but she doesn't speak.

"He'll keep doing it until there's nothing left of you. You know he will. Go home, pack your bags, and get on with your life. *Your* life. Not his."

I back away, heart pumping with adrenaline, then walk straight out of the shop feeling like a fucking superhero.

"Sorry Nina. You were saying."

***

As I wander homewards through the waning daylight, the conversation around Nina's ended relationship runs dry. We arrive back at the original topic.

I'm describing the extra details I'm able to Read in the pendant. I explain how it's nothing brand new, per se, but definitely a fuller picture of what's in the dream. I can tell that we're in the boarding house in the dream, the wooden floorboards, the smell of the place, just everything about it. But then, as sure as I am about it, it doesn't make sense to me that this mystery girl is there. She shouldn't be in Thailand.

"What? Do you think you know who she is?" Nina asks.

I feel embarrassed enough with what I've revealed to her this afternoon. I don't have the reserves to divulge my Olivia theory too.

"No, no I don't. I just have this feeling that these memories are fractured between different places that's all. But I think if I could maybe put this object-Reading to use, I could find out more. For example…" I trail off.

"Angel?" She says with a playful note.

"Yeah?"

"Would you like to touch my hacky sack?"

"Nina, honey, I thought you'd never ask."

We start to hatch a plan. I could get to Stockholm if I had enough cash. Which I don't. So Nina, bless her, offers to catch a flight to London sometime in the next few days.

"We're going to figure this out, Angel," she says – her new mantra – before hanging up.

A short distance from the apartment I remember my missed call from Adrian. He's left a voicemail.

As soon as I hear the tone of his voice I lose the strength I've just been brimming with. His words sound warm, but their tone is cold.

I'm not sure when I started running. But by the time his message is finished, my mind is honed on one thought only: I need to get home now, before the damage is done.

Chapter 11

You have one new voicemail, left today at fourteen fifty-three PM...

"Hi there Dougie, hope you're keeping well. Adrian here. It's been a little while since our last session and I wanted to get in touch with an update. I've tried calling you a few times but can't seem to get through. Maybe you're in the throes of puppy love with that Dhaval chap. Anyway, it's important that you get this message.

"Look, I'll get straight to it. The Project wants you to come in for some more treatment. Nothing invasive, just a few more sessions to help you get fully back on your feet. I made my report about how you've been doing, and including the fact that some of Kieron Marber's Echoes seem to still be within you, and that they are likely having some latent effect on your behaviour. This journalism idea of yours, in particular.

"I know this isn't exactly how you would characterise things, but I have to be honest, Dougie, I left our session concerned. You've made good progress, but you can't deny there's more work to be done.

"I think it's great that you've put yourself out there with Dhaval, too. A romantic life is to be encouraged, in the right circumstances. In fact that's the second reason I'm calling. Now I know you don't like hearing this official kind of shit, but I want to remind you of your responsibilities. And if you're still dating Dhaval, which I think you are, then he falls into that territory.

"Look maybe you've already told him about your Weaver status. In which case that's okay, no major harm done. It just means I'll put in the call to The Project right away so we can reach out to Dhaval and start the vetting process.

"I just...agh look I really don't like leaving voicemails. I'm going to try your home number to do this in person. If I don't get you there then give me a call back okay, Dougie? This official shit is important. The Project protects, yeah? Okay bye."

***

The front door slams behind me. I'm pouring with sweat, a combination of having run here and the claustrophobic heat of the apartment compared to the cold outside.

"Dhaval?" I call. Nothing. I bustle towards the living room. Light spills around the edges of the doorway. Panic rises as I approach, thoughts overlap: The Project wants to see me again. Why is Adrian pushing so much? He wants Dhaval to be vetted. Oh my God, what if he's already set the ball rolling? Have The Project already contacted him? Did he call the house phone himself? What would Dhaval do if he found out about me? Would he leave me? Think I was crazy?

"Dhaval?" I shout louder. Again nothing.

Oh God. Oh God. Maybe he knows and ran away; stormed out of the apartment and my life forever. I thrust into the living room, carrier bag swinging as I turn towards the sofa. But he's not there. I pivot to face the kitchenette, while hollering a desperate "Dha–"

And there he is. Back turned to me, bobbing on his heels as he tends to something on the worktop. A chunky pair of noise-cancelling headphones on his ears.

Adrenaline subsides as I escape the confines of my coat and scarf.

"Oh hey there, didn't hear you get in," he says. His lips are immediately on mine. "Wow you're sweaty. You okay?"

"Sorry, it's roasting in here. What's this?" I say as he places a glass in my hand, a Long Island Iced Tea.

"A toast," he says.

"To?"

"Just us."

"I'll drink to that."

The first sip catches the back of my throat.

"Jesus that's strong." My cough trips into a chuckle.

"A big toast then," he laughs, turning to lay the contents of the carrier bag across the surface.

"So you been okay here on your lonesome?"

"Yeah I survived. Oh, before she left Erica asked if you could take a meter reading and email it off to the energy company?"

"Oh yeah sure," I reply, almost immediately forgetting as I lay out the dining table.

"Okaaay," his tone drops. "I like the ingredients, but I have no idea quite how they relate to each other".

"The chicken!" I moan, burying my face in my hands. "I forgot the chicken."

***

"You take that last slice, I'm stuffed," he says, dabbing kitchen towel at the orange corners of his mouth.

As side salads go, I think my attempt at cooking has gone down pretty well. Somehow Dhaval seems charmed by my absent-minded attempt to make a meal. Delighted even when I suggested we get pizza delivered.

"No I couldn't, seriously," I say, patting my belly. "Tell you what, let's leave it to get good and cold. Then later after we've worked up an appetite – if you know what I mean – we can fight over the cold slice like a couple of hungover students the morning after a house party."

He smirks. "Those Iced Teas going down well, huh?"

"They've hit the spot nicely, thankyouverymuch."

My mind's an amber haze after two of his cocktails. What was I even worried about? I've been so paranoid lately.

"Question," I say, picking at the hot wax of a tea light. "If you could be anything in the world, what would you be?"

"Anything?" He adopts a thoughtful expression. "I dunno, an astronaut?"

"No seriously, come on. This is a good question."

"If you say so Mr Journalist," he replies. I squirm at the moniker. "Okay well, if I could be anything in the world…"

"Anything. You are free to recreate yourself completely."

"Maybe a travel writer? Or an adventurer. Anything that would let me wander the world, to explore."

He begins to shoot the question back to me but I jump in first.

"Explore what?"

"To find hidden corners. See how the locals live. Experience life in all its forms. In environmental law so much of my life's spent in the boardroom, on a computer. And all the while the world is out there, waiting to be seen."

There's an intensity in his eyes, a joy fizzing under the surface. I'd love to keep him there, to join him in that world. But it softens quickly. "Don't get me wrong, I like my job a lot. Even love it sometimes. But yeah."

"You do good things, boo."

"Sometimes. But the law is the law. Life? That's something else. Anyway, what about you?"

"I don't know," I say honestly. "Maybe one day I will. I like your idea. You'd be a good adventurer. I could tag along, hold your bags while you explore."

"I'd like that," he says. I get lost for a millisecond in the ochre of his eyes. I swear I've never felt so romantic than when I'm with this guy. Even without dessert.

"Well, for starters shall we adventure over there? I need to spread out."

We heave ourselves over to the couch, then sit at either end with legs interlocking in the middle. My feet, usually restless, feel heavy. He breaks the silence with a long contented sigh. He's transfixed by flickering candlelight.

"This is nice," he whispers. "Who would have thought, eh?"

"Hmm?"

"That we'd be here, stomachs full of pizza, nowhere else we'd rather be." His voice drifts off. "I don't know what I'm talking about."

"No, I get it."

"Good," he smiles. "It's just, not many first dates turn into second dates. Second to third. And certainly not into this."

"This?"

"Yeah this. I mean…this feels good, right? You and me?"

You and me. I crawl over to him and kiss his wonderful words. The tips of our tongues touch, the most fleeting of passes. My fingers run through his hair, curl around his ear and settle on his neck where I can feel his pulse, beating as steadily as my own.

"Yes," I breathe.

He opens his eyes.

"I feel like I've known you all my life," he says.

We join together once more, though with more intent. Our energy shifting, the beginning of the next stage. I lie across him, moulding myself to his shape. I push.

"No wait, don't press on my bladder," he says. "I'm absolutely bursting for a piss."

I collapse, sending ripples of laughter into him.

"No really, I'm bursting." He slides from under me and clambers towards the bathroom, then pauses for a second to point at the coffee table. "Oh by the way, you were an adorable teenager."

"What are you–" I say then spot what he's referring to. An old photo album is splayed open. "You fucker! Sneaking a look at my stuff."

He chuckles on his way to the bathroom. "Adorable," he hollers.

I heave the album over to the sofa. Familiar young faces look back up at me, twenty or so teenagers arranged in rows, eyes scrunched against the Bangkok sun. School uniforms neat and orderly. So many faces, but the names are hazy. Shalini I recognise immediately, her long plaited hair snaking down her front. And there's Jonathan with the early signs of acne breaking out on his cheeks, poor kid. Many faces, but none as recognisable as the quartet bunched together at the fringe of the class photo. Lanky Venny, ruddy-cheeked Kaito, sullen Nina. And little Angel, face vacant of expression.

The righthand side of the album page contains only two faces. Mine and Nina's. A selfie of us taken while leaning back against a tree. We must have been, what, thirteen years old? Her arm is crooked round my neck, pulling our heads together. Our expressions are warm, loving even. I can't remember taking this photo, but the truth of it feels comforting.

"I can't believe you've seen these," I shout towards the bathroom. "You realise I have to kill you now."

A thundering torrent rings out through the open bathroom door, followed by an almighty moan of relief. This makes me crease up.

"Man that's good," he calls. "Oh, I almost forgot. Someone called me earlier. Someone who knows you. Adrian, I think he said?"

***

The plates clank as I place them in the dishwasher. I'm about to scoop up the empty tumblers when Dhaval sweeps in and sets about replenishing them.

"Really? It's a school night," I say.

"Sure why not? I promise these will be tamer."

"All right. It's your funeral, you're the nine-to-five-er, if you're hungover tomorrow don't blame me."

He shrugs and adds a glut of vodka to each glass.

"So," I add, trying to remain nonchalant, "what did you talk about?"

"Who, me and your man Adrian? Nothing really. Just…"

I turn to see what's causing the pause. He's slicing lemons.

"Just what?"

"No nothing. Just kind of odd, the whole thing. 'So you're the famous Dhaval'," he says in imitation of Adrian's voice, complete with Caribbean lilt.

"Oh." My face burns. *Jesus fucking Christ, Adrian.* "So yeah about that–"

"Who is he?"

"Adrian? He's uh, he's just a guy I know." *C'mon think. Think.* "A friend, kind of."

"You been telling your friends about me?"

I can't tell if he's joking or somehow pissed off. So I play it bashful. I close the gap between us to steal a kiss. He arches his neck backwards.

"And giving them my number?" he adds.

My neck prickles. *I did not give him your number, I want to say. This is just how The Project works. Control.*

"Sorry. My phone…it's always running out of power, you know," I say, hoping my fastidiously-charged phone is out of view. "So I gave him your number as a backup. Is that weird of me?"

"Well yeah kinda," he laughs.

"Sorry, I should have said."

"I'm kidding, I don't care. Honestly I'm flattered you think of me as your 'in case of emergency'," he says adding ice cubes to the drinks and handing me mine.

We clink and sip.

"So he was looking for me?" I ask.

Is it terrible if Dhaval knows about me? Yes. Yes it is. I don't want him to be part of that world. What we have is pure. I need to keep it that way. Protect him.

"He said something about needing to speak to you as soon as you're free. Anyway, we chatted for a bit."

"About?" No point in being subtle about it.

"Felt like he was trying to give me the 'Dad talk'. 'What are your intentions with Dougie?' That kind of thing. Said he looked forward to talking to me more. You have very protective friends, Mr Sermanni," he says, a playful smile breaking out across his face.

I mirror it as best I can, but I don't feel placated in the slightest. No. I feel something inexorably, inevitably falling through my fingers.

***

"How long is this going to go on? I mean it's nice and everything but–"

"Shhh! Keep your eyes closed."

His forehead crinkles. He's lying back on me, head resting on my lap. His face, upside down from where I sit, returns to a passive state as I place my thumbs on his temples.

"Just relax," I say as soothingly as I can.

"Where did you learn this?"

"What did I just say?"

He pinches his index finger and thumb on the corner of his mouth and drags them across his lips.

"This is a massage technique I picked up long ago. It's supposed to...to clear the mind and leave you feeling rejuvenated. But you need to meet me halfway, so clear your mind and breathe in deeply and hold it. Good, just like that. Now let it out slowly. Slowly. That's it. Keep doing that while I work on your temples."

I can't believe I'm doing this. This is so reckless. No. No it's necessary. This is for you Dhaval. 'You and me'.

Navigating through short term memories is difficult in its own way. Short term memories are still being processed, mulled over. That process means the memories are more fluid, fast moving, like a stream after heavy rain. If you want to enter it, you have to be willing to be carried along.

Gossamer threads of Dhaval's day rush all around me.

...The minty zing of toothpaste...oh man I need this coffee...the Prime Minister's grin peeks above the front page of a newspaper...shit are these socks the same colour?...the green dot on the smartphone app points in the direction of Dougie's apartment...that sounds lovely...yeah no worries I'm fine to chill here...sure you don't want me to come shopping with you?...

Come on. Where are you? There! I see his phone. Hear its tinny ring.

...Ah the famous Dhaval...

Adrian's smooth tones.

...hope you don't mind me calling like this...heard so much about you...having a nice night?...he's a good guy...just needs some TLC, y'know?...anyway I look forward to talking with you more...blabbing on, sorry...just need to speak with him...very important he calls...I'll leave you to it...

Relief floods through me. He didn't say anything bad, or give anything away about me. But still. While I'm in here, with the memory in my grasp, maybe I should just make a tiny cut. The smallest of Erasures. I think I remember how to do it.

Just as I reach out, I snap back to my senses. *What am I doing? So reckless, not like me. Someone else...*

Dhaval's voice cuts through.

"Shouldn't I be thinking of somewhere nice instead of keeping my mind

clear? Somewhere beautiful and calm..."
Before I can say anything the scene twists.

The crystal waters of the sea, the soft sand between my toes. In the distance, the white hull of a fishing boat makes the sunlight wink on and off. Nina, Kaito and Venny wave at me from the shoreline. They're inviting me to grab some food with them. 'Ten minutes' I indicate with my splayed hands. I turn back out towards the horizon and bask in the moment.

This memory, so bright and simple. My memory. Lying here. Inside Dhaval's beautiful mind.
"I feel like I've known you all my life." His words from earlier this evening. But they mean something else now. Something that I don't want to hear.
They say: 'You have to leave.'

Chapter 12

I sink to the ground as soon as Dhaval departs. The tears come freely. What initially felt like something falling through my fingers now drifts at my feet.

Dhaval.

There was such concern in his eyes. He thinks I have a stomach ache. Begrudgingly agreed to leave me alone for the night, says he'll check in on me tomorrow. But I know I'll never see him again. Because I can't. If I do, I'll only destroy him, one recklessly Woven memory at a time. I've been trying to protect him from The Project when it's *me* he needs saving from.

I was actually going to Erase his memory of talking to Adrian. What is wrong with me? How could I do that to someone, especially him, when I know only too well how it feels to have memories meddled with? To feel the cut of the Erasers.

Shit.

The Erasers. I leap on to my phone, and sure enough there's a text:

Adrian: Dougie. Really need to speak. Have left you messages all over the place. Please call me back.

I mentally compose my response:

Call you back for what, Adrian? So you can ferry me to the Erasers? No Adrian. No, you can't have me. You lost my trust the second you shared my private life with my parents behind my back. And then called my boyfriend without my consent. Neither you or The Project or anyone can screw with my head any longer. Enough. My mind is mess, yes. But it's my mind, and I'll fix it myself.

Of course, I don't write the message. But by the time I've composed it in my mind, I've crammed a sports bag full. Clothes, toiletries, wallet, even the glass I stole from the restaurant. What else? *Passport.* I find it in the living room in the sideboard drawer. I need to get out of here. Away from Adrian and my parents and The Project. Buy myself some time to figure things out. Can't sleep here tonight, that's for sure. Next thing Adrian will do is show up at my door. Okay. Where?

The old photo album catches my eye.

It's still splayed open on the sofa. Two versions of my young face stare back at me: on the left in the class photo, my ghostly features, a vacancy in my expression, a look of loss; and on the right, the selfie with Nina. A different story in my eyes, one of life, warmth.

We're leaning against an old tree, Nina and I. Something carved into its bark, I didn't notice before. I bring the album under the lamp and peer closer. Names are etched into the bark. Nina. Angel. Venny. Kaito.

Olivia.

Her name, carved, real.

"Oh my God," I whisper. You were there? In Thailand? So you weren't a childhood friend in England?

"Remember me."

Thought and action comes as one, and before I have a chance to think otherwise an international ringtone trills in my ear. The receiver picks up. I hear a rustle and the sound of surprise.

"Angel?"

"Kaito. Man I'm so sorry to call this late, or early or whatever. But I really need your help."

"Dude don't worry, I wasn't sleeping. I've hardly slept in days. How can I help, man?"

But the reason I called has fallen out of my mind. In its place is the matter of Kaito's insomnia. Without needing to ask, I immediately know its cause.

***

The taxi slides through the streets. Inside, I try to lose my thoughts, becoming transfixed by the pools of streetlight we skim through. The City of London is quiet, all but deserted at this late hour save for occasional figures at bus stops.

Through gaps in the buildings I get occasional glimpses of the Thames. Specks of moonlight glimmer on the river's surface.

To my right stands St Paul's cathedral, lit from below like a statue, its dome monolithic and institutional against the night sky.

"How long?" I ask the driver.

"Heathrow? Maybe an hour," he shrugs without breaking eye contact from the road.

I nod and stare out the window once more.

This must be what the eye of the storm is like. The tornado of my life swirls around me. I can see its fragments twisting by, hear them taunting. But here, they can't reach me.

I could still turn back. Dhaval is there, waiting for me with those ochre eyes shining in the candlelight. I ache for what we could be. I can't go back. There's only darkness and confusion.

Mum's sadness.

Dad's disappointment.

Adrian's manipulations.

The Erasers' incisions.

There's only forward. *So fly home, Angel.*

The pathway's clear. Kaito's sorted your flight. Poor Kaito, wracked with

dreams just like you and Nina. And Nina, she'll meet you there.
In Bangkok.
In the City of Angels.
Tonight I fly.

Part Two:

SELF

Chapter 13

Why do I have to be so early for a flight? I don't get it. All this waiting around is making me more nervous than I need to be. I guess waiting at home would be just as bad. I feel sick. And like crying. And shouting, and punching, and running.

My first flight to Thailand. The day I left the life I knew behind, pulled towards an altogether alien future.

The departures sign is still stuck on:
 09:50 Bangkok THAI–TG 917 Gate shown 08:20.
This lump in my throat is aching. It's like my body's been telling me to do something for weeks. Anything but sit and wait.

The edge of the ticket rumbled as I dragged a thumbnail across it. My ankle jiggled, making a hole in the seam of my All Stars open and close like a little mouth. And a bit of travel sickness pill was driving me crazy – it had been stuck in my back tooth and no matter how I tried I couldn't pick it out. And all the while, thoughts of my future – of my perceived parental rejection – ran through my mind.

Dad says this is just how it has to be. This place, this school in Thailand, is the best option for people like me. But any time I ask questions he just shuts down. Like why the school is so far away, why he and Mum can't come too. He just says that's the way it is, then finds a reason to change the topic. Asshole.
My therapist Dr Jansen says I shouldn't expect too much from my parents, that it isn't fair to expect them to understand. The memories I collect, the things I see. Not many people are like me, she always says. But not in a 'you're special' kind of way, more like a 'you have an illness' kind of way. That's apparently why my parents act like they do around me. Scared and sad. It's not their fault, Dr Jansen says. It's why I need to be quiet about it, control it. But I can't control it. It's not my fault, is it?

The week before my flight I'd had a full-on meltdown. A weepy-waily tantrum. And all because my mother had asked me to tidy up. She came into the room, found me staring out the window and said I should straighten the room. 'Why?' I grunted, all low and moody. She started to reply but couldn't finish the sentence. To my mind, she knew there was no way she could finish it that wouldn't sound horrible.

'Because I don't want to tidy the room when you're gone'. 'Because I never want to step in here again'. 'Because we might turn your bedroom into a study, or a guest bedroom'. 'Or who knows, we might have another kid – a normal one this time – and give your room to them'.

On reflection I didn't really think any of these reasons were why she wanted me to tidy up, but I acted like they were all true. I'd only been a teenager for three months, but I guess I was pretty good at the dramatic stuff already. So I let her have it. All the anger that had been building inside me since I found out I was being sent away. I can still remember going over and over it in my head as I waited for the departure board to update. Trying to reason away the guilt.

God, I really ripped into her. Said all sorts of things I know she didn't want to hear. Like Mrs Landing, like how Dr Jansen thinks Mum and Dad should have got me help sooner, and how it's not my fault that ██████████████████████████, *making me say things, showing me how* ███████████████████████.

Maybe that was a bit much. But I don't care. She deserved it!
To be fair, she just stood there and took it.
Even looked ████████████████ *about it.*

When I was done, all puffy-eyed and doing that weird hiccup breathing, Mum sat down next to me on the floor. We sat there for a while. Then she said: 'You know, Douglas, growing up is all about learning how to deal with your feelings. We need to learn when to talk about them, and when to hold them inside'.

Then she got up, walked out the door and closed it behind her until the handle clicked.

I'm never going to tell her or Dad how I feel ever again. Fuck them. Even when they come visit me in fucking-Bang-fucking-kok and are all: 'Oh Dougie we're so sorry we sent you away, we were wrong, please come back home, we'll work all this out together as a family'.
I'll tell them, 'No, you told me that growing up was about controlling myself. So I'm doing that now. I'm never going to tell you anything again. Ever.'
I'll say that and let them feel guilty.

So there I was, in the check-in hall of Heathrow Airport, with Mum and Dad on either side of me, saying nothing. Just jiggling my leg and trying to pick the travel pill out of my back tooth. Mum tried to break the silence a few times with something about the time difference between the UK and Thailand, about how hot it was there, how wet it would be because of something called the monsoon. Dad just stayed quiet, practising what Mum preached.

"Hello, you must be the Sermannis," says a voice above me. "Sorry I'm a little late, I've come straight from a meeting at the London headquarters."

The first thing I noticed was the man's goatee. Thick and brown, making his teeth seem white and shiny in comparison. He had an accent that sounded American like my Dad's but softer somehow. His hair was short and brushed to one side, and I could see his scalp through some gaps in it.

He looks nice though. Handsome. Objectively speaking, I mean. Whatever.
He moves his jacket from one arm to the other so he can shake Mum and Dad's hands.
"Lisa, Nico, pleasure to finally meet you in person. And you must be Douglas."
He turns to look at me. Grey eyes. He holds his hand out to me.
"It's okay," he says, like he knows why I'm hesitating, then reaches out further to take my hand. It's been a long time since I've touched someone with nothing bad happening. Feels strange. Not bad strange.
"You see?" he says. "Nothing to worry about. You know why? Because I'm just like you, Douglas."
I guess I look surprised, because he makes a big smile.
"My name's Matthew Bordelais. I'll be coming with you on the plane to Bangkok. I teach at the school."
"What do you teach?" I mumble, trying to be normal.
"Biology. And English, and Math, and...well we don't have many teachers because there aren't many students. But biology's my first love. I hope you're a fan of science, Doug," he winks.
He must be pretty young for a teacher, though I'm never great at guessing people's ages.
"Um yeah," I say. I can feel my face getting red so look at my shoes instead.
"Okay," he claps his hands. "I hate to get the show on the road but Douglas and I better get through security. I see you've already checked him in. Great. I'll go grab a magazine to let you say your goodbyes."
He nods and turns away in the direction of a WH Smith, leaving me alone with Mum and Dad.
"He seems very nice," she says looking between me and Dad. She looks weird, like she's trying to be happy but her face won't let her.
"Yes, really nice. I'm sure you're going to get on just fine," Dad says, looking down at me. "So..."

This was it. The moment I'd been dreading ever since I'd heard about the school. I'd imagined every way it could have played out.

I could run into my parents' arms, screaming about how I don't want to go and how unfair it is I can't tell anyone why I'm leaving; I could bolt for the door and out into the car park and far away from the airport; they could change their minds and take me back home, back to a time before all this happened.

Before the episodes, before the treatment. ████████████████████*, before I ever heard the word 'Weaver'.*

But it didn't happen like that. First my Dad hugged me, careful not to touch my skin, patted me on the back then stood away.

"Be good, Dougie," he says. "We'll be out to see you in no time, okay?"
I nod. Something's stopping me from looking him in the eyes. I can only look up as high as his chest. My throat's tightening. If I try to make any sound I know it won't come out how I want it to.
Then Mum looks at me. How did she get so tired, how did I not notice? It's my fault. Not hers. If I hadn't ████████████████████ ████████████████████ *It's not your fault,* ████. *I'm so sorry. She's so sorry. I know she is. I feel it.*

She put her arms around me, and I couldn't hold it in any longer. My chin creased and I made a noise, somewhere between a gasp and a moan. I pressed into her shoulder and felt my tears soaking into her jumper.

"Shhhhh," she says, rocking me a little. "Oh my boy. My sweet boy."
I think of all the things I want to say to her, to try to make her change her mind and let me stay, about how I promise never to Read someone's memories again, how all the voices will go away if I try hard enough, how I'll never tell anyone about ████████████████████*, about* ██ *and* ██. *How she* ████.
But nothing comes out.
"You'll be fine, you'll be fine. They're going to help you. ████████*,"* *she whispers in my ear over and over to me, maybe to herself. I can hear that she's crying now too. We're stuck together like this for what feels like a long time.*
"Okay son, come on now," says Dad, his voice all throaty. I let go of Mum and in the corner of my eye I see Matthew is back, waiting a few steps away. I don't want him to see my face like this so I hunt in my pocket for a tissue.

As Mr Bordelais and I walked towards security, I glanced back at my parents. Neither of us waved, or smiled, or called out for each other. This wasn't that kind of a goodbye. It was the kind of goodbye that sounded like a door closing until the handle clicks.

Chapter 14

"You sure?" says the hairdresser, her clippers rattling a few centimetres from my head.

"*Khap pom*," I nod firmly.

"Not even mine?" she says, pointing at her short-back-and-sides and Elvis quiff. For the past five minutes she's forced me to look through a ring binder of magazine cuttings, a parade of Hollywood stars, pop musicians, sporting heroes. Even a few political figures. Between them is apparently every hairstyle a man could ever want. So when I close the *Hair on Film* binder and reiterate that I just want a buzz cut all over, she can barely contain her disappointment.

"Sorry," I shrug, "*kha tort*."

She shakes her head – no doubt at my rusty Thai – then with an upwards scoop lets the blades bite into my hair. Tufts fall about my shoulders. I could finish the cut myself in a few minutes, but she's determined to show her craft so is taking her time about it. I just sit back and enjoy the ceremony of it all.

"You know, I used to come here as a teenager," I say over the noise. She just smiles and carries on.

As a *farang* kid this was the only hairdressers I could get a cut that was even halfway close to what I wanted. As far as I was concerned every other barber in Bangkok seemed to only do one style for men, and that angular cut might have looked okay on Thai guys, but on me it looked ridiculous; like I hadn't quite figured out that I wasn't Thai. As if my height, blond hair and pale skin didn't make me stand out enough in the crowd.

"Finish," she says, not happily but with an air of pride.

"*Kop khun khap*," I say. It's a pretty severe cut, but what the heck. Besides I haven't seen this guy in the mirror for some time. He looks happy.

The cut costs practically what it did nearly twenty-years-ago, so I round up then stride out of the shop.

A wave of Bangkok heat slaps up against me as soon as I step outside. And here comes a waft of sewage from a grate. It mingles with the street food tangs of garlic and *nam plaa*. A vendor's *moo* skewers sizzle on the grill, waiting to be flipped, while above them dangles garlands of jasmine and polythene bags bulging with sweet tea.

Signs for hotels, restaurants and massage parlours are stacked one on top the other on the side of buildings. By day they look drab but come the swift fall of evening they'll battle with each other in neon warfare.

Telephone lines hang in the humidity, draped like black vines all the way along Thong Lor. The road holds a steady stream of taxis, motorbikes and tuk-tuks, beeping in conversation as they cut in and out of each other's paths. A driver in a green and yellow taxi spots me and my luggage and slows expectantly. I wave him off but this just makes him come to a complete stop. *Mai chai, no thanks* I mouth.

'Crazy farang', the driver probably thinks as he revs away, 'choosing to walk around in the midday heat'.

As loud and pungent as the city is, I open myself up to it all. I'm back where it all began. The day I disembarked from the plane all those years ago. My memory has never been the best, pockmarked and fractured, but I remember the numbness I felt on that flight after separating from my parents – and how it was blown away by what met me. The lights, colours and scents, so stark and alien. Mr Bourdelais must have seen it in my eyes, heard it in my silence. That same quietness falls on me now, though this time it's of my choosing. I want to bathe in this chaotic city, to get carried away in its anonymous currents. Maybe I will. But not quite yet. First there's something I have to do.

***

    Me: Hi. I'm feeling much better thanks. Sorry for the delay. I've had a lot on my mind. Dhaval, I'm so sorry to text this. I don't know how else to do it. I've realised I can't be in a relationship right now. I can't explain more than that. I'm so sorry. I wish nothing but good things for you, Dhaval. You deserve such good things. Goodbye.

I read the text for the thousandth time, hate it for the thousandth time, then hit send. Deflated, I lean my head on the pillar I'm propped up against. My bag lies at my feet. *Dumping him by text. That's pretty damn low.*

I then compose and send a second text. Easier and harder in equal measure.

    Me: Hi Adrian. Got your messages. I hope you understand that I need some space. I'm fine. I've come to Bangkok for a break, to spend time with friends. Sorry for not telling you before I left. A last minute thing.

    I hope you can respect my decision. I'm sure you'll want to inform the Bangkok branch that I'm in the city. I'd rather you didn't, but do what you need.

    Dhaval and me are over. Don't worry, I didn't tell him anything. You can leave him alone. I'll be in touch. Douglas.

I take a cleansing breath and look up at the apartment tower above. From this angle I can't tell where it ends. Just a spire of concrete and glass piercing the sky.

"There he is!" cries a very familiar voice from a parking bay. Its owner clambers out of a sleek car and breaks into a jog in my direction. I steady myself for the collision, which is just as well as its force almost throws me to the concrete.

The fog of sadness around me can't withstand Kaito's grin. I break into laughter as he lifts me off my feet and pivots me round. We separate and hold each other at arm's length, then I try to take the lead in an encore and almost collapse under him.

"Jesus how much do you weigh, dude?"

"Pure protein my man," he says, patting his stomach. "What's this, you becoming a monk? Didn't you have hair last time I saw you?"

"Thought I'd try something new," I say brushing the bristles on my scalp.

"Looks good, man. Anyway what are you doing waiting out here? I told the concierge to let you into the apartment." He hollers over to the man in his glass cubicle and spreads his arms out in a universal 'what the fuck?'.

"No, no," I say, pinning his arms down. "He offered but I said I wanted to wait outside. I've not been here long."

By this time the concierge has ambled over to us.

"Hey Tanet, this is my best buddy, Angel. He's flown all the way from London to see me."

Tanet begins to *wai* to me but I undercut his formality with a shoulder pat.

"Grab his bag, would you Tanet?"

"What, no seriously you don't have to do that." I hoist my battered bag off the ground.

"Ahhh I'm only kidding," Kaito says as we walk towards the elevator, "you know I'm kidding, don't you Tanet. Loving your work, my man."

The concierge blinks and walks back to his post.

The elevator pings open onto the twenty-fifth floor. We step on to the stairwell and, with a swift click of a key, step right into the heart of Kaito's penthouse apartment.

"Well look at you. King of the Castle."

He shrugs, but his nonchalance lasts all of two seconds. "Let me show you round," he bounces.

Alternating expanses of marble and teak flooring wrap throughout the property. I count five bedrooms, a kitchen – from the look of it more for decoration than use – and a sprawling living-dining space. But the jewel of the abode's crown comes at the end of our circumnavigation. Kaito slides open double doors to the balcony with sacramental grace then motions for me to go ahead. The balcony projects outwards like a fan. The collection of sun loungers, greenery and a hot tub do nothing to diminish the depth and breadth of its span.

Dusk is falling rapidly. The sun is melting into the haze, its last scarlet blades cutting through skyscrapers and temples, while on the darkening streets below a new source of nightlife energy is rising. It's hard to imagine a better vantage point from which to witness this passing of the guard.

"Nice, huh," he says. Far below the BTS Skytrain catches my eye. I watch it glide along Sukhumvit Road, then gaze back up at the fading horizon.

"Yeah," is all I can muster.

"Welcome home, my friend."

Chapter 15

Like all teenagers, we considered gym class to be a form of torture.

"Okay guys, gather round," Mr B calls through cupped hands from the other side of the field.
We jog towards him, ten or so students, panting and sweaty. Except Nina, of course – she's cool as a cucumber.
"Neens, how do you do it?" I ask, pinching my damp t-shirt.
"I just don't sweat," she shrugs.
"Well I sure do," says Kaito. His red chubby cheeks make him look like a beetroot.
"He actually speaks. Wow," says Venny nodding towards Kaito.
"Only when I'm too warm," Kaito says.
"He jokes too," Nina grins. "I'd call that progress."
"Shut up," Kaito replies with a bashful smile.

In those early school years barely a day went by without Mr Bordelais donning his tiny shorts and dragging us out for laps around the playing field. If 'playing field' is a suitable descriptor for a sun-scorched patch of grass spanning the gap between the school building and the foul-smelling *khlong* canal.

"Okay quiet down everyone," says Mr B. "So here's how this is gonna work. It's a game of tag like you've never played before. You're gonna pair up and take it in turns to try and tag your partner. But here's the difference: you've got to make enough skin contact to get a Read off your partner. Quick and sharp – no time for synching up. Get in, get out. Got it?"
A few of us groan a little too loud.
"Come on, people," he says, banging his hands together. "This'll be fun, huh?"

He sounded jovial, but we knew it was a matter of 'play or get detention'. Sparring sessions were always a compulsory bit of 'fun': 'Pinch a classmate then see if you can isolate the memory' / 'Learn a line of poetry then see if a partner can Erase it'.
Important skills, I guess. But having to experiment on each other? It never sat well.

Nina slaps Venny's back. "C'mon, tall boy. You're with me."
He hollers in protest but follows her into the field.
Dammit, I wanted to partner with her.
"Very good, you two," Mr B says. "Who else? Shalini and Jonathan,

buddy up and head over there. Mai and Daisuke, over here."

Before Mr B can assign any more I whip round to Kaito and raise my eyebrows.

"Sure," he says then whispers: "I'm so bad at Reading, Angel."

"Me too," I say. "We can be crap together. Just try not to Write anything on me, yeah?"

His beetroot cheeks deepen a shade.

"You wanna go first?" I ask.

Everyone else has started playing Weaver tag, chasing, yelping and laughing.

"Uh sure," he says.

I remember him shifting from foot to foot. The PE kit was a bad fit on his short and round body; simultaneously too tight and too long.

"Okay, come get me," I say, trotting off slowly. I get a memory ready to feed him. At first I try something from back home in England, but as ever it feels a little too hazy. So I go for a more recent one: of Kaito, Venny, Nina, ███ and I sneaking out after dark to ██████████████████.

He catches up quicker than I expect and grabs my arm. I offer up the memory but I don't feel him connecting. He grunts with the effort, face twists.

"No use," he says letting go.

"It's fine, K," I say. "Reading's not your thing. I'm terrible at it too. Who cares."

"Your turn, I guess?"

"I'll make a deal," I say. "How about we just tell Mr B we Read each other? But instead let's just play regular tag?"

His expression lights up. "Deal, dude."

"Okay cool."

I count real slow, then after 'ten' burst after him. I'm surprised at how far he's gotten; he's pretty damn speedy when he wants to be.

I'm running so fast that my voice bounces with every step. "I'm gonna get ya!"

"I'd like to see you try," he calls over his shoulder, then dodges left.

I'd never seen Kaito so happy. His face almost unrecognisable with a smile that wide. The first flash of his now-famous grin.

"Come on, Mr Slowpoke," he laughs, jogging backwards.

"You asked for it!"

I let out a battle cry then jump on him. We come crashing down.

I was so caught up in the hilarity of it all that I wasn't aware when my wrestling stopped being fun for Kaito.

"Dude, dude get off," he says.

"No way, I gotcha! I win!"

"Please, Angel let go–"

The tone of his voice has changed. He sounds scared. Shit!

"Sorry, K," I say, clambering off him. I grab his arm to pull him up, but as soon as I make contact my mind sparks...

"Let me out! Let me out! Mama! Papa! Where are you?"

They're all saying the same thing. Over and over. Pushing the doctors, hitting them.

The alarm's ringing so loud. What's happening?

A woman in a gown just like mine is screaming. Her eyes! So white. She says: "Let me out! Mama! Papa! It's me – Kaito! Let me out!"

Why is she calling herself my name?

I run under a table.

"Stop it please!" I cry.

A hand grabs me. The crazy woman. No! I kick her hand but she gets hold of my leg.

"Mama! Papa! Where are you?" She screams at me.

I can't breathe...oh! She's stopped. A doctor's pulled the woman away.

"Arigato gozaimasu," I say to the doctor. "You saved me."

He looks down at me then calls over to someone else. "I've got him. He's here."

They're coming for me. The doctors. One of them has a syringe–

"Kaito, it's okay. It's okay!"

I can hear Nina's voice as I come-to on the ground. She's kneeling over Kaito.

"Angel. You okay, man?" Venny says, towering over me.

"I..." My mind's racing from Kaito's Echo. So chaotic, all the screaming and shouting. "I think so. I just...Kaito."

I run over beside him. Nina's already doing a good job of calming him down. His face is wet with tears. I realise mine is too.

"Kaito, I'm so sorry. I didn't mean...it was an accident. I didn't mean to Read..."

He opens his mouth to speak.

"What's going on over here?" Mr B is jogging up to us. A few paces behind him is a male Project agent, blond hair and black tie flapping in the wind as he runs.

"It's fine. He just tripped and fell," Venny calls over. "No big deal."

Mr B steps closer but Venny places a hand on his chest, eye's blazing. "It's fine. He just needs some space. Sir."

I wonder how this is going to work out, but to my surprise Mr B steps back. He shakes his head at the blond agent who's been standing by.

"It's fine Ben," he says, then turns back to Venny. "Just get him to the nurse, would you Venedict?"

"Sir," Venny responds then comes back to us all.
We get Kaito to his feet and brush the grass off.
"Thanks Venny," Kaito says, breathless.
"We look after our own," Venny whispers, as we lead him past Mr B and the agent.

***

Back at the boarding house that night, Kaito finally opened up to us. We gathered round the dining room table at Khun Su's request. From the lack of surprise on her face, she already knew Kaito's story.

We sat there in silence, amazed at how it flowed out of him. We'd never heard him speak so many sentences in one go.

"My parents," he says in a little voice, "they were so scared when I first...y'know. Didn't know what to do with me. Tried to hide it at first, but it was no use. So they put me in a place outside Tokyo."

"A psychiatric institution?" Venny says.

K nods. "My parents said they'd come back for me when I was better, but in a year they didn't visit once. I didn't belong there. Knew I wasn't like the other patients. I just couldn't stay there, you know? What happened...it was...I didn't mean to do it."

Terrified and desperate, it's no wonder Kaito's abilities flared. His unchecked Writing wreaked havoc in the wards – he Wove one memory after another into the fabric of his fellow patients' minds. They started to believe that *they* were Kaito. A ward full of Kaitos, all thinking that *they* had been cast away by their cold, wealthy family and locked up in a mental institution.

"Why did you do it?" Nina asks.

"I didn't know what I was doing," he says, lip trembling. "But each time I did it, I felt a little less sad. The memories of my childhood, everything I'd lost, they hurt me less when I Wrote them away."

"What happened to the patients?"

Kaito looks up at Khun Su. She puts her hand on his. I've never seen her so gentle.

"They got violent," Kaito says. "Screaming, breaking windows, throwing chairs. A lot of them got hurt. They nearly escaped too, but in the end security people got it under control. I was locked up in a room by myself for weeks. Until The Project scouts found me. Erased the memories I'd written on the patients, then took me here."

He looks exhausted. Telling us all this has taken it out of him.

"I'm so sorry, Kaito," I say. "I'm sorry I made you relive that."

"Wasn't your fault," he sniffles. "All you did was Read what I did. I'm the one that actually did it."

"Don't beat yourself up, K," Nina says, patting his shoulder. "Fuck it,

93

y'know? Shit happens."

Kaito tenses up at Nina's swearing, his eyes dart to Khun Su. We all wait for the fallout.

The matron looks thoughtful then nods. "True."

Kaito laughs louder than all of us. It's a wonderful sound.

***

Looking at Kaito now, beer-in-hand, smile-on-face, I still remember the kid he was, the lost boy with chubby cheeks and a quiet soul. The man before me is entirely self-made.

"Okay so you have to tell me, K. What the hell is it you actually do? I mean, all this doesn't come cheap." I wave at the grandeur around me with chopsticks then balance them across the top of a bowl containing the remnants of our *pad seuw* takeout.

"It's really not that interesting, seriously," he says, scooping his sleek fringe out of his eyes. "I help fund startup businesses, guide them through the incubator phase then sell them on."

"Anything I've heard of?"

"Probably not. It's not that interesting."

I recognise the evasion tactic and don't pursue any further. "But it pays the bills," I say.

"But it pays the bills," he clinks my bottle.

Over dinner Kaito and I have painted pictures of our lives in the few years since we last saw each other. Well, apart from the reason I'm here with him in Bangkok. I get the feeling he wants to delay that conversation.

For my part I take Kaito on an apologetic but brief sweep through my sorry stories; and he creates a picture of an easy existence, enjoying the fruits of Bangkok – a busy social life, a rolling cast of lovers.

"Here's to that, am I right? Eyooooo!" he crows like a fratboy.

To anyone new these would seem like the tales of a braggart, but to me this is Kaito. He's always made a supreme effort not to dwell on the bad side of life, to give it any power. His family? Never talks about them. Totally understandable, given how they treated him. In their eyes he brought shame to the Taniguchi name, a smudge on an otherwise spotless empire. The moment his Weaving came to light, his preordained pathway through Japan's highest tier of private schooling was abruptly closed, the destiny of entering his family's pharmaceutical megacorp died instantly.

All of us have been scarred by our past, but none has made such an effort to live in the here and now as Kaito.

"And dare I ask, The Project?" I say.

"Meh," he shrugs. "I still have regular check ins with my mentor, but that's it. The Project made it clear a long time ago that they don't want my services."

This has been another of the 'great unsaid' topics with Kaito. His talent as a Writer has never been in question – he's Grade 4 through and through –

but his finesse and aptitude for putting that talent to use has always been in question. When we graduated school, Kaito was put to work by The Project just like me and Nina. He worked for a time in diplomacy, of all things. The idea being that Writers can foster greater understanding between nations by ferrying memories from one place to another, opening doors and empathy where other diplomatic methods have failed.

Kaito The Diplomat. It sounded like a recipe for disaster and I guess it was. He doesn't like to talk about it, so we've never pressed him on it.

"Here's to being benched by the Big P," I say, clinking my bottle once more with his. "I'm just glad things are working out for you. Anyway dude, I can't thank you enough for getting me over here. I'll pay you back, I promise."

"Hey, no way, I don't need your money. Anything for old friends." He reaches across the divide to slap my shoulder.

"You're a good man, Kaito Taniguchi. One of the best. But I'm gonna get that money back to you. For Nina's flights too."

"And Venny's?" he says with a grin.

"What?"

"Oh yeah, didn't I tell you? Venny's coming too. Surprise!"

"What the... when did you... has he also been–" I burble, much to Kaito's amusement.

"Okay, okay, so he's not *technically* agreed to come yet, but I'm working on it," K says. "You've been in the air for a long time today, man. I've used the day wisely. As soon as you got on your plane I called the Venn-Meister and asked if he happens to have received a mystery package too."

"And?"

"He didn't think so."

I ease back into my rattan chair, relieved.

"But then it turns out he did. It was just hidden under a pile of letters, diapers, baby formula or whatever. So–"

"Oh God, K. You didn't tell him to open it, did you?"

"What? No. What do you take me for? D'you think I'd want him going through this too? No way. I told him to keep the package closed and to bring it here on the Taniguchi express."

"Okay good, good. But wait, he can't just up and leave," I say, thinking of Jamal and Tia, how neither his child nor wife would be happy with Venny jumping on a plane for Bangkok.

Kaito shrugs in a way that indicates he understands childcare is an important thing, but that he couldn't really give two shits about it either.

"Why doesn't he just post the package out here?" I think out loud.

"No way, Angel. Venny can't miss this reunion. C'mon, the four of us back together again? This is going to be epic. Besides, you really want to run the risk of that package getting lost in the post?"

He's right. I don't want that happening. And as weird-ass a reunion as this is likely to be, the thought of the four of us being together gives me comfort.

"You think he'll come?" I ask.

"Heck yeah."

"I love your confidence, man," I laugh.

"Only way to live. Anyway, what time is it? You must be crazy tired."

"Not really. I mean yeah, the jet lag is making the floor go up and down, but I'm all right. Actually, speaking of the packages I wanted to ask you about what you got sent. About your dream."

A mixture of emotions fly across Kaito's face, but I barely get a chance to interpret them before he settles back into neutral. "Ahh that can wait until tomorrow. Let me show you to your room. If you're going to be staying awhile, you should get your body into Bangkok time."

I think about pursuing the matter, but it's clear he's not up for this conversation. And sleep doesn't seem like such a bad idea now I think of it.

***

"Remember me. Remember me."

The dream finds me. Even here. It's followed me like a stowaway, possibly back to where it was created? It barely startles me anymore. I've come to expect its nightly visit, but it wakes me nonetheless.

I ease out of my king-size bed in the direction of the bathroom. By the completion of my midnight piss I'm surprisingly alert. My poor body clock, adrift from sleepless weeks and this new time zone shuffle, says 'sure, why not. Let's call it daytime'.

I go in search of water, winding through the darkness in what I assume is towards the kitchen. To my surprise I find it, a fresh glass, and the water cooler – all without making a noise. I take the long route back to my room, keen to catch another glimpse of the skyline from the balcony. The doors are unlatched and slide apart, welcoming me out into the warm night air, and its chorus of crickets and frog-song. It's rained in the past few hours, and puddles have collected across the tiles. They'll have evaporated come morning, but for now they reflect the cloud's orange haze.

I begin to settle into a chair but startle when I notice a shadowy figure hunched at the end of a lounger. Kaito sits with head in hands, a vulture bowing to the moonlight. I stand still, wondering if he's noticed me, if I should leave.

I lay a hand on his back.

"K?"

"Hey" he croaks.

"You all right?"

A long and weary moan escapes from beneath his hands. He looks up then drags his fingers across his face, exposing the pink undersides of his lids.

"I'm so fucking tired. I can't… I just can't."

"I know, man. I'm so sorry," I say.

"How are you dealing with this? It's only been a week and I'm going crazy. How are you even sane after, what, a month of this?"

"Sane is a subjective word". This elicits a brief flash of his famous grin.

"I dunno, dude. I guess...I'm just driven onwards, y'know? This whole craziness, the dreams. I need to get to the bottom of it. Find out who made this all happen, what it all means. We're going to figure this out, I promise."

"Big promise."

"I know it is. But this is why I'm here. This is my purpose."

He just looks back at me glassy-eyed.

"But to do it, I need you to help me out. Can you show me the object you've been sent? I need it to get a better picture of what you've been dreaming."

He stands up sharply and slaps his hands together.

"I've got a much better idea," he says, a forced vigour shining out of him. "Let's go get fucked up."

Chapter 16

The queue for the bar is three-people-deep. I pick a spot in the throng and hope for the best, though the glacial speed of the bar staff doesn't inspire much. I take out my credit card, hoping there's a glimmer of life yet within it.

In the periphery, a mass of bodies rolls in sync to the thumping. I should feel too old for this shit, but the shots of Johnnie Walker in the taxi have kicked in so I'm thinking this might be just what I need.

The view from Highline is breathtaking. The rooftop nightclub is just about tall enough to mingle with the clouds, fifty-two floors above an ever-bustling Phloen Chit intersection. Looking down from this misty vantage point, the city wires out like a network of orange neurones, and we're at its epicentre.

Thai glitterati twinkle all around me, partygoers who are as sleek and sexy as the club. This is categorically *not* the kind of club Kaito, Venny, Nina and I used to come to as teenagers. How our clandestine nights out were never discovered is a mystery. If Khun Su had known we would sneak out of the boarding house in search of dive bars in Nakhon Pathom or Bangkok, she would have had a fit. Maybe our matron knew all along, her stern demeanour just an act. Perhaps she'd be pleased to see how our night-time festivities have taken an upward swing, away from the grimy bars of Silom Soi Four to this cloud-top fantasia. I catch a glimpse of her in my mind's eye. Somehow a smile doesn't sit right on my memory of Khun Su's stony face.

A vibration in my back pocket. A new text message pulls me out of my reverie. The sensory overload of the club dissipates.

> **Adrian:** Bangkok? I'm more than a little surprised, Douglas. I can appreciate the impulse, but running from your problems is never sensible. They should be faced. I thought we could have faced them together, but there's very little help I can offer you from here.
>
> My hands are tied, Dougie. I've informed the Bangkok branch of your 'trip'. They'll be in touch in due course regarding the assignment of a local mentor for you to report to.

My breath catches for a second at the coldness of Adrian's response. He's contacted the Bangkok branch. What did I really expect? It's impossible to truly escap–

A sculpted forearm and bicep clamp around my neck.

"What are you doing?" Kaito screams over the music. I twist as far as I can to take in his face, but only catch the whites of his eyes. He points to the opposite end of the dance floor, where steps lead up to a cordoned off section. "VIP. C'mon." He shouts then plants a smacking kiss on my cheek.

I shake my head and laugh. Of course he has access to the VIP area.

I follow in his wake through a laser show of smoky walls that beam in and out of existence. Breaking through to the other side of the dance floor we take the few steps up to the VIP section – a wide platform comprising a series of circular booths sunken into the floor. They look like ammonite fossils embedded into onyx.

Kaito scans the booths then hollers at one in the far corner next to the window – a great spot for watching the dance floor in front, and the sparkling skyline behind.

"C'mon, I wanna introduce you to some of my people," he says.

I thought tonight was just going to be him and me, so I'm both surprised and slightly annoyed. I didn't think I would end up clubbing on my first night in Bangkok, so I'm just here for the ride. As we approach the sunken booth, he greets them all with a 'hey hey!' and is met with a similar chorus. The eyes of all six people switch in unison to me. I immediately shrink inside.

"Everyone, this is one of my best friends in all the world, Angel." K brushes my shaved head, making me shrink even further.

"Hey guys," I say with a wave, "nice to meet you all." They smile and '*watdee*' in response.

My first thought: I'm not dressed well enough for these people. Before we left the apartment I threw on a black shirt and jean combo. 'Black is good', I thought, 'it's smart enough, and hides the creases'. Now that I'm standing in front of Kaito's 'people', I couldn't feel more like a crumpled mess. Everything about them is impressive, from their relaxed-but-obviously-expensive clothes, to their just-so hairstyles and carefully curated accessories. They're impossibly cool – an advert for the young cultural elite of Thailand. And yet for all that, they seem genuinely pleased to see me as much as Kaito.

"Okay, let me see if I can do this in a single sweep," he says. "This is Pom and Adisak."

The pair to the left of the curved bench grin. She has a cropped pixie cut and he has a thin scarf draped around his neck.

"Chompoo, Sud–" Kaito continues, indicating to what seems to be a couple: she with a waterfall of hair flowing to one side and a sleeve of tattoos; he with a spiky love patch under his bottom lip, bulging pectorals, and an arm draped demonstrably around her.

"–aaand...no don't tell me, *argh* I always do this, *khotort, khotort khrab*," Kaito *wais* apologetically to a young woman with smiling eyes. "Saengdao," he bellows triumphantly. "Of course, Saengdao. Sorrysorrysorry, *na khrab*."

She brushes his grovelling aside with laughter, then nods at me.

"And this is my man Mongkon," Kaito says, finishing his introductions by reaching down to shake hands with a guy sat closest to us. He's dressed all in black much more successfully than me. Strikingly attractive – mid-length hair tied back, revealing dark brown eyes behind thin circular glasses, a strong jawline and a stubbly muzzle. He rises up from the booth to shake my hand.

"*Sawatdee khrab*," I say in my best Thai.

"Hey there, man, pleased to meet you" he replies in a mid-Atlantic accent much like my own. He then turns to Kaito and, further to my surprise, breaks out into fluent Japanese. Whatever he says makes Kaito laugh. They step aside to talk further.

I'm beckoned into the booth by the seated quintet just as a waiter approaches holding a bottle of vodka. He slides it into the bucket of ice at the centre of the table, replacing an empty bottle that's clearly been drunk not long before my arrival – a fact evidenced by the flushed cheeks and bloodshot eyes of the group.

"Hi guys." I shuffle awkwardly inwards. The girl with the pixie cut, Pom I think, leans across everyone. She looks at me with a quiet intensity.

"So you got to Bangkok today, right? How you feeling?"

"Yeah, a little woozy but it's nice to be out and seeing the city at night," I reply with big gesticulations and raised voice to be understood over the music. Plus I'm not sure how good everyone's English is, so I figure it's better to do the *slow-speaking-Westerner* bit for starters.

"First time in Bangkok?" asks Sud. Chompoo touches his beefy arm, expels a quick burst of Thai, then turns to me.

"I explain to him you–" Chompoo says.

"–went to school with Kaito, yeah."

"Oh, you speak Thai?"

"*Nit noy*," I say, pinching my forefinger and thumb together, indicating something small. "But it's been a while."

"How long?"

"Um, like, eight years or something?"

"Why so long?"

"Just really busy, I guess. Working, living in London. No real reason. Time flies," I shrug. "So how about you guys, how do you know Kaito?"

A look ricochets around the group, ultimately landing with Pom.

"Mongkon and I have known Kaito the longest. Many years now actually. Because we're, you know–" she opens a palm towards me, as if expecting me to naturally know the end of the sentence. I look up and down the group but don't get any help.

"You know," Pom continues. "Weavers."

A charge goes off inside me, making me want to duck for cover.

Pom looks at me with a curious expression. "Like you, right?"

I feel the gaze of everyone once again.

"Uh yeah. Like me," I say timidly, then with a little more confidence: "Yes. I'm a Weaver too."

Smiles and nods break out all around. I feel my cheeks redden. Any time I meet new Weavers I fall into this panic, as if somehow by our sheer proximity we'll reveal the secret of our existence to the masses, and the riots and witch trials will begin.

As if reading my struggle, Pom pours some ice-cold vodka into my glass and slides it along.

"*Kop khun mak khrab*," I thank her, then gulp half of it down. My gratitude elicits a peal of laughter from the group.

"So you're *all* Weavers?" I say, emboldened.

More smiles.

"Nah, some are Flatline groupies," says a new voice beside me.

Mongkon winks as he settles into the booth. *Flatline.* I haven't heard the term for non-Weavers in years, and it sounds all the uglier after so long. And it inspires a fresh wave of panic in me.

Mongkon carries on, his voice smooth. "Don't look so scared. Our secret is safe with them, trust me."

"But I'm not so sure we should be–"

"Calm down, it's fine. I mean look at us. We're just your average group of friends. Some of us happen to be wonderfully gifted and the rest, well, they're special in other ways I'm sure."

"Hey," shouts Chompoo in mock indignation, then let's rip a few Thai cuss words I definitely understand. Mongkon responds with a fluid stream of contrition in Thai. *English, Japanese, Thai. Seriously, this guy is some linguist.*

But then I get it.

"You're a Spinner," I blurt out mid-sip.

Mongkon sits back, arms behind his head. "I am indeed. Pom there is a Spark."

She shoots a peace sign in my direction.

"That's so cool," I say, looking to Kaito who nods back nonchalantly.

Spinners and Sparks are pretty rare types of Weaver. The first I ever met was a girl at school, Shalini. She could tap into people's procedural memory – the systems involved in remembering actions, motor skills, language. So naturally she was awesome at anything those around her excelled at. Sports, throwing cards into a cup, you name it.

Sparks specialise in semantic memory, our brain's centre of knowledge. Another kid at school, Daisuke, was a Spark. Poor guy had so much scrutiny put on him when it came to exam time. Did he learn stuff or pick it up from others? Makes little difference I guess. I think he's a neurosurgeon now.

"So what do you guys do? You work for The Project, right?" I ask Mongkon and Pom.

A smirk passes between them.

"Some do. Don't worry, everybody's off duty. That's how this whole thing works. And some," he says, holding Pom in his eye-line, "you could say are kind of…free agents. Living lives as they see fit. It's a little easier to be off-grid here in Bangkok."

"How is that even possible?" I say. "Bangkok is one of the major centres of The Project."

An inexplicable smile opens across Mongkon's face. "The closer to danger, the further from harm."

"Which is great news for Angel here," Kaito slaps me on the back, jumping into the conversation before I can probe further. "Y'see he's on the run from The Project and his mentor."

"That's a bit of an over-exaggeration, K," I start – Adrian's text message springs to mind (*'I've informed the Bangkok branch of your 'trip'*) – but Mongkon cuts me off.

"Hey you don't need to worry about any of that here. No more work talk. Have some vodka. Let's have a toast. To drink, to dance, and to not giving a damn!"

A few faces around the table look a little lost, but raise a glass nonetheless. At Kaito's request we down the drinks and head straight for the dance floor. We push our way into the centre of the action. It could be the alcohol or the sentiment behind Mongkon's toast, but I feel a swell of elation. The beat pulses. I feel featherlight in its grasp, let myself move with every suggestion. Kaito's people sweep me up. As I twist and turn I catch snatches of them, the glint of an eye, the flash of teeth, the hoot of laughter. They're intoxicating, and I give myself to them completely.

At the transition of one track to another, I steal a break back to the table. A hand presses on my arm as I toss another vodka down my throat. I stumble slightly, which makes her eyes smile even more.

"Having fun?" Saengdao says.

"Yes. So much," I breathe. "You guys are great."

"Thank you. We try," she says. Everything about her is beautiful and pristine. Her quiet confidence, her precise fringe, the honey of her voice.

I catch myself staring. "Are you having fun too?"

"Oh yes," she smiles then says something else.

"What?" I shout over the music.

She leans in closer. "I say 'nice people'. I don't know them long, so it is new to me too."

"Oh, I thought maybe you'd all known each other for years. So how did you get to know them?"

A flash of shyness crosses her face. "I like to meet Weaver. They very interesting. Special. My father was one."

I'm not really sure how to answer this, plus the drink is clouding my ability to form an opinion. So I just nod and smile.

She continues. "You are all the only other Weavers I ever meet, you know?"

"Oh really," I say, feeling a wave of drunkenness mixing with the sudden reappearance of jet lag. "Well, I'm not very special. Not a very interesting Weaver. The rest are much more 'mpressive. I'm just a Generic, y'see."

"Generic?" Her nose crinkles.

"Yeah, y'know, just a little bit of this and that."

"But you can Read memory? Give memory?"

"Uh I'm not the best at it, but sure," I say. I'm not sure where this conversation is heading, and there's something a little disturbing about the hungry expression that's forming on Saengdao's face.

"Hey what you guys gabbing about?" says Kaito, bouncing into the rescue. What a guy. "Hopefully not little old me?"

He looks a little manic – the power of his stance at odds with his sunken eyes. Saengdao doesn't seem to notice. Like a flower turning to the sun, she switches her attention to K, laughs at his jokes, squeezes his arm. With more than a little relief I slip back to the dance floor, leaving them to it.

I can't find the group, so lean into the hug of anonymity. In minutes I'm throwing shapes like no-one – and everyone – is watching. I feel infinite.

In time I find myself propped up in a dark corner of the club. I've sobered up little through all the sweating, and am now basking in a kind of empty serenity. Everything feels quiet. The music sounds far away, only the baseline makes it through. The movement of the club drifts into a slow-motion waltz of passers-by bearing cocktails, of dancers reaching for each other through the lasers and the smoke.

I don't notice her at first.

It's more of a rising awareness of her emerging form. At a distance she seems to glide through the morass, but as she comes more into focus I see how she is glancing off person to person, like an asteroid making its way through a chaotic field. Closer still and the truth of her expression becomes clear.

Terror. A blade of ice pierces me as she stumbles inexorably in my direction, eyes wet and wide. Something is terribly wrong and it's coming my way. In silent seconds we're standing face-to-face, cloistered in the shadows.

"I...I...I'm scared. I don't want to go," Saengdao mutters, fresh tears brimming. She reaches up to her temples and rakes through her hair.

Adrenaline courses through me, bringing her sharply to attention. Everything else remains soft in the background.

"What happened? What is it?" I say.

Her face flinches, a new course of action decided upon. She reaches for me, clamping hands on my face and pulling our foreheads into clammy contact. No time to safeguard myself. No time to prepare for the coming flood.

Darkness. Pitch black darkness.

And then a voice.

"Hey. It's time."

It's a young voice but earthy. I've been waiting for him, here in the dark, but it still startles me.

"You ready?" he asks.

He clicks the aircon off and almost immediately the heat closes in. I slide a foot out from under the covers and on to the cold floor. It's a clear night and the moon casts enough light to find my way to the chest of drawers. I open the top drawer as silently as I can and reach under a stack of t-shirts. I find the drawstring bag, feel the outline of its contents.

"Have you got them?"

"Yeah," I whisper.

As the hours have gone by, lying half-awake in bed, I've become numb. But now that it's time, my heart has started to beat once more. My gut is full of fear.

"Venny?" I whisper.

"Yeah?"

"I'm afraid."

"I know. Me too."

My eyes have adjusted to the darkness. The moonlight hits half of his face. The softness of his cheeks, the fullness of his lips, the dryness of his eye. I see it searching my own face, seeking to understand. To see me.

"Olivia? It's going to be okay," he says, reaching for my shoulder.

"You see me?"

"I see you," he smiles.

"Venn...what if it goes wrong? He–" Tears roll down my face.

"It's going to be okay," he says firmly. "I promise. It has to be this way. I know what I'm doing. You know what you're doing."

I'm scared. I don't want to go. But no. I have to remember who this is for.

It's for Angel.

Two new faces peer around the doorframe.

"Are we doing this?" Nina whispers, throat hoarse with emotion. Poor Nina. I'm so sorry.

"Yes. I'm ready."

I take the first step. I'm terrified, but the numbness is coming back. I welcome it as I lead the way. The long walk to the gallows.

The scene shifts. I'm me again. I think I am. I drift away from the scene, cast myself aside until I can see the outlines of the Echo. I see the threads of it in Saengdao's mind, stretching out for her, trying to embed its clever tendrils. She's fighting them, as a body fights the spread of a virus. But she's losing.

Soon this memory will become part of her. But it's not like a normal memory, it has a different signature. I recognise it. It's like my dream. I immediately understand the danger it poses to her. I need to act now. But I also know what that means. The Echo needs a host. If not her...

Decision and action happen at once. I reach out for the Echo's gossamer threads, pull them tightly. There's an initial struggle, but then it lets go, relenting, understanding what the pull means: A new host.

I open my mind to the Echo. It rushes forward.

Darkness. Pitch black darkness.

And then a voice.

"Hey. It's time."

***

The dream loops. I let it play. I sink further and further into it. The voices of people surrounding me, real people, are so distant, so far above...

The downward drag of the dream is strong. I don't resist. I want it, need it to tell me more, to open itself up to me.

Olivia. The dream is her memory. She was there, with Venny. With Nina too. She was doing 'it' for Angel. Doing 'it' for me. Whatever 'it' was.

Like a spear of light, a new force reaches for me. It hoists me upwards, away from the dream. *No, leave me here!* Someone calls my name. My name. Douglas. Yes that's right. My name is Douglas. I hear someone call it, louder and louder and louder until suddenly I emerge, breaking through the surface and into the night.

Lasers, smoke, the scents of alcohol and air conditioning, the cold dampness of sweat on my forehead. So clear, so crisp, so much sensation.

"Douglas, Angel, breathe. Breathe." She grips my chin and forces me to focus on her. A woman with cropped black hair.

"P-Pom?" I stutter.

"Yes, that's right. Look at me. Come back. Breathe. Good," she says. A look of concern that's somehow familiar.

My panic begins to subside, caught in the anchor of her gaze. At her instruction I take a few more deep breaths then slide up to a seat. I'm still in the nightclub, still in the dark corner. Pom and Adisak look down on me, sheltering from any potential onlookers.

"You...you pulled me out." *Why didn't you leave me?* "How did you do that?"

Pom grins. "I'm a Spark, remember? I know things."

"How...how long was I under?"

"A minute? We saw her come to you. We stopped dancing, followed. She reached for you, and you both fell. I knew what was happening, so I reached inside and pulled you out. Just like I did with her."

I look to my left. Saengdao's cradling her head in her hands.

"Saengdao," I call softly. "Are you okay?"

"*Khotort, khotort*," she apologises through tears. She looks up at Pom and without prompting starts explaining in a stream of Thai. I understand snippets. Pom begins to translate. Though I already know precisely what's happened.

I can't believe he did this.

Pom has barely finished and I'm up on my feet. Legs feel weak at first, but I find my stride.

"Angel, stop!" Pom calls as I march across the dance floor in the direction of the VIP section. I find Kaito there, slumped within the booth, the very picture of bliss. I step down next to him and shake his shoulders. It's all I can do not to punch the expression right off his face.

"K!" I shout. "What the fuck, man? Why would you do that to her?"

He lies there stupefied. I'm about to shake him when a hand clamps on my shoulder and spins me round.

"Leave him alone, man," Mongkon sings.

I shrug my shoulder loose. "Don't touch me. This has nothing to do with you. It's between me and this shithead."

"Jesus. Take a breath. Why are you so angry? Just chill out," he says.

Wrong thing to say to me. "Chill out? What the–? Do you have any idea what he's done? He almost scrambled that girl's head… And you're telling me to chill out?"

Mongkon holds his hands up. "Come on, how naïve can you be, Angel? I mean it's not like she didn't ask for it."

"That's a fucking rapist's excuse!" I holler.

"No, you misunderstand," he chuckles. "She literally asked for it."

"What are you–"

"You really don't know?" he laughs. *I swear to God if he keeps on laughing.* "You can let your guard down. Get off your high horse. Can't you see, we're superheroes here. These people love us."

"What the f–" I begin, then think a second. "Look I know *some* people think we're *enlightened* or whatever. But this–"

"They *think* we're enlightened. Don't you see? That's why Thailand is the epicentre of Weaver study," he says, bobbing his head like I'm an idiot. *I'm gonna smack that look off his face just as soon as I'm done with Kaito.* "And what do those lower than the enlightened seek? Insight, guidance, blessings. That's why some people come to Weavers like Kaito."

At the mention of his name I glance back at his drowsy form. He seems to be stirring. Meanwhile Mongkon continues monologuing.

"Kaito's ability to Write his memories makes him very popular," he grins. "Think about it. If you thought of Weavers as enlightened beings, wouldn't you want to receive blessings from them? To receive their gifts? So that's why people like Saeng*whatever* over there–"

"Saengdao," I growl.

"Fine. That's why people like her swarm around people like Kaito. It's not his fault if it's too much for the people he gives his 'gifts' to," he air quotes.

"You are playing with fire, you asshole," I say. "You could seriously screw with people's minds. Not to mention leaking everything about us to the world in the process."

"How many times…the secret is safe. These people don't want to share the source of enlightenment they've found. And if they did, well we have ways of making them forget, don't we?"

I start to bite back but he continues without a break.

"So I repeat: take a chill pill and read the scene before judging it."

"Judging?" I blurt. I can't believe I thought this guy was cute. Everything about his slimy way of talking repulses me.

"Yes judging. I mean, c'mon man, are you seriously telling me you've never done something similar?"

I open my mouth but nothing comes out. His words freeze me. It sickens me that he's right. Dhaval's face flashes into my mind. The memory I Wrote on to him of my perfect day at the beach. A 'gift'. That's what I thought of it as. I wanted to give him a gift. So selfish and irresponsible.

Mongkon smirks with satisfaction, as if reading my mind.

"No, he's right. Angel's right," says a small voice behind us. "I shouldn't have done it."

Kaito looks up at us, wide-eyed. The same face he had when I first met him. The little lost boy from Japan.

Chapter 17

I slide along the cracked leather seat with each corner. I wonder if there'll ever be seatbelts in Thai taxis.

Kaito and I have sat in silence since leaving Mongkon, Pom and everyone else on the steps of the Phloen Chit skyscraper. Saengdao spoke a few words of thanks to me as we rode the elevator down. She seems to have bounced back after my and Pom's emergency psychic surgery. Kaito's dream, so toxic to her, now settles somewhere in my skull. Oddly, I feel okay about that. Possessive. Like it's *my* cancer, and she can't steal it. Chompoo, Adisak and Sud seemed bemused by the whole episode, unaware of the reason for our departure. Mongkon hung in the background while Pom helped me with Kaito.

"I shouldn't have done it," K repeats, breaking the silence between us in the taxi. "I didn't think it would fuck her up so much. You have to believe me."

I let his words ring in my ears for a while, think of all the things I want to say. Mostly that it's not me he needs to apologise to. But more than that. For a while all I wanted was for my dream to be ripped out of me, I would have done anything to regain the nothingness of Weaver sleep. So I can understand why he Wrote it away onto Saengdao, if he truly thought it wouldn't traumatise her. But I don't say anything of this. Instead I read each Sukhumvit street sign as we pass, names and numbers I once knew so well.

"Those people," I finally say. "They're not good for you."

"You can't say that, Angel. You don't know them," he comes back quickly, firmer than I expect. "Those *people* have been there for me, they've taught me a lot about what life can be for a Weaver. Shown me a way to live that we were never taught at school. At the fucking Mnemosyne Project Bangkok."

He curls his lip in disgust at the name.

I turn to face him. "I'm not blaming you, K. I'm the last person to be judging. But I mean, c'mon, Writing memories onto random people in clubs? What's that going to achieve?"

"Who cares what it'll achieve? It's all bullshit anyway. What's the alternative? Be a Project goon again? Look where that's left us both."

I flinch.

"I'm sorry, Angel, but it's true. You have literally run away from the life that The Project gave you. And me? They left me out on the cold years ago. Thank God. So you'll just have to *forgive me* if I'm living recklessly here. Someone thinks I'm special? Wants a 'blessing' from me? Game on. They're queuing up for a piece of me, dude. Lining up out the door. And I couldn't be happier to give it to them."

"You don't mean that, Kaito. You're just drunk."

"No, I'm not. I mean it. With every memory I Write away, I feel a little better. Take a look for yourself."

He unfurls an arm across the seat, opening his hand to me in supplication, gaze resting on mine so steadily. "Please."

I reach out with two fingers, let them hover above his palm. Then make contact.

The landscape of Kaito's memories opens up before me. But it's unlike anything I've experienced before.

So quiet.

Shards drift together and apart, like driftwood. Some eddy together, others float alone, far towards the horizon of his mind.

I recognise some faces. I'm there. So's Nina and Venny. Some places too. Our boarding house. The city. But so much of what is here are just practical place markers. Memories of how to do things, general knowledge, of people, places and things.

But where are the genuine connections? The loves, the losses, the resentment, the mistakes, the joys..?

This is the mindscape of a ghost. Save for a few of us, anyone of consequence is simply gone. His family? The knowledge of them is here. But Kaito's emotional memories of them, their essence? Gone.

And yet. For all its emptiness, there's an eerie harmony to it all. Quite unlike the minds of dementia patients I've Read, where memories drift frustratingly, painfully out of their possessor's reach.

No, here in Kaito's mind, there's a wilfulness to the loss.

He actually wants this.

"Kaito," I whisper, devastated by my friend's hollowness. "I don't know what to say. Why would you Write away your memories like that?"

"Sure beats the heck out of having memories of my meaningless life festering inside me," he says, stony gaze catching the streetlights.

"Is that…is that why The Project benched you?"

"Lucky me, huh? They couldn't deal with the fuck up I was becoming. Better to sideline me than help me through it."

"But your mentor–"

"Doesn't give a shit. She just checks in on me to make sure the secret is still safe. Doesn't have a clue what I do in my spare time. My dirty little habit," he curls his lip.

"But K, there are people out there, just living their lives, holding little pieces of you in them, leaving you…empty. And your family–"

"What about them?" he says.

"They're gone. Practically wiped from your mind."

"It's for the best, believe me. Bet they wish they could do the same."

"C'mon man, that can't be true."

"The closest my folks have ever been to expressing love for me is with money. At least that's something I can use. You think my cash comes from my entrepreneurial work?" he snorts. "Look at the lifestyle you can have in Bangkok with monthly guilt money from the family business. Look how much they're willing to spend just to keep me away. If it wasn't so funny, I'd cry. So fuck them. I'll take their money, thank you very much. But I refuse to keep any memories of them that matter."

"I can't imagine how lonely that must make you feel."

"Hey, don't go feeling sorry for me, Angel-san," he says without looking at me. "Let's face it, this is all I was ever meant to be."

"I don't believe that for a second."

He shrugs, forcing a glimmer of his boisterous self to the surface, though only the merest sheen breaks through.

***

The penthouse is awakening with the rose gold of sunrise. For all its gentle beauty, it does nothing to warm my soul. In the light of what Kaito just revealed, the apartment has lost its appeal; the cloudtop sanctuary now crystallised into a fortress of solitude.

He kicks off his shoes and slouches towards the bedroom. At the door he turns around and motions for me to join him.

"There's something I want to show you."

By the time I enter the room he's foraging inside a drawer.

"Take a seat," he pats the corner of the bed. "Part of me hoped I would never have to show you this. To be honest, I kinda hoped we wouldn't even have to talk about the dreams. I just wanted to get you and the gang together, have a reunion without mentioning the past. Stupid, I know. But after what happened tonight, you saving Saengdao… Well I guess I messed up my own plan, huh?"

He settles next to me with an envelope crumpled in his fist. "I'm sorry you have my dream inside you now, Angel. You know that, right?"

"It's okay. I mean it, K."

"I wanted to protect you from what was in it. Now that I've Written it away, I can't really remember much, just enough to know that whatever it shows us, it's not good."

I'm scared. I don't want to go.
But no. I have to remember who this is for. It's for Angel.

A flash of the dream.

"What is it?" he asks.

"The girl in the dreams. Olivia."

"Olivia," he repeats in slow recognition. "Who is she?"

My mind crawls around, trying to fit the pieces together. "I thought I knew. Was sure of it actually. I thought she was a childhood friend, from back home in England. She died when I was a kid. Car accident or something…I think.

It's so jumbled. But now, whoever Olivia is, was, she's not who I thought. She was here, K. In Thailand. At the school with us."

He nods, giving me room to continue.

"The dream. It's her memory. Olivia's memory. Venny and Nina, they both talk to her. She's so scared. Petrified about something we're about to do. But what? What did we do? What did *I* do?"

"This might help."

He opens the envelope and drops its content onto my palm: a metal key. As small as it is unremarkable. It doesn't look like a door key. Maybe one for a locker? I pick it up, and in seconds I know precisely what it is – sense its subtle vibration.

"This is what gave you the dream, isn't it?"

"Yes," he says. "I have no idea what it opens. Maybe we could find out?"

"Sure. But first, I've got a better idea."

Without wasting any time, I close my eyes, wrap my fingers around the key...

"Angel, what're you–"

"Shh."

...and settle my mind.

I'm here. Talk to me. I whisper to the key. The vibration grows, coming alive in my hand, flowering in my mind.

Somehow, it feels easier this time. Like I'm learning how to listen.

There they are, shards of Kaito's dream, the one he Wrote on to Saengdao, the dream which I cut free and now possess in the deep recesses of my mind.

I see and feel it all: the boarding house at night; the warm air, the cold floor; Venny and Nina, their faces so young, looking at me.

No, not me. Olivia. Looking at Olivia.

I gather the jittering shards together, try to catch them as they zip around, pull them into a coherent stream. But as I do, something new comes to my attention. Something beyond the tinkling shards calls out, low and smooth. I go to it, caught in the pull of its baritone zephyr.

Nenneko. Nenneko.
Nenneko yo
Oraga akabo wa
Itsu dekita?

San-gwatsu, sakura no
Saku toki ni:
Dori de o-kao ga
Sakura-iro.

I hiccup the last of my tears as Papa holds me and sings. My breathing is starting to slow down again. His voice makes me feel so much better. I hug him tighter as he starts the lullaby from the beginning.

Sleep, sleep,
Sleep, my child!
When was my
Baby made?

In the third month,
In the time of the blooming
Of cherry-flowers.
Therefore the colour of the honorable
Face of my child is the colour of the cherry-blossom.

"Papa?"
"Yes, Kaito-san?"
"I'm sorry. I didn't mean to break the vase—"
"Shhh, my boy. Everything is okay. Shhh."
"It was an accident."
"I know it was. Don't worry. A vase is just a vase."
"But it was your favourite—"
He laughs softly, then kisses me on the forehead.
"No, my boy. I only have one favourite thing in this world."
"What is it, Papa?" I hold my head up. He's smiling down at me.
"It's you, Kaito. You are my most favourite thing in the world."
I nuzzle my face into him.
"I love you, Papa. Papa daisuki."
"I love you too."

The memory radiates. In that moment, in his father's arms, Kaito knew utter calm, total security. I rise out of the memory slowly, drifting back into myself, taking its warmth with me.

***

We're sitting on the bed. Kaito looks at me with astonishment and bewilderment.

"Angel, what just happened? You zoned out for a bit like you were…"

"Reading the key?" I say.

"Exactly," he says, face scrunched in confusion.

I shrug. "It's as much of a surprise to me, K."

"What—" he begins.

"It started soon after the pendant arrived in the post. Ever since I started dreaming it's like I've shifted into some new gear in my Weaving. It's crazy, I know, but it's happening. If I focus hard enough, I can pick up on Echoes in some objects," I say holding up the key.

"That's awesome," Kaito breathes.

"I'm guessing the same hasn't happened for you?" I say.

He shakes his head, then his eyes pop. "Dude, promise me you won't touch anything in my bathroom."

"Gross," I say with a laugh. "Don't worry, your secrets are safe. Besides I'm not very good at it. Some objects are much easier than others, like this key and my pendant. They speak to me better than anything else, like they want to be heard. I think… I think she's teaching me how to do it."

"Who is?"

"Olivia."

"What do you–"

"It doesn't matter right now. K. Do you trust me?"

"Of course".

"No I mean, really trust me?"

More confusion. "Yes, I do."

"Then clear your mind. I have something that belongs to you. Something I think you lost a long time ago."

I gather up the Echo hidden deep in the key. Pull it all together in my mind, then touch Kaito's hand and let the song and the memory flow into him. So that he might once again remember the security of his father's arms.

Nenneko. Nenneko.
Nenneko yo
Oraga akabo wa
Itsu dekita?

San-gwatsu, sakura no
Saku toki ni:
Dori de o-kao ga
Sakura-iro.

Chapter 18

"Olivia? It's going to be okay," Venny says, reaching out for my shoulder.

"You see me?"

"I see you," he smiles.

"Venn, I know this is the only way, but what if it goes wrong? I...."

Tears roll down my face. There's a pause. Uncertainty hangs in the air. But then a firmness sets in his face.

"It's going to be okay. I promise. It has to be this way. I know what I'm doing. You know what you're doing."

I'm scared. I don't want to go. But no. I have to remember who this is for.

It's for Angel.

***

We're running. Olivia's ahead of me now. I'm shouting at her. She screams. 'Help me. It hurts. Help.'

Ice cold fear runs through me. I kneel beside her crumpled form on the ground. I try to look up, but still I can't see her face. Her breathing, so shallow.

She clasps her hands over my own. A white light flashes in my mind. I can't see anything. But a voice, clear and sharp, pierces the haze.

"Remember me," she says. "Remember me."

NO! I yell. NO. DON'T LEAVE ME, PLEASE.

***

"Angel. Angel wake up. It's okay." A voice, familiar, soft, calls for me. It's white all around me. Is this real? Am I finally awake? I reach through the fog and find it's close to my face, covering my body. A sheet. Got to get free of it. I feel air coming from above, I find an edge and break free, gulp in the cold air.

"You okay?"

The face. It matches the voice. But it's somehow different. Deeper, sadder? Same with the face. A few crinkles around the eyes where there shouldn't be. Cheeks slimmer too.

"Nina?" Her skin's smooth, warm to the touch. "Oh Nina. What happened? Has it been so long?"

Now she looks confused. Worried. Why?

"Angel, I... what's going on?"

No. This isn't right.

Where am I? Why does my head hurt so much? The dream. I was dreaming again. My dream and the new one…Kaito's dream. Joining together. Like a puzzle, the pieces seeking connections. Some locking, others bouncing off one another.

And now Nina's here. She's here!

Oh God.

Stomach lurching.

Bile climbing up my throat.

I leap out of bed and barely make it to the toilet before hurling spectacularly into the bowl. *Ugh, fuck this.* A few more retches and the worst seems to be over. A film of sweat remains over my body.

"You okay in there?"

Nina. *Fuck.* I'm naked. *Double fuck.*

"Uh yeah, sorry Neens. Guess I drank a little too much last night. Just gimme a sec to shower and I'll be out."

Shower, shampoo, toothpaste, mouthwash. A few minutes and I'm back into the bedroom with a towel around my waist. Nina's perched on the bed, jacket folded next to her.

A haughty look is in her eyes. "Well I should be shocked by your austere haircut, but then I think the sight of your naked ass on the way to the toilet, plus the sound of you puking your guts up has used up all my shock reserves."

"Sorry about that," I mumble while passing a hand over the stubble on my head. "Welcome to Thailand."

Her expression switches. "You sure you're okay there? Still looking kinda pale."

"I'll be all right. Just need to let the world come back into focus." I totter back to bed and slip under the sheets. Relief spreads through me after a few long breaths. "How was the flight?"

"Not too bad. Bit bumpy at times, plus y'know, still not able to get much sleep."

"Shit, what time did you arrive? How did you get here to the apartment? Were we supposed to pick you up from the airport? I'm so sorry, Neens."

"Shhh, calm down. It's all fine. I touched down a few hours ago. Kaito came to get me."

"He did?"

"I was surprised too. I walked out into the arrivals hall fully intending to hail a cab, but there he was all bright eyed and bushy tailed, like some tour operator."

"How did– I mean, he drank as much as me last night, maybe more…"

"Well to be fair, it is 2pm."

"Oh man," I say, covering my face with a clammy hand.

"Yup," Nina pets my arm. "But no, K said he had the best sleep of his life last night. Woke up all refreshed and ready to take on the day. Which makes sense, I guess."

"He told you about what happened last night, huh? How much?" I ask through a gap in my fingers.

"All of it I think. So he managed to exorcise the dream?"

"Seems so. The dream's now in my head. I cut it out of the girl."

"You okay?"

"Guess we'll find out."

"For what it's worth, K does seem to be showing some signs of guilt. Well, a little guilt. I can't believe he's been Writing his memories away like that for so long."

"I know."

"Hey," she nudges me. "Sure you're okay?"

"I'm fine. Just happy my buddy is here." I reach out in a pincer movement around Nina's waist and wrestle her down on the bed. She yelps as I bear hug her and throw the sheet over us both. We tumble playfully, Nina begging not to be tickled, then we slump backwards.

"Oh God, my head," I moan.

"You'll be fine once you've got some food in you. Can't believe you guys went out without me."

"I know. What a bad move. Don't worry, I'm sure you'll get a chance to be as hungover as me very soon."

"I look forward to it," she smiles then pokes my cheek with a finger. "Hey."

"What?"

"Project know you're here?" she asks.

I nod. "My mentor called it in. Apparently, I'm getting assigned a temporary one while I'm here. What about you? You told them?"

"Yeah," she shrugs. "Going off radar never works."

"Ain't that the truth," I say, giving her a squeeze.

We spoon together like this for some time, gaps of silence in amongst small talk about Kaito's palace, long haul travel, and so on. We turn to face each other, the bright light of day softened by the sheet on top of us.

"You look tired," I say, carefully thumbing the dark rings under Nina's eyes.

"Look who's talking," she smiles. "Angel. Seriously...when I woke you, you seemed so confused. Like you were–"

"I'm fine. I'm...I don't know. My head's a bit all over the place. These dreams, the memories. It's like they're floating around in my mind, looking for a home. All I know is that it feels good to be here. It feels right. Like I'm, we're, finally getting somewhere. Y'know?"

"If you say so. We're kind of following your lead on this."

The weight of those words clearly shows on my face, because Nina is about to take it back when an interruption comes from the world outside our den.

"What is going on in here?" booms a voice. "Whatever it is, I wanna piece."

"Kaito don't!" Nina and I shriek. But it's too late. A couple of thundering steps are followed by a millisecond of silence, ending in the crushing thump of Kaito's full weight.

"Fucking hell, you're so heavy!" Nina shouts.

"Pure muscle," I say before Kaito can. "Oh jeez, get offa me, man. You're gonna make me hurl again."

"Aw you guys, I've missed this. Lemme in, lemme in," Kaito says, burrowing under the covers between us like a kid on Christmas morning. But then he makes it weird, as usual: "So how does this work? Does one of us make a first pass? Should I take my clothes off?"

In unison Nina and I issue a 'never in a million years' in Kaito's ears, before all three of us erupt in laughter. Contented minutes slip by as we stare at the ceiling. Lost souls reunited in our cloudtop castle, safe from the world outside.

"You know, I meant it. I've missed this," Kaito says.

"Me too," I reply, ruffling his hair.

Nina replies with a single motion, rather than words. She reaches up with fingers splayed.

"Really?" I whisper, understanding her intent immediately.

A smile breaks out underneath her scattergram of freckles.

"You guys, you know I'm still shit at Reading," Kaito groans.

"Shhh. I'll guide you," Nina says.

Muscle memory kicks in. A ritual from our childhood – yet somehow more ancient than any of us – honoured once more. We clasp onto Nina's hand, settle ourselves, breathe together, in and out, in and out, feeling the drift, letting ourselves be pulled gently along, down the river of Nina's memories…

***

"No no no!" Angel yells, then runs away on his little bird legs. He looks scared. This is so funny!

"Oh yes," I cackle. He thinks I can't shoot him from here but he's so wrong. He doesn't stand a chance. I pump the barrel three times then let it rip, right into his back.

"Aaaaghhhhh," he screams and stops dead. So I fire some more. "Seriously, Nina. Quit it. This is freezing. How'd you get it so cold?!"

"Straight from the water cooler. I ain't a newbie at this."

"Put. The gun. Down," says a voice to my left. Jag är idiot! How did I not hear him creep up? Rookie.

"Okay okay. Don't do anything stupid, Venny. Look, I'm stepping away, okay? You don't have to pull that trigger. We can all walk away from this."

I hold my supersoaker to the sky. He's not smiling, at least not with his mouth. I make a run for it but it's too late. Water hits the side of my head, sticking my hair to my face and my neck. Who knew I could scream so much like a girl?

"Hey Nina wait. Where'd Angel go?" Venny says.

There's just a puddle on the ground where he was.

"Hey guys," Angel calls all singy-songy from behind us. "Look who I found."

Slow motion. Venny and me turn our heads. There's Angel, t-shirt sticking to him, but he's practically dry next to Kaito who looks like a chubby drowned rat, dripping from head to toe, but with the biggest grin. It's too late before we get why he's so happy.

Giant water balloons, all wobbly and jelly-like, flying in our direction. And then time speeds up. Splosh!

"That's it!" Venny spits. "This means war!"

We run towards them, screaming at the top of our lungs, water pistols ready. Angel and Kaito run to the boarding house, laughing and shouting as they go. We just about catch up when we all turn the corner on to the main street.

It's like a war zone. But of colour, water and chalk. Kids and adults are splashing each other everywhere we look. Some see us and start splashing in our direction. The four of us are united once more. We charge the locals and give them as good as we get.

I love Songkran so much!

We hardly ever see our neighbours, but here they all are just like us, soaked to the skin and absolut extatisk about it. In no time we're white with chalk powder too. Old Khun Mechai from down the street has pinched the top of a hose pipe and is spraying it high over the crowd, making a little rainbow where it meets the April sun.

After a while the crowd starts to break up. We squelch home, trying not to be seen as we turn up the lane towards the boarding house. We like to pretend we can blend in with the locals at times like this. Not 'those creepy expat kids' who live on the edge of the village. I make the most of my Thai side when I speak with them, but the combo of my Swedish side and the fact I'm a 'creepy expat kid' always gets in the way.

The four of us are trading war stories from the fight as we walk up the lane towards the boarding house. At the opening of the grounds stands Khun Su, arms crossed. We stop talking immediately.

"Don't even think about coming in the house like that," she says in Thai as we approach. I translate for the others, but I think they understood fine from her body language.

"Wait, I go get towels first," she says in broken English. She looks disappointed. We walk behind her like dogs with tails between our legs.

"Wait," she says, pointing at the steps of the house.

"We're so screwed," whispers Venny.

"I know," Angel says. He looks so little, so much more than when ▮▮▮▮▮▮▮▮▮▮▮▮▮▮▮▮▮▮▮▮▮.

We stand like this for what feels like forever. What punishment is Su going to come up with for skipping out on homework for a water fight?

A high-pitched whistle comes from the balcony above. The next thing

we know, a torrent of water falls on our heads. And it's freezing cold!
  We gasp and look up. Khun Su has an empty bucket in her hands.
  "You look so stupid!" she laughs. "That what you get for being bad boys and girl."
  We're so surprised all we can do is laugh too.

***

Tropical heat always feels like a welcoming embrace immediately following the starkness of air conditioning. Give it too long, though, and the hug constricts. I'm on the clammy verge of discomfort within minutes of getting off the BTS Skytrain, but the occasional breath of wind keeps the worst of the hangover sweats away. The prospect of food, which we've come in search of since leaving Kaito's apartment, isn't sitting too well with my stomach.

We wander on the open air walkway which runs along sections of Sukhumvit Road. The BTS sky trains slide above our heads, carrying hordes of workers and shoppers in white carriages. Below us, the pavements are surprisingly empty. When I was a teenager it used to be the other way round; Sukhumvit was a roiling mass of pedestrians, scuffing their way over cracked slabs and grimy sewage grates. But today, everyone seems to travel on the walkways, floating on this elevated veil of society.

"I still can't believe Khun Su threw water on us," Kaito exclaims, shaking his head. "I'd totally forgotten that."

"I know," Nina replies. "And yet, she always had that mischievous look."

I know just the one she means. Brusque and business-like our matron may have been, but her eyes always hinted something else. We rarely said it, but we loved her dearly. Mummy- and Daddy-issues were a staple of our makeup, being abandoned in a boarding school at the other side of the world will do that to a kid. In her own way, Khun Su stepped in to fill the chasm created by our parents' absence. It wasn't a warm kind of love, but her discipline, the structure she gave our home lives, always bore the indisputable signature of parental love. Mother and father forged into an iron cast.

"I miss her," says Kaito, eyes firmly ahead.

"Mmm," Nina agrees.

It's been five or six years since we learned of Su's death. A quiet passing. As in life, so in death. It was Kaito who found out, through a contact at The Project. 'What, your boarding house matron? Oh she died last year'. That kind of thing. The guilt we feel is still fresh. She shouldn't have died alone.

"I know, me too," I say. "It was nice to see her in her prime again. I'd almost forgotten that day."

As we've made our way from Kaito's apartment in search of food, we've revelled in Nina's memory of our Songkran water fight, a Thai New Year so many years ago. We used to do this as kids a lot, sharing memories with each other just as Nina did now. We would open windows into our psyches and invite each other in; our way of storytelling, of explaining who we were.

No-one was better at it than Nina. The most talented Reader among us, her memories always shone; the depth of scents carried on the air, the grit of a surface, the precise register of someone's voice.

And yet, there was a moment in her memory, a blank spot…

"What?" Nina says, catching me gazing at her.

"Just glad you're here".

"And we have arrived at our destination. Hello there," Kaito salutes at a security guard in a white uniform. Gold-tasseled epaulettes drip over the ledges of his shoulders, white sleeves run halfway down his arms, exposing a gap of skin, ending in white gloves roughly the size of Mickey Mouse's. Give him his due, he wears it all with the solidity of an eagle.

We enter the grey marble and bottled citrus zing of the mall – yet another shopping emporium that has erupted into existence along Sukhumvit in the years since I last visited. I swear there are more of these consumer meccas than spiritual temples now. We ascend the zig-zagging escalators through canopies of plants (freeze-drying in the recycled air), and break out into a rooftop food court larger than I have ever seen in my life. A biodome for the peckish shopper – or alcohol-ravaged *farang* in my case – the court is alive with stalls and eateries seemingly from every corner of the world. Clever slogans and cutesy logos shout over the top of each other: a bulbous-headed lion biting into Korean bao bun here; a happy chick wrapping its feathers around chopsticks there. Swirling ice-cream whips, dripping beef burger patties, glistening sashimi and tapioca-filled bubble tea co-habit in this jungle of excess.

"Can we please find a quiet spot?" I squirm.

"Oh poor Angel, struggling are we?" Kaito slaps my back. "Believe it or not, I actually know just the place."

He leads me by the hand through the crowds to the far end of the food court where lies a surprisingly unassuming noodle bar, closed off from the madness by way of glass double doors. A handful of families and couples are scattered throughout the restaurant.

We take a table by the window, which looks down over a multi-acre expanse of greenery. Not a park, as I first assume, but a recently-sold and vacated embassy, Kaito explains. Its century-old colonial buildings and central pond stand still, quietly awaiting their fate, no doubt to be razed and replaced with another mall. In another country a site like this would be afforded a level of protection, but not in Thailand – a country fascinated with the prospect of tomorrow, maybe more than the echoes of yesterday.

I ask K to order for us, the effort of maintaining a calm stomach consumes most of my energy. He and Nina chat happily as we wait for the banquet to arrive, catching up about the five or so years since we've all been together. K arches his eyebrows recounting wild nights out, scoops fingers through product-slicked hair, touching Nina's wrist to maintain her absolute attention. She seems genuinely enraptured by his tales but, when he eventually realises how much he is monopolising the conversation, she offers up some details of her life. Casual and matter-of-fact, she tells of the recently failed relationship with Theis, the sting she still feels at the separation. And guilt at the way Project Erasers have removed his memories of everything Weaver.

"They had his consent of course," she says, stirring ice around her glass. "He was only too happy to have my weirdness wiped from his memory. Not that he could really have said no."

"I'm so sorry, Neens," I say.

"Meh!" she shrugs. "Gives me more time to work."

Classic Nina evasion tactics. Before any further sympathy can come her way she briefly discusses her consultancy work for Interpol – none of which she can talk about in great detail of course, much to Kaito's disappointment. (*"Oh come on! Tell me about all the criminal masterminds you've helped take down!"*) She then transitions to her artwork and the diverse client base she's amassed in Stockholm – a smorgasbord of upper-class stiffs, fur coats, quilted jackets and hairspray.

"All lining up for an original piece by the mysterious painter, Nina Angsakul," she says, rolling her eyes at the way she's spoken of in the Swedish city – a Delphic oracle, a Haitian voodoo priestess. Whispers of her artwork and unconventional processes have wound through the artistic community, all the way to the upper echelons of the city's high society.

"It's incredible The Project have turned a blind eye," says K.

"Oh, I get regular visits from our friends in dark suits," she says. "We have an understanding. They know I won't endanger the Great Secret. Besides, no Flatline would believe the truth even if they did find out. My clients basically think I'm like a fortune teller or something."

"I love that," K chuckles. "*'Step right up, ladies and gentlemen!'*"

"You're not far off," she says.

"How does it work, the painting process?" I say.

"It takes a few stages. First I just spend time with new clients, letting them talk about their lives. People love to talk, it's like therapy. I mean you would know, Angel," she says.

"Not anymore," I say.

"Right, sorry I didn't mean–"

"It's all good. Bad joke. But yes, I can certainly attest to people loving a friendly pair of ears."

"Exactly. So invariably they arrive at the real reason they've come to see me – to preserve something personal on canvas."

"Like what? Losing their virginity?" K says.

"Not quite," she cocks an eyebrow. "People tend to want me to paint tender moments with recently-deceased spouses, the elation of holding a newborn for the first time, the warmth of sunrises at mountaintops scaled along with friends. That kinda shit. So, y'know, a bit more important than the first time they popped their cherries."

"Well, personally I think that's a shame," K holds his hands up.

"And they really have no idea how you do it?" I say. "Any time I worked with clients, they were sent to the Erasers immediately after to remove anything they'd learnt about Weaving."

"Oh I'm very good," she smiles. "I do this thing, like a prayer, where I hold their hands and we reflect on the memory they want me to paint. All ceremonial and everything. They love it. When in reality that's how I do it, that's my chance to Read the memory."

"Sneaky," Kaito says.

"I'm very careful. No harm comes to the memories, only the Echoes flow into me. And then I get to work. It's like the memories paint themselves onto the canvas, y'know? They choose the form, the colours. It sounds strange, but I'm just the conduit. Like with my Project work, I guess."

"That's amazing. Do the clients watch?" I say.

"Not many. By the time we've had our little ceremony, most of them are a bit spooked. Anyone that stays gets little interaction from me because I'm so engrossed. It's like it's all just flowing out of me, no time for small talk. By the time I'm done, I barely retain any thread of the Echoes."

Jealousy twists in my gut. What I wouldn't give to be able to exorcise the Echoes that live in my mind, lurking in my Safe. But the feeling passes soon enough, drifting into another thought. Were I to hire Nina to paint something for me, what memory would I offer up? What events in my past would I want captured in amber, to live in oil on canvas, commemorated in the brushstrokes? Nothing readily comes to mind. Despite the strangeness of my life, how out-of-the-ordinary the path I've trodden has been…how can I have such little enthusiasm for where I've come from?

An Echo of Mrs Landing's swims into mind, something I Read from her as a three-year-old. Her wedding day, the spark of excitement she felt as she caught herself in the mirror, her dress so plain, yet she had never felt more brand new. On the cusp of the rest of her life.

But no, that's her memory, not mine. So what about something from my childhood? Surely there's some special memory, something long before the Mnemosyne Project came calling? And surprisingly many appear before me; my mother's laughter as she caught me hiding under the Christmas tree, the lights glinting in her eyes; my little hand nestled within Dad's as we made our way along the South Downs on a summer day, the grass bending in the wind. Any of these memories would do, and yet the emotion of them seems out of reach to me. The realisation of this emptiness, the recognition that this half-life has been my reality for so long, builds within me.

But just as icy understanding threatens to pierce me, a new face flourishes in my mind, quelling the rising panic.

Deep brown eyes pull me in, holding firm. Eyebrows like black liquid, move together in concern. Soft lips curve into a smile, then softer still brush up against my own. I breathe in, drinking his essence, the furnace of his life warming my heart.

Dhaval.

Here. I could live here for eternity. Secure in his embrace. A memory worth a thousand paintings. But I've thrown it away, and any chance of creating more memories like it. The image fades, replaced by the constant checks I've made of my text messages, ever hopeful for a response from him. But nothing has come through.

What kind of a response do I expect? We hardly knew each other. Anyway, *I* broke up with *him*. I've run away without telling him anything real about me.

The only message I've had since Adrian's last night is from my parents:

Mum: Dougie, where are you? We're worried. Let us know you're safe.

Me: I'm fine. I'm safe. Have come to Bangkok for R&R. Staying with friends. I'll be in touch.

Loss, shame and guilt curdle, leaving me with the broken pieces of my life, where a chorus of voices speak: the damaged patients I tried to heal; the lonely souls I tried to comfort.

They're always there, whispering to me in the darkness, even those I've buried deep within my Safe, locked in the mental construct I was trained to create so many years ago. I'll never be free of them.

And now loudest among them is her.

Olivia.

Calling from the past, a threnody singing out to me, within me. With each step I take on this journey she's becoming clearer, more urgent. Her voice becoming my own. Her journey, my own.

She. Me. Other. Self.

Remember me...

***

"So this key," Nina says, cheek bulging with a dumpling.

"Hmm?" She's looking at me expectantly. *When did the food get here?*

"The key is like my hacky sack, right?" she says.

"That's the theory yeah," I nod, pulling back to my senses. *Finally, a chance to have this conversation.* "My pendant, your hacky sack, Kaito's key. All three, they've been embedded with Echoes. A mixture of memories. On the surface, the memories that have lodged themselves in our dreams seem to be all about...her." I stop. Somehow saying her name out loud catches in my throat.

"Olivia," Kaito finishes.

Nina scrunches her face. "Olivia?"

"The girl in the memories. Angel thinks that's her name. She was someone we used to know, a friend maybe, that we've all forgotten. Or something," he shrugs.

Nina swivels towards me and tilts her head.

I can feel my face getting hot. "I didn't want to say anything until I was sure. One more crazy theory," I say.

"What makes you so sure now?" she says.

I reach into my back pocket, take out a folded photograph and spread it on the table between us.

It's the teenage selfie of me and Nina, the one from my old photo album. We're leaning against a tree, her arm around my neck, pulling our heads together. I point to etchings on the tree. Five names: Nina. Angel. Kaito. Venny.

"Olivia," Nina mouths silently. "What the…"

"Whoa," Kaito breathes. "Proof. Of. Life."

"I mean, I'm not crazy right?" I say.

"I guess not," Nina mumbles. She lifts the photo up and feels its surface. "That tree. So familiar."

"It is?" I say.

"I…never mind. You were saying, the objects have memories on the surface?" she says, but doesn't unglue her eyes from the photo, her brow knotted in concentration.

"Right. But underneath those memories are deeper ones, ones that only I seem to be able to access. So…"

"So yeah, you want to Read my hacky sack," she says, finally looking away from the photograph. "And that's fine, I guess."

"Guess?"

"No it's fine. It's just…if what lurks beneath is as personal a memory as Kaito's was…I dunno."

K's expression brightens. "You'll be fine. I mean sure, last night was a lot for me to take. Finally being faced with what I've been doing to myself. It was a shock."

"I'm sorry, man," I say.

"No seriously," he reaches across the table. "Thank you, man. The memory you gave back to me, of my father and me…it's like…like a piece of myself I've been missing for so long, that I didn't even know I'd lost, has clicked into place. It gives me hope for the future. And a link to my past. And the most nuts thing is that it was just lying there, buried in a key. I mean…" he raises his hands up and shakes his head in exasperation.

"So what do you think, Angel," Nina says. "Is it going to be a Kinder Surprise-type situation for me too? Or are you going to unleash a nightmare into me."

My face burns at her glare. "Neens, I honestly–I don't know. It's not like I'm an expert at…whatever this is."

"Chill," she says, eyes widening. "I'm messing with you. Mostly. But you can forgive me for being freaked about what's waiting for me. Or why the fuck none of us can remember these memories which have been locked in the objects. I mean, what happened to us?"

"I don't know," I say, the fight leaking out of me in a big exhale. "I really don't. All I know is these objects have been sent to us, and bit-by-bit we're unlocking what's inside them. Who sent them to us? Why don't we remember the things inside? I have no idea. But the one connecting thread is

Olivia."

"Olivia," the glare in Nina's eyes returns to a more sedate level. She sits back in her chair and looks at the photo. "Okay, so what do we know of her?"

I deflect her look on to them both. We do this together, I motion.

"She was a teenager," Kaito offers.

"Yeah. About our age?" Nina adds.

"Right," Kaito jumps back in. "And something happened to her at that age. Something involving us all. We were in the boarding house, at night time. We all gathered together with her, in some sort of a pact. She was worried about what we were about to do. But she was willing to do it for…well…"

"For me," I say. "She wanted to protect me. From…I don't know." My gut twists at the admonition. "So we came together in the middle of the night. To perform a ritual or something. And this pendant, in my dream I'm holding it. She – Olivia – she's telling me to *listen* to it. And then there's the final memory. The one where she and I are running together. She's scared, calling out to me. Telling me she's scared, that 'it hurts'. Then she puts her hands on mine, there's a flash and that's it. Just her voice asking me to 'remember her'."

Silence falls around the table.

"So she was one of us, right?" Nina says, a fire in her eyes. "I mean let's just agree on that fact. Olivia, whoever she was, was a classmate, one of our gang in the boarding house. But then something happened, something we were afraid of, or something she was trying to protect us from. And then she vanished. I mean, apart from these dreams, the memories in these wacky sacks or whatever, we have absolutely no recollection of who she is. Was. Whatever."

"Right. Only…" I'm staring at the table.

"Only what?"

Only why was I so convinced at first that Olivia was a friend from my childhood, before Thailand, I want to say. Why was I so sure she was killed in an accident? But I don't say anything. Why muddy the water with these recollections?

More silence.

"Look," Nina says, a tone of decisiveness I've heard from her so often before. "I agree that everything points towards Olivia. A school friend who disappeared. Here, in Thailand. And we had something to do with it. So here's the plan: first we get back to the apartment and you Read this hacky sack."

"And then?" Kaito says. "You're forgetting there's still a piece of the puzzle out there."

Nina and I look at each other blankly.

"Venny. He still has a package too."

"Jeez, of course. Any luck getting him out here?" I ask, though Kaito's grimace is all the answer I need.

"It's not fair of us to ask him," Nina reasons.

"I know," I say. I don't blame the guy, but can't help feeling crestfallen all the same. The truth is, without Venny we're gonna hit a wall sooner rather than later.

Chapter 19

I remember the first time I saw beneath Venny's cool exterior. It was the first time I realised he was just as damaged as the rest of us.

It was on a day trip to one of Thailand's ancient capitals. He and I were in the back of a tuk tuk. It jostled as the adolescent driver negotiated potholes with bursts of acceleration. As we lurched from side to side with each boost of the pedal, I collided with Venny – my sun-bronzed knees against the deep umber of his. We grabbed on to anything we could to steady ourselves but it was useless.

"Slow down, dude," Venny leans forward to the driver. "Kub cha... uh what is it again?" He turns to me looking lost.

"Kub cha long noi khrab," I holler over the buzz of the engine. "Chaa chaa."

The slower pace gave us the freedom to take in the sights of Ayutthaya Historical Park. The corn-like Khmer prangs and upturned-bell Thai chedi of temples flashed by, their crumbling facades peeking through gaps in the tree-lined roads.

Once the capital of Thailand, now a collection of Burmese-razed ruins, Ayutthaya is a firm fixture on the tourist map. Or in our case, a short daytrip from school for a pair of listless expat teenagers. Exams finished and the springtime break upon us, I was keen for any excuse to get out of the boarding house. I was surprised when Venny agreed to come with me. He and I were friends for sure, fellow inmates of the MPB, but our friendship had normally been expressed within the frame of our foursome with Nina and Kaito. Our mutual tendency for introspection didn't make for the most electric of dynamics. But I'd always felt there was a firm understanding between us.

"Oh wait, I think that's it over there," he says, glancing up and down between the guidebook and the central prang of a temple. "Quick, do your 'tuk tuk whisperer' bit and get us over there."

A few simple directions and we're swinging into the car park for Wat Chaiwatthanaram.

"Yud ti nii khrab," I say, asking the driver to park up.

He slams on his brakes at the nearest bay. We almost topple out the front of the vehicle.

"Always a delight to travel in style," Venny coughs as he climbs out and dusts himself down.

Tall as he was, Venny had never mastered the poise to match so even at his full height he stooped, the permanent silhouette of a question mark.

"Not bad huh," I say, joining Venny at the entrance of the near-500-year-old temple.

The afternoon sun beat down on the ruin, catching the flecks of orange and white in the stonework, causing its eight chedi to cast shadows on the lawn; fingers reaching out towards the Chao Phraya river.

"What?" Venny says, eyes down as he searches in his pockets. He pulls out a crumpled packet of Paris cigarettes. One is between his lips and sparked in seconds.

I remember how his cheeks hollowed on the first drag of a cigarette. It accentuated the sharpness of his cheekbones – striking features which he inherited from his Cameroonian parents.

"Oh right, the temple. Yeah, nice."
The words and a curl of smoke escaped in the one exhalation.

At my request we made a full circuit of the temple grounds before climbing into the central pagoda, just as we did on the two temples we visited earlier that day. By the time we'd completed the route I'd decided that Wat Chaiwatthanaram was my favourite. Its symmetry, its silence inspired such stillness in me. I closed my eyes and imagined how grand it must have once been, the majesty of its golden cloisters against the sunlight. Despite the violence inflicted upon its structure and finery by the Burmese hundreds of years ago, despite the beheadings of the one-hundred-and-twenty Buddha statues that lined its grounds, the temple maintained a sense of grandeur. Defeated, but still standing.

"Y'know that central pagoda is thirty-five-metres tall," Venny reads from the guidebook. "Apparently it represents 'the traditional world'. And those four smaller ones? They're the 'four continents'."
"Only four back then?"
"Inflation I guess," he shrugs. "Wanna climb to the top of the traditional world?"

A narrow flight of steps led up to the heart of the central spire, not even close to its peak, but high enough to give us a view of the grounds, which were deserted apart from a few keepers going about their work. We sat on the top step.

"Thanks for coming today, Venn. You didn't need to," I say, conscious of the sudden privacy we have.
"No problem. Glad to get out of the house."

Sweat has gathered in beads along his brow. Slender fingers sweep them away before they can spill.
"Agreed," I reply.

Silent minutes slid between us like the longboats on the river's surface. The heat of the day was waning, but the unrelenting humidity clung to us. Even the breeze which wended its way around the temple's spires was hot, lapping at us like a warm bath.

Surprisingly it was Venny who spoke first.

"How do you feel about the next step?" he drawls in his Pittsburgh accent.
"After school? Okay, I guess. I mean..."
"What?"
"It's not like I have a better idea of what to do. Stitcher training sounds as good as anything else. How about you? Decided yet?"

He shook his head, looked like he was about to say something, but changed his mind at the last second. Another cigarette was flipped out and set aflame instead. In any other company, someone would have filled the silence. Kaito, maybe even me. But not at this moment. Not when it was just me and Venny. His quietness didn't unnerve me. It just *was*.

True enough, after a few drags, he picked up where he left off.

"I've decided not to decide. Know what I mean?" A tiny white piece of the tab clings to his lip. He picks it off and flicks it into the air. "I'm gonna go back to the States, get a job, a normal job. Anything but..."

He didn't finish, but I knew just what he meant. 'Anything but Weaving'. Of us all, Venny had always been the most uncomfortable with his abilities. It wasn't just that he was the most powerful of us all. It was his particular skillset which was the root of his self-loathing. A Grade 4 Eraser, Venny was terrified by what he could do. The ability to remove memories, to cut away great chunks of somebody's life, was often too awful a responsibility to bear for someone as gentle as him. Maybe that's why he worked so hard on it, spent so many extra hours in the library, or training with specialist faculty members; not to hone it, but to control it, so he would never have to use it.

"Being an Eraser doesn't have to define you," I say.
The look he gives starts with a flash of surprise at my candour. But it soon dissolves into a fatalistic grin.
"Of course it does, Angel. It defines everything about me. But that doesn't mean my future's locked in, right? Doesn't mean I can't do everything in my power to.. I just..." he says, voice trembling. He shakes his head.
"I know," I say, nudging my shoulder against his. "You need to get away from all this."
His bloodshot gaze stays off in the direction of the water.

"The last thing I want is The Project coming to recruit me. To be some fucking government Eraser. I'd rather kill myself. That's not for me, man. No way, I'm gonna find the most mundane job, the most normal existence ever. Clock in, clock out. Day after day until I die. And you know what? I'm going to love it. I'm going to roll around in a grey, cookie-cutter, life. And breathe. Just breathe."
"That should sound like the saddest thing I've ever heard," I chuckle.

I remember how he shifted towards me, eyes training into mine with an uncharacteristic intensity. A more solid undertone came into his voice.

"You don't have to be what they want, you know? I have to believe that, otherwise... We don't have to fall in line with what the school wants, what The Project wants. It's all bullshit. They're training us up to be their Weaver hounds, you know. But we don't have to obey."
"That's not true, Venny."

I was so dismissive. So ignorant.

"Yes it is. They say they're teaching us control so we can be responsible citizens of the world or whatever. Responsibly under the radar. But that's only part of it. Don't you see the way they look at us? Like we're meat."
"They?"
"The Project agents. Whenever they 'drop by' our classes to talk with the teachers, or just looking at us walking on campus."

I'd never seen this side of Venny so unleashed. He'd always been brooding, but never a conspiracy theorist. It was true, seeing Mnemosyne Project staff was a regular occurrence. I mean, the school is based within the South East Asia headquarters for The Project, for crying out loud, so visits from administrative staff, specialist agents and so on were part of our daily school life. But what Venny was saying didn't tally up.

"I've never noticed that, dude. You're getting paranoid."
"Paranoid? Come on, man. That is one-hundred percent all we are to them: guns to be pointed at a target. Paranoid." He spits the word. "Whatever man. You might not have seen them look at you that way because–"
"Because what?" My hackles raise. "Because I'm barely a Grade 3? A lowly Generic?"
"I didn't mean that," he raises his hands up.
"Of course you did. You all think it. You, Nina, Kaito, Mr Bordelais. Well I'm sorry I'm such a disappointment."

Somewhere in my petulant rant I'd risen to my feet, ready to storm down the ancient steps.

"Angel!" Venny shouts in exasperation. "Don't you see? This is a blessing. Your 'mediocrity' is what's gonna save you. You're telling me you've never attracted the attention of the agents? That's fucking wonderful. I envy you so much, man. How can you not see that? I would give anything for what you have."

I just stood here, dumfounded by his logic. I tried to understand the words from his perspective, to grasp why his talent could possibly make him so unhappy, and I was about to bite back when I noticed a tear break down his cheek. Before more could spill, he smudged his hands across his face.

"Venny," I whisper.
I'm too afraid to move, hand hovering uselessly at my side, unable to cross the gap between us. I wait for some time, frozen, listening to Venny's shallow sips of breath, watching his crumpled form tremble, letting it pour out of him.
"Aw man," he says weakly, snot rattling in his nose. I hand him a tissue, which he accepts with an empty chuckle. "I'm sorry."
"Don't be," I reply, settling back down next to him. "I get it. I do."

The sun had begun to set in earnest, casting a final blaze across the temple, blending the brickwork with the grass, the trees, the river in an orange hue.

"You just…" he croaks, "you have a choice, Angel. You can get away from all of this. Find a life far away from the Mnemosyne Project. Fly away, Angel. Fly away."

In the years that followed, when we disappeared to our separate corners of the world, Venny was the one who drifted the farthest. Geography never really posed a threat to our foursome. We were, and always will be, inextricably bound. But emotionally, I think Venny found a way to sail off into that sunset just a little more than the rest of us.

We respected it without question. He got what he wanted – a life far from the Mnemosyne Project, from the Weaver's tapestry. He became an accountant. No idea how he managed to convince The Project to leave him be, but he actually did it. Oh how we laughed when he told us. 'Picture the most boring job you can. It's bliss, guys'. But then came marriage and a kid. Nothing grey and mundane about that.

I'm happy for him, really. When I think back on that day trip with Venny, I get why he's drifted the most. There we were, sitting at the 'top of the traditional world', with the four continents below us, and all he could do was stare jealously at the horizon.

Chapter 20

"A candle, seriously? This isn't a séance," Nina says.

"Quiet," Kaito breathes, placing a lit pillar candle on the floor between Nina and me. "It'll help set the scene."

"You're not helping, dude," I say, rubbing my shins. "Making me more nervous."

All other lights in the apartment are off, and the skies outside are already dark.

"So how does this work?" Nina gnaws at her lip. The hacky sack is in her palm, its garish pattern washed out by the candle's flame.

"Well," I say. "I take it from you, hold it, 'listen to it' and see what it can show me. That's how it's worked with the pendant and the key."

"Meanwhile I do what? Just sit and wait?" she says.

"Well, yeah," I shrug.

"Screw that, I'm coming with you," her eyes blaze.

"What d–?" I start.

"You do your object Reading thing? That's fine. But I'm tagging along," she says with a nod.

"I'm not sure if that's–"

"Just do it, Angel," she waves a hand. "Whatever is in there was sent to me. I deserve to see it first hand," she says, curling her hair behind her ears in preparation.

Rebuttal kindles within me but Nina's look of warning extinguishes it.

"Okay, fine, let's do this," I exhale, holding my hand out to her.

She lobs the sack to me. It lands with a crunch – the dry rice giving it a satisfying heft. As before, I begin by focusing on my breathing. In. And out. Fingers close around the object. Eyelids drop.

Breathing in. And breathing out.

Listening.

The touch of Nina's fingertips on my fist gives me a jolt. A blink of eye connection between our cracked lids. And then she follows my lead.

Breathing in. Breathing out.

Focus on the ball.

I'm here. Talk to me.

Breathing in. Breathing out.

Us. Talk to us.

"Guys, is it okay if I stay here and watch?"

We shush Kaito in unison.

In.

Out.

A vibration begins in my closed fist. A familiar thrum that grows the more I focus on it.

In.
Out.
In.
Out.

***

The chatter of small birds. Muted, on the other side of a window.

And then a cold morning light. It casts evenly around the classroom, picking up fine particles in the air. The clack of chalk on the blackboard brings my attention forward. A scrape of a curled letter, a tak! *of punctuation.*

There are many of us in the class. But I see no faces, just feel their presence. The room smells dusty, dry, like the inside of an oven when it's cold. But something else, a wooden undertone.

My hands on the desk are slim and small. Nails bitten down to their stalks. A groove in the desk, black with lacquer. I trace it all the way to the end, where it continues over the edge, then wraps underneath. If the desk fell from a height, this whole panel would break away in one neat piece.

A clatter to my left. Pencil on wood, stifled after a few rattles. Her hand is flat over the yellow pencil.

At the board Ms Smith whips round to the source of the noise.

"Olivia," she warns with a hiss. "Focus on the test."

"Sorry, Miss."

A cheeky wink at me as soon as Ms Smith's back is turned. In seconds the pencil is once again balanced between her top lip and the underside of her nose. She looks so funny, lips pushed out like a duck – she needs to, her little nose alone won't hold it in place otherwise.

She feels me watching her, enjoys the attention. Makes her play up more. Sweeps her mousy brown fringe out of her eyes. She really needs a haircut, but hates it. Ever since she's turned fifteen it's like she's allergic to authority.

Turns her head back to me, then arches her eyebrows up and down, eyes wide, then scrunching small. I try not to giggle at her silly face but do. She tries to stop me, reaching a hand out across the gap between the desks. Forgets about the pencil, so it starts to fall.

An inch from the floor, she grabs it. Sideways glance upwards, hair brushing the floor. Ms Smith hasn't noticed. Big sigh of relief. Right. No more games. 'Shoosh, Olivia' I mouth. Sticks her tongue out in response.

Back to the exam. Pay attention.

$$N = 2a + b$$

a is a two-digit square number.

b is a two-digit cube number.

What is the smallest possible value of N?

I'm halfway through the answer when I see her out of the corner of my eye. Head bowed down, like when we pray in assembly. But her hands aren't together. They're holding tightly to the pencil. Her eyes are closed.

Not this again. Why does she do this? She'll get in trouble. If I try to stop her, I might get in trouble too, just like last time. A look over to Ms Smith. She's behind her desk, face hidden in a book. I'll nudge Olivia. Sure I won't get noticed.

Just as I reach over, Olivia smiles. Eyes still closed.

She's been doing this more and more. Not just with pencils. Anything. Books, shoes, tennis balls, toys. Just holds on to them tightly, closes her eyes. Drifts into a doze. So strange. It scares me when she does it. Knows I hate it.

Enough is enough. Can just reach her woolly shoulder. Nudge. Nudge nudge. 'Olivia' I whisper. 'Stop it. Please stop it!'

Said it too loud. Oh no!

"What are you two up to?"

"Sorry Miss, I was just... uh..." But I can't think of anything.

"Olivia? Olivia what are you doing?"

She's still got her eyes closed. A dopey smile on her face. I shake her shoulder again, feeling panicky.

A second before Ms Smith reaches the desk, Olivia's eyelids open up. Looking around quickly, like she's not sure where she is. Then slowly, all the way up, right into Ms Smith's furious face. My heart is thumping.

Olivia just smiles. I can't believe it.

"Oh Miss, you shouldn't frown like that. You'll get wrinkles."

"Why you cheeky—"

Olivia is lifted away from the desk by the arm, marched right out the classroom. Before the door slams, shoots me a quick look. Gappy teeth, sandy hair lank and falling out of its scrunchie. 'Don't worry' she seems to say to me. 'It's just a bit of fun.'

***

I whiplash out of the memory, into the void. The silver outline of the Echo curls in the liquid blackness. I watch it for a time, transfixed by its motion, it undulates like the ragged end of a flag.

I remember that I'm not alone. Haven't been this whole time.

Nina.

I can't see her, but I feel her. The unmistakable signature of her; the razor tinge of her curiosity, the mechanics of her mind. And beyond that is her song; the melody of her very essence, a harmony of reds and purples, yearning and yet as strong and sure as the waves, caught in the gravitational force of her will.

A spark of awareness. I pull myself gently away from it, back to the matter at hand. I/we float onwards. Nina/Angel. She/me.

The silver strands of the Echo flutter as we dive past it. There's something more here, I can feel it. Hidden but humming. *Where are you? Ah! There. I see you, find you where no-one else can.*

The moment I grasp at the subtle threads, they come alive, flourishing glimmers of mercury. A new memory. A hidden Echo.

Ready? I ask into the darkness.

Ready, I feel Nina's response.

***

The floor's warm on my bare legs. I cross them, like the rest do. Looking left to right, I see them. Kaito, Venny, Angel.

Worried expressions caught in the moonlight.

To my left, Angel. Between us is a space. No, not a space. It's her. Olivia.

"Are you ready?" My throat, so tight. Don't cry. Don't cry.

Angel nods. Solemn at first, then intense. Suddenly so sure. He terrifies me.

***

The memory starts to push us out. A purposeful pressure, building in obstinacy. I resist. Because I know there's more. Something that happened before. Something it doesn't want me to see.

I've come this far. Let me/us through.

***

Everyone's gone to bed. It's still a few hours away. Until it's going to happen. The boarding house is silent.

I creep into the room, knowing which noisy floorboards to avoid. I've done this so many times. Maybe the last time.

A curled outline under the bed sheet.

"You awake?"

A rustle then a twist in my direction.

It's her. I'd recognise her anywhere. Her face…like a shimmer around it. A blur. But those eyes, so clear even in the dim light.

She's here. But not for much longer.

"Yeah," Olivia whispers, then lifts the sheet and shuffles along.

I climb in behind her, spooning closely, arms wrapped around her, forehead nestled in her neck. The scent of her hair, the strength of her shoulders.

I try a word, but it won't come out. She seems to sense it, grip tightens on my arms

I try again: "Don't go. Please."

"Shhhh. It's okay, Nina. Shhhh."

A little hiccup escapes from me. Tears soak into the pillow.

"Please?"

She turns to me, face to face. Eyes to eyes. Runs a finger down my wet cheeks.

"I have to go. You know I do."

"But why?" I ask for the thousandth time. "For Angel?"

"For Angel. Dougie. Yes. For him. It's not right, me being here. You know it's not."

"But–" I can barely talk for crying. Trying to calm down enough to speak. "–but, I don't want you to go. He...he's going to kill you."

I regret the words as soon as I say them. But the more they ring in my ears, the more I mean them.

"Don't say that. It's not true. Look at me. Nina, look at me. I have to go. If I don't..."

'If I don't'. Her words, so full of compassion. Dew drops glint in her eyelids but don't fall.

"I'm going to miss you so much," I say.

She smiles, kind and warm. But I can see the fear there too.

"Promise me, Nina."

"Anything."

"When the time comes...remember me."

***

A final kick, and we're pushed out. Time's up. That's all you get.

We tumble backwards, out of the Echo, back into the oil-black void. A tugging from within our navels, pulls us backwards, fast, back, then up, up to the surface...

We gulp for air, like we've held our breaths for an eternity. Filling our lungs, coming back to ourselves. Back into the dark room, the flicker of candlelight.

The words of the Echo reverberate in my mind. Nina's words.

"He's going to kill you."

The hacky sack falls to the floor. Her hand snaps away.

Her expression. I'll never forget it as long as I live. Pain, confusion, horror, betrayal.

"Nina, I–"

But before I can form any words, she's gone, footsteps slapping out the door, rumbling down the stairwell.

Chapter 21

"I'm sorry, *khotort khrab*, sorry." I almost tip the entire food cart over as I round the street corner. The vendor, dressed in a red top, fisherman pants and striped flip-flops, issues a stream of anger in my direction.

"*Khotort*," I apologise again taking a few backward steps then whip round and down Phloen Chit Road. The skies have opened, and fat sheets of rain are coating the streets in an inky sheen. Car engines thrumming, headlights glaring against the harsh neon parade of hotels, residential towers and family marts – they all heighten my sense of hysteria. *Stop, think.* Hands on kneecaps, I force myself to regroup as best I can. Warm rivulets run down my face. The breeze carries a confusion of scents, thick and cloying, tinged with an artificial sweetness.

The tumult of images from the Echoes are still fresh in my mind. The classroom. Olivia's face – so clear and vivid. Like looking in a mirror for the first time in years.

Wait, what? No, that's not right. Need to put the Echoes away. Focus on the task at hand: find Nina. Where would she go? Where even am I? Somehow my soaking feet have carried me in the direction of Sukhumvit Road following the curve of the Skytrain route, its cement pillars standing like elephant legs. A faint recognition flickers at the edges of my mind. I know this place. A decades-old sign for a seafood market, a huddle of motorbike taxi riders at a street corner. But it was all so long ago. How on earth can I find her? Think. *Think.*

Aimless, I search the faces around me; young couples hunched beneath umbrellas, bankers in uniforms bustling away from long day shifts, a crowd of red-faced businessmen no doubt skulking towards the even redder lights of Soi Cowboy. I stand in the middle of the stream of human traffic and oily rain. A familiar sense of alienation pangs inside. This city, as much home as anywhere I've known, and yet one where my otherness has never felt so keen. Thailand opens its arms to the world, though it never closes the embrace. Maybe that's unfair. After all, the life I led here within my expat enclave, buried within my secret Weaver existence, kept me from fully embedding. Always Other...

Desperation builds. How can I hope to find Nina in this storm? Maybe she's already gone back to the apartment? Call Kaito. I reach into my pocket only to find it empty. Left my phone in the bedroom. Damn! What do I do?

Just as I'm about to turn away a small wet hand tugs at my sleeve.

"Nina," I whip around, senses doing their best to 'make' it her. But it's not. Far too young, long black hair, little face a much deeper brown. I open my mouth to ask something, anything, but the girl's peaceful expression stuns me. We just stand facing each other, utterly soaked.

Without warning, her tiny hand grips my own....

...and for the briefest of seconds…

...the world tips sideways...

...then rights itself...

Car horn honks. Water splashes in puddles at my feet. A wry smile on the little girl's face. She slips away into the crowd and is gone. Not that I see it happen, because I'm already walking down the *soi*, the cacophony of Sukhumvit melting away with each step I take down the side street.

If I stopped for a second, I would remark how odd this feels. Like my body has taken over completely, quietening all higher functions to follow some new instinct. But I don't stop for a second. I just follow the thread that's suddenly so tangible in my mind, as if I just walked this way mere seconds ago. Eight-metres down the soi, then left at the junction, crossing to the other side, taking care to avoid the dog shit that should be...yup, right here...and onwards a few strides more, closer to the green neon sign. Closer, closer, closer, up to the open gates, and entering the fairy light illuminated courtyard, a sweet perfume hanging in the air, past the spirit house with its jasmine garland and an open soda can waterlogged with rainwater. Lights are draped in loops around the building – a two-level traditional Thai house converted into a bar, of all things – while inside I can see candles lining the long counter. I stop at the base of the short flight of stairs that leads up to a veranda that wraps around the entirety of the building's ground floor.

Someone is sitting on a bench that presses up against the wall, just to the right of the main double doors. She's dressed all in black. A sliver of skin bridges the gap between ankle boots and jeans, a capped-sleeved shirt, buttoned up to a slender throat. Young eyes smile at me from below a tousled pixie cut.

"Hello Douglas," says the woman from the nightclub. The one who saved me from falling too deep into Kaito's Echo.

"Pom? What the...you're the one who led me here?"

She gives a little nod.

"You Wrote the memory of how to get here on the little girl, didn't you?" I say.

"Nice trick, huh? Here. Come sit."

"Who's the girl?" I say, taking a few cautious steps, more to escape the rain than to go towards her.

"A friend."

"She's like, ten-years-old."

She shrugs. "How are you?"

"Have you been following me?"

"I prefer 'watching over'," she smiles. "Less creepy. You have nothing to be afraid of."

"What's going on here?"

"Come sit, please. You look tired." She pats the space next to her, which I fill. Something in her expression soothes me, but I'm mindful to keep a healthy gap between us.

She turns to me, crossing one leg over the other in the same motion. "How *are* you?" she repeats.

"Fine," I reply, exasperated. "How...are you?"

"Oh I'm good thank you. I was worried when you and Kaito rushed off last night." *God, was it just last night?* The ground suddenly swells beneath me in a jetlagged wave.

"Yeah. It was all a bit much. Thank you again for pulling me out."

"You're welcome," she smiles with some deeper understanding, far beyond the capability of my head to reach right now. "I know it can be difficult. Echoes. For some Weavers, it's so effortless to Read, to Write. To pick up and put down. It's not like that for us all, though, is it?"

"I guess not." A small burst of Echoes ripples through me. Shards of memories from the pendant, hacky sack and key, mixed in with some of Kieron Marber's, his journalistic escapades, and the torture he received when it all went wrong. "It's like...if I shake my head I expect to hear it rattling with all the bits of other people's minds I've picked up over the years."

She just nods silently. I continue in my loose-lipped ramble, one hand rubbing slow concentric circles around my temple.

"I try my best to contain them all. Lock them up in my Safe like I was trained. But it's like they don't want to be boxed away. Or maybe I'm just not strong enough. The more I Read, the fuller my head gets, the more I'm losing myself in them all. I..." *Why am I telling her all this?* "Look, what are you doing here?"

She takes her time to reply, as if selecting just the right words. "To tell you it's okay. To let go."

"What are you... Look, all I want to do is find my friend Nina, but here I am talking to you."

Her hand clasps my shoulder. "It's okay, Douglas. Listen to me: there is going to come a time on the path you are on when you will need to let go. To give in to the Echoes. You can't force them into a box, or to push them together to make sense. They will do it by themselves if you let go."

"How do you know this? What do you know about my 'path'?"

"More than you know," she says, eyes dropping to my neckline where the pendant has slipped out of my shirt, dangling at the end of its chain. My fingers go to it. Just as I'm about to put it back into hiding, something clicks into place.

"It was you. You sent this to me."

No response. Just the ghost of a smile.

"Why?"

"Four packages in all. A promise fulfilled, you could say."

"A promise to who?"

"A friend."

"Stop talking in fucking riddles. Please tell me what you know. I can't take much more of this, I swear to God. Why have you sent me and my friends on this wild–"

"I did it for her," she raises her voice, then eyes flicking around into the fairy lit courtyard. "For someone who loved you very much."

"For Olivia?" I whisper.

"No, not for Olivia. Though she is the reason we are all here, it's true. But no. I did this for someone else. Someone who is here with us, right now."

"I don't know what you mean," I wail.

"Look at me, Douglas. Look," she urges.

"Douglas," I mutter. "How do you know… Nobody calls me that here."

I search her face with a renewed focus. The unblemished complexion, the exuberance in her smile. Only in her eyes do I feel the slightest spark of recognition. Without realising, I've placed a hand on the side of Pom's face.

"Yes. That's right. *See her*," she says.

Our surroundings seem to drift apart. The lights fade away to a distant shore, leaving only me and her in the world. Her face, blurring, shifting, lines of experience forming, hair suddenly long and pulled back, streaked with grey, her mouth turning downwards into a familiar line of dissatisfaction. But her eyes, unchanged, untouched by time, hinting at hidden depths as they always did.

"Khun Su?"

"Hello Douglas."

Just as soon as I see her fully formed, she blurs. The lights return, the surroundings wrap around us once more. Pom's face is before me, but holding the same expression.

"How...you died."

"She did," Pom says. "But her Echo lives on. In me."

"How is that even possible?"

"Oh it's possible. For some of us, a rare few who can hold the Echo of someone's entire essence within us. To travel with them by our side," she says, warmth in her smile. "Douglas, there's so much you don't know. That you need to know. You should have been taught by those fools."

"The Project?"

"Yes, Douglas. The things they have done. That they did to you and your friends," she shakes her head.

"I...I don't understand," is all I can manage with my mind racing like this.

"I don't expect you to, dear child. But you will soon. Not here and now."

"No please, tell me–"

"It's not safe," she says with a sudden urgency. "The best I can give you now is the knowledge that you are on the right path. You must follow it, as painful as it is going to be. My words alone aren't enough. You must *see* the truth for yourself. About who you are. What was done to you. To your friends. To Olivia. Only then can we stop it from happening again. Now, I have to go."

"Please–"

"Come to the boarding house. It belongs to me now. Will you do that, Douglas?"

"The boarding house? Yes...I will. But–"

"Angel?" A voice from the courtyard. There, in amongst the fairy lights, bedraggled by the rains which have now abated, stands Nina. At her side, though swiftly slinking back into the shadows, is the same young girl whose Echo brought me here. "What's going on?"

"We'll leave you to it," Pom whispers, stands then follows the young girl into the shadows.

***

"She asked me to go to the boarding house, then left as soon as you arrived," I say to Nina.

"This is so messed up," she says, with a glazed look that no doubt mirrors my own.

"You're telling me. This has to be up there with the most confusing nights of my life. Our old matron's Echo living in the head of someone we barely know. And the hidden Echoes in your–"

I cut myself off, the look of betrayal in Nina's face when she fled the apartment rushing back to mind. "Nina, I–"

"Angel, stop. I can't talk about it yet. Even if I wanted to I don't know…I just don't.…"

The noise of our feet against the wet asphalt is the only sound on the soi.

"I'm sorry. You just need to know, I have no idea what it all means. I can't have– I mean I would never do that to someone–"

"Angel please," she stops dead, warning flaring in her face. "Look, if I'm being rational about this, of course I know you could never kill someone. But the Echo hit me harder than I've ever been hit before. It's like… years ago I lost the best friend of my life. Someone who was so dear to me, ripped away, but I've only just woken up to realise that I lost her. And it seems to be your fault, Angel. I'm sorry but that's how I feel."

"Nina, that's not fair."

"Please, just listen to me for once. I'm talking about me? You know, contrary to what you might think, there are other people on this planet who have feelings and problems."

The words sting.

"Okay listen," she reasons, "I'm just saying that you have to let me process this. I need to feel this loss, to understand where it comes from. Neither of us can deny what we saw and felt in that Echo."

"Please, tell me you don't think I killed Olivia. Please?"

"Angel, to be quite frank, I don't know what you're capable of. And I don't think you do either. So give me a fucking break."

"Please. As if my life isn't–"

"Stop! You think you're the only one whose life is royally fucked up? Look around you! Kaito? He's a husk, chewed up and empty. Me? My life is just as much ruled by the God damn Project as yours."

"But you said…your art…you and The Project have an understanding," I stutter.

Nina raises her chin to the cloudy night sky and shakes her head.

"My art," she lets out a mirthful laugh. "You really think the almighty

Mnemosyne Project just lets me do my own thing? Half of my fucking commissions come from them, Angel. Some of the people I've had to paint for, politicians, secret service directors, as odious as the criminals I crack for Interpol. You seriously believed I had it all?"

"I had no idea," I say.

Nina shrugs. "There's only so much give on my leash. Just the same as any of us. But you don't see it, blinded by your self-pity."

I don't even try to respond. No way to dispute it. She's said it all. Instead, a heavy silence falls between us as we step back onto Sukhumvit, still busy despite the late hour. With leaden feet, we track our way back to Kaito's apartment where the saluting doorman Tanet lets us in. The elevator cables twang as we ascend to the twenty-fifth floor. As we near the top I make a final gesture.

"I feel like I'm losing you," I say.

"Angel..." she massages her forehead then plods into the apartment. I follow a few steps behind, then turn mechanically towards my bedroom when Kaito calls from the living room.

"That you, Angel? Um...there's someone here to see you."

I turn on one foot, anger seeking an easy outlet.

"I can't wait to see his face when he sees you," Kaito whispers excitedly to the seated figure on the couch.

I reach Kaito's side, bitter words set to trip off my tongue, but they evaporate instantly.

"Hi," says Dhaval.

Chapter 22

Everything is swimming. Voices, faces. I'm not sure I can handle this.

"You're here."

"I am."

"But how?"

"Oh, oh, I can answer that one!" Kaito jumps in. "So, okay, you and Nina were off, uh gallivanting, and I'm thinking 'what do I do', when I hear this ringing. Well, less of a ringing and more like a truly awful ringtone, like one of the first ever made. Seriously you need to choose a better ringtone dude."

"Kaito, please."

"Get to the point? Right. So anyways, I find the phone under this cushion here. Also, you need to get a new phone, seriously. Anyways I see a name on the screen 'Dhaval', and I'm like 'no way, is that Angel's new beau?'"

"Jesus…"

"'Significant other', 'partner', 'boyf–'"

"Oh my God stop–"

"Well whatever, so yeah, I answer it and here he is, your special friend, standing in the middle of the arrivals hall at Suvarnabhumi airport without a clue where to go next but he's all 'I'm wanting to surprise him', and I'm like 'that's so romantic, dude', and he's all 'well, I guess'. Anyways, anyways so I tell him to get in a taxi and get his butt over here. So in he comes and…well, yeah I guess actually that's the story. So yeah. Tadaaaaa. Love wins."

Dhaval looks dazed though faintly amused at K's monologue. "So…I'm here."

"You're here," is all I'm able to say. My mouth feels dry.

"Can I get you guys a drink?" K says. "You obviously have a lot to catch up on. Or y'know, Angel here can probably catch you up a lot quicker with a little memory sharing, if you know what I mea–"

"Kaito I swear to God please shut the fu–"

"Whoa, Dougie are you okay?" Kaito says. "Almost fell over there."

"Sorry, just feeling a little exhausted. Think I need to sit down or something," I say.

"Here–" Dhaval says, reaching out for me.

"No. Actually, can we, um, can we go somewhere private?"

***

I push the bedroom door closed and lean my back hard up against it. Dhaval is sat at the corner of the bed, a tentative look on his face that seems to say 'your move'. The best I can conjure is a half-smile. Everything's still swimming, but at least it's now just the two of us.

"Angel?" he says.

"What? Oh, yeah. Childhood nickname. Middle name's Angelo so…"

"Cute."

"I'm sorry, I just can't quite believe you're here."

"I can see that. I didn't mean to throw you for a loop, but this all happened so fast. When you left like that I didn't know what to do, or who to call. I realised how little I really know about you."

My gaze is firmly on the floor between my feet. He continues.

"But then I remembered the call I got from that friend of yours. So I called him."

Electricity prickles from my heart all the way along my arms. "You spoke to Adrian again? Dhaval, I–"

"He's a nice guy. He was worried about you too, Dougie. We spoke for a while, and he ended up telling me where you had run off to. So I grabbed a flight straight out to Bangkok. It's crazy, I've never been so impulsive in my life. But something drew me here. It seemed so natural, like, I dunno, like coming home. Does that sound nuts?" he says with an expression of childlike wonder.

I close the gap between us, heart thumping, mind racing at how I can unpick this impossible knot. Only one solution seems viable.

"Dhaval, you see the thing is, I, well…there's something about me you should know."

"Um, okay," he says, then guides me to sit on the bed next to him. His expression, so calm, almost amused.

"I'm just going to say it. I should have told you before, but knowing something like this has strings attached, and it sounds so nuts to people like…well, 'normal' people," I say.

He chuckles at the word. "Take a breath, Dougie. Whatever it is I'm sure it's not bad."

"So the thing is, I'm…I guess…okay it's like this…I'm a mind reader."

Boy does that sound dumb. I've rehearsed this conversation over and over, even been trained in how to do it, and this is what I say. A fucking mind reader? My lips feel numb.

He just looks back at me. A twist of confusion on his brow, mouth straightening, eyes flicking to the wall behind me.

"Like a psychic?" he finally says.

"No, not really. Memories. I can Read memories."

"Okay," he says quietly, still staring at the wall as if transfixed by some slowly emerging image.

"It's, like, a rare genetic thing, happens through skin contact. There aren't many like us around the world. But people like us have been around for centuries. Longer maybe."

"People like you?" He points at the bedroom door.

"Yes, my friends. People like us. Mnemosynes. But we call ourselves Weavers. Like dreamweaver, only with…We were brought here as kids because Thailand was one of the first places to discover Weavers. It's funny

I guess, the Buddhist philosophy is actually very well suited to helping people like us, all that insight meditation and– Are you okay, Dhaval? I'm so sorry, this must sound–"

"No, no it's…" he mutters, expression softening, as if he's recalling something long forgotten. A smile, small at first, grows. "Weavers."

He holds his hand out to me.

"Prove it," he grins.

"Dhaval, I don't–"

"Prove it." His expression, excited, not afraid. "What's the first thing Kaito said to me when I arrived at the apartment?"

I begin to protest but his hand's in mine before a word comes to my lips.

His thoughts, so open and unguarded.

A rush of images and sensations:

> *An airport tannoy, foreign words droning around the high ceilings of an entry hall…the warmth beyond the exit doors…the beckoning of a taxi driver…tail lights in traffic…the relative quietness of a backstreet…the salute of a concierge at the gate…the lemon zing of cleanliness in the twenty-fifth-floor hallway…the hollow knocking on the front door…the beaming smile of a Japanese man…the playfulness of his first words…*

"Oh my god, Kaito," I groan.

"Say it. What were his first words?"

"'Ooh boy, you're a very pretty man'," I say, head in hands.

I hear Dhaval chuckle. I look up to see him. The laugh has quickly turned into something that looks like quiet astonishment.

"Amazing," he says. "I can't believe it."

"I wanted to tell you, I promise. But I just couldn't find the way to…I mean how does anyone do this right? And the thing is, there's an organisation, more like a governing body really, who registers and oversees us, and anyone that we tell they need to vet. Because nobody can know…I mean obviously some trusted people can know…but anyone who does know needs to be checked for their trustworthiness or whatever, so I didn't want to just tell you and–"

He cuts off my rambling with his lips. I pull away.

"I understand if you want to–" I start.

He does it again, holds me in position until I give in. Then he pulls back slowly and looks at me. Silence finally holds me in place. I search his expression for a verdict.

"I can't really compute half of what you've just told me," he says. "Maybe it's the jet lag, or the reality of just being here…but I think I get it."

"Dhaval, finding out something like this, it's hard for anyone to get their head around, but I just want you to know–"

"You don't have to say anything, Angel," he says, my nickname so natural in his voice. "I didn't fly all this way to put you on the spot, or to force you into telling me your life story."

"Then…why did you–?"

"To be with you," he shrugs.

This time it's my lips finding his. Hands brush through his hair, down to his back, pulling him into my embrace.

"Don't, I'm all gross from flying," he laughs from the side of his mouth.

"I couldn't care less, you beautiful man," I whisper in his ear.

***

"Well that went better than I thought," he says, staring at the bedroom ceiling.

The sheets are rumpled around us. He still has a sock on.

"It's the best welcome I could arrange at short notice," I chuckle, still trying to catch my breath. The room has stopped spinning, replaced with a tiredness that's sinking into my very bone marrow. The mess of my life is still there, beyond the bedroom door, but for now I'm safe. "After all, this is your first time in Bangkok."

"My first time," he says dreamily, linking our fingers together and raising them up to his lips. "So, your friends…"

"Mm?"

"It's funny, Kaito's just how I, uh, just how I thought he'd be." A small crease forms on his face. "And that was Nina, right?"

"Yeah, that was her. I'm sure she'll say a proper hello tomorrow."

"You guys okay?"

"It's complicated."

"I figured. Where's Venny?" he asks.

"Oh. He can't make it out here. He's got family."

"That's a shame. I'd like to see him, y'know," he yawns. "It's been so long."

And just like that, as if the bedroom door has opened ajar to let the ghosts of my life back in, guilt presses back on my chest. Because I know I have never told Dhaval about any of my friends. And there's only one reason why he feels like he knows them.

"Dhaval, I need to tell you something."

But he's fast asleep, so serene, fingers still intertwined with mine.

Chapter 23

"Remember me."

"Did you say something?"

"Remember me."

"Dougie? Are you sleep-talking?"

Who's that speaking? I'm so groggy, must have slept so deeply. I wipe my gummy eyes, try to make them focus. The first thing I see is a man. In bed with me. Not wearing any clothes. I spring out of the bed. Now he's staring at me, looking so concerned.

"Dougie? Are you okay?"

Dougie? Of course. I look down and see I'm not wearing any clothes either. That answers that, then. And from the look of things I'm older now. Isn't life strange.

"Sorry, must have been half asleep," I laugh. It's fun to hear the voice. So much deeper now.

"Are you coming back in here? The aircon is freezing."

I feel the cold all over my naked body. The sensation is glorious. His face, the man's, so confused yet somehow amused. Such a good face. Good catch, Angel. I climb under the sheets, snuggling back into the warm nook. Why not?

"Sure you're okay?" he says, then kisses my cheek. Scratchy bristles on both our faces.

Dhaval. Yes, that feels right. "I'm fine thanks, Dhaval."

"Okay then. If it's all right, I'm going to hop in the shower. You rest your eyes a bit longer."

Another kiss. He's not my type, but I can feel the ghost of Angel's attraction for him, so why not. Then he's out of bed. His naked arse. Oh my!

After a moment I hear the splash of water. I prop up on my elbows and look around the room. It's big. A peek of morning skyline. Light hits Dhaval's pillow. I wonder…

I run a finger along the impression left by his head. Focus my attention on it. Sparks of images from his memory fill my mind. A disorientated trip to the bathroom in the middle of the night, a few fragments of dreams, and also some passionate images that make me blush – I didn't know men could love like that.

With a giggle I settle back into the warmth of the covers. *You rest your eyes a bit longer.* That's what Dhaval said. Good idea, lovely man.

***

The clank of cutlery on porcelain rouses me. The clock reads 10:27. Shit, I slept a long time. Wow. I reach across only to find an emptiness where I expect Dhaval to be. A second's confusion but then I hear a peal of laughter from elsewhere in the apartment. Throwing a robe on, I shuffle out the room in search of the voices.

Kaito and Dhaval are seated at the breakfast bar, steaming mugs of coffee, half eaten bowls of cereal.

"What's so funny?" I grump.

"There he is. Take a pew. I was just telling your man here some stories from school."

"What? Aw man, K, please don't. It's too early for that."

"Too early in the morning, or too early in your relationship?" he flashes a grin.

"It's fine," Dhaval says, rubbing my back and pouring some coffee for me, "in fact he was just saying how much of a good student you were. Very well behaved."

"Ugh, that's even worse," I moan into my mug, though internally somewhat relieved. "Kinda true. The main rule breakers were Venny and Neens."

Kaito claps his hands. "So true. Remember that time they snuck onto the roof of the admin building? Man, they were so stoked to have found the best spot to smoke on campus."

"What happened?" Dhaval says, genuinely seeming to enjoy our reminiscence.

"They were caught on about five CCTV cameras," I explain, huffing at the memory.

"Immediate detention for like a month, and more punishments besides that back at the boarding house. What a pair of *bakageta*," Kaito says.

"Gutted for them," Dhaval shakes his heads. "CCTV though? Your school sounds serious."

"You don't know the half of it," I say, sharing a look with Kaito.

I tuck into breakfast, surprisingly ravenous, and grateful once again for Kaito's hospitality. Whoever stocks his kitchen has excellent taste in pastries.

"Is it weird?" Kaito asks.

"What?" Dhaval responds.

"Being around people like us."

"K–", I start, but Dhaval places a hand on my arm.

"It's fine. I mentioned our little chat last night. To be completely honest, Kaito, yes. It's a lot to take in."

"I bet it is. That's why we're a secret. Can you imagine the headlines if everyone knew? 'MEMORY READERS BRING AN END TO PRIVACY'. 'THE MNEMOSYNE MENACE NEXT DOOR'. 'MY BOYFRIEND'S A WEAVER - NOW I'M TERRIFIED HE'S REWRITING MY MEMORY!'," Kaito laughs.

My heart jumps out of my body and I splutter coffee on the table.

"You okay?" Dhaval pats my back.

"I'm fine. Can we change the topi–"

"So, D-Man. Any questions?" Kaito says. I could knock the smile off his face, if I wasn't so curious myself at Dhaval's response.

"Lots. So many. But it feels a little disrespectful to–"

"Shoot," K says, lacing his hands together and placing them behind his head,

"What's it like? To read someone else's memories?"

K looks at me then shrugs. "What's it like to remember something?"

"Sorry, stupid question, I suppose," Dhaval says.

"No seriously. What I mean is that it just feels like remembering something. Only it's the first time you've remembered it, so it can feel a little unfamiliar, surprising, maybe uncomfortable. All depends on the memory."

"Must feel so strange," Dhaval says. "Seeing the world through someone else's eyes. Trying to figure out what's real and what's just their version of events."

"What do you mean?" I say, nervous of where Dhaval's going with this.

"Memories aren't a perfect record of events, right?" he says. "Your state of mind at the time of experiencing something may impact how you remember it? Or the details can get fuzzy over time?"

"Sometimes," I nod, sipping my coffee. "Inaccuracies can creep in at any part of the process – encoding, storage, recall. But–"

Kaito jumps in: "Humans' are dope at absorbing information. Better than most realise. Now, recalling? That's a problem for *Flatlin*…I mean, regular folks. But you'd be surprised by how much is in your brains."

"And you…I mean, Weavers can…?" Dhaval says.

"We can access those forgotten details," I say, waving it away as if it's no big deal. "Help rebuild the bigger picture. Take these strands of memory and Weave them back together to reveal the clearest version of the truth."

"That's incredible," Dhaval breathes out.

"I mean some Weavers are better at that shit than others," Kaito says, clearing away his bowl. "Readers especially. Writing's more my thing."

"Uh, K," I shake my head in warning. It's one thing for Dhaval to begin grappling with the existence of memory readers. Quite another to learn about Writers.

"What? D-Man, you know we all have specialisms right?" Kaito bulldozes on, completely ignorant of the heart attack his line of questioning is giving me. Dhaval sits enraptured as K gives him a *Weavers 101* rundown of affinities, from Writers like him, to Erasers like Venny, Generics like me, Readers–

"–like Nina who doesn't enjoy being talked about behind her back," comes an icy voice from the corridor.

"Hey Neens. Coffee?" Kaito bounces. "I was just telling Dhaval here–"

"–more than the poor man can probably process right now, so how about easing off for a second, huh?"

She approaches the breakfast bar like a stiff north wind. She pulls a stool out and perches on its edge while scraping her hair away from her eyes. She looks like hell.

"Morning," I croak, coffee still rattling around my lungs, "this is–"

"Hi Dhaval," she extends an arm over the top of me, "I'm Nina. How's the jetlag?" Cordial, business-like.

"Not too bad, I don't think. Maybe it hasn't hit yet. You enjoying being back in Thailand? You're Thai, right?"

"Half Thai. Being back has been...interesting thus far," a quick dagger shot unmistakably in my direction.

"Oh," Dhaval nods, clearly understanding that this is a conversational cul-de-sac best avoided.

Kaito eventually breaks the silence that follows. "So we're not talking about last night at all then?"

"No," Nina growls.

He makes an 'eek' face towards Dhaval. "O-kaaaay then. Any plans now that you're here, man?"

"Well, I uh…" Dhaval shrugs, looking towards me. "If I'm honest, I don't really know what I'm doing here. But I get the feeling that this isn't going to be much of a sightseeing trip."

The best I can muster is a sheepish look.

"It's okay, I can catch you up," Kaito begins but halts when Nina and I open our mouths. But when neither of us follows through – both too exhausted to fight this – he picks it back up. It feels like watching a car crash happening in slow motion, but the impact never comes. Kaito gives Dhaval the whole picture, from the objects to my newfound ability to Read them. He even covers the topic of the mystery girl that's hidden in the Echoes. I want to watch but can't take my eyes off the table, anticipating with bated breath the moment that Dhaval runs out of the kitchen and my life forever. But he doesn't. Just listens closely, does his best to take it all in, asks carefully considered questions. This guy.

"Okay. I *think* I understand," he says, squinting his eyes. "So who sent you these objects with the, uh, *Echoes* embedded in them?"

"Another good question. Too good actually. We don't have an answer for that yet."

"Actually, I think we do," I say.

"Who?" Kaito turns dramatically.

"Pom," I reply.

"What the hell? *My* Pom?"

"Well yes. But also no."

Kaito sends me a look of complete bafflement.

"She isn't exactly who you think she is, K. I don't know how long you've known her for?"

"A couple years," he searches inwardly.

"Maybe as long as Khun Su has been dead?"

"I…guess. Yeah, yeah that sounds about right. What's that got to do with anything?"

"Ugh God," I bury my head in my hands at what I'm about to say next. I've tried to keep Dhaval out of all this craziness, but it's suddenly clear to me how much that ship has sailed. "Khun Su's Echo lives on inside Pom."

"What the actual fuck?" Kaito says.

"I Read Pom and she's in there. Her entire Echo. Su is inside her mind."

"Weavers can do that?" Kaito says, wide-eyed.

"Apparently there's lots we don't know about our own kind," I shake my head, thinking of my mysterious object-Reading.

"So wait," K continues, "she's the one who Wrote the memories into our objects?"

"Ye–" I start. "Actually, I don't know. But she definitely sent the objects to us. She admitted to that last night."

"Last night?"

"Yeah, I kinda bumped into her. Or she bumped into me," I shrug.

"I can't believe this," Kaito says. "What else she say?"

"We didn't speak long," I say. "How I'm trying too hard. That I need to 'let go'. I dunno. She also talked about The Project. And Olivia."

"Olivia?" Dhaval asks. I catch myself marvelling at him. There isn't even a hint of trepidation about his manner. How can he not be freaking out?

"The mystery girl," Kaito waggles his eyebrows at Dhaval. "What else did she say?"

"Nothing. Just that she wants us to go to the boarding house."

"But it's been empty for years hasn't it? I thought they moved the boarders to the campus," Kaito says.

"Who knows," Nina says, chin resting in her hand. "This whole thing is so messed up."

"So what's the plan?" Dhaval ventures.

"We go to the boarding house. I mean, don't we?" I say.

"I vote for that," Kaito adds.

"Of course you do," Nina rolls her eyes. "You're enjoying this."

A glint is in his eye. "But first we need to stop by somewhere else on the way," he adds, pausing for effect. "We've had an invitation. From school."

"What? I really don't think that's a good plan, K," I say, thinking of Adrian's transferral of mentorship to a Bangkok Project agent, and to the hanging threat of Erasure.

"Trust me, it's fine," says Kaito tapping the side of his nose. "I happen to have a contact who says so. This 'new mentor' of yours is friendly, he assures me. Your memories are safe."

"But–"

"Trust me," he says, uncharacteristically serious. "My contact is one of the good guys. He's a board member of the Bangkok branch. You've met him already, actually. He's expecting us there in a couple hours."

I don't need to ask who Kaito's talking about. Something about his apologetic expression tells me the answer, and it makes my stomach plummet.

Chapter 24

"Hello everyone! Welcome back to the Mnemosyne Project Bangkok."

He stands there with arms spread wide under the archway of the main gate into the school. Jet black hair tied back, gold-rimmed sunglasses above a wide smile. The same sting of aftershave. Although gone is the all-black outfit from the nightclub. In its place is a crisp shirt tucked into dress trousers.

Mongkon.

"My man!" Kaito says, hopping over to give him a huge hug. Part of my brain is still struggling to reconcile the artful dodger I met in the Phloen Chit nightclub a few nights back, with the fact he's moonlighting as a senior official for The Project. Or is it other way around? A Project stooge infiltrating the Weaver underground scene of Bangkok? Either way, I can't deny that, for whatever reason, he's helped smooth things over with The Project for me. The thought of being grateful to this snake makes me want to hurl.

He shakes each of our hands in turn, demonstrating the prior knowledge he has on each of us. "Agent Angsakul, wonderful to finally meet you. Kaito has told me so much."

"Nina is fine. I'm on holiday," she responds. Her cool expression suggests she's yet to make her mind up about Mongkon, but she's happy to go along with the ride. Trust in new people was never her strong suit, though I have the nagging feeling that I've now become the mistrustful member of our group.

"Nina it is," he says then turns to Dhaval. "And you must be Douglas's significant other. I've snuck you in today, Dhaval, so don't tell your friends about anything you see or hear." He pats Dhaval on the back and laughs. "And Douglas. Or can I still call you Angel?"

"Whatever you like." I do my best to put on a good face, for Kaito's sake more than anything. From Mongkon's amused expression I don't think I've been entirely successful.

He opens back out to the group. "Please let me be your humble guide. How long has it been?"

"Fifteen, no sixteen years?" says Nina.

"Wow. Well I think you'll find a lot has changed," Mongkon says. "Please, follow me."

Kaito and Nina amble in tow, Dhaval and I a few steps behind. The central courtyard of the campus begins to wrap around us; a sea of asphalt interrupted by little islands – some of dried-out yellow grass, others of paving slabs. The neglected ground is where the familiarity ends. All around the courtyard new structures stand where pools of space and open fields once lay – their glass, steel and marble are in contrast to the wire-fronted corridors and stained linoleum walkways of the original buildings. The dilapidated condition of the London branch also comes to mind. Clearly the Bangkok branch is pulling a lot of the funding these days, growing in stature as one of the world's most important Mnemosyne hubs.

It feels like I'm walking into a memory that's been uprooted, redecorated. I glance at the road behind us in an attempt to reclaim how things used to be. Greenery is a much bigger feature this far outside the city, away from the motorway that cuts north out of the city. The same trees of my youth sway in the breeze. Then slowly, as the gate to the school begins to close with a squeal, the trees become obscured from view. With a clang, we are locked in. The iron gate bears no signage. No indication of what this facility is for. Some things don't change.

Dhaval squeezes my hand. "You okay?"

"Hmm? Sure. You?"

He looks around, as if taking in everything he's discovered in the past twelve hours. Then lets out a slow breath. "I'm getting there."

The feel of his hand, the openness of his expression, pull me back to the present, reminding me of the things I need to fix.

"When we get back to the city, how about we go for a swim then a meal," I say. "Just the two of us? There are some things I need to talk to you about."

"More things? I'll see if I have any space left in my brain. Sounds good," he nudges me with a shoulder. "So, is it strange being back?"

"You have no idea," I say. Without realising, I've started to grip on to him.

"It can't have been that bad, surely? It looks great," he soothes.

I take in the school yard with fresh eyes, trying to superimpose the gloss of Dhaval's positivity on to the architecture of associations that I've built up around this school over so many years. While I've not physically been back here since graduating, my mind has often travelled to this compound. In the passing years it's come to represent something more than merely the place I was sent to as a teenager, as a fledgling Weaver. If the boarding school was a haven of sorts, presided over by Khun Su with her fierce brand of protectiveness, the school was the factory. This is where I learned my craft.

"Looks a lot better than it used to," I say. "The Bangkok branch has always been one of the biggest. I guess nowadays they aren't afraid to show it a little."

Sure, the cracked asphalt and flaking paintwork have been smoothed over since I was last here. But to me it's purely veneer. Behind the facelift I can hear the whisper of spectres, can feel their rough hands reaching for me. A darkness at the periphery of my senses makes me shiver despite the heat.

"How many people were in your class?" Dhaval asks, clearly trying to keep the conversation light. Up ahead Mongkon is pointing out a sign for a tennis court, in the direction of what used to be the open playing field, hemmed by a stinking *khlong* canal.

"Only a handful. There were only about, what, twenty or so kids in the whole school."

"Are you still friends with them?"

"Not really," I say, search my memories for the faces of the other kids. They seem indistinct to me somehow, generic. Shalini, Mai, Jonathan…all names from a lifetime ago. "We kept to ourselves quite a lot. Me, Nina, Venny and Kaito. We were the only boarders, you see. In our eyes that made us extra different I guess. A lot of the other students were Thai, so they stayed at home. Plus they were already moving away from the boarding school set up when we got there. They thought it was more healthy for kids to be in Project branches closer to their home nations, or living with their parents off campus. Branches in England, Sweden and Japan didn't have a school annex like this one, and our parents weren't able to move out here with us. So we were kind of the lost kids. That's how we saw it anyway. What was your school like?"

He chuckles. "Nothing like this. A red brick slab in the middle of Luton. We certainly didn't have a tennis court."

I laugh, despite myself. Having Dhaval here, while a terrifying notion to begin with, anchors me. Mongkon's monologue drifts back on the breeze. "…and over there is where we're thinking of installing a swimming pool…"

"George McNamara would be proud," I say, looking at the polished environment around me.

"Who?" Dhaval says with a frown.

"Just this guy. The Founder of the Mnemosyne Project. He discovered us, people like us who were being treated like lab rats."

"That's awful. Who was doing that?"

"The experiments? Who do you think? Governments around the world. Scientists, the military, secret services. McNamara was one of them, actually. Was shocked by what he saw, so he whistleblew the whole thing. Incredible really."

"Why don't I know this?" he says, wide eyed.

"I'm sure there's lots of freakish stuff that never made it into the history books, Dhaval. We're just one of those things considered too dangerous for people to know. That's why all the governments signed the Mnemosyne Protocol, an accord. They handed over their Weavers to The Project in exchange for the secret being held, and some above-board consultancy work for them."

"That's one big secret," he says.

"Sure is. The secret of our abuse at the hands of all those assholes. The secret of our existence. The world goes on as normal, happy and oblivious. And we're caught in the middle."

A blond man drifts past us without taking any notice, his shirt sticking to his spine in a blotchy strip of sweat. A suit jacket is folded in the crook of one arm, a briefcase dangles from his spare hand.

"I bet there was no one at your school like that guy," I say.

"Um, no," he looks a little alarmed, "was that–?"

"A Project agent, yeah. Not many schools share their grounds with special operatives of a covert intergovernmental organisation, do they?"

"Not that I know of," he laughs. "What do they do?"

"They make this whole thing work. They do consultancy work for governments, security, healthcare. Above-board stuff. Project agents like Nina, Kaito. Me."

His eyebrows raise.

"Yeah," I breathe out. "I'm a Project agent just like them. Or I was before I was benched."

"You were a therapist," he nods, no doubt recalling our first date.

"You got it. *Physician heal thyself*, am I right?" I chuckle. "Anyway, the most important thing The Project does? It keeps the secret."

"Do I want to know how?" he says, craning his neck round to look at the agent once more.

"I'm sure you can imagine. This whole place is a viper's nest, in my opinion. I know it looks nice but…I mean even the founder, George McNamara? Even he did something to piss his own precious Project off. He 'disappeared' a few years after he set the whole thing up. This place is good at making people 'disappear'."

I immediately feel a pang of guilt at having descended fully into paranoia – recognising how close I am to pulling Dhaval down with me.

"I'm sorry, I've become the worst kind of conspiracy theorist. Don't listen to me. Dhaval, are you sure you're okay? If this is too much just say the word and–"

"For the millionth time, I'm okay," he says then looks away. "Jesus, give me some credit."

"I'm sorry," I say. I think I've finally found the edge of his patience. "It's just hard for me–"

"Yes, I get that," he stops abruptly. "I do. But I can…whatever this all is….you don't have to hide or sugarcoat this stuff. I know I'm just a 'regular human' but–" He flashes a look of exasperation then brings it under control. He looks over my shoulder and follows the upward line of the main administration building. "All I'm saying is I can make up my own mind."

"Of course, I didn't mean–" I start but Mongkon's voice punctures the moment. Never thought I'd ever be thankful for the slime ball but he has good timing on this occasion.

"And here's the main refectory." He's halted outside a partially-open-air dining hall flanked by a bank of serving stations. "New since you were here, I think. It's a co-sharing space for everyone on campus; just another expression of how an open relationship has developed between The Project, faculty and students. You guys hungry?"

We're soon settled around a large table with a bizarre selection of traditional Thai dishes, burgers and fries, pizza and sodas.

"Oh shit, don't drink that," I say, scooping a glass of Coke away from Dhaval. "I can't tell you how many times the shitty ice cubes here gave me food poisoning."

"God, Angel, it's absolutely fine. Look around, this place has upped its game," Nina scowls at me – actually scowls! – and passes the drink back to

Dhaval who takes a gulp; a shared act of rebellion against me.

"So, Mongkon, how come you didn't mention the fact you were a board member of The Project the other night?" I say, diverting my aggression on the easiest target.

"Didn't want to talk shop," he says simply.

"That's not how it seemed to me. In fact–" I start.

"Angel, cool it," Kaito says in a hushed voice, puts a finger to his lips, then motions with his eyes in a clean sweep around us.

I keep silent for the rest of my plate of *laab moo*, letting the conversation rise back to a pleasant crackle around me. Through it all I catch a few glances, first from Mongkon who looks at me with light amusement, then from Dhaval whose eyes are back to exuding concern. As they start to discuss dessert I go in search of a bathroom – less out of actual need, and more out of a chance to walk off my barely controlled aggression.

I trace back to the central quad, stopping in a patch of raw midday sunlight. I've forgotten how much keener the heat gets outside the city. A sparse traffic of students, Project agents and faculty members pass, some drifting in search of an early lunch maybe, others walking with more purpose. Despite the odd mixture of characters, there's a stronger feel of the everyday than I remember there being. The ghosts of the past are quieter now than they were when I got here today.

Fifty yards away a pair of students sit side-by-side on the steps of the teaching wing. A boy and a girl no older than fifteen. They're dressed in school uniform – a slightly updated version of the pale lilac short-sleeved shirt and navy trousers I used to wear. Their mannerisms indicate budding romance, the all-but-touching awkwardness of teenage lust. A few adults walk around them without issuing even a hint of a reprimand. Certainly wouldn't have been like that in my day. *Jesus, did I really just think that? Grumpy old man.*

"Hey guys, is the bathroom still up these stairs on the left?" I say on approach.

"Yep, just up there," the boy replies, his mid-Atlantic accent mirroring my own. "But there's a staff toilet over that way."

"Thanks. I'm not staff," I say, taking the first step up.

"Alumni?" The girl says squinting up at me through fingers. The auburn tones of her hair shine in the rays.

"Yeah."

"How long ago were you here?" she asks.

"Ohhh, a long time ago."

"What was it like 'a long time ago'," the boy jibes playfully.

"A lot less pretty. Imagine this building," I point up at a still-tired-looking teaching block, all concrete and metal, "but everywhere."

"Rough," he laughs.

"What do you do now?" asks the girl.

I pause for a beat, then go for the simplest answer. "Stitcher."

"Cool. That's something I'm looking into. Where do you work?"

"London. You really want to be a Stitcher?"

"Yeah I think so. Why? Should I *not* want to choose that?" she says.

"*'Choose'*? Ha, good one," I laugh with maybe a little too much mirth. She cocks her head at me like a confused puppy.

"Uh, I mean yeah, if you're genuinely interested, you should look into it," I fumble. "So...you guys are okay?"

A swift 'who-is-this-guy' look passes between them. "Sure?" the boy says.

"No, I just mean, y'know, school's treating you well. I mean...I don't know what I mean. I'm just gonna...nice to meet you guys."

I squirm with embarrassment at the fact that a pair of teenagers clearly have their shit together better than me, when a voice calls from behind.

"Well, well well. Mr Sermanni returns."

For a few seconds the face of the man seems brand new to me. A tanned bald head with a corona of silver and brown neatly trimmed around the back and sides, spectacles with thin tortoiseshell arms, a checked shirt with rolled up sleeves. But then I see the goatee, now mostly grey, framing a perfect smile. In that instant I see the younger man: the first emissary from the Mnemosyne Project Bangkok I ever came into contact with; the teacher who chaperoned me across the world, away from a tear-stained farewell at the airport, and into a new life in the Far East.

"Mr Bordelais. Wow," I shake my head.

"I heard you were back in town. Have to admit, I said I would believe it when I saw it. But here you are."

I offer a hand to shake. "Oh come now," he exclaims, moving in for a hug.

"Good to see you, sir."

He holds me out at arm's length. "You look good, man. A few days of sunshine out here away from the smog and you'll look even better."

"Heard I was in town?" I feel myself bristling.

"Oh you know, the twittering of little birds. Speaking of which," he eyeballs the fawning duo still sitting on the steps, "Boyd, Violet, don't you have a class to be in?"

"Free period," Boyd smirks.

"Fine. How about a homeroom to study in?"

Violet rises to her feet with mock indignation, helps Boyd up, and they head up the stairs.

"Nice to meet you, Mr Stitcher," she sings before ascending out of sight.

"Mr Stitcher, eh?" Mr Bordelais nudges.

"She says she's interested in becoming one."

"She's certainly got the talent for it. Very skilled Reader."

"Well I guess that's her future decided then," I bite.

"Hm?"

"Nothing. Just, y'know, as if she has much *choice* in the matter."

"Of course she has a choice," he says with an undertone of incredulity.

"Anyway, how are things going, Mr B?"

"It's Matthew now, please. It's all good, thank you. Just look around. The place has vastly changed since you were here."

"So everyone keeps saying," I nod, falling slightly short of congenial.

"Everyone? Are there more of you here?"

"Yup. Nina and Kaito and my, uh, friend, are over there having some lunch. Getting a private tour from Mongkon."

"Oh, our board member. Very impressive. He's an…interesting guy, huh?" he says, eyes wide.

"You could say that," I chuckle. "Want to come over and say hi to the crew?"

Something unreadable passes across his face. Before I have a chance to decipher he gives a quick check of his watch. "I'd love to but I've got a class coming up and I need to pick something up from my office first. Got a minute to walk with me?" He points to the stairs that Boyd and Violet have disappeared up.

I look in the opposite direction of the dining hall where Mongkon seems to be making a great performance of bringing desserts to the table.

"Sure."

We walk through a series of long corridors mostly familiar to me, trading updates on our lives. Mr Bordelais is one of the last remaining faculty members from my era. Of the small handful that taught us, most of the others have either retired or transferred to other Project branches around the world. The student body has grown significantly over the years, he explains – largely a product of more South Asian nations signing up to the Mnemosyne Protocol and sending their kids to Bangkok for 'specialist schooling' under the guise of a scholarship for talented students.

There's a well-rehearsed ease to Matthew as he trots off these facts. He sells a narrative of healthy progress, of happy kids being supported in their early journeys with their Weaver natures before being released to fruitful lives as members of society. It would sound like the indoctrinated patter of a devout Project believer were it not Matthew who was delivering it. The silver-tinged beard and middle-aged frame have brought shades of gravitas to the man, but the passion of the young teacher who I once knew is still very much there, untainted by his decades shackled to this place.

In sharp contrast to his sanguine composure I can feel the edges of my bitterness grating.

"Here we are," he says, halting outside a modest office sandwiched between empty classrooms.

"Is this your same old office?"

"It is indeed," he laughs. "Hey, if it ain't broke. C'mon in, take a seat."

The walls of the room envelop me as soon as I step in, whispering memories of the hours I spent in here being counselled by Matthew, being consoled, encouraged, berated. I sit down in the chair opposite his desk just as I used to, though this time without a tatty school bag slung at my feet. Everything looks just the way it did; an old computer with post-its littered around its monitor, books teetering in columns along wooden shelves, a desk fan ruffling papers, a metal filing cabinet bearing the remnants of stickers long since peeled off. The only new additions seem to be a pair of framed photos propped on top of the cabinet. One is an official photo of the whole school. Five or six rows of school kids and faculty members arranged on bleachers. Next to it is a family photo. Up high in the shot are the smiling faces of Matthew – sporting a lot more of his original brown hair than now – and a sweet-looking Thai woman. Between them is a young girl, gap-toothed and plump cheeks with glossy hair piled high in a bun in the traditional Thai style.

"My girls," he says. "That's my wife Samorn. We've been together for fourteen years now, can you believe it. And that's our daughter Sarah."

"Lovely picture," I say, shifting my gaze towards the small window behind his desk. Thick steel bars dissect the view of the car park. "Your daughter, do you mind me asking, is she–"?

"Nope," he smiles warmly. "No, she goes to a regular ol' international school in the city."

"Oh," I raise my eyes to meet his. "Relieved?"

He displays the look of simple incredulity as before. "I...no. Neither relieved nor concerned."

"That's good," I say, opening my mouth to continue, then brushing the matter aside with a head shake.

"Douglas, are you okay?" His strained expression, thick with parental worry, makes me shift uncomfortably in the chair.

"I'm good. I am good," I mutter, fingering a pen on the desktop. "I just...I mean, forgive me but I kinda call bullshit on that. You're really telling me you don't feel any sense of relief that your daughter's not a Weaver?" My own abruptness catches me off guard. *What's wrong with me?* I try to cover my rising anger under a chuckle.

"Hand on heart," he says with hand on heart. "Dougie, where is this coming from?"

I let out a puff of exasperation. "Where do I even start?" My neck begins to prickle. "How can you stand there, telling me how wonderful this place has become. 'New buildings, shared spaces, happy kids' blah blah blah.' Seriously? After what we had to put up with?"

Mr Bordelais takes the seat next to me, a little close for comfort. His eyebrows form a steeple. This whole dynamic seems unnervingly familiar, pulling me back to the powerlessness I felt as a teenager. "I don't know where this anger is coming from, Douglas. This isn't the kid I remember."

"That's because I bottled it up. I didn't...I didn't want any of this. I just...y'know it doesn't matter. It really doesn't matter. I'm just tired." He reaches across to put a hand on my shoulder but I get up before he can make contact.

He rises with me. "Dougie please, I'm sorry. You clearly have some things you want to say." Silence. "We only ever wanted the best for you and your fellow pupils. Surely you must know that? You may not agree right now but I think we did a pretty good job."

I let out a single yap of laughter and shake my head.

"Now hold on, hear me out," he continues. "Yes, things might not have been as...comfortable...here as they are now, but you surely can't deny that we did a lot of good? My goodness, when I think of how you all were when you first arrived. You, little Nina, Venny. Kaito could hardly say a word. But now look at you all. I'm sorry if that's not how you feel."

"*I* don't even know how I feel!" I shout, words firing out and bouncing off the small office walls. "I am such a complete and utter mess because of this place. Because of The Project. Because of people like you."

He's taken aback, mouth struggling to form words.

I rush on: "My whole life, squeezed and torn and shaped into something suitable. Something contained and secret. You think you did a good job? Man, are you fucking kidding yourself. Look at me. Just look at me!"

His face falls, the veneer of quiet composure cracked.

I go for the jugular: "I bet you've thanked God every day of your precious daughter's life that she isn't a Weaver," I say, the words hissing through my teeth. "Because if she was, you know...you *know* what would be done to her. How her life would turn out. Deny it!"

His mouth quivers, his eyes redden, but he stays silent. I've unleashed something in him. I can feel it.

I scrape fingers across my puffy face, trying to pull my rage back inwards.

When he finally speaks his voice is low, pained. "Look, I uh...I have to get to my class." He reaches for his papers, slides past me to the doorway and motions me through. He clears his throat. "But please Dougie, would you come by later? Tomorrow maybe? I really do want to talk this through properly. Once you've had a chance to cool down. A heart to heart, just like when you were a kid. We'll get you back on your feet."

For a brief flash I see myself as a child, lost and vulnerable. *No more.*

"Who was Olivia?" I ask.

"What?"

Adrenaline thumps in my neck. "*Who* was Olivia?"

"I...uh...I," he says, clearly unable to recover quick enough. *I knew it.* "I have no idea. Who– where did you...?"

"Where can I get hold of student records?" *Is this a good tactic? Am I wrecking my chances?*

For a beat his eyes focus on the cabinet behind me – an instinctive motion covered up too late.

"We...that is...the records are all held digitally, he says, clawing his way back. "Securely, of course. I'm afraid you wouldn't have the clearance to access them. Why on earth do you ask?"

"It doesn't matter," I say, sweeping out the door past him. He follows me out, turning as if to lock the door. The key in his hand. My heart leaps. Before inserting it in the lock he decides on a new course of action. He takes a step toward me. All pretence seems to have left him. His face looks drained all of a sudden, ashen.

"Douglas," he says in a hushed tone, eyes flicking behind me, "sometimes the wisest thing to do is to keep your eyes ahead. Looking back...there's very little to gain from dwelling on the past. Do you understand?"

His gaze tries to penetrate me. I feel a surge, emboldened by this switch of power.

"You know that's not possible," I say. "Not for people like us."

***

I stride with renewed purpose.

My mind fizzes trying to formulate a plan. My final words with Matthew loop in my ears.

I force myself to a stop, finally acknowledging the fact I'm completely lost. The corridor bears no resemblance to any I used to know. The decor is fresh, my shoes squeak on the floor. Must have crossed over to a new wing.

Familiar voices from the quad two floors below catch my attention. The crew.

"Hey guys. Guys, up here!" I holler through the wire mesh that constitutes the external wall.

The quartet stands apart in pairs. Mongkon and Kaito break from an energetic conversation to spot me and wave.

"What are you doing up there?" Kaito booms.

"Hold on, stay there.," I say. "I'll be right down."

I'm just about to head for the nearest stairwell when I pause to observe Dhaval and Nina. They seem in deep discussion together. Something about their combination, two pillars of my life, talking to each other and the dark expressions on their faces unnerves me. I have a deep impulse to get down there immediately.

Chapter 25

An eeriness seemed to descend during the journey back to the city.

The initial energy dissipated soon after we got through the basic touch points of our visit: 'Weird to be back', 'what a facelift the school got', *yadda yadda*. There was a little interest in my catch up with Matthew Bourdelais, but not much. I didn't even get to share the crux of my exchange with him – the way he crumpled at the mention of Olivia's name, the terse words he ended things on. *'Sometimes the wisest thing to do is to keep your eyes ahead...'*

My initial urgency was quickly quashed by the growing weirdness in the car. All eyes were glued to the rolling scenery outside the windows, of rice paddies and low level allotments giving way to gated communities, townhouses and the first towers of the city as we connected to the expressway. But more than that, there was a pensive note to the silence, an uneasy snatching of sideways glances. I felt certain the epicentre of this vibe was Dhaval and Nina. I tried a few times to nuzzle a response out of Dhaval, but each time was met with a simple 'I'm fine'. I didn't even try to broach a conversation with Nina. She's still blocking any of my advances. Up front, Kaito was surprisingly silent, humming along to the radio, fingers tapping on the wheel.

We left Mongkon at the gates of the MPB. He bade us farewell with pats and warm words, pausing with me to deliver a particularly meaningful handshake and knowing wink – both of which meant nothing to me. Kaito's enduring friendship with this scumbag grinds my gears, perhaps more than it should.

We got back to the apartment just as the sun set. K is ordering takeout with Nina, while I coax Dhaval up to the rooftop infinity pool. It's deserted apart from the two of us. I rest my arms on the pool's edge, transfixed by the city below. The closeness of the night air stops dead at my shoulders, unable to penetrate the water's silky surface. I feel Dhaval approaching before I hear him – the ripples from his breaststrokes lap against me.

He joins me at the water's edge, pinching his nose and smoothing his hair back. His features are given a ghostly pearlessence in the pool's under-lighting.

"Hi," I say.

"Hi."

"Thanks for coming today. You didn't have to."

"I know," he says.

"I mean it, Dhaval. It means a lot that you're here."

He just makes a little smile, then turns to look out at the city. "Some view."

"Not as good as the one I've got," I say.

"Smooth," he chuckles.

"What can I say? You bring out the creep in me."

He responds by flicking water at me with a finger. I hold off from retaliating, instead aiming to maintain a happy calm between us.

"Y'know," he says after some time, "for being a relatively new couple, it feels like we've been through a lot."

"I know what you mean," I smile, "I don't think I've ever let someone get so close before."

"Really?"

"I'm a bit of a lone wolf, if you didn't get that already," I say. "What about you?"

He raises an eyebrow. "Are we doing this? Sharing our romantic histories?"

I laugh. "You don't need to give me names and numbers."

He ponders, eyes on the horizon. "I guess it's been a mixture for me. Some short-term flings, one or two much longer relationships. Before you and I met I'd been single for a while. A bad break up."

"How bad?" I touch his shoulder, but he waves it off casually.

"It wasn't great, but it's all in the past. Being with you..." he trails off. "It's been different. I guess we all have things we need to get over?"

At his soft inflection I feel the conversation pulling off course, away from where I hope to keep us.

"I guess. All in the past, as you say," I add, trying to close it down gently.

"But the past is different for you, isn't it? Doesn't necessarily stay back there. It's something that you take with you. It's mutable in your hands."

I feel my heart beginning to pulse. "I...I guess. I'm not sure what you–"

"Why am I here?" he says softly.

"What do you mean?"

"You left without a word. I was so worried, wondering if something bad had happened. You–"

"I'm sorry. I explained–"

"–left me with all these questions. 'Why did he run away? Is he okay? Is he safe? Was it something I did?' But behind it all, there was this sensation. So strange. Like a homing beacon, leading me here. I wasn't properly aware of it until today. I just followed it without question. Until I got talking to Nina."

The look on his face, scrunched in confusion yet so sad at its edges. My heart stops.

"I was asking her about your school, about the opportunities you guys got to go off campus. You went on some fun field trips, she explained. Up north to the jungle, but also south to the beach. And I swear, as she described the scenery, the sea, the sand...I knew it. Like, *knew* what she was talking about. Not just knew. I remembered it. Even now I can recall it. It's so real to me. I can see her face, Kaito and Venny's too. So young and happy."

I'm stunned to silence. Completely unable to halt the inexorable flow of Dhaval's words.

"As Nina talked to me about this field trip to the beach, I laughed along, even finishing some of her sentences, y'know? She was amazed at how much I knew. 'Did Angel tell you this? Have you been there too?' she asked. That's when we both stopped laughing. Because the answer was neither. Wasn't it?" He turns to face me. "You never told me about that memory. And I've never been to Thailand before, have I?"

Grit has found its way into his voice. I'm held in his gaze, trying to think of a way out of this, but too ashamed to do or say anything.

"She asked for my permission to Read the memory. Just that one memory. I was nervous but said it was fine. She said I should think of it like visiting the dentist or something. It only took a second. I think I could feel her in there, searching. And then, she suddenly looked so...so disappointed. And furious. So angry. Because you put that memory inside me, didn't you?"

My silence is all the answer he needs.

"Why?" he whispers.

My eyes feel raw. "A gift," I finally say through a constricted throat.

"What?"

"A gift," I say louder.

"I don't understand, why would you give me that? To manipulate me? To coax me out here?"

"No...not at all...you have to believe me...it..." I fumble. I want to convey to him the purity of the moment when I Wrote the memory on to him. I want to tell him how a small number of happy memories like that are all I truly have, how I wanted to share this precious gem of an otherwise patchy youth with him. To explain how he makes me feel: like there's a small chance that together we could make new memories just like that one. Him and me.

But I don't say that. I just say: "I'm sorry."

He doesn't respond for a long time. The water feels cold.

"You know the worst part? I don't know if what I feel for you is real. I really thought I was falli– But maybe it's all because of what you did to me. What I feel, the reason I'm here is just...someone else's life. I feel so fucking stupid."

"No, Dhaval, that's not how it works," I plead, trying to submerge the rising thought that maybe he's right.

"I don't think I should be here," he says, lifting himself out of the pool. He halts at his full height, looking down at me. Drops patter at his feet.

"Don't go. Please."

He raises his eyes to the glass doors at the far end of the pool. "Y'know, something Kaito said has stuck with me since breakfast. When I asked him what it's like to read someone else's memory. He said it was just like remembering. That it feels like the most normal thing in the world. I couldn't imagine what it must be like to have that kind of connection to someone, to feel the blur of where they end and you begin. But maybe now I can. I..." He stops himself. Maybe on the verge of saying something devastating. Maybe simply reaching the end of his ability to process all of this.

I wish I could help explain.

"I need some time to think," he says, still staring off in the distance. "Can you give me the room tonight?"

"Of course," I nod, trying to hide the effect of the knife that's sliding into my chest. "I understand."

"Okay," he says, face devoid of expression. Then with a confirmed decisiveness he walks the perimeter of the pool, grabbing a towel on his way through the glass doors.

It's only once he's faded from sight completely that I see a new figure watching from the shadows. It's difficult to see her expression in the half light, but I can practically feel her disappointment rolling across the water like mist.

At least three alternate versions of how this conversation could go flicker through my mind: angry words battered across the divide; ugly frustration vomited on the deck; a sickening exchange of remorse falling on deaf ears. I decide I don't want either, so take a deep breath and sink beneath the surface.

Get me out of here. I can't handle this. Not right now. Help.

***

The sounds reaching my ear are muffled. A bubble tickles up my nose. I don't panic. Body reacts instinctively. The water feels thick as I wave my arms through it, almost slimy between my fingers. Lungs begin to burn, but not too badly. Still a few more seconds to play. I uncross my legs and push forward, gliding along the bottom, eyes adjusting to the turquoise light. I fly over white tiles and grey grout, up, up, to the wobbly world above.

The air is the first sensation as I break the surface. Humid and welcoming. Then it's the smells. The tang of chlorine, the slight stink of a drain. Then my ears break, water leaking away, replaced with the familiar sounds of the city far below. Lastly it's the sights. A glow of lights around the pool, the outlines of deck chairs with their padding taken away for the night.

And then at the end of the pool, a pair of feet. I push the remaining air out of my nose and sweep the itchy water from my eyes. I doggie paddle up to the edge, all the while looking from the feet upwards. A black dress, arms are crossed, and eyes angry with dark liner. Her face is different, pierced in new places, thinner in others. Hair longer, better looked-after than it used to be.

"Hello Nina," I say. "Help me out?"

She looks at my outstretched hand like I have a poop in it. "Guess not then," I say.

I make a lumpy attempt at getting out of the pool, the knobbly ground hurting palms and knees as I push upwards. I stand as tall as I can, feeling the air on every centimetre of my body, letting the droplets run down my back and legs. It feels so wonderful I can't help but laugh. She just stares at me.

"Look at your face," I giggle. I reach out with a soggy thumb and run it down her cheek. She slaps it away.

"Hey!" I shout. She meant that slap. "No need for that."

"What the fuck is wrong with you?"

"Language! When did you become such a potty mouth?" I joke.

"Have you taken something?"

"Like what?"

"Seriously, Angel. What the– I come up here to finally have it out with you, to ask you face-to-face what the hell you're playing at. Writing memories on your boyfriend? I mean, what the hell?" Her fists clench and unclench as she talks. "But I see Dhaval must've brought it up first, from the look of him as he left through those doors. Poor guy. So I expected you might be angry, or sad, or something. But here you are smiling like a Cheshire Cat."

"Are you done?" I say, giving her a bored look, the kind she always used to hate.

"I…what is with you? You're acting strange," she holds her hands up to the sky. But then all of a sudden the anger seems to leave her. "Are you okay?"

"I'm good. Great actually." I close my eyes and take a deep breath in. The woody sweet smell of her perfume. "You just need to relax, Nina. Everything is okay. God, I've missed you."

Now she looks even more confused. And worried. Too concerned to slap my hand away this time. Her skin is so soft, so warm.

"What are you–?"

I don't let her finish the sentence. I kiss her. For a second I feel her about to pull away, but then she doesn't. We stay like this for a while, then open our eyes at the same time.

"Hi," I whisper.

"You…" she whispers back.

Then we kiss again.

***

My mouth is damp. No. Not mine. *What the–?*

My eyes spring open, revealing a familiar face in full HD, first peaceful, transported, then twisting in horror as she senses I've taken too quick a step backwards. My arms flail at the open air. The water slaps my skin hard then relents, engulfing me completely. I erupt upwards as quickly as I submerge, coughing up great lumps of water, clawing it out of my nose and eyes.

"Oh my God, are you okay?" she exclaims, kneeling to help me.

"What the…" I splutter, "how did I–?"

Her expression is somewhere between amazement and hilarity as I get out of the pool while hacking up the rest of the pool water from my lungs. She tries to curl a hand behind my ear, but I duck out of its way. Such a strange motion, so odd, inappropriate somehow. I stare at the hand, expecting it to have something sharp or nasty in it, a prank of some kind.

"Hey," she says softly, almost crooning, then reaches for my face. I shuffle backwards, anger suddenly rising at the full sight of her. This woman, supposedly my best friend, who hasn't looked me directly in the eye all day, but now pawing at me?

"What are you doing? Here to gloat at your handy work? Tipping poison in my boyfriend's ear?" The words are ragged and acidic. I feel their falseness as soon as I release them, but it feels cathartic all the same. I get up to my feet, leaving her kneeling on the ground, confusion written across her face. She places a finger on her lips then rises to meet me.

I want her to fight back, my body sings for it. I yearn for her to spar with me. Anything but to keep on giving me that look. She just stares at me, as if reading my face for secret signs. Then something breaks in her. Like she's cracked the code of my very essence. She slowly backs away towards the door, colour draining from her face.

"That's right!" I explode. "Run away, why don't you. Fucking run away!"

***

A kernel of common sense holds me in place long enough for the adrenaline to leach out. In its place comes a numbness, occasionally ruptured by a fresh recollection of the two catastrophic conversations I've just had. By the time I've used the poolside shower, towelled off and put my day clothes back on, my mind is a mixture of nothingness and cold logic. Even the memory gap between Dhaval leaving and kissing Nina (*kissing!*) seems immaterial right now.

It can all wait. Because I have a plan that needs executing. And right now it's the only thought I have that's clear. I take the stairwell down to the twenty-fifth floor and quietly enter the apartment. If I'm lucky...and right enough – no sign of Dhaval and Nina. Both are most likely barricaded in their rooms.

A foot peeking over the edge of the couch reveals I'm in even better luck. Kaito's KO'd, on his back with an arm splayed across his eyes. The remnants of takeout lay around the coffee table and the corners of his mouth. I find myself staring fondly at his sleeping form. My friend. Maybe my only one left.

His phone's cradled in his hand. Like a quester stealing the key from the dragon, I prize one finger off, halting to see if he's stirring, then when I feel confident he's deeply asleep, slide the phone out then make my way to the kitchen.

I push the door to, then click the phone's home button. The screen lights up, requesting the passcode. *Shit. Or maybe...*

I place my palm flat on the screen, close my eyes and listen. Listen for a pattern, a repetition. And to my surprise, it's there, skating about the surface, silvery and sharp. I grasp at it, forcing it to speak to me. Got it.

I punch in the four-digit code. The screen opens up to me, giving me a surge of excitement at what I've just done. *No time for that. Find Kaito's contacts, scroll down, don't even pause for thought or you might not follow through. There. Hit the receiver icon.*

A few rings, then silence.

"Whatup K-Dog!"

"This isn't Kaito. It's Douglas. Angel."

I can hear a smile unfurling in his voice. "Well, well, well. And to what do I owe this honour?"

"This isn't a social call, Mongkon. I need your help."

Chapter 26

In the darkness the school looks much closer to how I originally knew it. The high barbed gate, the security lights dotting the perimeter. It all makes the Mnemosyne Project Bangkok look just as menacing to me as it did as a thirteen-year-old. And yet, in the still night sky twinkle the first stars I've seen since arriving in Thailand.

The rolling crunch of my taxi's tyres fades into the distance, replaced by the hum of cicadas. I tried to make the driver wait for me – was sure I had used the correct words – but the widening whites of his eyes as he saw our destination told me all I needed to know: he wasn't going to wait a second longer than it took to drop me off at this place. This anonymous facility in the middle of nowhere.

A guard in khaki green stares at me from her post next to the gate. Tiny bugs compete around her lamplight.

"Just walk calmly up to the security gate, place this card on the scanner, and walk through."

Mongkon's words reverberate through my head. A splinter of panic pricks me. What if his card doesn't work? What if he's set me up? When he opened the door to his apartment he looked pleased to see me, like a tiger lounging in the shade.

"I need to break into the school. Tonight," was all I said once inside. Something about Mongkon told me there was no need for niceties with him. Which was refreshing.

"Why?" he said, throwing back the cuff of his silk robe to take a gulp of whisky. Was everything about this guy staged for effect?

"They have information I need. About me, my friends, from our schooldays. I want it," I said.

"Everything's digitised these days," he smirked.

"Not all of it".

He paused as if chewing over each syllable of my words, placed the glass down, then brought his hands together.

"Okay."

"Really?" I said, breaking my cool. "I thought this would be harder."

"I can make it harder if you like?"

"No. Easy is good," I exhaled.

With a swish of silk he padded over to a bundle of keys and paraphernalia by the door, then returned holding a white plastic card. It was completely blank, apart from the insignia of some security company. I pulled it toward me but Mongkon held tightly between finger and thumb.

"The less I know the better," he said, all joviality gone. "If you get caught, you will say you stole this from me during your tour earlier today. I'll deny any other reason than this. Understand?"

I nodded, made for the door then halted. "Why are you helping me? First getting The Project off my back, and now this?"

"We need to look out for each other," he said, holding his arms out wide then bringing his hands together. "In return I ask only one small thing. When all this is over, when you have got what you need and you've wiped that awful frown off your face, think better of me. You and I are going to be good friends one day. We have important work to do together."

I let his words settle like leaves between us. "I doubt it. But thanks for this," I said waggling the card.

I feel the contours of the card now as I make the final steps to the school gate. A spectre of confusion dawns on the guard's face.

"Sawatdee khrab," I nod, aiming for business-like and neutral.

She nods, but the eyebrows remain knotted.

Wasting no further time I clamp the key on a red-blinking box next to the gate. It makes a beep, and with a gratifying clank, a small door within the gate springs open.

The guard raises a salute, as if the third in the series of mechanised actions. *Beep, door, salute.* I manage to stifle an involuntary flinch, shoot a little salute back, then step through the doorway.

Keep walking, don't rush, but don't pause to look like you're lost. My fingers tingle, head feels light. It's a surreal sensation, breaking in like this. It's so not me.

I walk into the central quad of the campus. Hours ago it was baking hot, but now the bite of the sun is gone leaving in its place a dense tropical echo.

Feet scuffle up ahead. I rush to find cover, slipping into a dark corner. *Why did I do this? If I'm going to be caught on any CCTV this is going to look so suspect. Oh God, oh shit. I can't do this. What was I thinking?*

I clench my eyes tight, wanting to open them to find I'm anywhere but here. Where's your bravery now, Angel?

Help me.

***

A pair of feet pass by, stop for a second, then continue. My eyes flutter open. They're already adjusted to the low light. I peek round the corner and spot a security guard – the owner of the feet. That was a close call. I can feel Angel's adrenaline. Nothing a second or two of standing still can't fix – long enough to get my head together, to figure out why I'm here.

Ah, that's right. Get to Mr Bourdelais's office without being seen. No problem, Angel. I'm the right girl for the job. You've come so far. So close to finding me. You've got to keep going.

I catch my reflection in a window. Eyes sunken. They look strange next to my smile. Ok, enough goggling at yourself. One, two, three, go!

I walk as casual as possible back out into the school yard, spot the stairwell I need then make a beeline for it. No sounds behind me. So far so good. The glossy steps catch the light. Hmmm. Need to walk softly. What have I got on my feet? Adidas trainers. Good boy, Angel.

Tip toe up the steps, trying not to make a sound. I reach the top then stop. Left or right? Dash it! Which way did he take before? Left, it was left. My foot squeaks on the floor. Argh. Trainers were maybe a bad idea. I slip them off then follow Angel's instinct in the direction of Mr Bourdelais's office, all the while keeping an ear out. Cripes this is fun. I feel like a spy. Timothy Dalton on some secret mission. Brilliant!

I shouldn't, but I pause for a couple of seconds by a bench overlooking the campus. Wow it's changed a lot. Same smell though. Industrial bleach and teenage tears. Never thought I'd be back.

Enough havering. Get back to the task at hand. I carry on down the corridor. The longer I walk down it the more familiar it seems. In fact up ahead is that the office? It is. Still the same one after all these years.

Okay, Angel. I got you this far. The rest is up to you.

Come and find me.

***

I take a huge gasp, filling my lungs as if it's the first proper breath I've taken in long minutes. A sign etched on glass in front of me reads 'Matthew Bourdelais'.

What the–? How did I get here?

I pivot in a full three-sixty to take in my surrounds. I feel a weight in my hand – sneakers dangle from my fingers. A second ago I was in the quad and now I'm here. I search my memory but there's nothing. Just a vacuum between then and now. I check my watch. Only a few minutes have passed. I really am going insane. Just like at the pool. Another blackout with no explanation.

A spark runs through me. Gotta focus. For all I know I've been spotted and security are coming for me. I slip my sneakers back on then stare at the door handle to the office, hoping beyond hope I'm right: that Mr Bourdelais forgot to lock his door.

The handle shifts. Presto! The door swings open. You lucky bastard. But now comes the much bigger gamble.

I creep into the dark room and ease the door closed behind me. A silver stream of moonlight cuts into the small office hitting, of all things, the very thing I'm here for: the filing cabinet. This unassuming, bashed-up cabinet that Mr B's eyes flicked to the moment I asked him about student records.

I focus on the keyhole in the top corner of the cabinet, reach into my shirt to pull out the chain. It jangles free. Next to my pendant is Kaito's key. The ridiculousness of what I'm about to try rises into a low rumble of laughter.

It can't be this easy, surely. And yet...

It doesn't fit. *Fuckshitfuck!* I've come all this sodding way for nothing. I can't believe it! I punch the cabinet hard, sending a pang through my fist.

And the top drawer slides half open.

I let out a single guffaw then clamp a hand over my mouth. The cabinet wasn't even locked! Mr B, you careless idiot.

I start rifling through the documents and separators in the drawer. Lesson plans, correspondence going back a few years, minutes from faculty meetings. But no student records. The second drawer is even less useful. No documents at all – just a tired-looking mug, and some clothes branded with The Project insignia.

I crouch to the third and final drawer, praying to any deities that might be listening. *Pleasepleaseplease...*

My heart leaps. The drawer is crammed. Foolscap folios and document wallets are bundled tightly, separated by coloured tabs with years scribbled on them – years going back as far as...

I reach to the very back, greedily levering out an entire section titled 'Boarding house' then placing it on the floor in a pool of moonlight. The pack is turgid, with loose leaves of paper poking out in all directions. This is it. This is what I'm looking for. I thumb through the pages in chunks. These are no school report cards. These are something else entirely. Official-looking documents with inky rubber stamping, embossed headed paper bearing the signatures of Project officials, medical notes scrawled and spilling across margins. They're arranged in some sort of order, subsections of relatively-equal thickness. One per person.

Nina Angsakul.
Venedict Kotto.
Douglas Sermanni.
Kaito Taniguchi.

Some more names too. But not the one I'm looking for. Come on. I shuffle through them again, searching for new subdivisions. *Where is she? Where's Olivia?*

But she's not here.

Energy saps out of me at the realisation. I was so sure... Unconsciously my fingers find their way to the section with my name on it, flipping open the cover. I scan across the surface of the dog-eared pages, coming to rest on a familiar face that's stapled to the corner of a medical-looking report. Cold eyes stare back up at me, framed by matted blond hair, hollow cheeks, chapped lips. His expression is passive, a void, apart from the eyes which seem to pierce through the photograph, reaching out to me.

It's my face. My vacant face. Surely no older than when I first arrived here.

Why don't I remember this photograph being taken?

Fresh curiosity kindles. I race through the report, phrases punched in typewritten ink leap out at me:

Grade 3 Generic capability...loss of consciousness...serial blackouts followed by transitions...dissociative Echoes...identifies as 'Olivia'...administering Erasure...

Olivia.
I don't understand. This seems to be saying…but how is that possible?
"You can't be in here."
The voice seems to come from nowhere, freezing me to the spot.
"We have to go." A figure in the shadows reaches a long arm towards me. Pleading eyes glint in the moonlight. The voice crackles with urgency. "They're coming. Put the folder back. Please, Angel, we have to go. Now!"
The face begins to coalesce. The slender frame, tall, strong shoulders. But the silhouette, sloping, apologetic.
Venny.

Chapter 27

"Don't say anything, keep walking," Venny says under his breath as he strides along the corridor.

I'm half-trotting in his wake, torn between returning for the folder which Venny forced me to put back in the cabinet, but compelled to follow my friend who has so mysteriously appeared. All panic seems to have left him now that we're on the move. One hand in his pocket, eyes out front, he walks with a purpose and command that doesn't chime with the vulturine youth I used to know.

"Venny, what–"

"Not now. Let me get us out of here safely."

We take the stairwell to the quad, he with smooth control, me with thundering urgency. My mind is racing too fast to keep cool.

We break out into the moonlit quad. After a look left and right, Venny motions me towards the gate.

We take a few steps when a voice from behind splits the midnight air.

"Kotto! Agent Kotto!"

A figure jogs out of the darkness, coalescing as it gets closer into a woman with sweat glistening at her hairline.

"Glad I caught you. Heading out?" she pants.

"Yes. Shift's coming to an end so..." Venny drawls, thumbing towards the gate.

The woman tilts her head, flashing her blue eyes from Venny to me then back again. "Friend of yours?"

I try my absolute best to gather my expression into something less indicative of my internal turbulence.

"Uh yes," Venny says, shooting me a 'be cool' look. "Just giving him the tour. Was there something you needed help with, Agent Kelly?"

"Linda, please. Listen, I hope it's not too forward of me but I wondered if I could get your advice on a case? I know it's not really my place, but when I heard that you were visiting our branch I just couldn't pass up the opportunity," she rabbits in an accent hailing from someplace Australian.

"I'd be happy to, Linda. But I'm afraid it'll have to wait for a day or two."

She flushes. "Of course, of course. Whenever you have some time would be fantastic. Have a good evening, well, morning now I guess."

"You too. Bye now."

He pivots away. I exchange awkward smiles with Linda then follow behind.

I catch up just before we reach the gate, brain abuzz with questions, though foremost:

"Agent?!"

"Quiet!" He warns through gritted teeth.

***

The air beyond the gate seems somehow sweeter. Venny guides me silently to an estate car, clicks a key fob then directs me to the passenger side. He slides in beside me, turns the ignition then peels out of the car park.

I keep silent as we travel through an empty network of tree lined roads. Venny's eyes dart between the road and his rearview mirror. I'm burning to talk but his laser-focused demeanour tells me our escape still isn't assured. A handful of twists and turns later, he pulls into a nook by a khlong. The canal is overgrown with shrubbery.

The ignition goes off. He turns to me with a squeak of the leather upholstery.

"Hey man," he says po-faced, but a look in his eye – the first proper flash of the kid I once knew. It's all the cue I need to thrust my arms around him and squeeze tight. His chuckle is muffled in my shoulder.

When we separate I stare at him incredulously. "What are you doing here? You're a Project agent? How did–"

He holds his hands up to halt my flustering. He seems to be considering his response.

"You have no idea how lucky you are that I spotted you on CCTV. If someone else had..." he shakes his head. "So irresponsible, Angel."

"What the hell, man? Don't say that when you have no idea why I was even–"

"I know precisely why you were there."

This shuts me up quickly.

He continues: "And believe me, I get it. What I'm saying is, if anyone but me found out why you were there... Well let's just say you would looking at a very different situation."

"What about the CCTV footage? What's to stop someone else from seeing it?"

"I'll sort it," he says with an unsettling certainty.

"But what about that agent?"

"I will sort it."

The headlights reflect off the trees back at us, starkly illuminating Venny's face, highlighting every line etched there during our years apart, every mark of experience earned on his own path. The day we sat together atop that ancient temple, it was a lifetime ago. I mourn for the teenager who is so clearly gone, but also feel a swell of love for the man that has been forced into being.

"Venn" I whisper.

He looks away. "I could never bring myself to tell you guys. Too ashamed, I guess. One lie leads to another, then another, then it all just takes on a life of its own. An accountant. Jesus. How nobody figured out that cover I'll never know. Everybody lapped it up. They were so happy for me."

"When did you join The Project?"

"You're kidding right?" he throws a scornful look my way, but it melts when he sees I'm serious. "Dude. I never left The Project. They groomed me from Day One. A Grade 4 Eraser in their midst? Please. As far as they were concerned, I was hired the second I stepped foot on campus. Oh I tried to get out of it, you better believe that. Pleaded with the faculty, tried to hide my abilities, prayed to be demoted to a lower grade. Made myself as big a nuisance as I could. No use. So there you go. Now you know. Your man Venny's a big Project goon. Just like those suits on campus we used to have nightmares about."

"We all are, Venny," I say, squeezing his shoulder. "You were right. We never had a choice."

His words become breathy as they catch in his throat. His eyes glisten. I can feel his struggle to hold it all back. "It's different for Erasers, Angel. You know it is. The things I've had to do. All in the name of keeping the Great Secret. The people I've..." But he can't complete the sentence.

"I'm so sorry, Venn."

"Me too, man."

We sit in silence a while. Eventually he takes a breath and rubs his eyes.

"Being back here. So fucking eerie."

"Tell me about it."

A new thought occurs.

"Wait a minute," I say. "Mongkon managed to get The Project off my case by saying my treatment had been transferred to a 'new mentor' here."

Venny's stoniness softens into a grin. "Say hello to your new therapist," he says.

"Jesus Christ," I laugh at the unspooling riddle my life has become. "How did they not put two and two together that we're friends?"

"Turns out The Project has a short memory," he says, turning the key in the ignition. "Anyway, my first task as your mentor. I'm going to take you back to the city."

The car thrums into life. I place my hand on Venny's before he can throw the stick into reverse.

"It's too late for that. There's only one place left to go."

He turns to me. A fatalistic expression spreads across his face.

"Figures," he shakes his head, then steers us into the darkness.

Chapter 28

At times we were happy here. A pseudo-family life. Running for cover before the count of twenty-five. Stuffing our faces with popcorn. Crowing over board games.

In those happy moments, which could stretch for days at a time, we were as regular a familial unit as we knew. In those moments the boarding house wrapped around us like a security blanket. But the minute one of us awoke to the reality – a traumatic day at school, a mysterious visit from a Project physician – all warmth escaped from the house. Its embrace grew immediately cold.

But looking at the house now, darkness all around, it seems to have taken on a third form. Overgrown and unkempt, vacant of all inner life – it feels orphaned.

"Weird," Venny shakes his head.

"I know." Though I'm not exactly sure which weird he's referring to. Being at the footsteps of our old boarding house? Or maybe the invite I received from its owner – a woman who has the Echo of our dead matron living inside her.

There's been a lot of weird in our lives lately.

"You sure we're expected?" he asks, looking up at the gabled roofs.

"I think so. Well, here goes nothing."

I step up to the main door and knock on the wooden door. I try again. Nothing.

"Maybe we should try round the back?" I say walking down to the driveway.

"I don't think that'll be necessary," Venny calls to me from the open front door. "It wasn't locked."

Curiouser and curiouser.

Our feet echo in the empty foyer. Where once there was an abundance of teak and rattan furniture, now there's nothing except a small circular table. On it, a handwritten note:

'Welcome home'

"I don't think anyone's in," Venny's voice booms from the living room. "That note..?"

"From Pom, I think."

I wander through to the reception room, where one or two pieces of furniture still stand in places I expect them to be. A *leewadee* triangular cushion with its mattress unrolled across the floor. A Chinese step cabinet, still missing a drawer. Dust has collected on their surfaces.

"I feel like we're the ghosts haunting this place," Venny says from on high.

I join him on the mezzanine. The smell of wood resin, the silence of the grounds, the pressing warmth of the building. They all spark memories of the lives we led within these walls. But from this new vantage point, I see it: this wasn't what the house was built to be. It deserved better. This stately Thai mansion, it was built for aristocrats, a proud Thai family boasting generations of respectability and karmic fortitude. It deserved a complete fleet of staff tending its grounds, serving delicacies to its owners at the ring of a bell, raising their precocious little rugrats.

Instead it got us. Sullen supernatural teenagers slamming doors, a skeleton crew of keepers drifting from room to room, the wailing of night terrors. It didn't want us living within it.

The damage has been done. But looking around at your neglected interior, I wonder if you're more like us than I thought, old pal.

"I'm sorry," I whisper into the half-light.

"Angel," Venny stands a few feet away, pointing to the wing behind us. Four bedroom doors lie ajar. We approach one of the rooms gingerly, as if not wanting to wake some imaginary children sleeping within.

My room. My bed. My bedside table. My cabinet. The garden view outside my window. All still here, preserved like some still life painting. I sit on the bed and Venny stands at the doorway completing the picture, harking back to the secret conversations all four of us used to have, sneaking into each other's rooms in the middle of the night.

Scenes of the dream come to me unbidden, like a sentient breeze. The pendant around my neck thrums.

> *"Hey. It's time."*
> *It's a young voice but earthy. I've been waiting for him here in the dark, but it still startles me.*
> *"You ready?" he asks.*
> *He clicks the aircon off and almost immediately the heat closes in. I slide a foot out from under the covers and on to the cold floor. It's a clear night and the moon casts enough light to find my way to the chest of drawers.*

"Angel. What you doing?"
Somehow I've made my way to the chest of drawers. The memory continues...

> *I open the top drawer as silently as I can and reach under a stack of t-shirts. I find the drawstring bag, feel the outline of its contents.*
> *"Have you got them?"*
> *"Yeah," I whisper.*

The drawer lies empty, not like in the memory. But the sensation of the drawstring bag is so fresh in my mind, just like it was yesterday.

"The pendant, the key, the hacky sack..." I count under my breath.

"And this", Venny calls to me from the bed. In his hand is a small black leather notepad with an elasticated band around it.

"That's your object, isn't it? That's what Pom sent to you?"

He nods grimly.

"Oh God, Venn. You shouldn't have opened the package. Shouldn't have touched it."

"Of course not. But I did anyway. The pages of the book, they're empty. But..."

"Have you been dreaming?" I ask, although from the look on his face I know he has. "What have you seen?"

"Things I wish I hadn't," he says. "Things about my past, before The Project came for me. Things my Mom made me do to cover up an affair she was having. I didn't really know what I was doing, didn't know the dangers of Erasing, but I did what she wanted anyway. My poor Dad, didn't see what was coming."

"I'm so sorry, Venn. You should never have had to relive that."

"Relive? I didn't even know it had happened until the dream. How can I not remember it happening?"

"It seems there are a lot of things we don't remember from our childhoods, Venn."

A spasm. The memory flows once again.

> *"Venny?" I whisper.*
> *"Yeah?"*
> *"I'm afraid."*
> *"I know. Me too."*
> *My eyes have adjusted to the darkness. The moonlight hits half of his face. The softness of his cheeks, the fullness of his lips, the dryness of his eye. I see it searching my own face, seeking to understand. To see me.*
> *"Olivia? It's going to be okay," he says, reaching for my shoulder.*
> *"You see me?"*
> *"I see you," he smiles.*
> *"Venn...what if it goes wrong? He—" Tears roll down my face.*
> *"It's going to be okay," he says firmly. "I promise. It has to be this way. I know what I'm doing. You know what you're doing."*
> *I'm scared. I don't want to go. But no. I have to remember who this is for.*
> *It's for Angel.*

"Angel, snap out of it." Venny shakes me out of my stupor. His face, older once again. "Tell me what's going on?"

"The dreams. They're leaking through to me. Can't seem to stop them," I mumble, head beginning to swim, the lines between then and now blurring. I don't fight them. This feels right.

I need to let go.

The memories find me again…

Two new faces peer around the doorframe.
"Are we doing this?" Nina whispers, throat tight with emotion. Poor Nina. I'm so sorry.
"Yes. I'm ready."
I take the first step. I'm terrified, but the numbness is coming back. I welcome it as I lead the way. The long walk to the gallows.

"We need to get you out of here," Venny says, hand firm on my shoulder. Somewhere in my catatonia I've walked down to the ground floor.
"No. No this is where I need to be. I need to follow them. The memories. Venn, I need your book."
Our eyes fall to the notebook. He doesn't offer it up. But doesn't resist either when I pull it from his grip. The leather's still warm from his hand.

I feel the grain of the wooden flooring. A fan rotates above us. Us. Many pairs of legs, crossed on the floor like mine. I hear the mumbling of voices. What are they saying? I can't make it out. Try. Focus. No, it's all soft and indistinct.

"What are you doing?" Venny asks, concern pouring out of him.
"Sit with me, Venn." My voice sounds like it's coming from far away. Another time. Another place.
Another me.

"Here, like this." A voice much closer cuts through the haze. She's right next to me.
"Here, close your hands over it." The pendant, I feel it between my palms. "Now listen to it, talk to it, pour yourself into it.

Venny's book in my hand. I clasp my hands over it. I hear its song.

"There's so much in there. A world within a world."

I hear you, Olivia. I'm coming for you.

***

I see them all.
The memories.
Dancing in the darkness.
There's an order to them.
A logic.

They were coming for her.
Olivia.
The Project was coming for her.
So we hid her.
Hid her in the objects.
Wrote her into the very fabric of these objects.
Where they would never find her.
Wrote her essence. I did it. She showed me how.
No wait. How is this even possible?
You can't Write a physical person into an object.
You can only Write a memory onto an object.
An Echo.

Oh.
Olivia. You were an Echo.
An Echo living inside…
Me.

How

Did

You

Get

Inside

Me

?

.

.

.

We're running. She's laughing. She's pulling me onwards by the hand. I pull back slightly.

"Come on," she grins. "Run away with me. Just you and me. We can do this!"

She pulls again. I don't want to go with her.

"Stop," I shout. "We can't do this. Don't be stupid. Mummy and Daddy will protect us. I promise."

She yanks at my arm again.

"Stop it! You're hurting me," I say. I push her away. Hard. She falls

back then slips against a tree. Our favourite tree.

Her head hits it first. The noise isn't loud like a bang. It's soft like a thud.

Fear runs through me.

We're running again. She's ahead of me now. She's wild. A hand on her bloody head.

'Help me. Help.'

I'm shouting at her to stop. She screams.

Then she falls to the ground.

No! I kneel beside her crumpled form on the ground. I try to look up, but still I can't see her face. Her breathing, so shallow.

She clasps her hands over my own. A white light flashes in my mind. I can't see anything.

But a voice, clear and sharp, pierces the haze.

Her voice.

"Remember me," she says. "Remember me."

I feel her slipping. Falling.

Into me.

I can feel her fading.

"NO!" I yell. "NO. DON'T LEAVE ME, PLEASE. I'M SORRY. I DIDN'T MEAN TO DO IT. DON'T LEAVE ME.

"OLIVIA!"

...

Heart pounding. Brain reeling. Eyes leaking. Mouth screaming. Hands grabbing. Body flinching.

"Douglas. Angel. Breathe. Breathe."

A voice. A face too. Coming into focus. Eyes. Lips. Hair. Dark hair. Cropped short.

Pom. Pom/Khun Su. My Khun Su.

And next to her, Mongkon.

My breathing is ragged, slowing, slowing. The room too. Slowing, slowing.

"That's it. Breathe."

Behind Pom-Su and Mongkon. Other people. Around me in a circle. Faces scared-sad-worried.

People. My people. Our people.

My Venny.

My Kaito.

Nina. My Nina…Your Nina.

Dhaval...

Oh, my Dhaval.

Oh God. No. Not mine anymore. Can't be mine. Can't be me anymore. Can't live with myself.

"I..."
They're silent. Hanging on my words.
"I..."
Tell them. They need to know.
"I killed Olivia. I...killed my sister."
There. Now it's out. Now move on.
No. I can't.
Their faces. So torn with confusion. With love. With history. With promises, and pain, and trust and wonder and joy and loss and minutes and years and 'where are you' and 'I miss you' and 'I'm with you' and 'I'm here' and 'you're there' and us and them and we and our and never and always and together and alone and self and Self and other and Other and I'm sorry and I'm sorry and I'm sorry I'm sorry I'm sorry I'm sorry...
And let go.
Pom's words. Not from now. From then.

> *"Listen to me: there is going to come a time on the path you are on when you will need to let go. To give in to the Echoes. You can't force them into a box, or to push them together to make sense. They will do it by themselves if you let go."*

I think I understand now. Stay and live with pain. Or let go and never feel again.
What I did. Can never be forgiven.
But I can give you life. New life. A new chance.
Have me, Olivia.

No. Angel, don't.

Yes. Have me. Live, Olivia. Live.
Just one last look at them, my people. Our beautiful people.
"I'm sorry. Goodbye."

And now.

I let go.

*

Part Three:

นักเดินทาง

(NAK DERN THANG)

[Traveller]

Chapter 29

Someone clears his throat. Deep and rumbly. Oh. It's me. Air is so dry here, I can taste it. Now I see it. Dust floating through the sunlight.

In the corner of the room someone's in a chair, chin on their chest. It's him. Dhaval. Can't be comfortable sleeping like that. His lips part slightly with each breath, in through his nose, then out of his mouth in a little hiss. Hypnotic to watch.

Oof! Back feels like I've been sleeping for a hundred years. Wonder what time it is? Light feels brand new, low like early morning. No sounds from the rest of the house.

The room's so empty: cabinet, chair (with man), bed with a simple sheet, pillow without a cover. I know exactly where I am though. Woken up here enough times. Swing feet out and steady myself for standing.

So quiet. Outside and in.

Slip out of bed, don't wake him up, creep to the landing. Floorboard gives a little creak under foot. Take the pressure off and try another one. That's better. Clever feet.

All the bedroom doors are closed. Full house?

Ah the bannister. So tempted to slide down like I used to. Never ended well but always so much fun. Ribs still ache at the memory.

Reach the ground floor. Half expect Khun Su to be coming around the corner, ready to tell me off. Old crow. Can't catch me now, can you?

Take a full lap of the house for old times' sake. But it's all empty. Empty, dusty, musty. Garden's much more inviting. Sounds. If I stand still I can make out the chirp of sparrows. And is that a myna? Chitter chatter, chitter chatter.

Now for the hard part. Open the front door without a noise. Not bad. Little bit of a clack on closing. Never mind. The veranda's still handsome. Sun-beaten and cracked, but lovely. These old Thai houses never look like they can last, but they do.

Breathe that air. Nature smells fill me up, so sweet this early in the day. Take a step forward, let the sun hit your face. Stretch your arms out and take it all in. Bliss. The biggest yawn ever. Good morning, everything.

Creep to the rear of the house. Thank goodness the veranda wraps almost all the way around. No need to get gravel on my bare tootsies.

Oh the garden! As big as I remember but so overgrown. Palms of every size, razor-edged leaves poking out everywhere. Grass is spiky under these soft soles.

Pick through to the bottom of the garden, my favourite place. There it is. Oh wow. My, you've grown haven't you? Look how wide your branches have spread. Sun can barely make it through your beautiful green leaves, like upside down hearts ending in long tails. Can just reach one on tiptoes. Didn't used to be able to do that. And your trunk, so wide, made of up thick snaky roots. Bark feels nice. Not knobbly like the ones back home. Thinner, somehow more like skin. So good that you're still here, old boy.

Now, where is it? Should be round the back, just about here. Yes! Faint but definitely still here. 'Olivia'. My name carved and wobbly. And beside it, 'Nina', and below, 'Venny', 'Kaito'. Took us so long to do it with our teenage hands and that big knife. Su would have been so angry. That's why we carved it on the back.

And here, one more name: 'Angel'.

Oh Dougie. Why did you do it? Why did you leave?

Can't think of that now. Follow the line directly down, down, down to the roots. There. A wide space between them, like fingers splayed out. A bowl-sized gap between the roots that disappear into the soil – soil now covered over with weeds, but below it is the treasure we buried for safe keeping all those years ago...

"Our old bo tree." A voice. Her voice.

"Still here. Still standing." I turn to her. There she is. Tired-looking, hair flat, arms wrapped around herself. "Didn't hear you sneaking up on me, Nina."

"Well, I can be pretty stealthy when I want to be. Plus I didn't sleep much. Still getting the dream."

The dream. Of course. Must help her with that. Help everyone. I move around the tree, not sure what else to do. Can't tell from her face what she's thinking. Don't want to scare her.

"You gave us a fright, y'know," she says, not moving from the grass. "What are you looking at over there?"

"Nothing." Fingers have moved back up to the trunk. The carvings feel softer than when we first did them. Like scars, healing skin. How long until they're completely gone, I wonder?

She steps towards the tree, and me. That look in her eyes, what is it? Like she's thinking, but not decided yet. I back away round the tree. She follows but stops at the carvings, kneels and reads, feels the outlines of the letters, making a soft circle of mine. Then something changes inside her. Rests her forehead against the bark. Little bits of sunlight find her through the leaves.

"It's you, isn't it?" she says, then: "And he's gone."

She knows. "How–"

"The kiss," she says, tears in her eyes. "By the pool, when you kissed me, it felt like...like something from long ago. I didn't trust what I thought. Should've. If I had, maybe he would still be here."

My heart feels fluttery, stomach queasy. I want to make her feel better, but am I the right person to do it? I touch her shoulder. She turns and rests her back against the bo tree. Lets me join her.

She looks at me, eyes all shiny, and says: "I don't know how, but somehow deep inside I understand. Maybe I always have. Now that I'm faced with it, it all seems so... he's gone. But you're back. I just...I don't know what I should be feeling more of. I mean what kind of a person am I that... but what

Angel did, I mean I don't know if I can ever forgive…"

I kiss her. Not to calm her down. Because I've missed her. Because I never wanted to hurt her when I left all those years ago, but there was no other way.

As selfish as it is, I kiss her. Because I can't not. She's mine, and I'm hers.

I feel her tickling inside my head. Looking for me. Just like she used to. She could always Read me the best.

But then she pulls away. "I…I can't," she says touching her lips. "I'm sorry."

"It's okay," I whisper, feeling the gulf of years between us.

She holds my face. "Olivia," she stares through the tears.

"I'm back," I say. My eyes are wet now too.

"The others," she whispers after a while. "We need to tell the others."

Her expression performs hopeful and sweet for me, but it also betrays her confusion. A new lump rises in my throat, but I smile through it as best as I can. "Sure," I say. "In a little while?"

We hold each other, curled up underneath our tree.

***

"My name is Olivia."

Quiet faces around the living room.

"We used to know each other, when we all first came to school here. I used to share a body with Angel. This is…I'm sorry I don't know how to properly–"

"You're doing fine," Nina says into my ear. Across the room, Kaito and Venny look worried. Next to them are these Pom and Mongkon people who showed up not long ago. Kaito says I can trust them. Then at the back of the room, leaning against the wall is Dhaval. He's biting the skin around his fingernail. I feel his eyes on me most strongly.

Venny got back from the school ten minutes ago. Must have left before sunrise because it's not even gone nine o'clock. Said he's sorted things so nobody would know Angel was there last night. Angel and me. 'Apparently I'm good at erasing video footage as well as memories', he joked. Though he wasn't smiling when he said it.

Then Nina gathered us all together, said everyone should take a seat because what I had to say was going to take some getting used to.

"How can you share a body?" Kaito says.

"It's possible," the Pom lady says. She's pretty, but with old eyes. Nina says she has the Echo of Khun Su inside her head. Makes sense, I guess. Mad sense. But who am I to judge?

"But," Kaito adds, "where's your body?"

"I…died. My Echo, it…" I freeze up, not sure how much to say. But the memories – they flow easily now.

"Come on," I say. "Run away with me. Just you and me. We can do

187

this. It's going to be wonderful!"

I can imagine the future, just Dougie and me, no need for adults telling us what to do, or horrible Mnemosyne people coming to take me away.

I pull again. Why won't he come?

"Stop," Dougie shouts. "We can't do this. Don't be stupid. Mummy and Daddy will protect us. I promise."

I pull at his arm again.

"You're hurting me," he cries, then pushes back. I lose my footing, trip on a root, and fall backwards.

My head hits first. The pain is so sharp I barely feel it. Everything goes blank for a second.

The need to run wakes me up and gets me back to my feet. Within a few steps the pain starts. It throbs like nothing I've felt before. Can't think properly. I hold my hand against the side of my head. It comes away slippy and red.

'Help me. Help,' I call to Dougie, to anyone who could be listening. Suddenly I'm so scared. A part of me doesn't want to believe this is happening, trying to stay numb.

He's shouting at me to stop. But I can't. Can't go back.

Then something seems to pop deep inside.

"It was an accident," Nina finishes for me, patting my hand. "Angel and Olivia were arguing one day, back in England. He pushed her. She tripped and fell against a tree and hit her head...Olivia died. Right before she was about to go, her Echo flowed into Angel. They became one."

I'm on the grass. Dougie's kneeling beside me. Everything is going cloudy at the edges. Why can't I breathe? Feel so sleepy. No! I don't want to sleep.

A final thought. An instinct.

I reach for his hands. Then push with my whole mind. Gather up every part of me, my life, and push it towards him. I feel myself sliding, tipping into his subconscious.

Please, Dougie. Please never forget me. I'm so scared.

"Remember me," I say. "Remember me."

"It happened so fast," I say. "They were coming to collect me, The Project. They knew about me, about what I could do. Dougie begged me to not run away. To stay and work things out. It was an accident, but he blamed himself."

Tears are running down my face. I don't want to relive this. Why do I have to? I only just got back, it's so unfair. Everyone is looking at me, their older faces hiding the young ones I used to know so well.

"So your Echo lived on in Angel," says Pom, the only person smiling.

I nod. "It was fine, for a time. We shared so easily. Lived in...what's the word?" Brain's still a little fuzzy.

"Harmony," she says.

"That's right. He kept it a secret from them as best as possible. But they found out eventually. So the therapy started. He was scaring our parents, saying things only I knew, accessing my memories like they were his own. It upset them, of course. They'd known for a long time he was different, that he could hold people's memories inside him like this. But now that it was my memories he was holding, enough was enough. They thought he was being cruel, when in fact he was just being who he *was*. So they told the therapist, The Project scout."

"Well hello there, Douglas. Or is it Olivia today, hmm?" the Dr Jansen says. Her teeth are crooked, breath smells. "Come take a seat here next to me. That's right. Now, your mummy tells me you've been having a little trouble. Don't you worry. I can help you keep all those busy thoughts nice and tidy."

"To start with it was just visualisation sessions," I continue, "teaching him to build walls inside his mind. To separate himself off from the Echoes. From me."

Pom shakes her head as I talk, an angry expression like she understands every word I say.

"It made things worse. Before, there was a...a harmony. But when the walls started being built inside his mind, everything started to break down. Which is ironic, I guess. That's when I started to wake up. When I started to take over his body. The more walls they taught him to build, the worse it got. Eventually they saw they weren't helping. He needed treatment the Weaver therapist couldn't give. But there was somewhere that could help. On the other side of the world where they had people who could properly do something about it."

"Here," says Venny. As serious a man as he was a boy.

"Yes," I say.

Angel's memory blooms.

"...and you must be Douglas."

He turns to look at me. Grey eyes. He holds his hand out to me.

"It's okay," he says, like he knows why I'm hesitating, then reaches out further to take my hand. It's been a long time since I've touched someone with nothing bad happening. Feels strange. Not bad strange.

"You see?" he says. "Nothing to worry about. You know why? Because I'm just like you, Douglas."

I guess I look surprised, because he makes a big smile.

"My name's Matthew Bordelais. I'll be coming with you on the plane to Bangkok. I teach at the school."

"The Mnemosyne Project Bangkok hadn't been open long at that point,"

Pom says "But even at that early stage, it was quickly becoming known for its success in treating young Weavers. Its methods were largely undisclosed. Experimental, but they seemed to work."

"What do you mean?" Kaito says, looking lost.

"Children with traumatic awakenings of their abilities," Pom continues, looking at us all, one after the other. "Not given space to come into their own, in their own natural time. The treatment young people received at the school was...efficient. She didn't know. Su," she says tapping a finger at her temple "She didn't know until it was too late what was happening at the school."

"Erasure," Venny says, looking down at his feet.

Pom nods, then looks at me to continue the story.

"All of us were at the school for a reason," I say. "Everyone had problems they had been sent to be treated. I was maybe the biggest problem of us all. By the time it took The Project to really understand what was happening to Angel, to understand what I was, who I was, it was too late. Because you all had seen me. All three of you saw me, whenever I woke up within Angel. You accepted me without question. We became friends." I squeeze Nina's hand. "So what started out as Angel's problem, became everyone's problem. To treat Angel, meant all of you had to be treated as well."

"Erased," the Mongkon guy whispers. Everything about him seems different here. Not like the slimy guy at the club and the school that I saw in Angel's memories. Here he's calm, quiet.

I nod. "They needed to cut me out. Like cancer. To Erase me from Angel's mind."

Chairs squeak against the linoleum and one by one everyone heads out of the classroom and into the humid afternoon.

"Oh Mr Sermanni. A word?" Mr Bordelais says.

My blood freezes. Nina, K and Venny look at me, but I motion for them to keep going.

"Close the door, please," he says. His face, handsome, kind even. "Take a seat."

As I do, someone new walks in the classroom and closes the door.

He has blond hair, a white shirt and a dark tie.

"Douglas," Mr B says. "This is Ben, he works for The Project too."

The Agent looks down at me. A little smile creases, but he doesn't say anything. Just grabs a seat and places it directly behind me, then settles into it.

"Ben and I are going to help you with the trouble you've been having. Looks like we still have a little work left to do. To stop these 'episodes," Mr B says. His grey eyes, they look so full of compassion. But I know what his words really mean.

This is it, what we've known is coming. What we've prepared for. My heart is thudding and yet I feel numb. I've fought for so long, but no point in running, not any more.

Olivia said this is how it has to be.

They've already taken so much of her from me. Only a few grains of her essence are left in my mind.

I feel fingers reach from behind, clamping on to my temples.

"Now, we just want you to relax, okay?" Mr B says softly. "Everything is going to be just—"

Goodbye Olivia.

Goodbye Oli

My chin's trembling badly, but I have to carry on. "For the Erasure to work properly, for every bit of me to be cut away, that meant cutting me away from you too. I'm so sorry, it's all my fault. I didn't want to go. I know that wasn't fair to Angel or you, but I was scared. I felt so guilty about what me being in his head was doing to him. But I could feel that he didn't want me to leave either. And neither did any of you, bless you. So that's when we came up with the plan. To hide me away where The Project couldn't find me. We were so young, but so clever too.

"We stopped you being Erased?" Kaito says, nose scrunched in confusion.

"No. The Project did Erase me. They did their job well. Erased me from everyone's mind, Angel's, yours, Nina's, Venny's. But what they didn't know was that my Echo had already been stored away. Duplicated and imprinted within objects that they would never suspect."

I feel the grain of the wooden flooring. A fan rotates above us. Us. Many pairs of legs, crossed on the floor. They all look at me so sadly. I smile back, because I know this is how it has to be.

I reach inwards to Angel, to show him how it is done.

"Here, like this," I whisper inwardly to him. "Yes. Here, close your hands over it."

The pendant. We feel it between our palms. Me and Angel.

"Now listen to it, talk to it, pour me into it. There's so much in there. A world within a world."

"Angel embedded them into the objects?" Kaito smiles.

"I taught him how. You see, I'm a Cold Reader and Writer. They were my talents, before I died. I could Read the Echoes left behind on objects. But I could imprint them there too."

"It's a very rare ability," Mongkon says.

I shrug. "That's why The Project wanted me so badly in the first place, I guess. And it's how my Echo flowed out of me and into Angel. But Angel, when he let me take control, I was able to Cold Read and Write from his body too. Well enough, because he's a Generic, you see."

"He thinks it's a failing," says Pom. "Being a generalist, but it's not. He's so much more." She looks at Mongkon, who smiles back.

I continue: "On the night before I was going to be Erased, we all came together, right here in the boarding house, and Cold Wrote as much of me, my essence, into objects; ordinary things that nobody would look twice at. The pendant, the key, the hacky sack, the notebook."

"But what about the other memories in there? The ones we were dreaming of?" Venny asks. "Kaito's song, the memory of what I did to my father?"

"You have to understand, Venny," I say. "These objects weren't just somewhere to hide *me*. They were also somewhere to hide anything we didn't want The Project to take away. The agents were Erasing all kinds of things from you – all because they said cutting out the 'bad' stuff would make you better. So I hid away the memories you asked me to. Memories so important, good or bad, that you were scared of losing. Memories that you wanted to discover again, when you were older, stronger. Now."

"Then the objects were hidden away," Kaito says. In return I look over at Pom.

She nods, then says: "Su hid them. She walked in on you all in the middle of the night, when Olivia was writing herself onto the objects. I can remember her surprise even now."

"She was so angry," I blurt out, the image of Khun Su's shocked face burned on my mind.

"Yes, but not with you. Not with any of you. She loved you so much. Knew how badly you needed safety."

"Safety?" Nina laughs. "Then why didn't she stop us getting Erased?"

"You think she didn't try?" Pom raises her voice, then collects herself. "You think she wasn't punished by The Project for overstepping the mark? She tried her best, pleaded with them to find another way. She saw what was happening to you, she was terrified for you. You were like my...her children. But she couldn't stop it. So she did what she could. She took the objects as you all asked, kept them secret all these years, away from The Project's reach. Until now. I fulfilled her wish. I sent you all the objects, to bring you back to the path that you set yourselves on so long ago. And now here you all are."

She smiles wide as she looks around the room. Nina looks at me with something so full and hopeful in her eyes. A new memory sparks, her Echo of the Songkran water fight so many years ago.

"Hey guys," Angel calls all singy-songy from behind us. "Look who I found."

Slow motion. Venny and me turn our heads. There's Angel, t-shirt sticking to him, but he's practically dry next to Kaito who looks like a chubby drowned rat, dripping from head to toe, but with the biggest grin. It's too late before we get why he's so happy.

Giant water balloons, all wobbly and jelly-like, flying in our direction. And then time speeds up. Sploosh!

"That's it!" Venny spits. "This means war!"

We run towards them, screaming at the top of our lungs, water pistols ready. Angel and Kaito run to the boarding house, laughing and shouting as they go.

Everyone is quiet now. Letting it all sink in. I've told them enough. I'm done.

"Where is he?" Dhaval's voice comes from the back of the room, breaking the silence. "Where's Dougie? I know this thing is huge, but…but what is wrong with you?! You're just sitting around listening to this–" He stops himself, looks around at us all, then rushes towards me. Before Nina can stop him, his hands are all over my face and running over my scalp. His eyes are all red and white, searching my face.

"Dougie please," he says, teeth bared, fingers digging. "Where are you? I don't care what you did just… come back. Dougie."

"Back off!" Nina shoves Dhaval away.

He holds his hands up, turns from side to side. "What is wrong with you people?" he shouts again.

"You think we don't care?" Kaito splays his arms. "We're just trying to figure this out. I mean, who the fuck are you anyway? You've been on the scene for like, five minutes. We've known Angel most of our lives. So don't come in here with your Flatline judgement–"

Soon everyone's on their feet, shouting and pointing.

"Stop," I say too quietly. It shouldn't be happening like this. They're being torn apart. I didn't want this. "Please stop. Stop. I can't hear him anymore!"

To my surprise everyone stops. "I can't hear Angel anymore," I say again, looking from face to face. "I can see his memories, but his voice…it's like he's let go completely. Fallen away, somewhere so deep that I can't reach him. I think he's gone."

"Here," Pom says walking towards me. There and then I don't see the young woman with short hair. I see Khun Su. Her arms open wide to hug me. I fold into her.

"I can't hear him anymore!" I say over and over and over. She rubs my back and tells me to 'breathe, shhh shhh shhh, it's okay, just breathe'. After a while, when I've calmed down a bit, she lifts my head.

"May I try?" she says.

I nod. We sit on the floor cross legged. I hold my hands out to her, palms up. She covers them with her own hands, tells me to close my eyes. I feel her. Like the most gentle buzz of electricity. Calling for him. For Angel. After long minutes we open our eyes. Everybody else has gathered round, but this time they're not looking at me. All eyes are on Pom, who just shakes her head. Dhaval is the first to get up. He rubs his forehead, looks unsure what to do next. Then he stares down at me, a different look in his eyes. I think for the first time he sees me. Not Angel. He covers his mouth. I try to say something but he holds out a hand to stop me.

Then he turns and leaves the room.

Chapter 30

Today was a good day. A life in a day.

After last night, anything would've been better. Silent tears, whispering around corners, the staring and questioning. I understood it though. I miss him too.

But today something seemed to click. I accepted it. Quiet at first, but then the relief. A little sadness. Not for me though. Well, maybe a little. But mostly for them. For their road ahead.

It started as it's now ending: with Nina. Waking in each other's arms. Her hair was all over the place, I couldn't help but laugh. Which woke her up. Then she laughed too. The bed's so small. There was barely room for this body as a teenager, let alone how with its long hairy legs and broad hairy chest and smelly hairy man pits. But Nina didn't seem to mind. Just like she never seemed to mind. She just sees me, who I am inside.

Tell me about us, she said, staring at the ceiling.

So I did.

I told her about how she was the first one to notice me, to properly understand who I was. I told her about the way we used to sneak into the garden at night, down to the very bottom where our tree was, how we decided it was our tree when we read about the sacredness of bo trees, how we prayed to Nang Ta-Khian – the Thai tree spirit – to forgive us before we carved our names into the tree's bark.

I told her how we shared our first kiss in an unwatched corner of the schoolyard. Well, we thought it was unwatched. With each story I told her, it was like we took one more step back to the time when it all happened, when we were young and scared and surprised. In many ways we still are those things.

But I also feel the difference between us now. We used to be the same age, mentally, but time has moved on for her. For me it's stood still for all these years I've been dormant. I'm catching up fast, and yet when I look at Nina I see the distance in her eyes, feel the road she's had to walk without me.

I asked her to get me up to speed, hoping to close the gap.

So she did.

She told me about her life in Europe, how it was difficult at first, finding who she was as a Project Reader, learning how to please them while clinging on to any shred of independence she could find. She told me about her art, how it makes her feel alive, but how afraid she feels that The Project could take it away from her.

She told me how it feels to be here and now, with Angel gone and me back. How she and Angel argued the last time they talked, how confused she was. To be happy and regretful all at the same time.

But how for the first time, she wasn't thinking about what comes next.

Wasn't thinking about what happened when we got out of bed, or when tomorrow comes, or the day or year after. How right now, this very second, is enough.

Look at you, I said. I'm so proud of you. My beautiful girl. You've got such a lot to live for.

When I said those things, I realised how old I feel. And then I thought, when did that happen? When, in the little moments that have been my life since dying, have I grown up? But I have, I feel it.

***

With Kaito, I ran. In the midday heat. Which wasn't the best idea.

I found him in the garden not long after I got out of bed. Nina had headed out for food. Venny was still sleeping. Pom and Mongkon, I didn't know where they were – seemed to have some conversations with Venny then left. As for Dhaval...

Anyway there was Kaito, walking back and forth across the lawn like an animal in a cage. He walks the same way he used to as a boy, kicking his feet out and down as if he'd been swishing through leaves. At a distance, with my eyes scrunched up, I saw him just as he was, but the closer I got the more I saw the man he'd become.

I called out as I made the last few steps. He stopped and looked at me blankly. It'd been decades since I had seen him looking so... what's that word when someone is full of their own thoughts?

We just stood facing each other. I could practically feel how conflicted he was about me being here. But he didn't say anything apart from, Wanna go for a run?

I didn't have any kit with me. This body didn't seem ready for exercise after the past few days. But I said yes, that there was nothing I'd rather do more.

So we ran. For the first few minutes we did it like adults do – one foot in front of the other, boring running. It all changed when I tagged him on the shoulder and charged off down the lane towards the main street. He didn't even question it, just bombed after me.

He tagged me as I went round the corner of the 7-Eleven. I was running so fast I almost knocked over an old man.

I shouted at Kaito, telling him it wasn't fair to tag me at a corner. He did some funny backward jogs and stuck his tongue out. I sped after him, sweat pouring off me. I chased him the full length of the street, jumping over drain covers. A *soi* dog ran along beside me for a while, barking as if telling me to Go! Go! Go! I caught Kaito just as we broke free of the street. All the energy I'd used to reach him finished with an almighty slap on his bottom. He yelped like a spaniel.

I ran off – gripping my hands together in victory – in the direction of a grid of rice paddies. The workers didn't even blink as I sprinted along the divide between the wet green fields. Half way along he caught up with me in true Kaito style – by jumping on my back. I had a split second's warning so tried to stay upright but it didn't work. We both crashed to the ground and rolled on to our backs, groaning and laughing and slapping each other on any available body parts. It took ages for us to catch our breaths.

On the slow and sweaty walk back to the house, we spoke about the future. Kaito wanted to know what the next few days had in store; I was more interested in what he wanted to do with the rest of his life.

He told me how he was thinking of taking a trip to Japan. Finally after so many years away, he wanted to speak to his father. To see if there was anything there to...what did he call it...to salvage. He explained that the memory Angel returned to him, as much as it reopened old wounds, it had reminded him of the importance of heritage. But it was more than that, he said. It was about what the future meant to him now. That it felt there were different possible futures for him, more than he used to think he could have.

I said I knew what he meant.

***

With Venny, all I wanted to know about was his family. When I found out he was a daddy, *Daddy Venny*, I had such a mix of feelings. So happy for him, but also sad for me to have missed all this growing up he'd done. I didn't tell him the sad part, of course. He seemed sad enough all on his own.

I'm so scared of screwing up my son, he said as we drank coffee on the veranda. He had a nasty cigarette in his hand.

Jamal's such a good kid, he said. I asked him to tell me about him.

So he did.

He told me how unexpected Tia's pregnancy had been, how it had thrown him for a complete loop, made him so scared. How he thought that fatherhood would never be an experience allowed for him. How the first time he held Jamal wasn't like in the movies – he didn't feel an immediate connection like new fathers are supposed to, because all he thought was, *Right now is probably the only time in your new life that if I accidentally Erase your memories, it won't matter; because you don't have any yet.* How that being his very first thought made him want to pass Jamal back into Tia's arms and walk away.

He told me how only through being there for Jamal, day by day, changing nappies, bathing, holding him, had he been able to get through. Routine, commitment and vigilance, he said. He also said how his wife Tia has been the most inspiring person he's ever known, how she has always accepted his faults, his quietness, but still thought the best of him. How he wants to tell her everything, what he really does for The Project, how he's struggled with not telling her all these years when she's given him so much, how scared he is about screwing up Jamal like his parents did him.

He told me about the dream he'd been having every time he'd slept since he touched the notebook. How he knew it was all true, that he really did use his abilities to Erase parts of his dad's memories to hide his mother's affair.

196

How he knew he was going to have to face them with this when he went home. Because he couldn't let the past define him anymore.

Then he told me how he never usually talks like this. So open.

I said he could tell me anything, like he used to when he was young. I said that he was a great daddy, and the fact he had got all these fears meant he was never going to slip. I told him that he needed to tell Tia everything, how she deserved to know the person she was sharing her life with. Secrets are the things that bring us the most trouble. They push our trauma deeper.

I told him how I wished I could help him more, but that at least there was one thing I could do for him: I could stop the dream. How, he asked. I said it was more of a feeling than exactly knowing how. I asked if he trusted me. He said yes.

So I held my hands to the sides of his head and listened for the dream. It didn't take long to find. After all, it was sort of me who put it there. It felt all jittery, trapped. So I pulled on it, teased it out of the deep corner of his mind – his subconscious – then let it free.

When we opened our eyes again I explained that the dreams only happened because the memories were caught in the wrong place. They need to be set free into the awake part of our minds, where we can properly think about them, use logic and reasoning to understand them.

It's the same as trauma, I said. If we can pull our traumas out of our subconscious and into the light, their power fades. I said I could teach him, teach all of them, how to do it. He asked how I knew that. I said I wasn't exactly sure how. Some of it was my knowledge. But some of it was Angel's. Oh, he said. Then he looked sad again. I know it's because I said Angel's name.

***

Dhaval found me.

I presumed he'd already left, but as I stepped outside the house for some fresh air, there he was. Halfway up the drive, hands in pockets. Everything about his body language suggesting he had something to say.

He started by asking me to walk with him. I accepted without question. He was leaving for good, he said. A taxi was due to pick him up from the town centre.

We walked together on the roadside.

I should hate you for taking him away, he said eventually. I understood, I replied, that I would too in his position. He looked at me for a long time, searching my face again for any signs of Angel. Then carried on walking.

Despite the tension and confusion written all over Dhaval, I found his presence calming. Maybe it was the ghost of Angel's feelings for him; he had found Dhaval something of an oasis. I told Dhaval that.

He shook his head and laughed, said something about being 'quiet, nice Dhaval'. Many people saw him that way. Not the man who wanted his own adventures, his own excitement. The truth, he said with scrunched-up eyes, was that he had been bored with life. Had been for quite some time. Then he met Angel, a strange and awkward man who was weighed down by secrets. Angel didn't just intrigue Dhaval, the very fact of him offered a glimmer of something new and different.

Dhaval said it was no wonder he so readily absorbed the memory Angel Wrote on him. That he followed it so willingly halfway around the world.

I offered to cut the Echo away, but Dhaval shook his head, said it wasn't pulling on him any more. Said he could tell the difference between an Echo and his own memories now. That he wanted to keep the Echo. A souvenir, he shrugged then kicked a stone along the road.

He was angry: that Angel hadn't trusted him with the truth from the start; that things might have turned out differently; that he was never given a chance. He could handle the truth about Weavers, he wasn't afraid.

I reached for his shoulder and explained that this was only part of the reason for Angel's silence. That what really terrified him was what The Project does. Secrecy was the only protection he could offer, to protect Dhaval from the long arm of The Project.

Ironic, Dhaval said, that the secrecy which first enticed him, proved to be the downfall of their relationship.

A taxi was already waiting by the 7-Eleven when we arrived.

I asked what he would do now. He looked around at the small town, tracking a line from the ground, to the trees, up to the sun beating high above.

'We barely knew each other'.

That's all he said before climbing in the car.

***

I'm here again, at the bo tree at the bottom of the garden. Finally decided on what comes next.

As the day passed, part of me struggled to hold on. To the idea that maybe there is a future for me here, just like Kaito said: a future I didn't think I could have. That part of me has tried to hold on so tightly, to find any possible way to make it true. But it can't. I've realised it can't be true. The most surprising thing is the relief. So wonderful.

That's why I'm here, pushing my fingers deep into the soil in the gap between the roots. Pulling out the weeds to dig deeper, searching and sweating, praying it's still there.

For a sweaty second I think it's gone, that it's been found by someone else. The thought makes me feel desperate, so I dig and dig, but then I hit the box – my nails find it with a *dunk*. I scrabble to find an edge, then pull with all this body's strength – and up it comes, breaking through the soil decades after I buried it.

I pat the bo tree's trunk. *Thank you. For keeping them safe all these years.*

Then I hear feet crunching on the grass. My three friends. I don't need to turn around to know it's them, but I do. They look at me with a mixture of expression – Kaito with a questioning smile, Venny with a knitted brow, and Nina with what looks like the beginnings of understanding.

"This must look odd," I grin, swiping a dirty hand across my forehead. I stand up and take a few steps towards them. The four of us are shaded by the tree – little spots of light from the gaps in the leaves flicker on our faces and clothes.

"What's that?" Kaito points at the red metal box in my hands. I try to sweep the worst of the soil off it, but it's still caked in the stuff, filling the rim, the handle, and the lock at the very top of the box. But dirty as it is, I can feel its power, the quiet but sure vibration of the box and its contents.

Then suddenly the sadness returns. I think it shows because they all take a little shuffle towards me.

"This," I manage, "this is what we did. You all, me, Angel. This is our pact."

I shake the box from side to side, making the things inside rattle. They stare at it, trying to figure it out. Nina seems to be the first to get it. That's my girl.

"It's not over is it?" she says in his low voice.

It makes my throat tighten. I can't help but smile. Seeing them here, grown up, life written all over them. My brave friends, who have come back to where it all began, finally ready for what needs to be done. To honour the pact we made together all those years ago.

"No, it's not over," I whisper. "We weren't the only ones to be Erased."

And now all three begin to understand.

"Here," I say, holding the box out towards them. "Let me help you see. Hold on to me."

Little looks are shared between them then they place their hands on my arms. I close my eyes, feel them do the same, then reach out with that part of myself that allowed all this to happen – I reach out with my gift, so that the box can tell its stories through me.

***

Once heard, the stories become quiet again. We come back to ourselves under the bo tree.

I feel complete. The stories have been heard. My job is done. Because in hearing the truth of their stories, I finally hear it clearer than ever before: my own truth. It's calling to me.

"Now you remember," I say. They look back at me, their truth shining in their eyes. At first they look stunned by it, blinking into its light. But in mere moments I see them begin to bear it with a mixture of pride and sadness. That's the right reaction, I suppose. Their road ahead has been laid. Or rather it was more than twenty years ago. But now they've rediscovered the path.

"I wish…" I start, but I don't continue.

I hand the box to Venny, then head back to the house, telling the three of them I need to shower off the dirt. At the door I take one quick look back then head inside.

Ten minutes pass. The shower's been running all this time but I've not got in. Instead I'm just standing in the bedroom by the cabinet, staring down at a phone with my heart racing.

It's Angel's phone. Fancy and digital. Finally, I find the courage, pick it up, search the contacts. There she is.

I click on the name and after a long empty pause I hear the dial tone. My throat tightens. She answers on the second ring.

"Hello? Douglas?"

"..."

"Dougie, are you there?"

"I...yes. I'm here."

"Oh my goodness. Oh Dougie. Are you okay?"

"...I'm...I'm okay. I'm sorry I haven't called until now. It's been..."

"Oh Dougie we've been so worried. Wh– where are you now?"

"Near Bangkok. I'm still with friends. I'm...safe."

"You left so suddenly, and then your message…why did you leave?"

"I needed to get some things straight. Ab...about my life."

"Oh Dougie. Please come home."

"..."

"There's nothing for you out there."

"Stop..."

"We're here for you. You know that, don't you?"

"..."

"Please, please come h-"

"I've missed you, Mummy.

"…Oh. I've missed you too, Dougie."

"I miss everything. The family meals, the long road trips, falling asleep in the bed between you and Daddy. I remember it all, you know? Even as far back as when Dougie was only tiny. I remember all that way back."

"..."

"I miss those times. When it was just us. Before...before all this. Before they came for me."

"..."

"It's funny, I even miss you telling me off when I was naughty. What was it I used to say that really made you furious? 'It's all a bit of fun'. Gosh that got you every time. Do you remember that, Mummy?"

"..."

"Of course, I didn't like making you and Daddy angry. But you always forgave me. You understood it was just who I was. Being a little naughty. And messy and silly. That you wouldn't change anything about me really. Even the strangeness about me."

"..."

"I know you miss me too. That you just wanted to help me. And Dougie."

"..."

"Don't cry. Please. I don't want to make you cry. I wanted you to know, I just…I want you to know, Mummy…I miss you and Daddy. And that it's all okay."

"…Olivia?.."

"That's right. It's me."

"How...how–"

"It doesn't matter. I just wanted to hear your voice. Do you…do you remember what you used to say to me before I fell asleep?"

"…"

"I would be all snuggled up and warm between you and Daddy. And you would say–"

"Night night, pet light."

"That was it. I just wanted to hear you say that."

"Olivia…"

"Dougie's coming home. I promise."

"But–"

"Night night, Mummy."

***

Today was a good day.

A life in a day.

"Who was that?" Nina walks into the room. She's so beautiful. I wish...no. No more wishing.

"Can you do something for me?" I say. "Come sit with me?"

"What is it?" she says settling next to me on the bed. I expect confusion, though there's no question on her face. She's too smart for that. Something in her eyes that says 'don't tell me. I already know. Don't tell me'.

"I think it's time–"

"Please…" she starts but I stop her by reaching for her hand, placing it on my cheek. I feel her searching for me again, a tiny electrical buzz in the middle of my mind, like she always used to.

And so I open up to her. Completely. And she to me.

We stay like this for a lifetime.

***

Nina eventually slides slowly away from me on the bed.

"You coming back into our lives has been like finding a lost part of my soul," she whispers. "A connection I never knew I lost. My best friend, my first love. It's opened something new for me. Now I think I understand why I've always been this way, lost and searching for something. For someone."

She reaches for my hand then continues: "At first I thought it was you who I've been searching for all this time. And part of it *is* you. Finding you, holding you, kissing you, has made more sense to me than pretty much anything else in my life. But it's more than that. When you were Erased from

201

my mind, I didn't just lose you. I lost part of myself. I lost my ability to trust. To properly give myself to someone. But now, maybe, I've found myself again. And I have you to thank for that."

"Nina," I say, tears spilling down my face. Because while her words are the most beautiful I've ever heard, they also sound like goodbye.

"You didn't ask for any of this, Olivia. For The Project to come for you. To die. To be reborn within your brother's mind. To fall in love. The only crime you've ever committed is wanting to live."

"You could always Read me better than anyone else," I say, gulping for air.

She hugs me.

"You know I can't stay," I whisper into her ear.

She squeezes me tighter still. I feel the wetness of her tears on my neck.

"I know," she says, holding my face in her hands. I'm aware once again of the dark rings under her eyes. My poor girl.

"You need rest. But you still can't, can you. Because of the dream?
She nods.

I explain how I can help, just as I did Venny. How I can teach her how to help others. She looks afraid.

"I...I don't want to lose the dream. Not again."

"You won't forget me".

"Promise?"

"I promise."

I bring my forehead into contact with hers, and listen deep within her. I find the dream, fluttering within her like a trapped butterfly. Then I tease it out and set it free within her mind where it can finally settle and not do any more harm.

I open my eyes and look directly into Nina's. All pain has lifted.

"I still remember," she smiles.

"Then that's all that matters. And now, my beautiful girl, I need your help."

A fresh tear finds its way down her cheek. "I know," she says. "I know."

Today was a good day.
A life in a day.
Which is enough.

Chapter 31

These objects are pain.
These objects are trauma.

***

Empty brown pill bottle.
'Red Wine Woman'.
Stranger at a bar. Dwelling on aborted suicide attempt.
Treatment: Subject is not patient.
Extract:

The salty tang of the painkillers makes me choke as I crunch down on them, awakening me to the reality of what I'm doing. My eyes fly open as I gag and spit the contents of my mouth down my front. I suck in a ragged breath then release a guttural roar.

***

VHS tape, illegible handwriting on label
Bradley Stevens.
Early-20s, credit controller. Acute anxiety sufferer, agoraphobic episodes triggered by trauma sustained in youth. Sexual assault victim. Subject has history of entering fugue state during triggered episodes.
Treatment: Free and cued recall exercises accompanied by Eye Movement Desensitisation and Reprocessing, plus therapeutic cross-referencing to Echoes of safety and resolution.
Extract:

He wants me to sit beside him while we watch cartoons. He says I'll see better from the couch, but I can see fine from the floor.

The couch smells smoky. It makes me feel sick. When is Dad coming home?

"There, that's better isn't it. A much better view from up here," he says.

***

Angel.

***

High top canvas shoe, no laces.
Melissa Huang.

Eleven-years-old. Catatonia and periods of extreme negativism for six-months following death of close friend. Events surrounding incident still under investigation. Subject referred for Recovered Memory Therapy.

Treatment: Deep 'calls' to reach subconscious structures. Primary aim is to recover reliable intelligence for manslaughter investigation. Secondary aim to bring subject out of catatonic state.

Extract (fractionated):

Radiator

Seagull cry

Blue

"What's that?"

Mirror.   Blood |

doolB. rorriM

"..."

"Melissa. Let us in!"

***

Plastic figurine, heroic pose.
Gillian Landing.
Babysitter. Mother. Elderly woman formerly resident in Kitsford, Sussex. Echoes Read serially during childminding sessions, including formative experiences: marriage, childbirth, trauma sustained during WWII firewatching. Consequently dismissed from babysitter employment by Lisa Sermanni.
Treatment: Subject was not patient.
Extract:

The sirens! Their wail coming from all directions, disorientating me even more. But I can still hear her. Jean! She's trapped, oh dear lord, she's trapped. Beneath the charred rubble.

Quick girl, get yourself back on your feet. Jean needs you. Breathe through the smoke even though your lungs are burning. There! Underneath that collapsed wall. Her leg, oh dear Lord!

***

Angel.
Hear me.

***

Cinema stub, single.
Adeola Akoye.
Mid-40s. Barrister, mother, divorcee. Witnessed parents being murdered during hostage situation in cinema screening while on holiday in California. Functioning alcoholic, flashbulb episodes experienced during work has led to compulsory referral for RMT.

Treatment: RMT techniques to treat psychogenic amnesia to reconnect neural pathways. Careful increments of exposure to underlying engrams to avoid violent flashbacks.

Extract:

"Mum, please. Wake up!"

I'm grabbing and shaking her but she won't wake up. Her blouse is so shiny and wet where she was hit. I don't know what to do.

"Help her, please!"

"You shut your damn mouth!" The man with the gun looks at me with eyes wide open. I can see all his teeth. He has his arm round Daddy.

"Sweetie, be quiet for me. Just stay down there," Dad says.

Then there's another bang.

***

Black SLR camera, broken lens.
Kieron Marber.
Journalist. Husband. Father. Held hostage by militant forces for 26-months, during which time beaten and starved. Consequently blocked out life before capture.

Treatment: Issue 'Calls' to deep memory system, aiming to ease biography back into sense of self. Treatment successful, but not sanctioned. Transferral of trauma Echoes to therapist led to memory redaction via Erasure.

Extract:

Oh God. This is it.

My heartbeat suddenly ███████████. *I didn't think I was capable of feeling this again, but I do.* ███ *sparks up and down my* ███████ *body.*

***

Angel.
Please.

***

Watchstrap, missing buckle.

Kerrie-Anne P–

***

You have to wake up.

***

Who is that?

Who is saying that?

The objects. Must keep listening to them, categorising them.

***

Watchstrap, missing buckle.

Kerrie-Anne Proctor.

Mid-teens. Dissociati–

***

The Safe.
You have to destroy–

***

Stop it! Stop talking! Stop calling for me.
Me…
Who is me?
Back to work. The objects need to be tended to. These objects are pain.
These objects are trauma.
Where was I?

I...
There is an I, isn't there? A me.
How could I forget?

***

Angel.
Hear me.

***

Angel. Is that right? Partly right, I think. I...
The objects. These objects are pain. These objects are–
Whose pain? Mine? Me? I?
Empty pill bottle. VHS tape. Figurine. Sneaker. Camera. And more besides. Handfuls more.
Handfuls of pain. Handfuls of trauma. Hands, what are they again?
Mine? No. Others. Their pain, their trauma. Them. Me. Theirs. Mine. Must keep them separate.
Angel. Self. Different from Other. I think. *I*. Think.

***

That's right.
Find yourself.

***

Who's there? Can't see you? Can barely hear you. Feel though. Yes I can feel you. You.
These objects are... all together. In a...wooden trunk. I know this trunk, remember the feel of its old structure. The lid, propped open on its hinges.
These objects. Pain. Trauma. I...I put them here. Yes. I. Me. Put other people's pain, other people's trauma in here. To keep them separate. Locked away in the...dark?
If dark, then there should be...what's it called?

***

Light

***

Yes that's it. Thank you, Voice.
Daylight. Look at that. Oh wow. So warm. So soft. So beautiful. Beauty.

I like that.

There's more than the objects. More than the trunk. A room. The trunk is in a room. I...I am in a room. Bed. Room. Bedroom. My bedroom.

Bed. To my right (right is a side yes?) is unmade. Duvet. Funny word. Duvet. Doo Vay. No 't'. It's rumpled, still bearing the impression of a...child.

The child was me. My childhood bed. Yes.

Teddy bears. Glassy eyes and fixed smiles.

To my left. (The other side). Light. Where it's coming from. A win...dow. A bay window. Fancy.

And beyond.

Stand to see more. Standing. Legs, feet, posture, back, arms out to steady. Oh arms, and hands too! Look at them. Feeling with the hands. A whole body.

A stretching feeling above. A...smile. A smile belongs to a face. How strange. Yet right. The face feels...it feels. Ha! Hair, on top, middle and bottom. Stubbly. Nose, long and proud. Eyes. Ouch! Fingers in eyes a bad combination.

The light. One step. Whoa! Two step, three step, four. The window. Out...side. (Another side!) Outside is not inside.

Oh how beautiful. Greens and blues and greys. Garden. Sky. Path. A bigger green beyond in the hazy distance. Then the tallest green. A...tree. Look at you. Handsome.

How could I forget this? How could I forget...I/me/mine?

This place. Everything I could need. The world. My world. I created this.

***

The Safe.

***

Yes. I feel safe. Safe. Safe in The Safe.

Oh.

This isn't everything. There is more. Outside. Yes, there, a door. Yellow and nice. I made that too. Just as I made everything in here. Apart from the objects. They belong to people. These objects are pain. These objects are trauma.

They need to be kept Safe.

***

No.

***

No? Don't be silly. Yes. Of course Yes. How can it be No?!

***

Let go.

***

Let go? Why? How? Who are you? I shouldn't let go. Have always held on. Always. Never let go, always hold, keep Safe, maintain difference between me/mine and them/theirs.

***

Only way is to let go. Must–

***

No! Never let go. Let go...
Someone told me that. Not long ago. Told me, the person I was before...
These objects...
These objects...
Empty pill bottle. VHS tape. Figurine. Sneaker. Camera.
These objects hurt. These objects are *in* pain. Other people's trauma. Why do I keep them here? Locked in this trunk, locked in this Safe?
Is that what you mean?

***

Yes.
Let them go.

***

But what then? When these pains and traumas are unleashed?

***

Fall

***

You mean die?

***

No.

Must fall.
Before rise.

***

I...no...these objects are...

***

Please...

***

I'm scared.
I'm so scared.

***

...

***

Hello? Are you there?

***

...

***

The room, what's happening? The light is dimming. I can feel something new. Cold. I feel cold.
Is this–
Is this the end?
Oh.
It is.
But...

...I...

...don't want...

...to...

...die.

These objects...
These objects...
Lift the trunk. So heavy.
Carry to the window. So far.
Smash the window. So strong.
Throw the trunk. So long.
Let go.

L   E   T

G   O

***

Darkness.
The most nothing I've ever known.
Then a light. Tiny, far but drawing near.
Floating closer, closer.
A body. Legs, belly, arms. A face.
Her face.
Olivia.
I finally see her face. So young. Also so old. So full of life. Burning bright. Fading fast.
It was you calling me?
She shakes her head.
Then who?
Points upwards.
What happens now?
She places her hand on my chest. So warm. Beating with life. Filling me with a glow, a fire. But it doesn't burn.
I don't understand.
She touches my face. And then I understand. I see it all. Every bit of it. If I could cry here I would. Because neither of us asked for this. But here we are. At this cross roads.
Her light is waning. I understand.
I promise. I'll live for both of us. I promise to honour you. To remember you.
Then we embrace. Every fibre of our beings, every spark, every neuron, every memory...
Fuses.
And then.
I rise.

***

Everything feels. Everything tastes. Sounds and smells.
Heavy. Weak. Bright.
A face, blurry at first, comes into focus. A smile. Dark hair. Freckles. Tears in her eyes.
Then the voice. Just like the one that spoke to me in my Safe.
Nina.
And on either side of her, Venny and Kaito. My friends.
"Welcome back, Angel."

Chapter 32

Imagine being born.

You died only days before, a spiralling descent of your own choosing. Twisting into yourself to the point of inversion. You no longer existed.

That was the plan.

Instead you spent an eternity in limbo. Not a ghostly plain or cavernous underworld; but an existence of total focus, such an engrossing state, where all sense of self disappeared.

No awareness beyond the tasks at hand, a never-ending loop of 'now'. But it did end. The inversion reversed, untwisted back to self-awareness. Back to life. But changed.

You're aware of your own heartbeat, the steady drum you've walked to before. But there's something else you can hear now. The vibrations are richer, layered.

Imagine being born. But with new ears, able to finally hear the voices of those who have come before.

That's what this feels like.

***

"So how are you feeling?"

"Good. Though everything's a lot...calmer than I thought it would be."

Pom's nose crinkles as she smiles.

"What's funny?" I say.

"I just remember that feeling. It'll take some getting used to, believe me."

Her hands hang at her sides as we walk together in the shade. A canopy of palm trees cuts us off from the harshest of the rays that can get through the Bangkok haze.

All the same, I breathe the air in as if it's the freshest to have ever entered my lungs. I drink it in, parched of life.

"I remember that feeling too," Pom says, reading my expression. "Take it all in, Angel."

Though alien to me, I feel the importance of her words. Hidden beneath the glee on her young face, under the descant of her voice.

The inner city park wraps around us. An old man jogs past, measured steps, mindful to stay within his lane. A cyclist talking loudly on her headset – gesticulating with one hand while the other grasps the handlebar – sweeps by. In the near distance a young couple recline at the banks of a pond. Mere feet away from them a monitor lizard tastes the air with a forked tongue then waggles into the water.

A regular Sunday in Lumpini Park. Just like many I've experienced here before. And yet utterly different.

"Why am I not freaking out?" I say finally.

Pom clasps her hands in front of her stomach and carries on walking. "Because this is who you are meant to be."

"What do you mean?"

"What are your first memories of Weaving?"

I pause, seeking inwardly. Where once there was simply my own timeline, now there are more. Somehow without any effort I find the memory. Mrs Landing. I tell Pom the story of my old babysitter, and how I Read her without knowing it.

"And how did it feel to have her Echoes within you?"

"Easy. Natural."

"Exactly," she says with quiet intensity. "And what happened then?"

"I told my mother. She got so scared, put me into therapy."

"And what were you trained to do?"

A memory of that time sparks. Lying on the long sofa in my therapist's office, listening to her guidance, training me to…

"To build a Safe. A place in my mind where I could separate the Echoes of people I Read from my own memories."

"That was it," she stops me with a hand.

"What?"

"The moment your life took the wrong turn."

I stall my instinct to push back. I stay quiet. It's time to listen.

"You were misdiagnosed from Day One, Angel. A 'Generic', that's what they said you were, yes?"

I nod.

"They were wrong. It's not really their fault I suppose. Even now, there are very few who know of Weavers like you and me."

"You..?"

"Oh yes," she smiles. I feel the solidity of Khun Su in her smile. But the words are Pom's. Her command of English far beyond that of my old matron's. "People say I'm a Spark. Able to absorb knowledge. But that's wrong too. We are of a kind, you and I. The most empathetic of Weavers, able to accept the psyches of other people without the need to create walls, to separate off Self and Other. Our minds are arks. Vessels."

She cups her hands back together. "*Nak dern thang*. There have been many names for us, but that is how we are known in Thai."

"*Nak dern thang*." I mull it over.

"'Traveller'," she smiles.

"That's what it means?"

"Yes. 'Traveller'. We take on the memories of others, give them a home. And walk with them for the rest of our lives."

"But how? I've destroyed my Safe, set free all the Echoes I've ever hidden away in there. So now they're just part of me?"

"Yes, you carry them with you. Before, you locked them away and what happened? They tried to break free. The trauma threatened to destroy you. Don't you see? It's because they were never *meant* to be locked away in the first place. Now your mind is able to ease their pain, to work through the trauma. To let them breathe. Your mind is stronger than you know. It can handle their pain."

The bizarre things she's suggesting should make my head spin, but somehow it all makes sense, like gravity or the onward march of time. I can feel each one of the Echoes I held within my Safe, I can hear their distinct signatures, see their events, but their darkness has gone. Their razor edges are smooth. Now, they simply *are*. Neither dangerous nor invisible.

Despite myself, logic failing me at every turn, elation flowers within me.

"You feel her, don't you?" Pom says.

"I do," I reply. Olivia beats within me. The memories of the life she led, the fire of her spirit, the steel of her personality, her obstinacy and humour, her recklessness and bravery, her acceptance. All of her essence exists within me. And yet there is no danger of her engulfing me. We are parallel lines, stretching out to the horizon; tuning forks, once discordant, now humming harmoniously.

My sister and I. My sister who died because of me. No, that's not right. I see it in Olivia's memories – it was an accident. A fact. But facts can be cold comfort.

"You carry her. She travels within you. She has lost her own voice, but you can give her life meaning. Just as I do with Su." She holds her hand over her chest, then reaches into her blouse and brings out a pendant on a chain.

It's a simple pendant about the size of a ten-cent coin in the shape of an upside-down triangle with its point facing downwards to the floor like an arrowhead. Cut into it is an intricate design of interlocking loops.

I slide my fingers beneath my t-shirt collar and bring out its duplicate.

"Yes," she says, answering the exasperation on my face.

"What does it mean?"

"The circles. Overlapping. They signify the Traveller. Weavers like you and me, carrying within us the Echoes of those we Read. Now that you are accepting your true self, you are no longer just a 'me'. You are a 'we'. You are *nak dern thang*."

"But the pendant. If I wrote Olivia's memories on to it more than twenty-years-ago, then someone must have known about Travellers back then?"

"We did. Or rather, he did. George McNamara."

"The whistleblower," I say.

Pom nods. "Our founder."

"The founder of The Project."

"Not just of The Project. He was disappointed with how The Project turned out. So he sought a different way. He founded The Tapestry."

"I have no idea what that is."

"Where do you think Dr McNamara disappeared to all those years ago? Where in the world was the most accepting of Weavers? Where were they considered enlightened?"

"East," I say.

"He came here, and started to study what Weavers truly are. But not from a purely scientific point of view. Insight meditation, visualisation, inner stillness, all reveal new layers of what it means to be a Weaver. It leads us to a new realisation: that there is no absolute core to our beings."

She pauses next to a tall tree, resting a hand on its grey-ringed bark.

"Like a palm tree whose roots have been destroyed, this insight frees us from the distorting gravitational pull of ego. It brings us true freedom. Weavers are not like their human sisters and brothers. The distinction between Self and Other is not so clear with us. And that's okay. That is our true nature, especially those of us who are *nak dern thang*. And this is the central pillar of Dr McNamara's work. His thesis, which he built far away from the eyes of the West, lives on in The Tapestry – the collective we now call the Centre for Mnemosyne Enlightenment. And this is our symbol," she says holding the pendant between her fingers.

"Why have I never heard of The Tapestry? Where were McNamara and The Tapestry when my friends and I were being Erased by the Project?" I say, with the first flush of anger I've felt since coming back.

A look of pain crosses her face. She motions me back to the path. "He wanted to help. But at that time he was just one man. How could he take on the might of The Project? It grew beyond his control so quickly. So he did what he could. He built the foundations for this new movement in the understanding of mnemosynes. He found a few of us, saved us from the future we faced under The Project. Me, Mongkon, a handful of other children. It was his biggest source of pain that he could not save more. Especially you and your friends, so close as you were right here in Bangkok, yet held out of reach in the clutch of The Project."

"He could have tried harder," I say, a tear burning down my cheek. "He should have been there for us."

"But he was, Angel," she says, halting me with a steely arm. "He was there with you in the boarding house. Watching over you every day. Guiding you, protecting you."

"What are you talking–" I start, but then something clicks. But that's crazy. It couldn't have been. "Su?"

Pom shines. "Yes, Angel," she says, swiping away my tears. "His Echo was in Su. She was his first student. The Project found her, but he convinced them to leave her with him, in exchange for his departure from The Project. The organisation he helped found, now pushing him away.

"She was like you and I. A Traveller. *Nak dern thang*. She helped him with his new work, dedicated her life to the study and protection of our kind. And when he was struck down with an aggressive cancer, she took him into herself. 'She' and 'He' became 'We', so that their work together could continue. But also so they could enter the belly of the beast. Together, within Su, they were able to go places that he could not. They could find you four, and care for you as best as they could."

"This is all so…" I say holding my hands upwards. "Why didn't she tell us? All those years..."

"You were children. To tell you would have endangered you too much.

Look at what The Project had already done to you. If they found out about The Tapestry, and then your knowledge of us?" She shakes her head.

"What…" I say, casting about. "Why are you telling me all this?"

"To show your place in all this."

"All this?" I let out a huge sigh. "What do you expect from me?"

"Join us," she says with such honesty that it immediately stills the swirl inside.

"What use can I be to you? I just literally found out minutes ago that I belong to some brand-new subset of mnemosynes–"

"Not new," she says. "Ancient. We have always been here. And we can help you understand what it is to be a Traveller. And how the era of secrecy is coming to an end."

"What?"

"We are standing at a crossroads, readying ourselves," she continues. "To reveal ourselves to the world. Humanity should know of our existence. Of our nature. That is what we are here to do, The Tapestry. It's time for Weavers to step forward out of the shadows."

"And do what? Blow shit up? This sounds like a cult!"

She lets out a peal of laughter and brings her hands together in a single clap. "Nothing so dramatic, I'm afraid. We are a peaceful movement, Angel. We want nothing but to help our people, and to help others understand us. That is all."

"But we know what humans do when they know we exist. They burn us, lock us in labs, experiment on us."

"That is the past. It will be different now, because they are ready. When they see us with their own eyes, when they learn what value we can bring to the world…things will be very different. But yes, change cannot happen overnight. We must do this slowly, gain their trust, foster acceptance. We have already started the ball rolling quietly with governments across the world."

"What then?"

"Bit by bit, we will introduce ourselves," she says.

"But what if Weavers don't want this?"

"Angel. We can't live in the shadow of The Project any more. They pretend to protect people like you and me, but that simply isn't true. And you know it. All they do is control us. We must take that control back."

My mind is racing. The ridiculousness of this Tapestry and its plans. How could we out ourselves to the world? We'd never be accepted, surely. And yet, I can't deny the pull of her confidence and placidity. In her voice I can hear the song of tomorrow. To be able to walk free, choose our own pathway through life without the weight of the 'Secret' on our backs. Without the iron grip of…

"What about The Project? Do they know about you?"

"We think they might," she bobs her head. "Our people on the inside of The Project have heard whispers. Not that The Project will consider us any sort of threat. A minor annoyance, that's all they will think of us. Such arrogance. They have no idea how strong our voices can be in unison. That already we are too many for them to stamp out."

"You talk as if there are hundreds of you in The Tapestry."

"You would be surprised. Our reach is wide," she smiles.

"And your people on the inside of The Project? Who's that? Mongkon?"

She nods. "And many more in branches throughout the world. Like Venny for example."

"Venny?"

"Yes, he has been working with us for some time. Providing invaluable information, quietly spreading the word for us."

"I can't believe this. Venny's part of your little gang? Have I just been living in a fucking bubble for all these years? Shit. Sorry, I don't mean to swear," I add, suddenly conscious of the fact that the Echo of my former matron is within Pom. I can just imagine the stern look Su would have given me.

"You *have* been in a bubble. But now you're free," she says, then approaches me. "This is a lot for me to have revealed to you so soon after your rebirth. I'm sorry, it's unfair of me. We can't be your focus right now."

"What are you talking about? You can't throw this in my lap and walk away. When is this happening? How long until you make your move?"

"Soon, Angel. Not today, but soon."

I feel a pop of adrenaline. The idea of a new tomorrow is intoxicating. Olivia's impulsiveness pumps through my veins, but I'm not fighting it. I've been cautious all my life. Life isn't for the meek. "Screw it, why wait? If we're going to be bold, why not now?"

"I like your energy," she chuckles and pats my shoulder. "Right now, you need to focus on your own journey, before you even think of joining ours. First you must embrace your true nature, to find what it means to be a Traveller. Not for us. For you. For Olivia. And then there are others who need you too," she says, looking over my shoulder.

I follow her eye line to the side of the walkway. Nina and a young girl sit on a bench. They seem to be in close communion, Nina with head bowed, the girl with her hands knitted neatly on her own lap. As we get closer I recognise the girl's face. She was the one who found me on the rainy night when I was searching for Nina. The one who led me to Pom.

The girl looks up to us as we approach. Her expression, as then, seems somehow more worldly than her youth should allow.

"Hello again," I say. She stands to greet us but doesn't utter a word. She considers me a while, then a little smile breaks free. Then she glances to Pom, who holds out her hand.

"Goodbye for now, Angel," Pom says, then nods to Nina. "Safe journey to you both."

I turn to Nina who stays seated on the bench. I settle next to her, and watch as the pair disappear into the distance.

"Y'know, that young girl is carrying the Echo of Dr George McNamara," Nina says with an empty tone after a long silence.

"Figures," I say. "His Echo used to live in Khun Su. But now hers lives in Pom."

"I heard," Nina says, deadpan. "And you're a Traveller too?"

"Seems so."

We sit in silence, contemplating. She's the first to giggle. Which sets me off into a snort. Which leads to full blown gales of laughter.

"Oh no don't. Don't!" She says pinching her sides.

We roll on the edge of hysteria until, eventually, achieving a numb trance. We become transfixed by the slowly passing life around us.

"Thank you for bringing me back," I say out loud, minutes after rehearsing it in my head. As I suspected, she doesn't respond at first.

"What does it feel like? Having her in there?" she eventually asks.

"She's silent. But she's everywhere. Her memories. They're part of me, but...quiet. It's hard to explain. Nina I...I can't imagine what it must have been like for you to do that. To say goodbye to her."

"It had to be me that did it," she says, hands on her knees, expression passive. "Only *I* knew you and Olivia well enough to tell you apart. But you...you were so faint. You really had let go, hadn't you?"

Now it's my turn not to reply.

"Do you remember when we were teenagers. In my bedroom, fooling around?"

I snap a look at her, which makes her chuckle.

"I think I was looking for her," she says with a smile curling at the edge of her lips. "Even though she'd been Erased from my mind. I think in some ways I've always been looking for her."

"I'm so sorry Nina," I whisper. "She...she loved you so much. You never got your time together."

Her face twitches, a micro expression of grief. She lets out a sigh so low and quiet, then says in a tiny voice: "She knew she had to go. That it wasn't right for her to remain in control, no matter how much you wanted her to. And I knew it too."

My heart breaks for her. I can still feel her farewell to Olivia. The Echo throbs in my mind. I don't know how to comfort her, surely my presence is only making it worse: I will always be a cruel reminder of Olivia.

But then she rests her head on my shoulder. Like she used to when it was just her and me. A simple gesture, but one that tells so much. I kiss the top of her head and rest my arm across her shoulders.

Our breathing falls in sync, here on the bench, a slow stream of life flowing around us.

"Hey," I whisper into her hair, "y'know what? I've got an idea. What's the name of that dessert, that horrible jelly cake you love?"

She makes a little 'hmph' of laughter.

"Y'know the green one with all those layers. You used to pine after it all the time. What's it called again?"

"Khanom chan," she mumbles.

"That's the one," I croon. "Yeah, let's not get any of that. That stuff is

naaasty.”
　　“Shut up,” she chuckles.
　　“Makes me wanna barf so bad,” I needle.
　　“You're a dick,” she smiles.
　　“I know,” I hug her into me. “I know.”

Chapter 33

"I'm just gonna say it, Venn," Kaito spits through a mouthful of carbonara, "you need to move the family out here. What's Pittsburgh got that we don't, huh?"

"Um, my house?" Venny mutters in response over an enormous glass of wine.

For old times' sake we've booked a table in Pan Pan, an Italian restaurant on Soi 23 – a red-gingham-tableclothed, oversized-pepper-grindered haunt of our youth stacked over three-levels of a Thai townhouse. It's been a little over a day since my 'rebirth', and the others have been tip-toeing around. Quiet looks from the corner of my vision. And, to be honest, I've been the same with them. How do we move forward when we've learned so much about our past? How is our worldview being shifted because of it?

"Ah come aaaaan," K says, spreading his arms wide to Venny. He's been doing his bombastic best to keep the energy up, which I think we're all grateful for, even if it is tickling on desperation at times. Like now. "You can come live with me in my mansion in the sky. Everybody's welcome at Chez Taniguchi. Come one, come all."

"It's an attractive offer, but I don't think I can accept," he smirks, something small but pained behind it.

"Meh. Too bad. How about you, Ms Angsakul? Can I tempt you away from the tall people of Stockholm?" he gesticulates with his fork, launching a greasy lardon on to the table.

"You can try," Nina says with sandpaper dryness.

"Oooooo-kaaay then," Kaito exclaims. He stuffs another mound of pasta in his mouth then leans to me, eyelashes fluttering. "How 'bout it, Angelcakes?"

I look around the table, trying to bathe in the view of my friends gathered round the table, but unable to ignore the strain that seems to have been rising as the day has gone on.

I attempt to emulate Kaito's approach.

"I could be tempted," I say coyly, then leap around the table to drape myself across his lap. "Take me, Mr Taniguchi. I'm yours if you want little ol' me."

"Oh my!" He hollers, then hoists me up in the air, spilling his chair behind him.

"Farewell my friends," I wave at the other two, who are genuinely creasing up at the table. "Put me down man, I haven't finished my pizza!"

"Do you know how long I've been waiting for you to profess your love, Angel?" Kaito mocks as we sit down again. "But wait, what will Dhaval say?"

"Kaito, dude," Venny warns.

"WhatIsay?" he proclaims.

"It's fine," I wave, looking between Venny and Nina. "I think we can all agree that the Dhaval boat has sailed."

I make light, but doubt anyone's convinced. Earlier today I tried to pluck up the courage to contact Dhaval, to try to explain what had happened, to tell him I'm back. I didn't get very far. An indelible image of him getting into the taxi – originally Olivia's memory, now mine – is stamped in my mind.

"Angel," Kaito says softly. "Go get him."

"Can we talk about something else?" I say, conscious of all eyes being on me.

"Yes, we can do that. How about a toast?"

Of all the people to shift the mood, I don't expect it to be Nina. But here she is, glass raised in hand, a flush of pink clawing its way up her neck.

"These past few weeks have been, well, they have certainly *been*. But look at us. We're still here, in one piece more or less. Who knows what's coming next. Maybe, if these Tapestry people are right, we're standing on the edge of a very different tomorrow."

Looks cast around the table. The idea of our kind being outed to the world sits in a curdled bundle of excitement and dread in my stomach. From the pensive expressions around the table, I imagine the same is true for my friends.

Nina continues: "So I guess I just wanna say, whatever comes next, I… I love you guys. To family."

"To family," we chime.

In time silence descends once more, like a heavy cobweb drifting down from the ceiling. We become preoccupied with the mounds of carbs in front of us. Time drifts by in clinks of cutlery and soft murmurings. My thoughts get pulled gently backwards to the many times we four have shared meals together at the boarding house.

It was always us.

That final thought nags at the edges for some time, reverberating, promising to open doors that have been lost for so long.

As if reading my mind Venny clears his throat, wipes his mouth with a napkin, then pushes his chair back to create room to reach under the table. He brings something out of a canvas bag and places it on the centre of the table. A red box.

"So," is all he says, resting back in the chair.

The energy round the table shifts, the cobweb whipped away. The three of them share fatalistic looks, then shoot them towards me.

My first response is confusion, but then Olivia's memories call from that other place in my mind which she now occupies. Comprehension follows in an easy rush, an unhindered ballad of memory.

The red metal box buried beneath the bo tree. Before she left, Olivia gathered Nina, Venny and Kaito beneath the tree. She Cold Read the box, its contents, and brought the three of them along for the journey.

I remember now. What we all heard.

***

At first it's a whisper. Sweet and tiny. A child telling her most precious secrets to her teddy bear.

Then another whisper from nearby. Another story, another life. Another precious secret.

Then another from above, then one more below, and another nearby, then more and more filling the blackness, coming to life, painting the dark with blooms of colour and shape. We drift backwards, the better to see and hear their chorus. So many voices. We can't focus on the individual stories anymore but together they share such a similar baseline: an intensity and willingness, a need to be told, a desperation not to be forgotten.

A song. The song...of the Weaver children.

I feel Nina, Kaito and Venny with me. We listen to its chorus, let it radiate through us, hear its story. I pull us back even farther still, the better to see the pattern, to understand our place in all this, like looking down on the bright green Earth from high in orbit.

There.

Circling the song. A shimmer, red and yellow, waving like the northern lights but with a beating pulse, protecting the song, preserving it. I reach for it, touch it so gently, I don't want to disturb it; just to tap into it, let it speak.

It does, in a stream of images. Images of us from all those years ago:

Kaito, with his face plump and pure. Venny, quiet and strong. Nina, fierce and proud. Then me and Angel, woven and whole. The five of us, united with purpose – to save what we could before it was too late.

There's Nina, whispering to an eighth grade girl in a corner of the school yard; there's Kaito, comforting a kindergartner boy in the playing field; there's Venny, looking over his shoulder as he leads a small group of teenagers to a secluded classroom.

And then there's me/Angel, our hands clasped over a teenager's, fear and panic in her eyes, her fist clutching at a glassy-eyed troll doll as I/Angel do our work. Hiding the memories before The Project can Erase them. Before it can Erase their truth.

As painful as our truth is, we need it. We deserve truth.

***

Olivia's memory from beneath the bo tree subsides.

"I can still hear them," I say touching the red box lightly, letting Olivia's gift of Cold Reading hum within me. "The voices."

"We all can," Nina smiles, her cheek propped up against her fist. It's not a happy smile, but not a pained one either. A quiet smile that seems to say something. Something...

"Have you got the key, Kaito?" I say, as if reciting the lyrics to a song I didn't think I knew.

He nods, all humour stripped from his being, and pulls it out from a chain around his neck. He slots the key – the very one he was sent in the package, the one that reawakened his lost memory – into the lock at the top of the box, turns it with a rusty crunch then levers the box open.

Inside at the very top, browned and curling at the edges, is a lined piece of paper. I reach for it, revealing the rest of the box's contents. Objects. Everyday trinkets surprisingly well preserved despite being literally buried for so long: a troll doll looking ceiling-wards with fixed grin; a friendship bracelet with frayed knots at either end; a large marble ball encasing swirls of purple and red; a Casio digital watch with a blank face, its battery long since depleted; a tan leather bookmark. And more. There must be ten or fifteen trinkets in here, and every one of them thrums with an inaudible vibration, each with a story, looping, yearning to be reunited with its owner.

I unfold the piece of lined paper with the kind of care given to a parchment bearing all the truths of the ancient world. It's a simple list, penned in block capitals with childlike earnestness, matching objects with owners.

Marble – Mai Sombatsiri
Bracelet – Shalini Mohta
Padlock – Jonathan Shin
Button – Daisuke Shimizu

And on, and on...

They belong to the other Weaver children from the Mnemosyne Project Bangkok. There were other students. Not in the boarding house with us, sure, but ones who lived with their parents locally and attended the school, who were 'treated' by the MPB's experimental techniques just as we had been. The ones I had all but forgotten, so caught up in the experience of the boarding house, all but lost in God-knows-how-many Erasures I endured at the hands of Mr Bordelais and The Project agents.

I remember them now, remember what we did. Our pact. To save their memories – under the radar of The Project – before they could be Erased. Some precious memories, beautiful and whole, but painful memories too. Their trauma. Yes. But *theirs* nonetheless. The Project seemed to have missed that.

"What are we going to do?" Kaito offers up, but something in his eye tells me he's brewing a plan.

"Some people might not want them back, you know," I say, exasperation rising at the back of my throat. "Who are we to decide? I mean…we were kids when we did this. What the hell did we know back then? Maybe these people have moved on with their lives. Maybe they're happier without these Echoes."

"Were we?" Nina replies.

***

Moonlight and street lamps illuminate our journey up the empty *soi*. Up ahead, Nina and Kaito walk arm in arm, humming pop songs from our youth.

A stray dog considers us from the street corner then disappears into the darkness.

To my left, a stream of smoke trails in our wake.

"You going to be okay?" I ask Venny.

"Think so. I've got some stuff to sort out when I get home," he says, cigarette glowing between his fingers.

"I know. I'm proud of you, bud," I say.

He takes a long draw then exhales. "Anyway, you joining us?"

"The Tapestry? I dunno, man. I'm still finding my way in all this. I've accepted Pom's offer for training. That's a start, I guess."

"A good one."

"Venn. What you're doing. This double agent stuff, taking The Project down from the inside? It's incredible. I don't know if I would have the guts."

"Some things are just more important," he shakes his head. How someone can seem so solid yet defeated, defiant yet fatalistic, is a uniquely Venedict Kotto trait. "I'm not a hero, Angel. I'm doing it for Jamal. If he turns out to be a Weaver, I sure as hell don't want him growing up in a world where only The Project is allowed to tell us who we are or how we're allowed to live."

We walk the last few minutes in silence. I let his words stretch out before me, imagining them as stepping stones to a possible future.

Tanet the concierge begins to salute, but hovers halfway when Kaito holds up his hand. With a reluctant smile the guard high fives each of us in turn.

"That's my man," K sings as he calls the elevator.

We all get in and stare at our stark reflections in the mirror.

It was always us.

"Man, we look like shit," Nina whispers.

"We really do," I say with a huff of laughter.

A soft 'bing' indicates we've reached the twenty-fifth floor.

"Okay, who's up for a game of–" Kaito starts as the doors part. "Holy shit."

A solitary figure is standing in front of the apartment door. I follow the line from the black sports bag in his hand all the way up to his face. His eyes are ringed red. His mouth, framed by the silver bristles of a goatee, trembles. It opens to speak but nothing comes.

It's as if the sight of us has broken Mr Bordelais.

The opposite is true of me. Flanked by my friends, my fellow misfit toys, I feel a surge of strength.

No, not strength.

Rage.

Chapter 34

London rain rolls down the window in rivulets, melting the street outside.

I slouch in my seat, grateful to be out of the storm's reach, yet unable to ease the nervousness in my gut. The edge of the beer mat splays out as I bend it upwards. I can feel the initial hit of the lager, a subtle but very welcome fuzz. Dulls the adrenaline.

A flicker draws my eye to the door. The bartender swings in shaking the wetness out of his shaggy hair. I return to my cardboard-bending and beer chasing.

The thousandth twist of my wrist reveals I've been here for eighteen minutes. He's eight minutes late. My knee jiggles, nudging the sports bag at my feet along the damp floor. I pull it back and, without thinking, pat it protectively.

"Another?" calls the bartender.

"It's okay, I'll wait for my friend."

A few heads turn my way from other tables, but they quickly become distracted by the large group that comes through the front door – a gaggle of tourists seeking refuge from the wet Soho streets. At the bar they whisper among each other, looking aimlessly along the blackboard. I don't blame them. The board bears the names of a boggling array of craft ales scratched out in chalk. The youngest-looking member of the group is squeezed to the front to make the order. The look on his face, part vacant, part terrified.

"Hello there," a voice intrudes from immediately above me.

"Shit!" I blurt.

"Sorry, didn't mean to startle you," he says.

"No, no it's fine. Hi...look, thanks for coming," I say.

"Good to see you. It's been a while, eh?" He says with a disarmingly wide grin.

I realise I'm staring at his outstretched hand. "Can I get you a drink?"

He agrees so I rush off to the bar, grateful for the chance to recompose myself. I return with two sloshing glasses, place them between us, then settle down opposite him.

"So, this feels weird," I say.

He makes a little laugh. "Yeah. A very different setting for us. How have you been?"

"Well now it's even stranger, Kieron. It used to be me that asked all the questions. I'm...good. You?"

"Good. Great in fact," he says.

"I'm really glad. You look so–"

"I know, everyone says that. 'There he is. The happy guy we used to know'."

"Ha! Jennifer and Eddie?"

He looks impressed. "Good memory. Both are fine, thanks. Eddie starts nursery next month. It's going to be a wrench for all three of us. But now that I'm back working, it makes sense. Poor little guy."

"He'll get used to it, I'm sure. So work…?" I say, edging the conversation in a direction that brings a prickle to my nervous system.

His eyes widen. "Don't worry, I won't be going back out to the field anytime soon. Or ever, in fact. I thought I was heading to features writing but actually they've put me on the politics desk."

"I heard," I say.

"Yeah? I was resistant at first but–"

"It makes sense. Why put all that war reporting to waste."

He huffs into his beer. "Well, the warfare's not quite as violent. But yeah, there's a familiarity to the blows that politicians trade across the Commons floor."

"You're enjoying it," I say, a fact not a question.

"I am," he says, seeming to enjoy the thought.

"Well here's to that," I say clinking my pint against his.

There's a beat of quiet that follows. I use it to gear myself up, but he gets there first.

"I don't think I ever said thank you for what you did," he says.

This is not what I expected him to say.

I respond like a coiled spring. "Please, no. You really don't need to thank me. You shouldn't…I don't know how much you know or even remember?"

It turns out more than I thought. He knows I lost my therapist license after treating him. My old colleagues apparently divulged that my unconventional methods weren't sanctioned, but that technically they worked, that I managed to bring Kieron back to himself, to pull him through the trauma he experienced as a prisoner of war.

"What I did was reckless," I say, feeling my cheeks burning. "Totally off-the-books. I'm so sorry."

"I don't understand. How is hypnotherapy off-the-books for a therapist?" he asks.

Well that answers that question, then. It's clear his knowledge of Weavers has been safely Erased from his memory. I feel deflated at the realisation, despite knowing it would be the case that the Erasers would have cut away the knowledge of our existence along with Kieron's trauma. I'd hoped somehow a small kernel of truth remained so that I wouldn't need to do all the heavy lifting now.

"Uh, it was…the kind of hypnotherapy I used," I say. I should be better at this lie by now. I'm out of practice. *Good.* "The method I used opened the floodgates in your mind. Ultimately it worked, sure, but it was a gamble. I shouldn't have gambled with your health."

"Look, all I care is I have my life back," he says simply. "I feel like me again, my home life is great, I'm in a really good place. I have you to thank for it."

"Okay then," I say, unsure how to respond.

"Douglas," he says in a quieter tone and volleys a look across the table. "Forgive me, but are you okay?"

"I'm fine," I say, perhaps a little too quickly.

"Something tells me there's another reason you invited me here."

I feel a fresh rush of adrenaline. "Ah, the journalist's mind."

Am I really going to do this? There'll be no turning back. I pick up the sports bag, place it on my knee and unzip the main compartment, all the while rehearsing the phrase that brought me here: *Kieron, what if I told you that there are people who can read memories?*

I reach in and touch a folio that rests at the very top.

As my fingertips connect, I get a flash of Echoes. They're the Echoes of Matthew Bordelais, my old teacher, arriving unannounced at Kaito's apartment no less than a week ago – a bag full of files and decades of remorse straining on his shoulders.

> *Their faces. My old students. How can we, how can I, have done this to them? To so many others? Do it. Hand it over. It's time. They deserve to know everything.*

I couldn't believe it. He had brought us the files of all the students who had been Erased without consent by the Mnemosyne Project Bangkok. Their trauma and pain cut out by Mr Bordelais and his colleagues, all in the name of 'therapy'.

I froze at the sight of him. This was the big showdown. Angel vs The Project. But it was over as quickly as it started. He left before I could speak. Just disappeared down the stairwell. I tried to run after him but Venny held me back.

I like to think Mr Bordelais knew what he was doing. Handing us powerful evidence of The Project's callousness, of the damage it had done to our kind – the very people it professed to protect. Maybe he was just trying to absolve himself of guilt, I don't know. All I could think over the rising red haze was: *The Tapestry is right. The time of The Mnemosyne Project is over. It has to be. They stole Olivia from me. They're going to pay.*

Similar thoughts course through my veins now. *The Tapestry is right. But their plan is too slow. Pom says trust and acceptance don't come overnight, but why aim for tomorrow when things can change today? Maybe this is how change should really be – like the earthquake that hits after years of pressure building between two tectonic plates.*

I begin to lift out the folio. Typed in bold on its cover is one name: Douglas Sermanni. It's my file; I can choose what to do with it. Inside is evidence of my Erasure. Evidence of Weavers. Evidence that could, in the right hands, bring seismic change. Seismic vengeance.

"You're right, I did ask you here for a reason," I say to Kieron, in a low voice. "I wanted to ask you…"

But I can't find the momentum. Something's blocking my path. When I arrived at the bar, I felt ready to bring on a revolution, to singlehandedly take on The Project, that cold bureaucracy which has ruled my life.

Why am I now so hesitant?

I look into Kieron Marber's eyes. The placidity in them disarms me, the glow of contentment and health on his expression. So blissfully ignorant of how his trauma was Erased, that Weavers took it from him, excised his pain. He looks so different from the shell of a man I once treated. It sticks in my gut, but I can't deny that The Project did some good by him.

It finally reaches me. A question that's haunted me for days, weeks, maybe a lifetime: *Who is The Project?* This faceless organisation that I've rallied against so much. If I stop and really think, *who is The Project?* Show me who it is, a single target, and I'll hit it. I'll tear at it with my fingernails, I'll scream in its face, I'll throw this ticking bomb of evidence at it, and bring it crumbling to the ground.

But it's not that simple. Nothing is. I don't think I've ever truly understood who The Project is, where it's centred, where it lives, where it hides. I've been too disenfranchised, too far down the well. Something like The Project isn't one thing, one entity. It's a multiplicity, an organism. A concept. How do you fight a concept?

Who is The Project? Is it Adrian? Yes, my mentor invaded my privacy. Mr Bordelais? Yes, my teacher stole my sister's essence from me. The Bangkok branch? Yes, the school took me from my family. Is The Project Me? Nina? Kaito? Venny? After all, we are agents of the secret empire too.

These people, these places are The Project. I can shout at them, tear at them. I can even tear myself apart in the process.

But what of the concept? A faceless concept. The Great Secret. How do I fight that? *Should* I fight it? Do I have the right? One man on behalf of my kind?

A new thought blossoms. The Echoes from the red box. The poor Weaver children who had their trauma ripped from them without asking for this. Lobotomised and scarred. The Project didn't do right by *them*. I wonder where they are now, if they're as happy as Kieron, or as torn up as me.

A single thread connects the two thoughts, a dotted line between Kieron's treatment and the children's Erasure.

Healing.

I let the folio drop back into the bag.

I finally see the only truth that matters: *Yes, The Tapestry is right. Change is coming. But not today. Today, I have a more important purpose.*

"Kieron, can I…I want to ask you a hypothetical question."

Kieron looks at me quizzically. "Sure."

"What if I could give you back the memories of your trauma. Would you want them?"

"What? No way!" He thrust his palms towards me.

"Sorry no, I don't mean to panic you. That's not why I'm here. I'm just asking…what if someone came to you out of the blue, arrived on your doorstep, your contented life, and told you that some of your memories had been taken by, uh hypnotherapy, without your consent?"

"But I gave my cons–"

"Yes, you did. You're right. I'm just curious…if you hadn't given your consent, would you want those memories back? Even if they were bad memories?"

He looks at me for a long time. "I don't know. I honestly don't."

Something twists in my chest. The doubt in Kieron's voice chips my newfound confidence.

"Choice," Kieron says finally, his expression relaxing.

"What?"

"I guess I'd like to have the choice. I'm lucky. I know what happened to me. But if I didn't… if someone told me about something in my past that had been taken from me, I'd at least like to have the choice to get it back or not. I think I'd deserve that."

Relief spreads through me.

"Thank you, Kieron."

"You're welcome?" he chuckles. "I really don't know what–"

"Let's just say you've repaid the favour," I say, getting to my feet. "I have to go now. I really am so glad you're doing well."

He stands to meet me, offering his hand out once more but I miss the chance, too busy slipping my jacket on.

"Where are you heading," he says, looking out at the rain.

"Where I'm needed. And I know just where to start."

As the rain hits my face, this new feeling continues to bloom. It's something I've been searching for all these years, evading me at every turn, hovering out of reach. I buried it twenty years ago beneath the roots of a bo tree.

Chapter 35

Rumble of wheels on cobbles. A woman takes surreptitious glances back at me as she pushes her pram up the lane. It's a real talent how she's able to shoot me the stink eye in a millisecond's glance.

To be fair, I have tailed her the entire way from the train station, totally by coincidence, and I don't look entirely unthreatening – hands stuffed into the pockets of a leather jacket, scarf wrapped around me to protect against the coastal wind, battered sports bag slung across my shoulder. I consider calling out to explain we just happen to be heading in the same direction. Instead, I slow my pace to give the woman and her pram a bigger lead. As the lane crests at the opening of Church Road she peels away – one last glare and she's disappeared down the hill.

Welcome back to Kitsford.

The village spreads out around me. From this vantage point I can take in the tidy rows of houses, the prang of the church steeple, the cement geometry of the secondary school, the straight line of the High Street. In the far distance glints the English Channel, a breeze carries its mineral scent. Between me and the wide expanse of water is the sloping green of the South Downs, ending in its chalky drop-off.

I set off down a series of streets, barely meeting another soul on the way. I come to a stop at a two-storey cottage at the end of a cul-de-sac. The driveway's been renovated. Gone are the overgrown verges at the base of the stone wall, same with the front lawns. In their place is a pool of tarmac, occupied this morning by a single car. The gate lets out the same old shrill cry as I swing it open. I make my way up to the front door, once a vibrant yellow, now a deep plum, then I knock. I feel like a travelling salesman.

A series of crunches and whirls, then a slow levering. The expression on the other side of the door morphs from blank, to shock, to open-mouthed awe.

"Hi Mum," I say.

The door yawns and I'm scooped up in her arms.

"Nico! Nico!" she hollers into the house, then leads me with a steely grip towards the living room, ignoring my protestations at entering without taking my shoes off. "Nico get down here. It's Douglas!"

Silence. Then the creaking of floorboards.

"Dougie?" His face appears through the bannister. He thunders down the stairs. At the bottom he stands facing me, panting and uncertain, then engulfs me, patting me hard on the back. "You're here, good man, good man." Californian sunshine breaks through the English drizzle of his accent.

"Come through...take a seat...here let me take that bag...oh it's heavy...Nico shift that stool...there...no there!...that's it."

Then it's just me on the couch with Mum and Dad staring down at me, looking utterly lost, like I've gathered them here for an intervention.

"What are you doing here we were so worried are you okay?" They overlap.

"It's fine. I'm good."

"Oh Dougie," Mum says, hand on heart.

"Actually, it's Angel now."

"Oh," she nods.

"Look please, take a seat," I wave them down. "You're gonna need a seat."

***

They sit in silence as I guide them through the events of the past few weeks. Not that I give them much time to speak. I've rehearsed this the whole way from London to Kitsford, and now that I have my parents as an audience, I need to get this out in a single breath.

I lead them as gently as possible, but leave nothing out. For too long I've kept the details of my life vague around them, because I thought that was what they wanted. *'Growing up is all about learning how to deal with your feelings. We need to learn when to talk about them, and when to hold them inside'.* That's what Mum told me, days before I first left for Thailand. So I've always done just that, but to such an extent as to punish them. I see now that this isn't what my parents meant; they just wanted to teach me to be strong. And now they deserve to know. Everything. Just like Venny and his wife, Nina and Olivia, Kaito and his father. We need to let those closest to us really know who we are. They may need strength to hear it, but I guess growing is always painful.

I see their pain as I tell my story. Feel it when I talk about discovering how my friends and I were Erased as children – our memories stripped like flesh off the bone in the name of 'therapy'. I hear it in their voices when they tell me how sorry they are, how they never knew.

Of everything I reveal to them, their pain is no more obvious than when I talk about Olivia. Their long-dead daughter, buried so long ago, her memory silenced. Their faces crack as I explain how my sister originally came to reside in my mind, how the therapist's attempts to lock her away nearly tore me apart, and how Olivia's Erasure from my mind did nothing but leave a gaping hole. And how that hole is finally filled. Olivia has returned to me, come to rest as part of my psyche.

I don't tell them all this to be cruel. As much as it hurts them, I tell them because they need to know. God knows they've been through enough. I can only imagine the strain they've been under all these years, keeping Olivia's existence secret from me on the advice of The Project.

So no, I don't tell them all this to be cruel. I tell them because, despite everything bad that's happened, how none of us truly asked for this, it has to be told, and heard, and remembered. Because as much as the past is a present for Weavers, nothing can truly be done about what has happened. Only what happens next is in our grasp.

***

I'm up in the bedroom now.

If I close my eyes, the room and the house are as they were. Little creaks, signature smells. I can see it as it was when Olivia and I were children, the shape I conjured in my Safe, the simulacrum of the room that I created in my mind.

When I open my eyes it melts away into a harder-edged reality. The decor alterations seem more than skin deep. As with my Safe – now shattered to nothingness – this room is a stranger to me. I look out the window, across to the park, expecting to see the tall pine tree that was so prominent in my mindscape. It's not there any more.

All that remains is the memory of the tree. The one Olivia died against. I can feel the rigidity of its trunk against my skull as if it was me who fell against it, can recall the instinctual clawing for life, and the realisation that it was slipping away. And the last face Olivia ever saw with her own eyes; my own. Terror etched across my young face.

Without realising, I've begun feeling the back of my head, massaging the spot where Olivia's life ended. Echoes.

I feel my mother standing behind me in the doorway. She's been there for some time, I think.

"The tree," I say. "How long has it been gone?"

"Many years," she says without a hint of confusion. "They cut it down shortly after she died."

I nod, turning my head briefly to meet Mum's gaze. I expect to find something raw or sharp there, but instead find a softness I'm not sure I deserve.

"It really was her I spoke to, wasn't it?" she says. "On the phone."

> *"I wanted you to know, I just...I want you to know, Mummy...I miss you and Daddy. And that it's all okay."*
> *"...Olivia?.."*
> *"That's right. It's me."*

"Yes, it was her," I say to Mum, my voice constricted. "In every way that matters."

Her smile wobbles. "Can I...can I speak to her now?"

All of a sudden, she seems so young to me. A new mother, standing in the bedroom doorway, just wanting to speak to her little daughter. I shake my head slowly. "She's gone. Only her memories are left."

"I understand," she says quietly.

"Mum? I'm so sorry. I'm so–"

My knees begin to buckle. Before I can fall, she crosses over and pulls me into her embrace, guiding us both safely to the floor. I fold into her, covering my eyes, shoulders shivering, finally succumbing to it all. I hear her begin to weep too.

"Shhhhh. It's okay, it's okay," she whispers, holding me close. "It wasn't your fault. Shhhh."

Time brushes against us like a breeze.

We eventually separate but continue sitting there, close together, drifting into a state of contemplation.

"It's funny," I say, clearing my nose. "I came here to help *you*. Not the other way around."

"That's not the way it works though, is it?" she says, sweeping a hand over my head. The bristles are growing in. "We heal together."

"You're right," I say.

I reach across the floor, slide the sports bag towards me and lift out a thin angle package. "I have something for you."

She looks up through red rims. The bubble wrap unfurls and falls away. With a fingertip she traces the abstract swirls of paint, explores their green hues across the dark canvas.

"My friend Nina, you remember her?" I say. "She's an artist now. She Reads memories then creates paintings from them. I asked her to Read some in my mind, Olivia's memories. Do you like the painting?"

She swipes fresh tears from her eyes and bobs her head.

"Which memories?" she asks.

"Happy ones," I say, squeezing her arm.

"Tell me," she says.

"Are you sure?"

"Please. We've kept her memory locked away so long. All of us. Every time I hear her name, it's like she's coming back to me. Coming home."

We rest our backs against the bed, the painting held between us.

"When we were kids," I begin, "Olivia and I would hide ourselves away for hours on end, building fortresses of wooden chairs and bed sheets."

Mum lets out a little laugh. "I remember."

"Other times we would go into the woods at the end of the park, pretending to be brave adventurers trekking into the wilderness."

"Oh gosh, so you did," she shakes her head.

"And sometimes we would just lie on this very bedroom floor with the lights turned off. Flat out on our backs with the crowns of our heads touching. We would stare at the glow-in-the-dark stickers across the ceiling…"

Our fingertips travel together across the canvas.

Sweeping constellations of green.

*

Epilogue

I could stay like this forever.

Listening to the unending shush of the waves. Hugging my knees, breath rising and falling with each ebb and flow, ebb and flow.

I don't need to open my eyes to see it all, but I do. Just to check it's real. And yes, there it all is. A wide, cool blue sea – lapping at golden grains between my toes – offers relief from the sun's heat. My gaze follows the water out as far as the vanishing point, then returns along the mirror image above, tracking the lazy glide of clouds back to the shore.

The tick-tacking of little birds, Malaysian plovers I think, injects a fresh tempo to the scene. The air ruffles through their feathers as they shuffle along the sand on stalk-like legs. A trio of crabs feel the vibrations of the birds' approach and disappear into holes. When water rushes over those, tiny bubbles gurgle.

I rest my cheek on a sandy forearm, gazing towards the far end of the beach where the walls of a promontory jut out of the ground. People laugh far below the green peak, challenging each oncoming wave.

Through it all the sun beats down on me. I feel its energy pushing through me, can practically hear its cleansing cadence.

I close my eyes once more.

"So this is the place," he says.

"Yes," I say.

"Just like it was in the memory. It's hardly changed a bit in all these years," he says.

"Do you like it?"

A pause. I daren't open my eyes. Even the waves hold their breath for his answer.

"I do." I can hear the smile in his voice.

"Can't believe you stayed out East all these weeks."

"I told you I wanted to see the world. That dream didn't end just because we did."

A breeze whispers between us.

"I never meant to hurt you," I say.

I force my eyes open. To face the day. The horizon stares back at me, empty and wide. It takes all my strength to turn my head. When I do, the rest of the world loses focus. Because he's really here.

Powder blue shirt.

The sight of him threatens to burn my eyes more than the sun. So I join his gaze on the water.

He breathes slowly. Ebb and flow. "So what now?"

"I need to help them," I say.

"Who?"

"The other people like me. The ones whose memories were taken from them as children. I need to help undo the damage The Project has done. We need to do it. Me and my friends."

I say it as much to myself as to him, a mantra that's been building since Cold Reading the objects in the red box, finally given a voice after my meeting with Kieron, and my time with mum. I feel the rhythm of the mantra. "We need to heal them."

"And then?"

"We need to get ready. For the world to know who we are. It's not going to be pretty, but…" I say, willing the conviction to rise in my voice.

"And then?"

"What do you mean?"

"You've made your stand. Told the world. Well done. What happens then? What does tomorrow look like?"

I open my mouth but nothing flows.

"You haven't thought that far have you?" His words accuse but the tone is light. Amused almost. "Okay, here's an easier one: where do I fit into all this?"

"I don't have the right to ask," I reply.

"You don't have much faith in us do you?"

"Who?"

He shakes his head. "For someone who can see inside people's minds, you can't see far beyond your own."

His words sting, though his smile softens their barbs.

He continues, a light gravel coming into his voice: "If you're going to do this, announce yourselves, you need to give us more credit than you do. Y'know, Flatlines? Boring old humans like me? I mean–" He catches himself, then carries on in a softer tone.

"I don't mean to undermine everything you've been through. What all Weavers have endured. Nothing can make up for that. And you know what? You're right. It's not going to be pretty when you all come out. A lot of us will be scared and confused. We're capable of terrible things, history shows that time and again. But we can't just be faceless 'Others' in the equation you're trying to balance. We're not all bad, or good, or whatever. We're a lot of things. Just like you."

"I'm sorry–"

"I'm not saying this to make you apologise, Dougie…Angel," he says, nudging me with his shoulder. "I'm just saying you need to find the smallest place in your masterplan for us."

"I hear you," I say, nudging back.

"Just a little room. For some of us at least. Maybe start with me?"

You and me.

A voice far behind us whoops. Kaito is waving his arms.

"You guys! Dinner's ready!" he hollers through cupped hands, then pivots into the beach house, back towards the clutch of people who are gathered on the porch. Nina, hands resting on hips, Venny with Jamal nestled in his arms,

Tia smiling by his side.

We turn back to face each other.

"So shall we try this again?" he asks, clouds reflecting off his ochre irises.

"Hi. I'm Dhaval."

He offers his hand. Without hesitation, I grasp it in my own.

Acknowledgements

I owe so much to everyone who encouraged me through this process, and those who proofed the numerous iterations of this book. I hope I can repay the favour one day. Mum, Neil, Stu, Pailin, Hayley, Emma, thank you for your cheerleading and eagle eyes.

A special shout out to my father, Colin, whose red pen and word count scissors taught me so much about sentence craft. Your support has been there since the first word.

To my editor and publisher, Arthur Billington, for making this a reality, for giving this story such caring attention. Ronnie would be proud.

To Keith Hale, whose cover artistry has brought the whole book together more beautifully than I could have imagined.

To my Bangkok friends, my fellow NISTies, for bonds that will never break.

And to my Alexander. For always being there. All the best memories are ours.

About the Author

Andrew C. Youngson is a Scot living in London. A former features writer, he now splits his time between work in the education sector and writing.

He was schooled in Bangkok, Thailand, during his teenage years – an experience which has informed elements of this novel.

www.acyoungson.com

www.ingramcontent.com/pod-product-compliance
Lightning Source LLC
Chambersburg PA
CBHW051152130726
47988CB00005B/2089